Spectral Promises

Orion Labauve Novel 2

by

L. L. Blacke

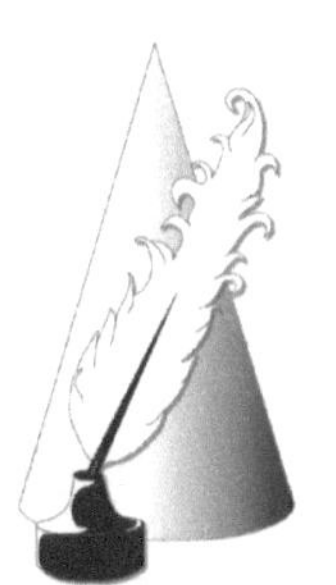

Foolscap & Quill

ISBN 978-1-938143-65-6

Foolscap & Quill
P.O. Box 1018
Morrison, CO 80465
http://www.foolscap-quill.com

Table of Contents

Chapter 1
Dreams and Battle Scars

Mommy told me to stay inside and hide in the secret place she showed me if anyone came to the house. She made me promise. She said she'd only be gone for a few days, but it's been so long. I'm still waiting for her to come back, and I'm scared all the time.

I watched Mommy drive away through the curtains of the front room bay window. She said she was going to talk to Daddy to work things out. I didn't understand what that meant. Daddy was always so mean. He hit Mommy a lot, and he would hurt me. Mommy would try to make him stop hitting me, and then he would hit her even more. I'm scared he'll hurt her when she talks to him.

She told me not to let anyone outside see me in the house. Every day I sit and look out the window, waiting for Mommy to come back. A kid riding a bicycle looked at the house. I moved back so he wouldn't see me, but I think the curtain moved. Did he see that?

I used the crayons to fill up all the coloring books Mommy left me. Then I started drawing on the walls, but the crayons ran out. The wheels on the truck I brought broke and now it won't roll. Now I just look out the window at the people in the neighborhood. I wish I could go and play with the kids outside, but I can't. They'll know I'm in the house and ask a lot of questions, and then bad people might come. I'm so alone.

Mommy left two loaves of bread, a full jar of peanut butter, and a full jar of jelly. She told me not to eat it all in one day. After a few days, when she didn't come back, I ate only one piece of bread with a little peanut butter and jelly each day. When I was down to my last piece, I used my fingers to scrape the last of the peanut butter and jelly from the jars. There were small gray spots on the bread. I picked them off. I was hungry for a long time after that. I drank big glasses of water so I wouldn't feel so bad.

I stayed in the secret hiding spot every night in case someone entered while I'm sleeping. I know it's morning when a sliver of light comes through a crack. If I didn't hear anyone, I'd come out. I lay in the dark and cry for Mommy every night before I fall asleep.

Then it became hard for me to get up, and I stayed in the secret place all the time. When the light tunnel came and tried to pull me away, I didn't go. I promised to wait for Mommy.

Now it's easy to get up. I'm never hungry, and I don't feel tired anymore. But now that thing is under my blanket. I don't want to touch it, so I cry in the corner.

Then one day, I heard the front door open and lots of people came in. Mommy told me that Daddy might send bad people, and I should hide in the secret place. Are these the bad people? I heard them coming in and out and making a lot of noise. I think they're moving furniture into the house. I cry for Mommy all the time. When the people went away, I left the hiding place and watch out the window.

I jolted awake, tears scorching down my face. The nightmare hit me again, an unending loop of a frightened child trapped in a shadowy house, desperately waiting for his mother's return. In that intensely vivid dream, it felt as though I were the boy, helpless and forsaken.

Wiping my eyes with my left hand, I sat up, my right arm cradled in its cast, a constant reminder of the battle scars from the psychic conflict two months ago with my grandmother, the Voodoo Imperatrice.

My arm was still in a brace from being shattered during the destruction of the Labauve signet sapphire. This mysterious artifact was part of my family's twisted legacy. The magical conflict with my grandmother nearly cost me my life, and my right limb would be in a cast for months. Even after surgery and weeks of physical therapy, the constant pain remained a cruel companion. I could barely move my fingers, and most nights, sleep was hard to come by.

Webster Turner, the ghost of my paternal grandfather, sat vigilantly in a chair beside my bed. His spectral image was that of a frail, balding, 70ish-old man with a hunched back. He may have been good-looking in his youth, but now his face and body were gaunt, just as they appeared at the time of his death from cancer.

Bound to me by a curse—punishment for killing my great-grandmother, another powerful voodoo priestess—he could never stray more than fifteen feet away, which forced him to follow me everywhere, just like he did with my father for thirty-five years. After I visited my father's grave, Webster had to stay close, since I am part of my father. The curse, a legacy of my family's tangled and violent history with voodoo, keeps us linked until I can break it. Once my right arm is healed enough to perform the necessary magical movements, I'll set him free.

Webster's spectral presence flickered as I wiped away the tears.

"Orion, did you have it again?" he asked gravely.

"Yeah," I muttered. "It has to mean something. Why else would I keep dreaming about this kid? The Duke said I had work to do, so this has to be part of it. I need to figure out where the boy is. I'm sure he's dead and a ghost."

My determination to unravel this mystery remained unwavering despite the challenges. Duke Shamedi, the voodoo Lwa Spirit God, and my *God* father, never makes things easy, as shown by the cryptic dreams that provide no clues about where the spirit child is or who he is.

"Can't you use your Finding ability to track him down?" Webster asked.

I possess a unique talent, a gift from the spirit God, to locate people and objects, which has been my profession for the past seven years. This ability enables me to locate even the most challenging targets. It's a form of supernatural tracking; however, it doesn't work on ghosts, which has been a source of agitation in my current situation.

Frustration simmering, I shook my head.

"You think I haven't tried? It doesn't work on spirits. It's useless in this case."

The dream started haunting me three weeks after I returned from the hospital. Not a nightly occurrence, but each time it manifests, it leaves a deeper scar. I still couldn't grasp how Duke Shamedi believed I could achieve anything with an almost useless arm.

The aching in my arm flared. I hunched over, grimacing, cradling it close, wishing it would cease.

Webster leaned forward, his ghostly brow furrowed.

"Why don't you take those pain pills the doctors gave you?"

Bitterness spilled out before I could block it.

I snapped, "You know why! I'm not ending up like my mother, hooked on pills and worse."

My deceased mother died of a drug overdose. Pain meds were her drug of choice for several years, and later, after developing a tolerance for them, she switched to heroin. This addiction proved to be too much for her heart, and she passed on five years ago. After seeing what these drugs did to her, I refuse to use them unless absolutely necessary.

I took deep breaths to calm myself and stop yelling. He was only concerned about me.

"Sorry for shouting. I'll talk to Rose about doing a voodoo healing ceremony. Maybe that could help."

Over the spring and summer months of 1982, so much happened that it seemed like years had passed. Since my twenty-fifth birthday in March, and after the Duke anointed me with the knowledge to use the powers he bestowed upon me, I can perform magical actions to call Lwa entities from the spirit realm to heal injuries or achieve whatever I require. However, I need both arms and hands to complete the proper enchanted configurations. I'm unable to fully extend my right arm for some of the required movements, and my right hand and fingers are unable to form the magical symbols.

Something has to be done. Between my arm aching continuously and these unsettling dreams, I don't get much sleep, and I'm always exhausted.

It was 4 a.m., and I realized I wouldn't sleep any more that night, so I went to the main floor of the 190-year-old plantation mansion, built in the late 1700s, and turned on the TV.

Rose entered the living room and asked, "Would you like some coffee?"

Rose was the ghost of a voodoo priestess and mother of Paul, the spectral yardman. She had created the Labauve signet and cursed the estate in 1813 when she was alive as an act of revenge for the death of her son. The priestess's spirit now resides at the L'Enfant Haven mansion and assists me as commanded by the Lwa Spirit God, Duke Shamedi, as penance for her possession of me while searching for the Labauve signet. I've forgiven Rose for the torment she inflicted upon me. She was a pawn, manipulated by my deranged grandmother—the Voodoo Imperatrice.

Today, the priestess not only cooks for me but also offers valuable advice, which I sincerely appreciate. I listen carefully, fully aware that her mastery of the Lwa religion far surpasses my limited understanding of it.

"Yes, please," I said, grateful for her presence.

She served me coffee, and I watched an old movie. I dozed off for half an hour until the pain in my arm roused me.

Upset that the pain once again disrupted my sleep, I begged Rose, "Aren't there voodoo healing spells that can help to heal my arm and reduce this constant ache?"

She explained, "Yes, but they need special plants, herbs, and blessed talismans to make a good one. I don't have any charms or herbs. It's possible to craft them, but that requires other specialized items I don't have. I've watched you suffering and searched the house and plantation grounds for plants and herbs that can help, but have found very few. Why don't you call Lwa from the spirit realm to handle this?"

"I can't call them because I must use both arms and hands to perform the magical movements, which aren't happening."

Frustration surged once more; I struck the sofa cushion with my uninjured left fist.

Rose paced back and forth, contemplating the problem and eager to assist.

"I wonder if Doris can do anything with her crystals. Could you call her and ask her to come over so we can discuss this?"

Rose couldn't make the phone call because spirit voices don't easily transfer through telephone lines.

"Sure, I'll phone her a little later when she gets into the office."

Doris Owens works as the secretary to Andrew (Andy) Butler Jr., my attorney and friend. She's also a crystal witch. This amazing ability was discovered when she helped create a crystal light protection barrier around the mansion during the psychic encounter with my grandmother. If this barrier hadn't been set up, the fight would have been much shorter, and we might have lost. The light wall slowed the Voodoo Imperatrice's advance, allowing me to destroy the cursed sapphire, which broke the curse on the L'Enfant Haven plantation. This freed the ghosts bound to the property.

Duke Shamedi gave all the specters the choice to either stay and help me or pass through the tunnel of light to the other side. I was surprised that most of them decided to stay with me. It made me love them even more as my family.

I called Doris later and explained the difficulty I was having.

She said, "I'm sorry you're in so much pain. I'll come over after work."

The secretary's willingness to help was a comforting reminder of the support around me.

Later that afternoon, the dark-skinned crystal witch burst through the front door with her usual enthusiasm and placed her voluminous purse on the couch. Coming from work, she wore a professional-looking dark blue dress, with her reading glasses hanging from a chain around her neck. A second silver chain, adorned with a two-inch clear crystal, also graced her neck—a vital part of her magic.

Doris and Rose disappeared into the library to discuss the issue. The two women remained for an hour and emerged smiling.

After returning from the spirit realm, where the Duke had implanted the knowledge to harness the powers he bestowed upon me, I equipped Doris and Andy with Spirit Sight. This allowed them to see, speak to, and interact with specters at the L'Enfant Haven mansion. Now others understand that I'm not insane, and the ghosts at the plantation and everywhere else are real. Doris and Rose became close allies, and their mutual respect for each other's magical systems created an unlikely bond.

The two supernaturally endowed women exited and Rose said, "We've discussed your problem and have come up with an idea we want to try. Since I can only perform less potent voodoo rituals because I'm dead, I can't summon a Lwa healing spirit. Doris can conduct a crystal ceremony, but her magic isn't particularly strong for healing. Because you can only perform the magical movements with your left arm and hand, this limits its power. We think that by combining all three of our diminished levels of magic, you may be able to call a Lwa over."

I pursed my lips, unsure about this proposal.

"Fine," I said, resigned but hopeful. "All we can do is try it. When can we do this?"

"First, we need to buy some supplies, and Doris needs to acquire a few unique crystals. She has a friend who owns a store that specializes in occult materials. We can go tomorrow. You must let me inside you while we shop for the required items. I'll need to smell the herbs and plants to ensure their quality."

I nodded, eager to move forward to ease my torment.

Doris said, "I'll drive since you can't. I'll come by tomorrow at nine to pick y'all up."

SPECTRAL PROMISES

Chapter 2
The Star Occult Shop

After weeks of isolation, the idea of visiting a mystical shop sparked a flicker of excitement in me.

Upon returning home from the hospital, I visited a high-security, specialized bank in New Orleans with Andy. This financial institution was exclusively available to customers who required discreet banking and financial services. The sign on the door read Harcourt and Jameson Financial Services, with no mention of it being a bank.

Webster Turner kept a secret account there during his lifetime. My grandfather's ghost provided me with the passwords and phrases, which were the only identification needed to access the account and safety deposit box.

The account and box were cleaned out, and the items were placed into two metal suitcases that my attorney had brought. The account contained one million dollars in cash, and the container held stacks of stock certificates from various high-end investment companies. These would be worth several million dollars in today's market when sold. My attorney worked with a covert network, which Webster told us about, to forge a codicil to Webster's will, ensuring that my father was the sole heir and I, as his son, was his heir.

I keep a substantial amount of the money in the house safe for easy access. I took some cash from the mansion's library safe while my grandfather watched over my shoulder. I don't mind Webster always being around. It's comforting to have someone to converse with amid the chaos. Most living people steer clear of me because of the disturbing sensations I emit—caused by the magical abilities the Duke 'Blessed' me with. 'Blessed,' yeah, right—more like cursed.

The other ghost who had previously followed me was my former best friend, Cyrus Labauve. Cyrus was my multiple great-grandfather and the one who had initially been the cause of the L'Enfant Haven plantation curse. However, I had only discovered that fact a few hours before the psychic battle with my grandmother. The attic is now his usual hangout.

Cyrus knows I still haven't fully forgiven him for what he had done, keeping the location of the signet sapphire a secret from all of us in the house for his selfish reasons. He said it was because he was gay, in love with me, and didn't want to go to the other side. He wanted to stay with me forever. This situation upset me.

Doris drove her black Honda Accord to the front of the mansion. I climbed into the front passenger seat, and Webster and Rose, the two ghosts, moved to the back seat. All house ghosts can now come with me off the plantation if I permit it. Before I broke the curse, the only one who could leave the property was Cyrus, but he had to remain near the amulet. At that time, I carried the amulet with me because I liked having Cyrus near.

I took two pain pills for the trip. I didn't want to grimace in pain around strangers. Normal people get ominous vibes from me, and showing a painful expression won't help.

Drugs can impair my ability to perceive spirits, but two of the prescribed medications were not enough to reduce my abilities. Anything more, and the specters would start to appear transparent, and it would be hard for me to hear them.

It took us about an hour to get to the Star Occult Shop in Shreveport, Louisiana. We parked a block away because there were no parking spaces available on the street in that part of town, which features several small shops of various kinds.

Before leaving the car, I told Rose, "Okay, go ahead and enter me now."

I inhaled deeply, exhaled, relaxed, and allowed the priestess to take possession of my body. I jerked slightly as she maneuvered herself into my flesh. My skin flushed, and the hairs on my arms rose briefly as the occupancy occurred.

This wasn't a deep possession like the first time she entered my body and took it over. This low-level occupancy I could control if I wanted to, and I could extract her when needed—one of the many powers the Duke gave me.

Both of us were using my eyes the moment I opened them. I sat there blinking, trying to make sense of the new presence inhabiting my body. It was like walking through dense fog, disorienting. Yet, I pushed through the confusion and regained control.

Doris's eyes locked onto mine; concern etched across her face.

"Is everything okay?" she asked softly.

I swallowed hard, forcing a reassuring smile.

"Yeah, I'm alright."

Rose, speaking through my vocal cords in a tone infused with her essence, chirped, "Let's go! I've been dying to shop again!"

Strolling ahead of Doris, she swayed my hips with feminine grace.

The crystal witch sidled up next to me, her voice a low murmur.

"Orion, maybe you should take over the walking—unless you're okay with everyone assuming..."

She let the implication hang, her tone teasing.

I took over walking and opened the door for Doris, just as Nanny Helen taught me.

A prominent sign hung on the shop's door: 'THANK YOU FOR NOT SMOKING IN THESE PREMISES.' I smiled at this because I didn't like being around smokers either.

Webster followed behind me, staying quiet. A bell hanging from the door rang as we passed through the entryway.

The crystal witch grabbed two baskets from a stack near the front door, one for herself and one for Rose and me.

"The herbs are over there," she said, pointing to the far corner.

I headed in that direction, while Doris made her way to the crystal display near the front.

Only a few people wandered the aisles. A woman glanced my way, her eyes lingering with a curiosity that felt out of place—neither fear nor unease, just an almost knowing intrigue, a different reaction than I usually get from people. Why was it different here, when everywhere else I went, people always shied away?

The air in the small store was thick with incense and the soft hum of unseen energy. Shelves filled with occult curiosities pressed in from every corner while a beaded curtain hinted at secrets in the back. Unusual paintings depicting occult objects, places from a unique perspective, or ordinary items surrounded by strange patterns of light hung above the shelves on the walls around the room.

Rose started gathering different plant and herb bundles, taking deep inhalations of their scents. I recognized the names on only a few of the tags. Jars and bundles soon filled the basket. We might need a second one.

I occasionally glanced at the artwork on the walls as we moved through the aisles. One picture caught my eye, depicting a wooden door with a lion-headed knocker and a ring hanging from its mouth. The partially open door emitted light streaming through the cracked entrance. I stopped and studied it. It resembled the door of my house. The knocker seemed identical—I could have sworn it was smiling at me—and the patterns in the wood panels appeared familiar.

At that moment, the doorbell tinkled, and Doris shouted, "Seren! I'm so glad you're here."

I looked toward her to determine who excited the crystal witch. Doris hugged an auburn-haired woman dressed in a mid-calf-length Indian paisley print peasant dress with an open neckline that slipped off her ivory left shoulder. Cinched at the waist with a macramé belt, it accentuated her curves.

When I looked up, the woman had her back to me, but something about her felt familiar—her auburn hair, thick with long waves and curls. I wanted to run my hands through it. I could almost feel it flowing between my fingers, which tingled at the thought. The way she leaned on her right leg seemed so intimate. She was taller than Doris, and I liked that.

The two women talked, and the tall redhead laughed, a sound I recognized from somewhere, but where? It made me smile, and I felt ready to laugh with her. I pursed my lips to hold back my laughter.

The woman named Seren turned and walked toward the back of the store. She was stunning, with milky skin, a radiant smile, and sparkling eyes. One red curl fell over her left eye, and she brushed it back with her hand. I wished I could do the same.

I couldn't look away from her. Every subtle movement she made seized my attention—the sway of her hips, the gentle rhythm of her stride. An almost magnetic pull drew me closer, as if her hand belonged in mine. My eyes followed her as she passed through the shop and the beaded doorway, unable to tear myself away. I kept staring at the spot where she had last been, craving her return with an intense longing.

This wasn't like me. Typically, I hide behind self-consciousness and never dare to look at someone this way, even women I find stunning. So why did I do this?

Then, Rose said in my mind, '*Orion! Orion! Come back to this plane.*'

I answered, '*Oh, I'm sorry. What else do you need?*'

I felt a little embarrassed at my infatuation with the redhead.

Webster leaned over to me and said, '*She's a looker.*'

I nodded. Every cell of my body agreed with him, and I glanced back at the beaded curtain she had just passed through.

Rose asked, '*Can you move over to the charms and talismans on the wall behind the counter? I need a couple of those.*'

'*Sure, no problem.*'

Rose reached out with my left hand while I approached the counter and grabbed three boxes of chalk from a shelf.

I asked the clerk to retrieve a couple of the talismans that the priestess requested in my mind. The pretty young Black woman pulled them off the hooks, and the ghost priestess inspected them in minute detail.

Seren pushed through the beaded curtain, slipping smoothly behind the counter with ease and confidence. I looked up at that moment, and her full lips curved into a knowing smile that made my stomach tighten. Her eyes—an electric, vibrant green—locked onto mine. I found myself yearning to drown in those emerald pools, to press my lips to hers, to run my fingers through her fiery red hair. Every fiber of my being was screaming. Why am I so irresistibly drawn to this woman?

Doris suddenly appeared next to me. I wasn't aware of her approach, as I was so captivated by the redhead's radiance.

"Seren, I would like you to meet Orion Labauve, a friend and client of my boss. Orion, this is Seren Griffyths."

The beautiful redhead smiled and extended her hand. I awkwardly shook it with my left hand since my right arm was still in a cast and sling. I'm sure I had a silly expression on my face.

When our hands touched, I was someone else and somewhere else with her.

We walked through a field of tall grass, exchanging loving smiles and holding hands. I had been away longer than expected on my business trip to the Caribbean and missed being with her. My heart pounded with happiness at being back in France, next to the woman I loved. The sun was shining, and I carried a basket in my other hand.

We climbed over an old stone fence. I took off my long coat and laid it on the ground for her to sit on. I sat beside her, pulled a bottle of wine from the basket, and uncorked it. We both drank from the bottle. I leaned over and kissed the lips I longed to feel on mine for months, savoring the taste of wine still there. Her tongue entered my mouth and...

Seren unexpectedly pulled her hand away.

"Jenny, can you take care of these purchases? I need to do something in the back."

She hurried out of the room and through the beaded curtain. I stood there with my mouth open, leaning over the counter where she had just been. I watched her go, confused and unsure of what had just happened, with my hand still extended for the handshake.

Seeing my puzzled expression, Doris asked, "Are you alright?"

I wasn't sure what had just transpired between Seren and I. I returned to myself, shaking my head and blinking my eyes to refocus them. I glanced at the crystal witch.

"Yeah, I'm alright. Is this everything you want?" I said, trying to deflect further questions.

She had two cases of candles and a box filled with various mounted crystals. I had a basket overflowing with Rose's selections, releasing aromas that overwhelmed all other scents at the counter.

"Yes," Doris said, furrowing her brow, wondering what was

happening.

"Okay, I'm paying for everything, and I want the picture of the door over there. Is it for sale?"

I pointed to the far wall.

Jenny, the clerk, said, "Yes, it is. Okay, give me a minute to pull it down."

She walked through the beaded curtain and returned a few minutes later with a step ladder. She placed it under the requested piece of art and carefully lifted it off the hook. She returned and handed me the picture.

I held the 12-by-18-inch painting, signed 'Seren,' admiring its craftsmanship. An unusual feeling ran through my fingers as I examined the artwork.

The clerk rang everything up.

One of my business cards slipped out of my wallet and onto the counter when I was taking money out. Without thinking much about it, I grabbed a pen from beside the cash register and wrote my phone number on the back.

I asked Jenny, "Can you give this to Seren and ask her to call me sometime?"

I had never given a woman my number. Why did I do this? For some reason, I felt compelled to do this.

Doris piped in, "Hand me the card."

She added, 'Ghost Expert,' on the back. I raised my brows at her, wondering why she would put that on the card.

With a huge grin, Jenny took the business card.

"Sure, honey. I'll make sure she gets it."

I stacked the three boxes and lifted them with my left arm. Doris grabbed the extra-large brown paper bag filled with Rose's items and the painting. We exited the store.

I looked over my shoulder as we left, hoping Seren was there, but felt disappointed when she didn't return. We placed our purchases in the trunk of the Honda, and I arranged the artwork to protect it during the trip. Was there something unusual in the light coming through the door? I shook my head and closed the trunk. We headed back home.

I sat in the passenger seat, and Rose withdrew from me with a jerk.

I gasped as she pulled away, blinking several times to clear my vision.

As she drove, Doris asked, "Orion, what happened back there? You looked like you were in a trance and somewhere else when you touched Seren's hand."

"I don't know what happened. Seren felt so familiar as she walked into the store, and I couldn't keep my eyes off her. When we touched, we were somewhere else, holding hands, walking through a field, dressed in 18th-century clothing. We sat down and drank wine from a bottle. I kissed her, and the vision suddenly ended when Seren released my hand."

Doris hesitated, her eyes scanning the distance along the road before she spoke.

"Orion, I think what you experienced was... a glimpse of a past life."

"A what?"

This statement stunned me. Familiar with the concept from stories and movies, I never thought it was real.

Doris explained, "A past-life experience is when someone remembers and experiences an event from a past life in another time and place. You and Seren must have known each other in a previous life."

"Is that a real thing?"

It was hard for me to believe this explanation.

"With what you've been through and seen, you don't believe in the possibility of reincarnation and previous lives?"

"I thought when you died, you just went to the other side and stayed there for eternity."

Rose piped in from the back, "While that's true for most people, some souls are destined to have multiple lives to fulfill their ultimate Soul Mission."

"Soul Mission? So, you're saying I have a Soul Mission because I may have had a past life."

I thought, 'Wonderful, something else to complicate my already crazy life.'

"Yes, I am. Orion, aren't you curious why your life has been so unusual?" Rose asked.

"I just figured it was all because of the Duke."

"That's partially true, but why did he choose you to have exceptional abilities? There are other Gods above him who guide mid-level Gods toward influential paths, as the mid-level deities manipulate us for reasons we don't understand," the ex-priestess explained.

"While I was in the spirit realm, the Duke mentioned Bondee. Is he…she…it a higher God?" I asked.

"Yes. One of many."

"Did you meet 'God' when you were on the other side?"

"Only the Voodoo mid-level Gods. It all depends on your beliefs and your soul's enlightenment," she said.

"Oh, man, this is making my head spin. I guess I have a lot to learn."

"Yes, you do. The Duke instructed me to teach you. You just had your first lesson on universal spiritualism. While you were experiencing your past life, I felt your love for the woman from the past. I sensed the emotions. Something was happening between you two."

"Wait a minute. Doris, why did you put 'Ghost Expert' on my business card?"

The crystal witch said, "I sensed that Seren would need one soon."

I've known Doris since I was three, and she was always just the Butler's secretary. I keep forgetting she is a witch and probably psychic as well. Andy and I discovered that she was a crystal witch a few months ago.

After this profound discussion, I remained silent for the rest of trip home. Gazing out the window, my mind raced with this newfound knowledge, feeling as though I was just touching the surface of a vast, universal iceberg. Could Seren and I have known each other in a past life? Is that why I feel an irresistible pull towards her?

I couldn't get Seren Griffyths out of my mind. Her stunning image kept invading my thoughts. I wanted—no, I needed—more information about her. And that painting signed 'Seren.' How could she paint a picture of my front door? She's never visited the mansion. I would have remembered someone so beautiful and vibrant as her.

SPECTRAL PROMISES

Chapter 3
Man from her Dreams

The bell's welcoming tinkle greeted Seren as she entered the Star Occult Shop. Returning from errands, the sound was always comforting, a sign of home. But today it also hinted at something extraordinary.

Doris Owens, a fellow member of the Occult Cabalistic Club, waved enthusiastically and called to her. The psychic approached her friend with a big grin and hugged her.

While conversing with the crystal witch, the psychic struggled to focus on her friend's words. She laughed at something Doris said, but the memory of the joke faded as quickly as it appeared. Like the touch of an unseen hand, an unsettling sensation washed over her body. She felt as if she were being watched.

Seren headed toward her office in the back storage area beyond the beaded curtain and felt eyes watching her as she brushed an errant curl from her left eye. She placed her patchwork leather purse under the desk and checked for any messages Jenny might have left while she ran errands. There was nothing urgent.

Hidden behind the beaded drape, Seren's gaze sharpened as she surveyed the room. A striking man with tousled dark curls, wearing a Star Wars T-shirt, stood casually near the counter. Something shimmered beside him—perhaps a spirit? His outline flickered ominously as he inspected a voodoo talisman in his hand. Possessed? No, this was something far rarer, something utterly unique and potent.

As she approached the counter, Doris introduced the man as a friend. A sudden wave of recognition crashed over her as Seren gazed into his piercing blue eyes, flecked with gold—a striking, unforgettable sight. His dazzling gaze held her captive. And that distinctive white curl of hair, a clear sign of some past trauma, seemed to shout at her. She recognized him from somewhere, or at least her instincts told her she did. She grinned and stretched out her hand to him. He awkwardly took her palm with his left, his right arm in a sling.

As their hands touched, the shop faded away. She found herself elsewhere, holding the hand of someone she loved beyond reason.

The field stretched endlessly under a golden sun as she clasped her lover's hand; they laughed. His loose, sun-kissed hair framed the warmth in his eyes. He left it unbound this morning, not pulled back and held with a leather ribbon at the nape of his neck, which was how he typically wore it.

They were going to have a picnic. He had been away for over three months and had only recently returned to France. They climbed over the old stone wall, and he removed his coat, placing it on the ground for them to lie on. He took a wine bottle from the basket, uncorked it, and they both took a sip. He leaned over and kissed her. She welcomed it longingly, feeling the heat of the kiss on her lips and tongue as she explored his mouth.

Seren grasped the truth of her feelings with a painful clarity. It had to stop—now—before it spiraled out of control. She sharply pulled her hand away from his grasp.

She asked Jenny to take care of the customers and rushed to the back, pushing through the beads, her heart pounding. She braced herself against the wall beside the doorway, her breath catching in her throat. The person she shook hands with was the man in her dreams, whose face always hovered just beyond recognition—until now. The fragments of those visions shattered into certainty the instant her hand touched him. Her chest clenched painfully, caught between elation and dread.

Her ears rang with intense sharpness. She longed to be with this handsome young man, but caution stirred, warning her that something was wrong. This longing wasn't part of her life. This sensation was from a previous existence, an illusion from someone else's love. Her heart raced with emotion and desire. She trembled, torn by a haunting memory. An internal battle left her unsure of what to do next.

During a past-life regression at one of the Occult Cabalistic club meetings, Seren learned about Abelard Ozane. Aimee, a member of the club who specialized in past-life regressions, offered each member the chance to experience it. Seren was aware of several previous lives she had had but only remembered brief glimpses of them: a psychic, a witch, and a priestess. The regression of her life with Abelard, the man she loved in that distant time, was the most vivid, intense, and tragic.

Her name in that life was Chloe Padou. Abelard, the man she adored, was the son of a wealthy landowner and merchant. She was the candle maker's daughter. They fell in love from the moment they met in her father's shop. After six months, the couple planned to marry, but they knew Abelard's family wouldn't be happy with their son's choice of bride.

His family wanted him to marry a wealthy merchant's daughter and had a few potential matches arranged for him to meet. He always made excuses to avoid exploring these options. He traveled to the Caribbean islands to handle business for his father, but when he returned, something about him had changed: he seemed more anxious, cautious, and uneasy.

There was something different about this Orion, too. The past-life vision kept her from learning more about him. The only thing she sensed was that ghosts seemed to be near him, and he had some kind of power, possibly voodoo magic, since he was looking at voodoo talismans. This only increased Seren's curiosity about their past-life connection.

Jenny came through the beaded curtain and saw Seren leaning against the wall.

"Are you okay?"

"Yes, I felt a little dizzy, and it really frightened me at first, but thankfully, it's passing now."

Jenny paused for a moment, gazing at her friend, then she grabbed the stepladder to retrieve the painting a customer requested.

Seren watched, wondering which picture he had chosen. He wanted to buy 'The Door.' What drew him to that one?

The shop owner waited until Doris and her mysterious friend left. A broad smile appeared on the clerk's face as she approached Seren to give her the attractive customer's business card.

"I think you have an admirer. He said you should call him sometime. His phone number's on the back of the card."

The psychic examined the card: ORION ANISTON LABAUVE— Finder of Things and People. Printed at the bottom was: Agent: Andrew Butler Jr., along with a telephone number. She flipped it over, revealing a handwritten phone number and the words 'Ghost Expert' inscribed by someone else. An ominous sensation ran up her spine, heightening her curiosity about this mysterious man.

The business card felt cold against her fingertips. A vision manifested of Orion standing before a plantation mansion, hurling glowing energy orbs at a voodoo priestess who retaliated with hex-laden pouches. The ominous perception blurred—was it the past or the future? She couldn't tell. What kind of power is he hiding?

"Thanks."

She placed the card in the register under the cash tray to stop the unsettling images. Still reeling from the past-life vision, she felt uneasy.

Jenny said, "He's handsome. You should call him. He gives off a weird vibe, but it's nothing bad. You need to go out with a man. You haven't been with a guy for quite a while."

"There's something... unusual about him," Seren admitted, her voice distant. "But I'm swamped right now. Starting something with anyone isn't in the cards."

She shouldn't even consider starting something with someone from a previous life; that's a path fraught with danger. Stories circulated about people reconnecting across lifetimes only to be doomed by old problems that refused to stay buried. When past-life issues surfaced, they tore relationships apart, and those unions rarely stood the test of time.

Jenny shook her head.

"Okay, I'm just saying, honey, you shouldn't be alone."

"I'm not alone—I have you."

Seren smiled at her best friend, knowing she was right about everything.

Remembering Seren leaning against the wall, the clerk asked, "What was really going on in the back when you were leaning against the wall?"

The psychic knew she couldn't hide things from Jenny.

"I think I had a past life vision when I touched Orion Labauve's hand. It surprised me, so I went back to calm myself."

"Past life, eh? That's interesting. You might want to look into that more."

"Maybe I will, later."

A customer came through the door, and Seren hurried around the counter to help them, needing to focus on something else.

SPECTRAL PROMISES

Chapter 4

Women: Distant Untouchable Dreams

When I returned home, Rose went into the kitchen to prepare lunch. I leaned the painting against the wall in the front hall, its presence weighing on me like an unanswered question. I stared at it, struggling to understand how the redhead could have created something connected to me and why.

Doris brushed past me, ready to leave, but I begged, "Please stay for lunch and tell me more about Seren."

She agreed, and we shared chicken salad sandwiches at the kitchen table. The smell of rosemary and freshly baked bread did little to erase my growing unease.

"I need to know more about Seren Griffyths," I said, urgency slipping into my voice.

Doris set her sandwich down, looking thoughtful.

"I don't know much about her. I've been buying most of my crystals from her store over the past few years, and I joined the Occult Cabalistic Club she started. Like you, Seren is an incredibly strong psychic and has had these abilities most of her life. She's well-versed in various mystical practices and religions. She's very personable and friendly, with a wonderful sense of humor. I enjoy being around her.

"Seren once told me that she helped the Shreveport police with a couple of cases."

While Doris spoke, I found my mind drifting—not away from Seren, but toward her, recalling the spark I felt when her hand touched mine.

Doris raised an eyebrow, an amused smile playing on her lips.

"You like her, don't you?"

"There's something about her..." I trailed off, shaking my head as the thought refused to manifest.

She didn't press the issue and moved to another room to talk about the upcoming ritual with Rose. I excused myself to the porch, needing the fresh air to process the day's revelations.

I sat alone on one of the wicker chairs, picking at the fibers sticking up on the left arm, and letting the truth wash over me. Seren Griffyths fascinated me; her presence tugged at me in a way I didn't fully understand. But what chance did I have with someone like her?

My history with women—or, rather, the lack of it—has always been marked by brief, awkward encounters—knowing that my very presence unsettles people, especially when they're sober. Women only wanted me to stay overnight when alcohol dulled their senses to the strange, unnatural aura I can't shake.

Because of the danger that my life attracted, I couldn't picture a future with Seren—or anyone, for that matter. The Voodoo Imperatrice's manipulations served as a brutal reminder of what loving someone can cost. Andy Butler Jr., my attorney, learned that lesson the hard way when she made his wife sick just a few months ago, forcing him to betray me to save her. Caring for someone wasn't just a risk; it was a weapon to be turned against me. The dream of a woman who might accept my strangeness and me as I am wasn't possible. Not for me.

I'd never had a girlfriend, but girls always fascinated me. By high school, that fascination grew into something hard to explain. Girls were like a beautiful mystery I didn't know how to reach. I admired them from afar. Meanwhile, I felt like a shadow, invisible unless someone needed a target for their jokes.

Around twelve, I became aware of changes in my body. I'd wake up feeling flushed, confused, not understanding what was happening to me. One morning, as I sat at the breakfast table, my mind raced with questions I was too afraid to voice. Summoning every ounce of courage, I asked Doc Albert what was happening to me. His answers were clinical yet gentle, and for the first time, I didn't feel dirty or strange. Still, the raw reality of growing up hit me like a punch in the gut.

Girls weren't just pretty faces anymore. They were dreams.

Distant, untouchable dreams. It remained a mystery to me how a man and a woman would ever get together, given that all the girls at school always shied away and never wanted to be near me. Even in classrooms, there were a few times when fights nearly broke out because no one, male or female, wanted to sit next to me. I always sat in the farthest corner beside a wall to avoid upsetting anyone. My desks displayed chipped corners from where I nervously picked them.

Eavesdropping on locker-room talk shattered my innocence and introduced me to the mysterious realm of sex. One night at home, armed with a stolen magazine I found discarded in the trash, I surrendered to curiosity. What started as strange and awkward quickly transformed into an explosion of sensation. As I approached the edge of the unknown, a surge of energy ignited within me. For a few fleeting moments, I wasn't the outcast; I was truly alive.

One day, when I was sixteen, it happened. I had just grabbed my lunch bag from my hall locker when Cyrus, my ghostly companion whom no one else could detect, warned me that someone was coming my way.

'*Heads up,*' he exclaimed in my mind.

I closed the locker door, expecting some teasing or a prank, but it never happened. I turned, ready for trouble. Instead, Norma Meyers stood beside me with a curious smile curving her lips. She was in a few of my classes and was pretty, with wavy brown hair and light, mischievous brown eyes.

"Your name's Orion, right?"

Her smile was so unexpected that I thought it might be a trick. My first instinct was to be suspicious. People didn't talk to me unless they had a reason to laugh.

"Yeah."

I stood and waited for some curse or slur, but all she said was, "Are you going to the cafeteria?"

"Yeah."

"Cool, me, too. Can I sit with you?"

"Sure, okay."

I looked around, expecting something more to happen. I didn't understand what was going on. We walked together to the cafeteria, my heart pounding. I strolled down the hall beside a girl like any other guy. I looked around. How could this happen?

She headed for the line, picked up a tray, and I followed her, but didn't take one. I rarely had money, so I always brought my lunch.

Beside me, Cyrus said, '*Why is she doing this?*'

I whispered, "I don't know," irritated by him bothering me.

Norma turned around with a smile.

"What did you say?"

"Nothing," I said, trying to look casual.

She bought her lunch, and I found an empty table in a far corner, assuming she wouldn't want the other students to see her sitting with me.

She said, "You don't talk much, do you?"

Still in shock that a girl would speak to me, I struggled, unsure of what to say.

"No, I don't," I replied, my head down, studying the stains on the table, scratching at them, afraid to meet her gaze.

"Why's that?" she asked with a slight frown.

"People don't like me and don't want to talk to me, so after a while, I just stopped trying."

I opened my lunch bag and removed my sandwich.

She leaned forward, resting her chin on her hand.

"You're that guy who finds things, right?"

"Yes."

I raised my head, thinking she might want me to find something for her. I charged the students to find things. It gave me some spending money since I never received anything from my mother.

I ate my chicken sandwich and offered her a slice of my apple. She took it and slowly nibbled, lost in deep thought. I waited to hear what she needed me to find, but the question never came; only a curious expression appeared.

"How do you do that?" she asked.

"It's hard to explain," I hesitated, debating whether to tell her. "I can sort of feel things, like a pull in my stomach. It gets stronger the closer I get to it, and I sometimes feel sick."

She seemed to think about that as she finished her lunch.

"Wow! That's weird."

'Yeah, that's me, weird,' I thought, 'Here it comes. She'll say something mean.'

"You drive that old Rolls-Royce, right?"

"Yes."

I was still trying to understand why she even spoke to me.

I had passed the driving test and received my driver's license just a few weeks ago. I had been operating vehicles since I was ten, but only on the plantation property. The driving examiner fidgeted in his seat while we were in the car. He passed me to get rid of me as quickly as possible, rather than honestly evaluating my skills.

The first day I drove into the school parking lot in the Rolls-Royce, everyone stopped and stared in amazement. As I parked the luxurious vehicle, the surprised expressions of the students and teachers made my heart skip a beat. I smiled, knowing that no one else owned a car like this. I had always been the kid with hand-me-down clothes and no money; now, I possessed something no one else had.

Norma asked, "Could you give me a ride home on Monday?"

Her words hit me like a jolt of electricity.

"Yeah, sure."

I stared at her.

She stood looking to the other side of the room.

"Okay, it's a date. I gotta go now. I'll see you on Monday at your car after school."

"Alright," I said hesitantly.

My potential first date sauntered away and approached a group of girls on the opposite side of the room. When she walked over, they all gathered around her and began giggling.

I sat with my mouth open. Did Norma say it was a date? I had a date with a girl. A date. The word lingered in the air, heavy with possibilities.

Cyrus appeared beside me as she walked away, his voice low and teasing.

'Well, look at you, Romeo.'

I nodded, still in shock from what had just happened. The bell rang, and I slowly shuffled toward class, still lost in thought about getting together with a girl. Arriving late, I took my detention slip in a daze.

The rest of the day went by in a fog. I couldn't stop thinking about Norma. Was she serious about the ride? Was it truly a date? The word felt strange, as if it didn't belong in my life. And yet, she said it so casually, as if it were the most natural thing in the world.

Driving home from school after detention, my mind spiraled. I was dating a girl. What should I do? Maybe I could steal a kiss or even make out. Perhaps I could go further. No way. I could never be that lucky.

I entered through the back door and shuffled past Bertha and Doc without saying a word, my eyes fixed on the floor. I had never acted that way before. My mind was still reeling from the thought of having a date and trying to figure out what to do. Bertha, the ghost cook, and Doc Albert, the spirit of my distant cousin, exchanged glances.

The ghost doctor called to me, "Orion, what's wrong?"

I stopped and turned, "What? Oh...Nothing."

"You didn't even bother to say hi when you walked in the door. What's going on?"

Concern flickered in Doc's eyes, highlighting the gravity of the moment.

"Oh, I'm sorry. I was thinking about the date with Norma."

Doc shouted, "You have a date with a girl?"

A big grin appeared on his face.

"Kinda… Norma wants me to drive her home on Monday after school. She said it was a date."

"Well, okay. It doesn't sound like much of one, but it's a start."

"Doc, what am I supposed to do? I don't know what to do with a girl. I mean, I know how it's supposed to be done. But I don't know…" I trailed off, on the verge of being upset.

Albert said, "Come over here and sit down."

I plopped onto the couch, worried that he might say I can't go out with her. Doc sat next to me.

"Don't get upset, and don't count your chickens before they're hatched. She may only want a ride home. But if more happens, don't move too fast and scare her. Girls can become scared easily. They are more sensitive than boys. Just start with a gentle kiss and place your hand on her arm. If she enjoys that, then you can go for a more intense kiss."

"But Doc, I don't even know how to kiss a girl."

My lower lip began to tremble as I thought about not knowing how to make out with a girl.

"Okay, we'll teach you what to do with a girl."

The ghosts always seemed to know what I was thinking and feeling.

"You're going to teach me," I pushed away, not wanting a man to show me how to kiss a woman.

"Not me. Milly and Philly will show you. They know how to be with a man. They are the experts in this house. They can show you how to have sex with a woman."

I sat in shock. I hadn't yet touched Milly or Philly on their death anniversary to uncover their past. When I touch a ghost on that day, I experience the tragic memories of their lives and understand why they are stuck in the L'Enfant Haven mansion.

A year later, I discovered, on the anniversary of their deaths, the horrifying truth: Milly and Philly had been snatched from the streets at just fifteen by Gregor Labauve, a distant relative from the 1880s. He placed them into a high-end New Orleans brothel, where they learned all things sensual and sexual. After years of brutal instruction, they were sent to the L'Enfant Haven plantation where they served as maids and secret lovers to Gregor himself, until both of them became pregnant. In a desperate attempt to cover his actions, Gregor hired a shady character to perform abortions, which tragically went horribly wrong—both girls bled to death.

Gregor was the sickest of my relatives; his depravity knew no bounds. If he hadn't died in a hospital, I'm convinced he would still be lurking among my family, poisoning everyone with his evil.

The two spirit maids stood beside me. Each took one of my hands, and with broad smiles, they led me up the stairs to my bedroom.

Over the next two days, they gently taught me everything I needed to know—every nuance of lovemaking and what truly pleases women. Despite my eager, enthusiastic focus, I couldn't shake the feeling that this wasn't normal. I was engaging in intimacy with ghosts. All I truly yearned for was to be with a real, living girl.

When I went downstairs, Doc warned me, "Be sure to use condoms for protection, and don't get a girl pregnant."

I thought, 'I've only got a couple of dollars from my finding money. Is that enough to buy condoms?'

Doc came out of his office and handed me a five-dollar bill from his secret stash of cash in the library desk.

"Thank you," I smiled.

I drove the Rolls to the drugstore and waited in the car, peering through the store's window until the customers left. I entered and nervously roamed the aisles but couldn't find the prophylactics. Finally, there they were, hanging on the wall behind the counter. SHIT!

I approached, and the gray-haired pharmacist, who had a permanent scowl and a cigarette dangling from his mouth, glanced up from his magazine.

He placed the cigarette in the ashtray on the counter and growled, "Can I help you?"

I stammered, "I...I...need a box of condoms."

He glared at me.

"What size?"

What size? Oh, my God. How was I supposed to know what size to get? REGULAR was prominently printed on several boxes.

I blurted out, "Regular."

I could feel myself blushing.

He asked, "Lubed or non-lubed?"

What on earth did that mean?

I answered, "Non-lubed."

He turned, grabbed a box off the hook, threw it on the counter, and rang up the sale. My hands trembled slightly as I paid. I hurried to the car, drove off, and took deep breaths.

I took the container into the house, ran to my bedroom, and read everything on the container and the insert. I took one out and experimented that night. I lay in bed, having difficulty falling asleep, hoping I wouldn't mess up the date.

The final bell rang on Monday. I hurried out to the parking lot, my palms sweating. I leaned against the front of the Rolls, trying to appear relaxed and casual, but my stomach cramped with anticipation. Norma approached, walking quickly, almost jogging, her hair flying behind her.

I stared—my first date. She was so pretty.

I thought, 'Don't mess this up.'

"Hi," she said, moving directly to the car, barely acknowledging my presence.

She opened the passenger-side door and jumped in as if she didn't want anyone to see her enter my vehicle.

I jumped when the car door slammed, and I ran to the driver's side.

"Hi. Where do you live?"

"Off Smith Road, but I want to go somewhere else first."

"Okay, where's that?" I asked with a big, stupid smile.

"On Riverside Road by the bridge."

I wasn't sure where that was.

"You'll have to give me directions."

"Just go south on Ralston and then left on Riverside. I'll tell you when to pull over."

I followed her directions, and we ended up near the overpass down a dirt road behind a grove of trees, hidden, where no one knew what we were doing.

I turned off the engine and sat, unsure of what to do next.

Then, I asked Norma, "Do you like Mr. Olson's history class?"

"Sure, it's fine."

She leaned over, grasped my shirt firmly, and pulled me into a fierce kiss. An electric shock shot through my body from my lips straight to my groin, leaving me breathless. Doc warned me to proceed cautiously with shy and sensitive girls, but Norma was anything but timid.

Remembering what Milly and Philly taught me, I slowly scooted over to her side of the front seat and gently kissed her. I wrapped my arms around her, kissed the soft skin on her neck, and sucked on her earlobe, hoping I was doing it right.

She started rubbing my semi-erect dick. Again, this shocked me, and I jumped when the pressure of her hand touched it.

She suggested, "Let's go in the backseat where there's more room."

I leaned over and opened the door. She got out and jumped into the back seat. I opened the glove compartment, pulled out a condom packet, and tucked it into my pocket.

I leaped out, and by the time I got in the back seat, she already had her pink blouse unbuttoned.

I hopped in, and she grabbed the edges of my white T-shirt and forcefully tugged it over my head. This was different from what I had anticipated.

I started kissing her more excitedly, having a hard time controlling my actions. I grasped one of her small breasts and gently kneaded it. I moved my tongue inside her mouth and explored around.

We continued to kiss and explore each other's bodies with our hands and mouths. A lavender scent permeated her hair, probably from the shampoo she used. I kissed down her neck and between her breasts. She sighed when I did this.

My confidence increased, and I glided my right hand under her plaid skirt, sliding it up and down the insides of her silky thighs. My digits tiptoed between her legs and over her already-wet panties, moving my fingers amongst the sensitive areas. She gasped and moved her hips around, getting more excited by my sensual manipulations. She really seemed to like this. I guess I was doing it right.

I was so hard by this time; I thought it would burst out of my pants. I was on fire and wanted to go all the way, but I knew to hold off as long as possible.

Norma grabbed my belt, frantically unbuckled it, and unzipped my jeans. I pulled them and my underwear down to my knees and ripped open the condom package with my teeth. As I rolled it on, she removed her panties.

She lay back, her eyes begging to go all the way, "Now! Do it now!"

For the first time, I felt another person enveloping me. It was clumsy yet exhilarating. Still, it felt incomplete. Even amidst this incredible experience, something was missing.

Norma shouted, "Faster, faster!"

I went for the gusto, closing my eyes and trying to maintain control, but I came soon after, and she followed almost immediately, yelling, "Yes! Yes!"

Afterward, I lay on top of her with my face between her breasts. We were both sweaty and panting.

I relaxed and leaned up to kiss her, but she pushed me away, saying, "Get off."

I sat up, confused.

"What's wrong? Did I do something bad?"

"No. Just take me home now, please."

"I thought maybe we could do it again."

Anticipation mounting along with other parts.

"No, I just want to go home."

I got out of the back seat, threw the spent condom into the bushes, and pulled up my pants as she put her panties back on. I replaced my T-shirt while she buttoned up her blouse.

Still confused, I asked, "Did I do something wrong? I thought it was wonderful."

She snapped back at me, "Just take me home, now."

"Okay."

What happened? Why was she angry with me? I drove back onto the road, and she gave me directions to her house. She didn't say anything else during the whole trip.

When she moved to get out of the car, I grabbed her hand and asked again, "Please, tell me if I did something wrong."

She shouted, "Let go!" as she forcefully pulled her hand away, slammed the car door, and ran into an empty house.

I sat in the Rolls, completely confused, watching the lights inside the house turn on. I slammed my palm on the steering wheel several times in frustration, not understanding what I had done wrong.

On my drive home, I thought about what should have been an incredible experience and couldn't understand why Norma didn't feel the same way. She seemed to enjoy it, as shown by her sighs, gasps, and moans when she came.

My ghost friend Cyrus was with me during this event because the amulet was in my pocket. I found him and the amulet in the attic when I was eleven, and he always followed wherever it went. He was always around, and being so used to it, it didn't embarrass me that he was there during my first experience with sex. I told him to stay silent while I was with Norma, and for once, he listened.

I asked, "Cyrus, what did I do wrong?'"

"You did nothing wrong. You did everything perfectly. There's something not right with that girl."

This didn't just disappoint me; it shattered my confidence—tormented by the relentless thought that I caused this terrible turn of events. Upon returning home, my stomach twisted with dread, convinced I had completely ruined everything. What should have been a glorious moment transformed into a catastrophic disaster. I retreated to my room, rejecting any hunger, paralyzed by regret. I believe Cyrus was the one who leaked the information about what happened to the other ghosts.

I tried to talk to Norma the next day, but she looked at me with an expression I couldn't quite understand. Was it an 'I can't believe you're talking to me,' or 'Please don't talk to me,' look?

She shouted, "Get away from me, you freak!" and stomped off.

Everyone turned to stare; their expressions filled with disgust. I hurried outside and sat alone at a picnic table, picking wood chips off it, missing my history class. The world was collapsing around me.

I didn't say anything to anyone for several days, and then it happened again. A different girl approached me and started talking. She asked for a ride home, and I fell for it again.

She was blonde, her name was Joy, and she was a joy. With this second girl asking for a ride home, because I had no experience being with girls, I wondered if this was what happened to other guys. Girls come up and ask for a ride. Was there a double meaning to this?

Like Norma, she took the lead. As we kissed, I could taste cigarette smoke on her lips; she was a smoker. Far more energetic than Norma during intimacy, Joy gyrated around a lot, grabbed my ass, and screamed when she reached her climax. Thank God we were in the middle of nowhere.

I tried to persuade her to give it another shot. She thought about it for a moment but then brushed me off.

"No, take me home."

I drove to her house, again baffled. What was I doing wrong?

Cyrus said, "Don't worry about it. She's a dog and has a big nose."

The following week, a third girl named Karen, who was a bit heavier than the previous two girls, approached me for a ride. Once again, we had a wonderful time in the back seat.

While we were getting dressed, she said, "The others said you were terrific, and they were right."

This statement shocked me, and I flippantly said, "If I'm so good, then why do you all just want to fuck and then go home?"

Karen laughed.

"You're the freak that everyone never dares to touch. If we can stand being near you and do it with you, we're in and can join the Good Girls Club."

Her words landed heavier than a slap, and for the first time, I wished I could haunt someone.

This angered me. I almost wanted to make her walk home. I didn't say anything for the rest of the drive to her house. Cyrus was ready to shove her out when she opened the car door, but I grabbed his hand and stopped him. He probably wouldn't have been able to push her because the ghosts don't have much power to move things when away from the L'Enfant Haven property.

I screeched the tires as I drove away.

When a fourth girl asked me for a ride, I yelled at her, "Go fuck yourself. My services are no longer available to the Good Girls Club."

I turned and stormed off. Classmates stared as I hurried down the hall. Maybe I should have kept offering my services.

I didn't have sex with another woman until I was eighteen, when I picked up a drunk college girl a few years older than me at a dance club. We went to her nearby apartment and had a fantastic time. However, in the morning, when she woke up and started feeling uncomfortable around me, she told me to leave. After that, when I picked up a woman, I would leave after they fell asleep.

SPECTRAL PROMISES

Chapter 5
Calling a Lwa

On the day we agreed to perform the ritual to summon a healing Lwa from the spirit plane, Rose and Doris spent the whole day preparing for that night's ceremony, which coincided with the full moon's rise. They chose to do the ceremony then because, as the priestess explained, that is when the veil between this plane and the spirit realm is thinnest, making it easier to open a portal and summon a Lwa.

The sharp scent of burnt sage lingered in the air as Rose and Doris prepared for the full moon ritual. They rearranged the living room furniture, leaving ample space in the center. Rose knelt on the polished hardwood, a stick of chalk in hand, whispering as she etched a perfect five-foot circle onto the floor. At the circle's cardinal points—north, south, east, and west—she drew intricate sacred voodoo symbols with white, pink, and green chalk, their precise lines seeming to hum with latent energy.

The crystal witch arranged black and red candles around the sacred circle, their wicks already trimmed for the evening's work. Crystals placed at the cardinal points inside the white circle caught the fading sunlight from the back windows, casting fleeting rainbows throughout the room. She positioned a clear quartz crystal at the northern point. It refracted the light like a frozen sliver of sunlight.

Days before the ceremony, Rose and Doris had prepared bundles of various plants and herbs, tying them with burlap twine. The ghost priestess chanted in the god language, took a mouthful of blessed water, and blew it onto the talismans and charms to bless them. Now, the voodoo priestess placed them next to the quartz crystal.

Early in the day, the crystal witch found a quiet spot on the veranda where she meditated and soothingly hummed before the ritual, while stroking the crystal that always hung around her neck.

Rose called upon her son, Paul, the ghost yardman, for help. She moved him to the side, placed an old wash tub upside down on the floor, and showed him how to beat a specific rhythm on its bottom. Paul practiced while the women prepared other items for the ceremony. The sound echoed through the house, faintly vibrating in the soles of my feet as I waited.

I watched these preparations from the dining room, seated at the end of the table.

Doc Albert approached.

"Do you think this will work?"

"I don't know. We hope all this magic will be enough to pull something from the spirit realm."

"Being a man of science, it has always been hard for me to believe in this mumbo jumbo, but with everything I've seen in this house, I now understand it's all real and can work if done properly."

"Well, that's what I'm hoping for. If I can call a healing Lwa over to heal on my arm, that would be a godsend. I've got to do something about the continuous aching."

Rose approached.

"It would be good if you went somewhere quiet and meditated before the ritual. Concentrate on the movements you must make. I'll call you when it's time."

I nodded and went to my bedroom. I sat on my bed with my legs crossed, breathing slowly in and out, trying to meditate on the actions I needed to take. The ache in my arm made it hard to concentrate. I tried to relax beyond the pain, but it kept drawing my focus away.

Paul continued hitting the washtub downstairs, and I used the rhythm to calm my mind. The drumbeat reverberated in my bones, and I found myself somewhere else and as someone else.

Once again, I was Abelard Ozanne, entering the candle maker's shop to order several dozen candles for the Ozanne household. After returning from university a few weeks earlier, my mother asked me to run a couple of errands for her in town. It was a beautiful, clear day, and I welcomed the opportunity to walk to Falaise village, even though I could have ridden a horse.

The village of Falaise was positioned atop a forty-foot seaside limestone cliff. This location offered residents stunning views of the ocean and the coastline to both the north and south. A staircase was carved into the cliff to access the piers below, where fishing and supply vessels could dock.

As I stepped into the cozy shop, a bell hanging from the door rang, and the most extraordinary woman I had ever seen emerged from a back room.

"How may I help you, sir?"

She had thick, wavy auburn hair with wild curls that framed her face. Her full lips curved into a radiant smile that seemed to light up the room. I was instantly smitten, my heart pounding. Her green eyes shimmered like sunlight dancing on the ocean's surface, mesmerizing me. For a moment, I was so captivated I forgot how to speak, struggling to find words to answer her question.

I stammered, "I...I... need five dozen long candles delivered to the Ozanne household."

"Is that all, sir?" she asked, smiling with her green eyes twinkling.

"Yes, and I must know your name."

"Chloe. And yours is?"

She smiled and stared down at the counter shyly,

"Abelard Ozanne."

"Ah, you are Monsieur Ozanne's son. I should have recognized you."

"Have we met before? I'm sure I would have remembered you," I asked curiously.

"I used to go with my father to the Ozanne estate on deliveries and saw you several times before you went to school."

He remembered her now, the shy, red-haired little girl who would accompany Monsieur Padou.

"Oh, yes. My, but you have grown up while I was at school."

She smiled.

"So have you, sir. I'll have the candles delivered within the next few days."

"Will you deliver the candles?" I asked, hoping to have an opportunity to be near her again.

With a twinkle in her eyes, she replied, "I can do that."

"Good. I want to accompany you on a walk around the estate to show you some of the changes."

"I would like that."

Her smile made me want to stay and talk to her all day, but I couldn't; I had other errands to run. Reluctantly, I left the shop, glancing back through the window at her as I moved on to my next errand.

She arrived at the estate three days later. From my second-story bedroom window I saw her, driving a battered cart pulled by a weary old horse. Heart pounding, I hurried down the stairs, and a surge of anticipation and urgency engulfed me. She expertly maneuvered the wagon to the back servants's entrance, where all deliveries were made.

Without hesitation, I pushed past the servants to rush to her side, determination fueling my every move.

A shiver of intense pleasure and exhilarating excitement surged through my body as I firmly wrapped my hands around her slim waist and lifted her effortlessly off the cart. She placed her delicate hands on my shoulders as I gently set her down. The stunning girl smiled timidly, and my soul dissolved completely into her piercing, vibrant emerald pools...

Rose was shaking my shoulder, saying, "Orion, Orion. It's time.'"

I said, "That was so weird. I think I had another vision of that past life."

"You did?"

"My name was Abelard, and I loved a woman called Chloe. I met her in a candle shop and was immediately attracted to her."

"That's interesting. Your interaction with Seren must have opened a door to that past life. So, it wasn't just a one-time event. We'll need to investigate that later. We are ready for the ritual."

I followed her downstairs as the house seemed to hold its breath.

The living room had been transformed by nightfall into an ominous sanctuary. Only the flickering glow of candles cast twitching shadows, their flames dancing wildly in the faint currents stirred by unseen forces. The chalk circle on the floor gleamed faintly, its symbols pulsating with an eerie, ethereal light. The scent of burning herbs thickened into a heavy, intoxicating haze that made my head spin and sharpened my senses.

Rose pointed to the center of the circle.

"Sit there, listen to the rhythm of the drum, relax, and meditate on the movements of your arms. As the ceremony's climax approaches, I'll let you know when to summon the Lwa. Then you can begin your arm and hand movements."

I nodded, closed my eyes, relaxed, and swayed to the rhythm of the tinny drumbeats Paul produced.

Rose moved with deliberate intent, her steps pounding in sync with the drumbeats, each strike echoing like a fierce heartbeat through the room. She raised charms in her hands, her voice soaring in the ancient, God language—sharp, guttural, and primal. Though I didn't understand the words, their potent resonance shook me to my core.

Doris's unmistakable, haunting hum sliced through Rose's chanting, piercing the air. Her voice blended with the crystals, which pulsed with a radiant glow, casting fiery, shifting colors that painted the room. Every note struck deep within my chest, resonating, awakening a raw, primal energy.

Rose moved around the circle with purpose, calling out to the different Gods. At each cardinal point, she took a heavy swig from a bottle of rum, then mercilessly sprayed the fiery liquid through her lips at me. The scorching droplets struck my skin, causing me to jerk and twitch uncontrollably. She repeated these motions, completing her circuit. With every spray, the intensity grew, as if it sought to sear into my soul.

At the northern point, with the last spray, I opened my eyes, aware that they were now golden as the link to the spirit world manifested. Waves of magical energy drifted through the air. I felt a deep vibration, a resonance that coursed through my body and settled in my bones.

The ache in my right arm flared as I began the magical movements.

Doubts clawed at my mind: What if I failed? What if nothing emerged from the portal?

Rose didn't have to tell me when; I knew instinctively—it was time to start. I moved my left arm and hand into the precise configurations, the gestures flowing seamlessly as if guided by an unseen force. I called out for a healing Lwa in the sacred God language; the connection solidified instantly. Now, I could speak and understand the ancient dialect with clarity and power.

I executed the magical movements through five intense cycles. As I concluded the last, I sharply extended my left limb, palm open, and a small, multicolored, undulating portal erupted into existence—visible only to my heightened Lwa sight. With a clenched fist, I reached out and contacted something from the other side. A searing buzz coursed through my palm, accompanied by a tingling heat that surged fiercely through my arm. The air before me shimmered violently, rippling like a restless fire.

I sensed I was holding something on the verge of crossing into this plane. Pulling my fist to my chest and clinching it over my heart, I watched as my open hand released a radiant, pulsating glow. From it, a small, fuzzy orange being emerged—playful and shimmering with life. In an instant, the portal snapped shut, sealing its mysterious passage.

I exhaled, feeling dizzy, and nearly fell over. Rose caught me and helped me sit back up.

She asked, "Did it work?"

I opened my eyes. Sitting on the cast of my broken arm was a small, fuzzy orange Lwa with a shy smile. It didn't have a recognizable face, but I knew it was smiling at me.

I nodded, unable to look away from the tiny being perched on my cast.

"Yes, I have something."

I smiled back at the little guy.

"What's your name?"

It communicated with me in the God language, but since the connection to the spirit realm was no longer open, I couldn't understand it anymore.

I said, "You're a cute little fuzz bucket, so that's what I'm going to call you, 'Fuzzbucket.'"

The creature spun in a delighted circle, emitting a soft, high-pitched trill, and exclaimed, '*Yea! The Small Duke gave me a name. I have a Small Duke name.*'

The Lwa all called me Small Duke.

This filled the entity with joy, but the others were unaware of its jubilation, only observing me as I looked up and smiled.

I laughed and performed the formations with my left hand to summon it, and it landed in my palm. Using my thumb, I stroked it. The little fuzz ball enjoyed this and purred like a kitten.

Doris asked, "What are you doing?"

"I'm petting it. It's purring. Here, put your hand over mine. Can you feel it? It feels like angora."

She closed her eyes.

"Yes, I sense something a bit fuzzy and tingly."

She smiled, pulled her hand away, and stared at it. She could hardly believe she felt a spirit entity.

"He's small, but we'll see what he can do."

I stood up, and Fuzzbucket flew to my right shoulder and perched, ready for whatever I asked him to do.

I turned to Rose, Doris, and Paul and said, "Thanks for doing this. Hopefully, he'll be able to help me. I'm exhausted from using my power to pull him over. Heck, I'm always drained."

The Lwa chirped, '*Yes, sleep, sleep. Good sleep.*'

I glanced over at him and smiled. I liked the little guy.

I ascended the stairs to my room, undressed, and lay on the bed.

I implored Fuzzbucket, "Please try to heal my arm. At least try to keep the pain down so I can sleep. Anything you can do to help me would be wonderful."

He flew to my head and rolled amongst my curls. He purred and gently vibrated. This calmed me, and I started to drift off.

The fuzz ball hummed, '*Small Duke, sleep; Fuzzbucket fix arm.*'

The next morning, I woke up stunned to realize I slept peacefully through the entire night. A wave of refreshment washed over me. The tiny creature rolled softly back and forth along my right arm and hand.

The dull, persistent pain in my limb had finally eased, replaced by an unexpected, warm sense of comfort from the little friend now perched on my cast. I tentatively moved my fingers, and to my astonishment, they responded more than usual—more agile, more hopeful. That little guy truly made a difference.

From his usual overnight spot in the chair next to the bed, Webster asked, "How are you feeling today? Did the Lwa help?"

"Yes, I think he did help. I feel good, and I slept through the night. Thank you so much, Fuzzbucket."

Fuzzbucket darted around my room, humming a cheerful tune that sounded like a child's lullaby mixed with a distant wind chime.

It landed on the painting of the door I bought at the Occult Shop a week ago. I had hung it on the wall opposite my bed. The more I stared at it, the more I became aware that faces appeared in the light streaming through the cracked opening. The orange fuzz ball hovered over the lit-up part of the picture, which seemed to intrigue him as well.

Chapter 6
Learning to Drive & Walter's Tragedy

After getting some restful sleep, I decided to check on Walter's progress with the antique automobile restorations and headed to the garage.

The accident in April had left the Jaguar in terrible shape. Walter Sherman, the ghostly chauffeur and mechanic, had been working tirelessly to restore the 1939 Rolls-Royce when I wrecked the red 1949 Jaguar. While the Rolls was almost finished, the expensive antique Jag had to be taken down to the chassis, with a detailed list of replacement parts.

Since then the Rolls-Royce restoration had been completed; the results were stunning. The shiny black paint sparkled under the lights, and the polished chrome trim shone perfectly. Inside, the restored dark leather seats and panels were flawless, featuring hand-tooled details that took the most time to reproduce.

"You've outdone yourself, Walter," I told him, running my hand along the smooth leather. "It looks like it just rolled off the showroom floor."

Walter smiled modestly.

"I can't wait to take it for a spin once my arm and hand are usable again."

"It'll drive like new. I gave the engine a full overhaul."

A smile of pride appeared.

"What about the Jaguar?" I asked, glancing at the partially assembled vehicle in the corner.

"I'm still waiting on a few parts," the chauffeur replied. "Marti has been fantastic at tracking down almost everything on your list. Andy dropped off the last batch a week ago, but we might have to source some pieces from England."

"Damn. That's going to take a while."

Walter nodded in agreement.

I glanced at my right arm, still in its brace, and sighed.

"I wish I could help with the assembly, but this arm is still useless."

"No worries," the chauffeur said reassuringly. "I've got it under control."

I inspected the work completed on the Jag and recalled when I learned why Walter was a ghost at the plantation and when he started training me to drive the sports car.

At thirteen years old, I found out why the chauffeur became a ghost and was compelled to stay on the plantation. One day, I found him staring at the wall in the far corner of the carriage house garage. I knew this must be the anniversary of his death—a day when ghosts often relive the events that bound them to the earthly realm.

I approached cautiously, hand extended, ready to touch him. Should I invade his privacy? He'd never know if I didn't say anything. I learned at eleven, on Nanny Helen's death anniversary, that touching a spirit on such a day could reveal their past. That first experience plunged me into Nanny Helen's tragic life and death.

Now, I was curious about Walter. We spent so much time together in the garage maintaining the estate's automobiles, yet he never spoke of his life.

When pressed, he would say, "That's gone and doesn't need thinking about anymore."

However, once a year, it haunted him.

At thirteen, curiosity seized me, and I rested my hand on his shoulder, instantly transported into the memories that Walter could never escape.

Walter Sherman's life was extraordinary yet tragically flawed. His remarkable journey included roles as a race car driver, automobile designer, and engineer. By the age of sixteen, he started working at the Ford Motor Company and rose from assembly line assistant to design engineer. He had a natural gift—a genius—for mechanical devices and absorbed everything about automobiles in a very short amount of time.

He created engine designs and eventually gathered enough courage to show them to the Ford mogul himself. Walter's designs impressed Henry Ford, earning him a coveted spot on the racing design team. He made several upgrades, resulting in even greater horsepower and speed.

The team competed in most track and speedway events across the U.S. Walter's big break came unexpectedly when the regular driver for a race in Indianapolis showed up drunk. Walter offered to drive—and he won the coveted trophy for that race. From then on, he became the team's top driver.

His skill on the track, combined with his engineering talent, made him a legend in racing circles. Invitations flooded in from wealthy sponsors, and a lifestyle of endless receptions and admirers followed.

The high life caught up with him; Walter drank more than he should and barely stayed sober for the races.

One morning, after a wild night at a sponsor's estate in Kentucky, the race car driver woke up in the sponsor's daughter's bedroom. Still drunk, he panicked, knowing the scandal could ruin his career. He ran off, stumbling into his car at dawn.

The winding country road blurred as he fought to keep control of the vehicle. Suddenly, a dark shape darted into his path.

BAM!

Walter slammed on the brakes and skidded to a stop. He jumped out of the vehicle and hurried over to the crumpled mass in the middle of the street. He crouched down and realized it was a kid.

He had hit a boy. He rolled the boy over; he couldn't be more than fourteen. The child was dead, with his eyes open and a three-inch bloodied gash on his head, turning his blond hair red. The driver stood up and stumbled back, tripping over the bent bicycle and landing on his butt. Newspapers scattered and blew across the road.

Walter panicked. What should he do? He couldn't let anyone know he hit a kid while drunk; it would ruin his reputation. He staggered back to his Ford and sped down the street. The guilt-ridden race car driver parked the Ford and entered the hotel lobby. Luckily, no one was around. The night clerk slept with his head resting on his hands at the counter.

Walter crept up the stairs instead of taking the noisy elevator. He stumbled into his room and rushed to the bathroom to vomit. He paced the room, haunted by the horrifying image of the boy on the road. Sitting on the bed, he cried. Driving while drunk, he hit a kid on a bicycle. Why was the kid out so early in the morning? As he remembered the newspapers scattered across the asphalt, he realized the boy was delivering them.

Walter lay on the bed with his arm over his eyes. He couldn't get the image of the injured boy's face out of his mind—the terrible result of his reckless choice. Eventually, he fell asleep, not waking until someone pounded on his door.

He shuffled to the door and cracked it open. It was his friend Anton. He opened it the rest of the way.

Anton said, "Why aren't you up? You're late for the meeting downstairs."

"Oh, crap. I drank too much and fell asleep."

He got dressed, and the two hurried downstairs. His head felt like it would explode, and his stomach churned as they descended in the jerky, creaking elevator. He entered the conference room, and everyone glared at him for being late.

Walter muttered, "Sorry, I'm late," with his head lowered.

He took a seat and stayed silent for most of the gathering, the haunting images of the boy's bloodied head flashing through his mind.

After what seemed like hours, the meeting finally ended, and all he wanted was to go back to bed, but he couldn't. The maintenance team needed him to supervise the engine overhaul for the next race. Anton drove him to the rented garage.

His friend said, "Did you hear about the kid who got hit by a car this morning?"

Walter's stomach turned. Oh, no! It wasn't a dream.

He shouted, "Pull over now. I'm going to be sick."

His friend pulled to the side of the road, and Walter rushed out, bending over and puking into the ditch.

Anton asked, "Are you okay?"

"I think it was bad shrimp at the party last night."

He couldn't tell Anton the truth.

Walter spent most of the day sleeping on the office couch while the crew worked on the engine.

The next day, he couldn't focus on racing because images of the dead body on the track made him swerve unnecessarily, almost causing a few wrecks. He lost the race, finishing near the back of the pack.

His disappointing performance continued through the next few races until the Ford racing team manager called Walter into his office. The guilty driver entered, and Mr. Tucker indicated a chair.

Tucker frowned.

"Walter, I'm sorry, but I must remove you as the team's lead driver. Your placements have been terrible lately, and we can't afford to let this continue. I'm putting Monty Ripple in as the new driver."

This didn't surprise Walter. He half expected it. He couldn't drive without the image of the dead kid appearing on the track.

"Okay, sir. I understand. Am I still part of the engineering team?"

He half expected to be pulled from it as well.

"Yes, you can still work in that area."

"Thank you, sir."

He left and went to the bar, drowning his depression by drinking all evening.

The next day, he was late for the engineering meeting. This unacceptable behavior continued for two months until Mr. Tucker dismissed him.

A few months later, Anton discovered Walter heavily intoxicated and staggering along the sidewalk toward his apartment building.

He shouted, "Walter, Walter!"

Walter turned, nearly stumbling, and smiled when he saw his friend. It had been a long time since he had last seen his friend after his dismissal from the Ford Racing Team. Delighted, he waved.

Anton parked his car and helped his friend to his room. The room was a complete mess, filled with a strong smell of urine, vomit, and alcohol. Empty bottles and dirty clothes covered the floor and furniture. Anton lay his friend on the bed and covered him with filthy sheets; the ex-race car driver then fell asleep.

Walter was aware that his life was miserable. He began attending AA meetings. The meetings proved helpful, leading him to stop drinking for six months and motivating him to look for a job. However, none of the other vehicle manufacturers would hire him as an engineer after hearing about his issues.

He was down to his last dollar when he found an advertisement for a chauffeur in a New Orleans newspaper. It was in a small town in northern Louisiana, and he thought the job would be perfect— no pressure and quiet. He wrote an application letter and met the plantation owner, Gretchen Labauve. She hired him, and he worked for her for a few years until Anton arrived at the estate to visit him.

His friend insisted they go out for a couple of drinks. Walter wanted to believe—one or two would be fine, but it proved to be more difficult than he expected. After Anton left, the chauffeur continued having one or two drinks daily, and his consumption increased.

One night, he drank far too much. Thoughts of the boy he killed came back, and he swerved the Labauve Rolls-Royce, crashing into the right oak tree in the plantation's front yard, smashing his head into the steering wheel of the car. By the time the ambulance arrived, Walter was dead.

His ghost manifested next to the Rolls, and he watched as they covered his body. The other ghosts—Paul, Milly, Philly, Bertha, and Hugo—appeared. He had heard the other servants at the estate speak of the spirits, but he had never encountered them.

Bertha stepped forward and explained the curse and why he must remain at the plantation.

Walter said, "I deserve to be here and punished for what I did to that poor boy. I've been punishing myself for years over it."

He shuffled to the carriage house garage, where he spent most of his time wallowing in depression until the child Orion moved into the mansion and showed an interest in automobiles. The ghost chauffeur was overjoyed to help and teach the boy everything he knew.

I pulled my hand away from Walter's shoulder and hurried to

my room, not wanting the other ghosts to see me cry. I felt deep pity for Walter and what he endured during his lifetime. He went from being the top race car driver and engineer in the country to a drunken chauffeur, all because he hit a newspaper delivery boy on a bicycle and the guilt gnawed at him.

The next day, I approached him.

"Walter, can you teach me how to drive the Jaguar?"

The former race car driver taught me how to drive when I was ten. I could only operate vehicles on the plantation property because I wasn't of legal age. I hadn't been allowed to operate the Jaguar before that, because, as Walter put it, I was too young to handle a vehicle with that much power.

He thought about it for a few moments.

"Sure, I believe you're old enough now. However, you need to take it slow at first, as this type of car can quickly get out of control. It's fast. I'll show you how to take corners properly at high speeds."

I smiled, knowing I was being trained by one of the best race car drivers in the country.

SPECTRAL PROMISES

Chapter 7
Dancing with a God

I left the carriage house garage and entered the mansion. As I stepped through the back door and passed the kitchen entry, my gaze fell on someone I'd rather not see—pouring coffee into a cup. It was Duke Shamedi.

In this realm, the Voodoo Spirit God appears as a tall, slender Black man dressed in a dark tuxedo with tails, shirtless, and wearing a top hat that heightens his imposing stature. His face, usually covered in white makeup or maybe something else, remained uncovered. This stark face was only visible during voodoo ceremonies, where it served to awe practitioners sensitive enough to detect him and symbolized his dominion over death and the spirit world.

"What are you doing here?" I asked, my tone annoyed.

I didn't want him around. His so-called 'Endowments' had already screwed up my life.

He swiveled toward me, flashing his unnaturally bright, toothy grin, and said, "Not bad coffee, but Rose should add some cinnamon next time to give it a little extra zing."

I snidely replied, "She didn't make it; I did. I'll think about it. What do you want?"

I knew he wanted something. He didn't just show up for a friendly chat.

"You've been cooped up here for too long. We need to do something together. Let's go out and party. You need to get out and have some fun."

He almost sounded friendly. What did he care about my life? He must be planning something else.

"Party? Really? You think I can go anywhere with this busted arm?" I shouted, pointing to my braced right arm. "I can hardly move it. It's a little better since Fuzzbucket has been working on it, but it'll still take weeks before I can use it properly and drive."

The Duke moved his fingers on his right hand, and Fuzzbucket zipped from my shoulder—where he always sat when not actively working on healing me—landing in the God's palm. The poor creature shrank to an even smaller size. Was it afraid of the Duke? The voodoo God stared at the Lwa, and I assumed he was speaking to it.

Staring at the minuscule Lwa, he asked, "Is this what you really want to have around to help you?"

"Yes, I like the little guy, and he has helped me," I said with an annoyed tone.

Fuzzbucket shot out of the Duke's hand, materializing on my right shoulder, and darted into the curls at the back of my neck, trembling with fear. I grimaced, furious at the Duke for terrifying the creature.

The Duke grinned slyly.

"I've got something to fix your arm."

His eyes bulged unnaturally before he gagged and spat a small white object into his hand.

"Eat this," he said and held out the disgorged item.

I recoiled.

"You want me to eat... that?"

My stomach churned as I stared at the glistening object, bile rising at the thought.

"Yes. It's a piece of fruit from the Tree of Life. This was the only way I could bring it to this plane."

I wanted my arm to be healed. From my time in the spirit realm, I understood that the fruit's magic could heal my body, but eating something regurgitated, even from a god, was unsettling.

I decided I had no choice but to do it. Summoning all my courage, I stepped forward and grasped the revolting item from the Duke's hand with my left index finger and thumb, trying to touch it as little as possible. My stomach churned as I hurried to the sink, holding the disgusting object under hot water, desperately attempting to wash away any lingering Lwa Spirit God puke or saliva. Although nothing was visibly on the magical item, the very thought of it repelled me, sending a shiver down my spine.

I leaned against the counter, popped the piece in my mouth, and chewed. Once again, it was the most delicious thing I had ever eaten. A smile spread across my face as I swallowed. I trembled and shook from head to toe. The magic of the fruit flowed through every part of my body. I screamed in both pain and pleasure as my chest flashed three times. I stood there with my eyes closed, panting afterward. I felt strong and energized, as if I had just been reborn. The mystical energy moving through my veins began to fade.

I raised my right arm with a sudden, determined motion, flexing my hand and fingers in and out with no obstruction. In one swift move, I slipped my arm from the sling and forced it downward, smashing the cast against the edge of the old ceramic sink. The cast shattered into countless pieces, scattering across the kitchen floor with a loud crash. My right limb was finally free and fully healed. I moved it deliberately, testing for complete functionality, a triumphant smile on my face.

I became aware of my erect dick jumping in my pants. I rubbed it, trying to calm it down. This was a side effect of eating fruit from the Tree of Life—the immediate need to have sex with someone—something—anything.

The Duke said, "You had better go and take care of that," nodding his head at my groin.

He was right. I had to do something to appease it. Getting anxious and shaky, I called Milly and Filly and ran toward my bedroom. I stripped and copulated with both the girl ghosts, fast and hard, multiple times, screaming each time, not stopping until sated.

They understood what to do from the first time this happened when I returned from the spirit plane after eating a piece of the magical fruit. Thank God they were there to help me. I don't know what I would have done without them. Having sex was the only way to satisfy the overwhelming lust that came with eating the mystical fruit and being on this plane. Afterwards, I fell asleep.

At 7 p.m., I woke, and the Duke stood beside the bed, saying, "Go clean yourself up and get ready to party."

I scowled at him, irritation flickering in my eyes, as he tried to boss me around. Despite my annoyance, I knew I desperately needed a shower. My body was sticky and clammy from sweating after the wild time with the girls. I swung my legs over the bed and stormed to the bathroom. I showered hurriedly, shaved roughly, brushed my teeth, and stumbled back to the bedroom, still wrapped in a towel around my hips, feeling defeated and gross.

The Duke was in front of the armoire, pulling clothes out and tossing them onto the floor, saying, "No. No. Nope. My god, boy, don't you have anything decent to party in?"

I'm not a clothes hound. Jeans, T-shirts, and basic button-up shirts are my usual attire. I don't go out much and rarely socialize, so I only need the essentials.

Finally, the voodoo Spirit God smiled.

"Here's something."

He pulled out the only suit I owned.

"Here, wear these," he said, tossing me the black dress pants and a white long-sleeved dress shirt.

I quickly slipped into them as he scrutinized me.

"We need something more… something that makes a statement."

Without a word, he disappeared, then reappeared a few moments later with an assortment of elaborate, embroidered vests made of silk on velvet. He held up several and finally settled on a stunning purple one.

"This is your color," he declared confidently.

I asked, "Where did you get these?" as I pulled it over the shirt.

"From Cyrus' trunk. He has good taste in clothes."

I approached the mirror at the back of the door and evaluated myself. I looked good in this outfit. I unbuttoned the top few buttons of my shirt, revealing my now muscular chest. I pulled the collar out over the shoulders of the vest and rolled up the sleeves to my elbows, which made it look less formal.

The Duke said, "There you go, boy, now you're getting the right idea. Okay, let's go."

"Wait! Is that what you're wearing?"

I glared at him in his usual dark attire.

He gazed into my eyes and said, "No, I'm wearing YOU," and a huge grin appeared.

"Wait!... What...?" and he jumped into me.

A cold surge of dread shot through me as the God forced his way in.

My limbs trembled uncontrollably, my head snapping back violently as if yanked by invisible strings. For a moment, chaos reigned inside me, then silence.

I felt the Duke inside me. No, it was me trapped within the Duke. The God seized control of my body. Fury erupted within me, and I lashed out, telling him exactly how angry I was.

'You didn't say you were going to take over my body to go partying. I want you out. Right now!'

I was angry that he took dominion without informing me.

'Calm down. Do you think I was physically present on this plane? No, I must use an avatar. You're my perfect avatar.'

He said this as if it were the most obvious thing in the world and I was foolish even to ask.

'I'm your WHAT? You never told me any of this.'

Shocked by this revelation, I attempted to push him out. It was like pushing against a thick brick wall.

He laughed, *'That's a price for receiving my endowments.'*

'I never had any choice in the matter; if I had, I would have said, HELL NO!'

Seething, I pushed him as hard as I could. He didn't budge.

'You're right; you had no choice. Avatars never do. You were born to be my perfect avatar, able to hold me for hours or perhaps even days. Any of the Lwa Spirit Gods can possess others, but only briefly. A perfect avatar can carry a Lwa Spirit God for an extended period with no unfortunate side effects.'

I didn't like the sound of that.

'What side effects? What if I wasn't... perfect?'

'You don't want to know. It's not pretty, and the avatar often dies violently.'

'But I thought my grandmother was the one who set up the meeting between my mother and father to create an heir with my abilities.'

'Yes, but who do you think gave her the idea?'

'So, you were involved with my creation from the beginning to have a body you can take over whenever you feel like going out and partying? You fucker. This makes me hate you even more.'

I pounded on him in frustration from the inside.

'*I could dump you in the in-between if you want. This isn't bad. We're going to have a good time together. You'll see.*'

I wanted to avoid being stuck in the in-between. The cold was so intense that I thought I would freeze solid during the two times I found myself in that void. It wasn't a physical freeze; it just felt like it. You must endure the frigid void until the Duke takes you to the spirit realm or returns you to the mortal plane and your body. There were no acceptable options.

'*No, I don't want that.*'

'*Don't worry, I'll let you surface and have fun, too.*'

'*Gee, how nice of you,*' like that should make me feel better.

'*It is nice of me, isn't it?*' he said, smiling.

He placed my wallet and house key in my pants pocket and went downstairs. He opened the safe and took out several hundred dollars in cash. When he possesses me, he knows everything about me: my thoughts, memories, and feelings. An overwhelming sense of violation washes over me. I hate it.

The ghosts realized that the Spirit God controlled me and looked concerned with furrowed brows as I left the mansion. The Rolls was parked and running by the gate. The Duke must have told Walter to prepare it.

I said, '*I'm driving. I don't trust you behind the wheel.*'

He said, '*Okay, boy. You know the clubs to pick up girls.*'

He turned to Webster, who had been following us the entire time, and said, "But you aren't coming. You stay here."

My grandfather stopped following us. The Duke was able to lift the curse on Webster that had forced him to follow me that night.

I knew the leading clubs I usually visited when I felt the urge for sex. He let me drive, and I headed to the 'Hustle Heaven' dance club in Shreveport.

I parked the Rolls beside a lamppost, making it hard for anyone to steal it unnoticed. A line of people stretched down the block.

I said, '*It's going to take hours to get in. Maybe we should try another place.*'

The Duke replied, '*Don't worry about it. We'll get in.*'

The spirit God controlled my body as we approached the club

entrance. A massive bouncer, his muscles nearly bursting through the sleeves of his yellow Hustle Heaven T-shirt, stood beside the door with his arms crossed. He scowled at us intensely, but then a big smile appeared, and he unclipped the velvet rope barrier.

"Nice to see you, sir. Go right in."

Shocked by this, I asked, *'How did that happen?'*

The Duke smiled.

'People know me.'

He radiated an undeniable aura of curiosity, drawing the attention of nearly everyone as we strode by. We approached the bar, and the striking blonde bartender's eyes caught ours, prompting a warm, inviting smile. Without hesitation, he pulled out my wallet and confidently handed her a hundred-dollar bill.

He said to her, "Darlin', start a tab for me. Here's the first hundred."

"What would you like?" she asked.

"A Long Island Iced tea, heavy on the vodka."

"You got it, sir," she smiled.

"Call me Duke."

"Okay, Duke," she said, tapping the counter twice.

He leaned back, my elbows resting against the bar as he surveyed the scene. Smiling and laughing, people bounced up and down to the loud, overpowering beat of the music in the crowded venue. A massive disco ball spun from the ceiling, and a spotlight aimed at it caused small squares of light to flash throughout the room. A haze of cigarettes and other types of smoke swirled over the gyrating bodies.

'Who do you think we should go for first?' he asked me.

'I don't know. I usually wait for the girl to approach me.'

'We could do that, but it would be a long, slow night. I'll show you how it's done.'

He spotted a group of five girls sitting in a booth across the room.

'Ah, that's what I'm looking for: a small harem.'

Surprised, I asked, *'What? Are you going for all of them?'*

'You have to think big, boy.'

He grasped his drink tightly and swaggered toward the cluster of women with undeniable confidence. As we advanced, their eyes widened in surprise, acknowledging our approach. We moved with purpose, cutting straight through the dance floor's chaos to the group of women. I could feel the powerful ripple of his presence emanating from the Duke—not from me—like a shimmering wave rolling around us. Unconsciously, the dancers instinctively shifted aside, recognizing our commanding aura without a word. We strode through the sea of bodies, swaying to the music's relentless beat like unstoppable waves crashing on the shore.

We approached the booth, and the God called out to the women over the music, "Which of you lovely ladies would like to dance with a god?"

They all giggled. The brunette raised a hand.

"If I'm your Goddess, I'll dance with you."

"You are tonight, darlin'," he said with a broad grin, offering her his hand.

We glided to the dance floor. The Duke placed his right arm around her waist, took her right hand in his left, and gazed into her eyes. We moved in fluid motions across the floor. I'm not a good dancer; I bounce around to the beat of the music. It was astonishing how the Spirit God danced like a professional. His moves blended ballroom and disco, featuring twirls, dips, and an occasional lift.

The girl was hesitant, unsure of how to move so elaborately. But the moment the Duke's piercing gaze locked onto hers, everything changed. She synchronized her movements with his, their dance becoming a seamless, mesmerizing flow. Other dancers instinctively parted, recognizing the magnetic connection between them, as if entranced by an unspoken command.

After the song ended, we led her back to the table and slid into the booth with the other girls.

One of her friends said, "Barbara, I didn't know you could dance like that."

Barbara said, "I didn't know I could either until I was with him."

She seemed to be in a daze.

The Duke quickly finished his drink and lifted the empty glass overhead. A waitress appeared and took the glass.

"What would you like?" she asked.

"The barkeep knows what I'm drinking. Ladies, what would you all like?" he asked, peering at the bevy of beauties.

They all seemed to melt from his gaze, and piped in, "The same as him."

"You heard the ladies, and it's on my tab."

The next song started, and we picked another beautiful one from the group, smoothly moving to the dance floor. Once again, we danced as if we had been together for years. This time, we added a few more lifts and a couple of flips. I liked the moves the Duke performed and hoped some of his skills would rub off on me. The movements were so smooth that it felt like we were floating an inch above the floor. Maybe we were.

We all drank, laughed, and danced for the next two hours. I was snockered entirely by then. I had never consumed so much alcohol in my life. The drinks didn't affect the God at all.

After a while, he stopped dancing and started making out with each woman in the booth.

He leaned closer to the dark-skinned girl and whispered, "Do you want to dance to a different beat in my car?"

She smiled and nodded.

We stood up, took her hand, and led her out toward the Rolls.

As we passed the bouncer at the door, he said, "We'll be back in a little while."

The bouncer grinned knowingly and nodded, unhooking the rope to let us through.

We approached the Rolls-Royce.

Impressed by the opulent antique vehicle, the girl asked, "Is this your car?"

Duke Shamedi replied, "It's the boy's; I'm just borrowing it for the night."

We opened the back door and got in. At that moment, being so drunk, I blacked out, but the Duke continued.

The dark-skinned beauty rested her head on my shoulder when I woke up. She was straddling my lap, and we were both breathing heavily.

The God patted her perfect ass and said, "That's all for now, sweetheart. Tell your blond friend she can come out if she wants to."

She scooted over, pulled her panties back on, opened the car door, and returned to the club.

The God said, '*It's about time you woke up. I thought you were going to miss all the fun. I told you we'd have a good time.*'

'*Did you do something to her to make her want to have sex with you?*'

'*No, that's all on you.*'

'*What do you mean, it's all me?*'

'*It's your handsome face and fantastic body that are attracting the women.*'

'*I've never attracted women like that.*'

'*Only because you never made the right moves or said the right things. I did, and that was all it took.*'

A knock on the car door interrupted our conversation; I leaned over and opened it. The blonde with a please-take-me smile peered in. The Duke took her hand and helped her in. He let me step forward, and the girl and I made out and had fantastic sex. It seemed more intense than usual. Was this because the Spirit God was inside me?

After she left, the Duke commented, '*See, wasn't that fun?*'

He zipped up my pants, tucked my shirt in, and went back to the disco. We handed the bartender another hundred-dollar bill. As we passed through the crowd of dancers again, the harem all stared at us with lustful eyes. He took the short girl's hand, and she followed him to the dance floor.

I was so blasted that I drifted in and out of consciousness, only catching fleeting glimpses of drinking, dancing, kissing, and sex. The club closed by the time the last girl swung the Rolls' back door shut—she was probably the bartender.

The Duke said, '*Time to go home, boy.*'

I quickly opened the back door, stuck my head out, and puked on the asphalt.

'*I can't drive like this. I need to sleep this off first.*'

I rolled down the back windows a few inches to let in some cool air, curled up on the back seat, and quickly fell asleep. It felt like I had just closed my eyes when someone knocked on the window.

With my eyes shut, I slurred, "No more tonight, girls."

Then I heard a male voice say, "Are you okay?"

I opened my eyes and glared at a police officer beside the car. Then, I rolled down the window.

He asked, "Are you alright?

"Yes, officer. I just had too much to drink and didn't think it was safe for me to drive home."

"You can't stay here."

He stood looking down at me with his hands on his hips.

"Can you give me a couple more hours to sleep this off, and then I'll leave?"

The policeman hesitated for a long moment.

"Alright…but you have to leave then."

I don't know why the officer didn't haul me off to the drunk tank. Maybe it was because the Duke was still there inside me.

"Thank you, officer."

I rolled the window up and went back to sleep.

A couple of hours later, although it felt like only a few minutes, the policeman came back and knocked on the Rolls' window. I sat up and recognized him.

"Okay, okay. I'm going."

I moved to the driver's side back door, and a wave of nausea hit me hard. I doubled over, retching violently, clutching the back fender for support. Unable to hold it any longer, I staggered and urinated on the lamppost beside the car, the whole scene grotesque and humiliating. The cop watched silently, unimpressed by the chaos. As I struggled to steady myself, I realized there was no way I could drive.

At that instant, the Duke stepped forward.

He stood up straight, zipped up my pants, and turned to the cop with a broad smile, saying, "Thank you, officer. I'm heading home now."

He jumped into the driver's seat and drove the Rolls out of the club parking lot. I don't remember anything after that. I woke up with my head on the steering wheel, the horn blaring, and the vehicle parked by the gate at the plantation. Webster was shaking my shoulder.

I lunged desperately at the front door and hammered my fists against it. The door swung open, revealing a ghostly figure, and I staggered into Doc's arms, gasping for breath. The spectral apparitions hurriedly supported me, guiding me into my bedroom and helping me into bed.

I finally woke up late in the afternoon, my body heavy and my mind racing. My grandfather's ghost sat in the chair beside my bed, his usual calm replaced by a worried frown. Cyrus hovered nearby, his arms crossed.

"I feel like death," I croaked. "Never again with the Duke."

Like I had a choice.

My stomach turned violently, and Webster was quick with the wastebasket as I heaved into it.

I started to sit up, saying, "I need to take a piss."

Webster said, "Here, go in the basket."

He held it as I urinated.

I lay back, my head pounding like the back beat of the loud music at the club.

"The Doc said you should take these when you wake up."

He handed me two pain pills and a glass of water. I took them and lay with my left arm across my eyes.

I asked, "Fuzzbucket, can you do anything to get rid of this hangover?"

'*No, Small Duke. Not until the alcohol is out of your system.*'

Cyrus asked, "Did you have a good time?"

"My God, can he drink and never feel a thing? It only affected me. I was so drunk that I wasn't aware of what was happening most of the time. He smooth-talked a group of girls into dancing and screwing him most of the night. I have to say he's an incredible dancer."

Cyrus said, "You fucked more than one girl last night."

"Yeah, I think it was five, no—six. There was the bartender, but I'm not sure. I was passed out half the time; I don't even remember driving home. I guess he drove. Now I have to suffer with the hangover from his good time."

The pain pills were starting to take effect, and I wanted to go back to sleep.

I told Webster and Cyrus, "I'll share everything I can remember tomorrow when I feel better."

I rolled over and fell asleep immediately.

It took me two days to get back to myself. I told the ghosts about what happened with the Duke. The maids giggled, Cyrus and Walter smiled, the others just shook their heads, and Doc said, "I hope you don't get a venereal disease from that escapade."

My grandfather stood off to the side with a frown.

"What's wrong?" I asked.

"I don't like how the Duke used you."

"I don't like it either, but I'm stuck with him. To change the subject, are you ready to pass over?"

He stared, surprised I had asked the question.

"Can you do that now?"

"Yes, now that I can move both hands and arms."

"Okay, I'm ready. I've been here too long."

He glanced at the floor with a depressed frown.

I told him, "Stand here," and placed him in the center of the living room.

I steadied myself, drawing deep, shuddering breaths before performing the ancient magical gestures to pierce the veil to the spirit realm. A wild, turbulent swirl of mystical energy erupted in the room. I summoned the God language with force, commanding the Lwa—those spirits bound by the curse placed on Webster Turner—to return to the supernatural realm. Then, I executed a series of potent, deliberate magical actions. A shimmering portal yawned open; the purple Lwa—faithfully tethered to Webster for over three decades—darted into it. In an instant, the passage snapped shut with a thunderous bang.

I looked at my grandfather.

"The curse is broken; the Lwa returned to the spirit plane. You're free."

The tunnel of light and love appeared behind my grandfather. He turned and gazed at it.

I told him, "You can enter now," recognizing some hesitation.

He stared at the tunnel with an intense, lingering gaze, as if torn between fear and resolve. It has been over thirty years since he died, yet not a single moment of peace has touched his existence since that day. The torment my grandmother inflicted upon him should have been enough to break his spirit forever.

He confided in me a few months ago, as we sat in the quiet graveyard by my father's final resting place—the very spot where I first met him—how tormented he felt over the horrific acts he committed—killing my great-grandmother, raping Renee, my grandmother, and many other despicable actions he committed. His guilt was overpowering, and he knew he deserved punishment. Now, the weight of his choices pressed down on him: he must decide whether to cross to the other side or remain trapped on this plane of existence.

He finally made his decision.

"Thank you. I'll miss you, son."

"I'll miss you, too."

When my grandfather turned around, my father, Antoine, appeared in the tunnel, his arms outstretched with longing toward Webster. As my grandfather entered, father and son locked eyes and embraced for the first time, a heartfelt reunion filled with emotion. They then walked down the tunnel together, and in an instant, it vanished into nothingness.

I watched with a gentle smile, a sense of relief washing over me as Antoine finally forgave his father. I desperately hoped this was the kind of work the Duke trusted me with—healing broken spirits and mending fractured bonds through forgiveness.

The chair beside my bed, once occupied every night for over fourteen years, at first with Cyrus, then with Webster, now sat empty. The absence of a watchful presence made my sleep feel fragile and strange.

Chapter 8
The Haunted House

The phone rang while Seren sat at her desk, entering receipts into her ledger—a task she performed every Thursday.

She picked up the telephone.

"Star Occult Shop, how can I help you? "

"May I speak with Seren Griffyths?"

"This is Seren."

"You were recommended to me by Detective Brian O'Reilly. He's a family friend and said you might be able to help me."

A strange sensation coursed through the psychic—this request felt unlike any she'd ever received.

The psychic vividly recalled her tense collaboration with Detective O'Reilly on two grueling cases for the Shreveport Police Department, where she served as a consultant. She bravely assisted in a heartbreaking missing person case and wrestled with the grim identification of a murder victim buried deep in the woods. Both assignments pushed her to the edge, unleashing violent visions that haunted her for weeks, shaking her to the core. In the aftermath, she was deeply hesitant to involve herself in any more emotionally taxing and disturbing cases. But Brian was a friend, so she listened.

"Oh, Brian. Sure, how can I help you?"

"My name is Johanna Mason, and my husband and I just bought a house in the Stoner Hill district...."

She paused.

"Well, we think it's haunted."

"A haunting?" Seren's tone sharpened. "What makes you say that?'

"The sound of a child crying comes every night and sometimes during the day. There are no children living in the houses next to ours. The sound is pathetic, and we can't sleep. We've been staying in a nearby motel to get any sleep at all. Brian told us you might be able to help."

"Sure, I can come over and do an evaluation and it's possible I could do an exorcism. That will cost more. When can we meet?"

They discussed the matter further, and Seren arranged to meet Johanna and her husband, Ron, at the house on Friday at 2:00 p.m.

The psychic arrived at the address, her old Toyota groaning ominously as it halted before the Victorian mansion. Once pristine, the house's peeling, tattered paint hung in ragged strips, exposing the gray, weathered wood beneath. Overgrown bushes writhed across the neglected yard, and despite a recent mow, the yard exuded an undeniable aura of neglect. Johanna and Ron loomed on the porch; their anxious expressions tinged with dread.

A chill ran over Seren. Someone—or something—was watching her from inside.

The psychic stepped up the stairs to the porch. Both owners smiled and reached out their hands to shake hers. She could tell they were nervous and a little scared.

Johanna said, "We're so glad you could come and look into this."

Anxiety was evident in her eyes.

"I see why you bought the house. It has the potential to be beautiful."

"That's what we thought. We wanted a fixer-upper, and this looked like a perfect project for us."

"Shall we go in?"

"Oh, sure."

Ron pulled the key out of his pocket, unlocked the door, and opened it for the ladies to enter.

As she entered, Seren detected a sliding noise.

"What was that sound?"

"We don't know. Quite often, when we come home, we hear it, too. We could never figure out what caused it."

A freezing dread clawed into Seren's bones as she stepped into the vestibule, the air suffused with an overwhelming sorrow that bore down on her chest like an iron vise.

She told the couple, "First thing I can tell you is there's something here. It was watching me as I drove up."

She moved into the living room on the left, feelings of sadness and longing everywhere. Furniture was stacked in the center of the room, covered with a plastic tarp. The couple must have been planning to paint the room. She wandered through the space, inspecting the crayon markings and drawings on several lower wall panels—images made by a child.

The scenes on the walls dragged at her chest with overwhelming sorrow and anguish. The final panel showed a lonely child with disheveled yellow hair. A cascade of blue blobs obscured his face and dripped down to his feet. Was the boy crying? This was the most gut-wrenching of all. She fought desperately to hold back her tears, feeling her heart fracture with every passing second.

Each panel was subsequently marked and scrawled with long, furious, angry strokes.

She peered at the homeowners.

"Do you know who drew these? Were children in this house?"

Johanna said, "No, they were here when we arrived. We also found five children's coloring books with all the pages filled and an empty box for crayons. The crayons were all gone, but the paper wrappers were everywhere."

Seren asked, "Can you show me the rest of the place?"

"Yes, of course."

They escorted the psychic through every room in the house. None emitted the sadness and fear that she sensed in the living room.

While being escorted around the house, she asked, "Who lived here before you?"

Johanna explained, "No one has lived in the house for years. We spoke to the neighbors, and one of them told us that someone had been here for a few weeks, drove away, and never returned. Perhaps they heard the child crying, too."

"Do you know who owned the house previously?" Seren questioned.

"It was foreclosed on by the state four years ago for non-payment of property taxes."

"So, somebody must have been paying for the place for part of the time it remained empty."

She wondered who that could have been.

"I suppose so," he said hesitantly, voice trailing off.

"But you don't know who that was?"

Her eyes sharpened with a hint of challenge in her voice.

"No. I guess you may be able to find out at the housing records office."

Seren told the Masons, "This house is haunted, and I think it's a child. This might be difficult to exorcise because children don't always understand what is happening to them and don't react the way an adult ghost would."

Johanna asked, "When can you try the exorcism?"

"I'll give it a try tonight. I have to return to my shop and pick up some necessary items."

Ron asked hesitantly, "Do we have to be here for this?"

The psychic knew he didn't want to be present for the purging.

"No, you don't have to be here, but I'll need the keys. This may take several sessions."

The Masons gave her the house keys and drove away.

Seren stood frozen in the living room, the air heavy with a suffocating sorrow. She closed her eyes, desperately reaching into the house's very fabric, seeking any sign of a presence. A faint, pitiful sob echoed through her mind, more haunting and desperate than before.

"Don't be afraid," she whispered, her voice trembling. "I'm here to help you move on."

The sobbing only grew louder, a heartbreaking wail that pierced through her very soul.

She returned to the shop and picked up the items she needed for the exorcism. She didn't believe that a demon was causing the haunting; she thought it was the spirit of a scared child. She collected holy water, a crucifix, a Star of David necklace, a sage smudging stick, and a bag of salt. Putting everything into a basket, she headed back to the haunted house.

After conducting several house cleansings and one demon banishment, Seren believed this cleansing would be straightforward if she could convince the child's ghost to listen to her.

Upon her return, the sliding sound happened again when she entered the house. What was that?

First, she opened a window to give the spirit an exit route. She then sprinkled salt and holy water evenly across the floor. She wore the Star of David and a crucifix around her neck. Next, she lit the sage smudge stick and circled it clockwise while walking around the room. Throughout the preparations, she felt the frightened spirit watching her.

She chanted the ritual words: "Child spirit, listen to me. I mean you no harm. This house is no longer your home. You must move on to the spirit world, where your loved ones await you."

The incantation was repeated three times, and the child's sobs filled the air.

Prayers for the spirits to move on, repeated three times in English, Latin, and Hebrew, were unsuccessful in removing the ghost. The child continued to cry.

She started from the beginning, imploring the specter to pass on and reciting the prayers. Nothing was working.

The psychic grew frustrated because there was no response.

"Why won't you pass on?"

The word 'Mommy' floated through the air, and the crying grew louder.

Tears welled uncontrollably in Seren's eyes as the child's raw anguish crashed over her like a relentless storm, each agonized sob twisting a deep knot of despair in her chest. Heart pounding fiercely, she broke into a frantic, desperate flight, fleeing from the overwhelming weight of sorrow she could no longer bear.

Arriving home, she reflected on the incident and how upsetting it had been. The child's sobs set her determination to help this spirit pass on and find peace. She needed more information about who had previously occupied the house. The next day, she called Detective Brian O'Reilly.

"Hello, Brian. It's Seren Griffyths."

"Oh, hi, Seren. Did Johanna and Ron Mason get a hold of you?"

"Yes, they did, and I went to their house. A child is haunting the place."

"Really? Can you do anything about it?"

"I attempted an exorcism last night, but nothing happened. I need more background about the previous occupants. Is there any way you can find information about that for me?"

"Technically, I can only search records if they concern a case."

"Well, a child died in that house. Is that enough for an investigation?"

"Any evidence?"

"Pictures are on the walls with crayons, showing the mother driving away, leaving the child alone."

"I may be able to make that work. Give me the address."

She relayed the address to him.

"Thanks, Brian. I'm sure something terrible happened to a child in that house."

"Okay, I'll see what I can find."

She hung up the phone and hoped the detective could find some information.

Two days later, the detective returned Seren's call.

"Seren, I searched but didn't find much about the house. Wilma Newman owned it for 50 years, and her niece, Darlene Newman, inherited it in 1972. Since 1977, no information has been available about Darlene Newman; a car hasn't been registered in her name since that year, she hasn't had any credit checks, and no taxes have been filed. Another intriguing detail is that she had a son named John Newman in 1972, with no father listed."

"Thank you, Brian. Maybe those names will help me."

She hung up the phone and went back to the shop.

She told Jenny, "You can take off now. I'll close out the cash drawer."

She followed Jenny to the front door, locked it, and turned the sign to "CLOSED."

She returned to the register, pressed the keys to generate a daily report, and removed all the money from the cash drawer. She lifted the cash tray to take the checks and high-denomination bills, discovering Orion Labauve's business card.

Looking at the back of the card, 'Ghost Expert' immediately seized her attention. Could this enigmatic man truly be an expert on ghosts?

That was precisely what she needed, an expert who could make a difference. Without hesitation, she decided to call him. Something deep within told her this was the right move. Because of their past life connection, she knew she would have to be cautious around him, but she was desperate to do whatever it took to help the child's restless spirit.

Seren took everything to her desk, including the business card, and called the number written on the back.

Chapter 9
The Phone Call

It had been months since I went jogging, but I decided that day was a good time to start up the practice again. With life settled down and my fitness improving, a jog around the plantation seemed perfect. My stamina wasn't what it used to be, but I had to start somewhere.

After the run, I went into the garage and helped Walter assemble the Jaguar with the parts we had. Although we didn't have everything, we managed to finish a few small sections.

We completed items in the morning, and I went into the house, ready for lunch. The answering machine light flashed as I walked through the front hall on my way upstairs to wash up.

I pressed the rewind and play buttons. Seren Griffyths. Just hearing her name made my stomach leap. She had called.

"Hello, Mr. Labauve. This is Seren Griffyths from the Star Occult Shop. You left your card and asked me to call you. The back of your card states, 'Ghost Expert.' I could really use one of those right now. Please call me to discuss my ghost issue."

She had left her number. My hand trembled as I wrote it down.

It had been three long weeks since I last set foot in the Star Occult Shop, and I never imagined I would hear from that beautiful woman again. Yet, unexpectedly, she contacted me about a haunting. Doris said Seren would need someone with my rare abilities. Without hesitation, I rushed upstairs, quickly washed up, and changed into clean clothes, feeling the weight of the impending conversation.

She called; she really called. After returning downstairs, I took a few deep breaths to calm myself. I didn't want her to feel my excitement when talking to her. I dialed her number.

A woman answered after a few rings.

"Hello, Star Occult Shop. How can I help you?"

"Yes, Seren Griffyths left me a message to call her. This is Orion

Labauve."

"Hello, Mr. Labauve. This is Jenny. Just a minute, I'll get Seren for you."

"Thank you."

I waited anxiously, craving the sound of Seren's voice again.

"Hello, this is Seren."

Her lively voice echoed through the receiver. My breath caught—an involuntary reaction that left me struggling to regain composure. I started to cough.

She asked, "Mr. Labauve, are you okay?"

I sputtered, "Yes… I'm okay. I just got a dry spot in my throat. I'm returning your call."

"Yes, Mr. Labauve, your business card indicated you're a ghost expert. Is that true?"

The rich tone of her voice was so familiar, as if we talked frequently.

"Yes, I guess you could call me that."

"I need someone with a greater understanding of ghosts than I do. I was hired to exorcise a ghost, which isn't proving easy. Do you perform those services?"

"Not exactly, but I can come and see what I can do."

What an excellent opportunity to be near her once again.

"I believe it's the spirit of a child that won't leave a house. I think his mother left him there alone, and he died."

I said nothing, my mind troubled by the relentless dream invading my nights. The vivid, unsettling images had haunted me for weeks—now, they felt eerily familiar, overwhelming me, so close I could almost touch them.

She asked, "Are you still there?"

"Yes, I'm still here. Is there a bay window in the front of the house?"

"Yes."

"Is there a secret room?"

"I don't know."

"Were full coloring books scattered around and a toy truck?"

"Yes, there were coloring books, but no toy truck. How do you know this?"

"I saw it in a dream. I've had the same one for weeks. When can I come over?"

"Whenever you want."

"Where should I meet you?"

"At my shop."

"I'm leaving right now."

I hung up the phone and headed for the garage. I grabbed the Rolls-Royce keys from the hook and took off. The road to Shreveport blurred beneath me as I pushed the car faster. The dreams wouldn't let me rest, and now I understood why. A child was waiting, and I had to help him. And almost as important, I would get to be near Seren again.

Seren hung up the phone after speaking with Orion, her heart pounding in her chest. When Jenny announced that Orion was on the line, a surge of adrenaline shot through her, and she lunged to answer, her voice trembling as she fought to appear composed despite her racing breath.

As she detailed the spirit child haunting the Mason house, a chilling realization hit her—this enigmatic man already knew everything she was saying—and even more. He was coming.

Excitement bubbled up, and she fought to suppress it.

'Stop it, Seren. That's Chloe's longing, not mine,' she reminded herself. 'He's not Abelard. He's coming because he's a ghost expert, nothing more."

She returned to the shop and placed price tags on items. Her hands trembled, aware that he would be there soon.

The shop's doorbell tinkled sharply, piercing the quiet. She jerked her gaze upward, her heart pounding as he strode into the store— much sooner than she anticipated. Inhaling sharply, she forced a smile, feeling a mixture of surprise and nervousness. He looked even more captivating than she remembered, his black curls framing his striking features. A single white streak caught the light like a beacon, drawing attention. His piercing blue eyes, flecked with gold, seemed to glow with an almost hypnotic intensity.

"Orion," she greeted, extending her hand out of habit.

They both hesitated briefly, recalling the vision from their first meeting. Seren pushed past the awkwardness, reaching out her hand more firmly, and he took it. This time, no vision appeared.

"Didn't you have a cast on your right arm when you were here before?" she asked.

"Yes, but the arm is healed now."

He held up his right arm, perfect as could be.

She asked Jenny to close the shop and told Mr. Labauve, "Come upstairs, and we can discuss my ghost issue."

He nodded and followed her up the stairs.

Chapter 10
The Apartment &
Leaving for the Caribbean

I sped down the road to Shreveport, anticipation building with every mile, to meet Seren Griffyths. I repeat her name silently, 'Seren Griffyths,' allowing it to roll over my tongue.

The moment the name took shape, a thrill shot through me; a wild, uncontrollable smile spread across my face, filling me with an unexpected burst of happiness. Why am I feeling this surge of joy? I almost want to leap out of my seat, shouting in excitement. But I held myself back. Remember, this is just a business meeting—nothing more.

I parked the Rolls in front of the Star Occult Shop and entered the store. Seren stood behind the counter, greeting me with a smile that lit up the room.

"Orion," she said, offering her hand.

We both hesitated, the memory of our shared vision lingering in the air. However, when I finally took her hand, nothing happened.

She spoke with Jenny and then asked me to follow her up the stairs. I followed Seren through the beaded drape, past a desk, and she opened a door that exposed a staircase. While ascending the stairs, I ogled the beautiful, perfectly formed mounds of her backside in tight jeans, swaying alluringly with each step. I wanted to grab that ass so bad. I clenched my fists, keeping this crazy urge in check. We entered an apartment at the top of the stairs.

The apartment sprawled across the second floor of the old building, emanating an aura of mystique. Inside, a meticulously furnished one-bedroom showcased an eclectic collection of occult items: shimmering crystals, delicate dream catchers, ethereal angels, whimsical fairies, serene Buddhas, and hauntingly beautiful occult artwork adorned the walls.

The air was thick with the aromatic scent of burning incense, enveloping the space in a spiritual haze. Near one of the front windows, a painting easel stood ready, likely awaiting the gentle sunlight to inspire a masterpiece. A cluttered small table beside it teemed with paint jars, tubes, and brushes, suggesting ongoing creative chaos. A charcoal sketch of a colonial house, alive with detail and shadow, captured mid-creation, adding a sense of unfinished mystery to the scene.

She offered me a seat on the sofa.

"Would you like some tea?"

"Sure."

She went to the kitchen, and I could hear her filling a kettle with water from the faucet and placing it on the stove.

She came back and sat across from me in a cozy chair that looked inviting. God, she was stunning. I could sit and admire her beauty all day. She looked at me. Was she feeling uncomfortable about my presence and thinking twice about having me over?

She commented curiously, "There's something unusual about you. I don't know what it is yet, but I can tell that you have a lot of power."

I said, "That's nice of you to put it that way. Most people don't want to be near me because of it and tell me to get out, or they leave as soon as possible, practically running for the door."

"Some people feel the same about me. They sense that I know things about them that they don't want anyone to know about, and don't want to come near me."

"I wish that was all that happened to me. I've been beaten up just because people didn't like the sensations they get from me."

"Have you always given off these... 'sensations'?"

"Yes, and since my twenty-fifth birthday, it seems to have worsened."

She stared at me briefly and squirmed in the chair. Unsure what she was thinking. I hoped it wasn't something terrible.

"Excuse me," She said.

She returned to the kitchen. I heard her pulling something from a cabinet.

While alone in the dimly lit living room, I scrutinized the scattered items surrounding me, each one a silent reminder of the supernatural. A painting on the wall opposite where I sat caught my eye—it looked eerily familiar. I got up and moved closer. It was an impressionist piece depicting a plantation house wreathed in fog, with towering oak trees and a small boy standing on the front porch. The image seemed swallowed by a thick, suffocating fog, as if hiding secrets. I squinted, heart pounding. Could that be my house? My reflection? The young boy I once was. No, it couldn't be—but the unsettling feeling lingered.

I returned to the sofa, my eyes settling on the enormous purple crystal on the end table. I rubbed my fingers over its sharp facets, and a jolt of the same tingling sensation that would flash from Doris's desk crystal shot through me. Nearby, a clear crystal ball sat atop a black pedestal, almost calling out to me. An overwhelming urge seized me—I had to hold it, to peer into its depths.

As I gazed into the ball, the world around me dissolved, and I found myself somewhere else—someone else.

It was a bright, sunny day at the port of Le Havre in France when I heard my name called as I approached the sailing vessel, Sainte Marie. The ship was a well-known merchant trading frigate, with the crew bustling about the decks and climbing up and down the masts, getting ready to depart for Saint Dominque Island.

"Abelard, Abelard!"

I turned and saw the most beautiful woman in the world—at least to me—running down the dock. Her thick auburn hair streamed behind her as she clutched a green knitted shawl slipping off her shoulders.

I smiled as my love approached. Panting, flushed from exertion. I wrapped my arms around her.

"Chloe, what are you doing here?"

"Don't go. Please don't go."

Her emerald eyes were pleading.

"What do you mean? I have to go. I must finalize the purchasing agreements that my father promised Mr. Pasteur months ago."

"I know that, but I've had a vision that something terrible will happen to you if you go to Saint Dominque."

"You've been saying that for weeks. Your visions don't always come true."

Chloe occasionally glimpsed the future, especially when danger loomed. She had never been so confident about her predictions as she was with this one.

"But I went to Fairy Hill and prayed to the Fairy Queen to help me understand the image more clearly. Abelard, she revealed to me that you will die due to what occurs during your trip to Saint Dominque."

"I won't die because I'm going to a Caribbean island. It's just business. I promised my father I would take care of it for him. You know he's been having health problems, and a long trip like this would not be good for him. Please calm down."

I felt bad. I didn't like seeing her this way, but I had to take this trip.

Tears welled in her eyes, and her lips trembled.

"I know Abelard, but I'm begging you. Please don't go."

"I have to go," placing a kiss on her forehead.

"Last call for boarding the Sainte Marie," the officer's voice echoed, a stark reminder of the imminent departure.

"That's my call. I must leave. Everything will be okay."

I kissed her soft, full lips passionately, knowing I would miss Chloe terribly during the next couple of months.

She made one last plea, tears streaming down her cheeks.

"Please stay here."

Guilt tightened my chest—I hesitated, torn between my love for Chloe and my duty to my father. But I had to go.

I turned to leave when she grabbed my hand.

"Take this to protect you."

She placed a crystal she found a few years ago on top of Fairy Hill in my palm. I clutched it in my fist and held it close to my heart.

"I love you," I whispered before rushing down the dock, becoming the last person to board the vessel.

Two dockhands lifted the boarding ramp and shifted it away from the vessel. Other dock workers released the mooring lines and tossed them toward the ship, where sailors caught the ropes. The merchant ship departed from the pier.

As the Sainte Marie sailed away, I stood on the deck, watching until Chloe's figure vanished from view. A cold shiver ran down my spine. Doubt gnawed at me, fierce and unrelenting. Was I making a mistake?

86

Chapter 11
The Ghost Issue

As Seren ascended the stairs to her apartment, a flicker of anticipation stirred in her—she imagined Orion's arms wrapping around her, his lips hot on her neck…

She abruptly shook her head, trying to shake off the wandering thought.

'This is Chloe again,' she murmured, blaming her lingering memories from a past life.

She showed him to the couch and offered him tea.

She filled the kettle with water and placed it on the stove. She returned to the living room, where Orion sat with his hands folded, his eyes fixed on her. Their gazes met, and the intensity of the moment made her stomach flutter.

She couldn't shake the uncanny, magnetic energy that radiated from him. It pulsed with an intensity she had never felt before. Having encountered many people with psychic abilities, Seren prided herself on recognizing their signature psychic sensations, but Orion's was entirely different—raw, primal, and impossible to ignore. Was it a remnant of their shared past life, or something darker, something altogether new? No ghostly shimmers lingered this time, yet his presence was downright surreal yet not threatening. She knew she had to delve deeper.

They spoke about how their psychic abilities had profoundly shaped their lives, a connection that was just beginning to ignite with an electrifying spark.

The urge to close the distance between them and kiss him became an overwhelming, almost uncontrollable craving. Her heart pounding, Seren abruptly excused herself and fled to the kitchen. She busied herself with a tray of cookies, thinking that Abelard always loved small pastries. But instead of comfort, another memory of Chloe crashed over her, unbidden and sharp.

The kettle's piercing whistle shattered the silence, jolting Seren back to reality. She had been in another past-life vision of Chloe and Abelard making love in a field of grass. Her trembling hands fumbled as she hurriedly lifted the scorching kettle off the burner. She doubled over the sink, panting heavily and crimson-faced, her body still tingling from the haunting memory.

"Calm down," she whispered harshly to herself. "It wasn't real."

After steadying herself, she poured the hot water into the teapot, placed it on a tray with mugs and cookies, and returned to the living room. This is about ghosts now, she told herself firmly. Nothing else.

Orion took the chamomile tea, which was interesting. It's uncommon for men to choose chamomile tea; they seem to prefer stronger teas.

She asked, "You like chamomile, eh?"

"I got used to it after the poss…," then he trailed off.

This piqued Seren's curiosity. Possession? She wondered if that was what he was about to say but didn't press him.

Seren explained to Orion everything she had perceived at the Mason house and how the exorcism had been unsuccessful. Amazingly, Orion already knew most of the information she understood about the ghost and knew even more than she did. He said he received the details from dreams. It was amazing that these images were so detailed. She would also have prophetic dreams that came true, but they were never as vivid as his.

The kettle shrieked in Seren's kitchen, jarring me out of the past life memory stirred by the crystal ball. I fumbled to place the fragile orb back on the pedestal, nearly dropping it in my haste. I forced myself to appear calm and casual, but inside, a turbulent storm raged. Why were these visions invading my mind?

Seren returned carrying a tray with a teapot, two mugs, a bowl of assorted tea bags, and a plate of cookies. She looked flushed, likely from bending over the hot stove while waiting for the kettle to boil. I selected a chamomile tea bag and poured hot water over it.

She commented on my liking of chamomile.

I almost mentioned, 'since my possession.' Why do I feel so comfortable around her and willing to share things I would never tell anyone else?

I sat back, sipped my tea, and munched on a couple of cookies as she detailed everything she observed, sensed, and knew about the haunted house and the ghost that resided within.

After she finished, I told her, "Most of what you've shared with me, I've seen in a dream. However, there are a few details you may not be aware of. For instance, he sleeps and hides in a concealed room or a closet off the living room. He calls it the secret place. He's often terrified and cries every night for his mother."

She said, "I asked him why he wouldn't leave, and I think I heard, 'Mommy.'"

"He promised his mother he would wait for her, and it seems he has. He wouldn't enter the tunnel of light to move to the other side after he died because of that promise. Do you know anything about the previous owners?"

She answered, "I asked a detective friend from the police department to look into the matter. He found that Wilma Newman lived in the house for 50 years before her niece, Darlene Newman, inherited it. Although property taxes had been paid for several years, no one occupied the house during that time. Four years ago, tax payments stopped, and Darlene Newman's name was no longer on any vehicle registrations or income tax filings. It was as if she had disappeared. The current owners spoke with neighbors, who recalled that someone stayed in the house for a few weeks, about four and a half years ago, before driving away and never returning."

I informed her, "His mother went to speak with his father, or Daddy, as the kid calls him. The father used to beat him and his mother. He was afraid his father would hurt his mother when she left."

"You got all of this from your dream."

She furrowed her brows, curious how I received this information.

"Yes. It felt like I was the kid in the dream and could feel everything he did. I'd wake up crying my eyes out every time. I knew I had to help the boy, but I didn't know where he was. I tried to do a Finding on him, but it didn't work."

"A Finding? What do you mean?"

"When I search for something, I feel a tight, queasy sensation in my stomach if I'm on the right track. It disappears when I find it. I got nothing when I tried to find the kid's ghost."

"Oh, that's why your business card says Finder of Things and People."

I nodded. It was so easy to talk to this woman about my weird abilities.

She continued, "Well, let's head over there so you can get a feel for the place. Did you bring supplies with you?"

"I don't need anything."

She stared at me with a questioning expression.

I knew she didn't understand how I could do anything without the typical items used by exorcists.

"Okay, we'll take my car."

I followed her through the bedroom and out a door in the back. Noticing the bed with a multi-colored quilt on top as we passed, I wondered what it would be like to make love to Seren on top of it, soft and warm.

Metal stairs descended outside the red brick building to an older white Toyota Corolla parked below. We entered the vehicle, and she backed up, went down the alley next to the structure, and exited onto the street.

She noticed the antique Rolls-Royce parked in front.

"Is that your car?"

"Yes. Technically, it's owned by the L'Enfant Haven Trust, but I can drive it whenever I want."

"How nice."

And she smiled.

Chapter 12
The Ghost

It took nearly twenty minutes to reach the house, each second stretching uncomfortably long. An eerie sensation overcame me, a premonition that something was about to happen as we turned onto the street where the house loomed. When we finally pulled into the driveway, I sat rigid in my seat, eyes fixed on the house. A strange familiarity washed over me—a recognition that sent a chill over my body and filled me with an overwhelming sense of unease.

Seren realized I was staring at the house.

"Are you okay?"

I didn't answer for a moment.

"Yes. I feel like I know this house."

"Let's go in."

She opened the car door and leaned down, looking at me still sitting in the passenger seat, wondering what was happening.

I finally stepped out of the Toyota and slowly stepped up the stairs to the porch, each step heavier than the last. Tears brimmed in my eyes. I didn't want to go inside—afraid I might never find my way back out.

Seren said, "What's wrong?"

"I told you when I had those dreams, it felt like I was the kid. I'm feeling the same way now."

She unlocked the door, took my arm, and led me inside.

A scraping sound erupted from the adjacent room.

I hurriedly asked her, "What was that?"

"Yeah, I hear it every time I've entered. I don't know what it is."

We entered the vestibule and turned left into the living room.

Seren said, "This is where I feel the ghost's presence the strongest."

Inside, the air was heavy with raw emotion. As tears streamed down my face, my hand clamped over my mouth. I moved slowly, my eyes dissecting the walls—portraits of joy between the boy and his mother—the heartbreaking image of the mother driving away, leaving the boy alone and crying. The chaos of anger erupted in wild scribbles and jagged slashes over everything, a visceral outpouring of pain.

I said, "This is so sad and pathetic, but I don't see his ghost anywhere. He must be hiding in the secret room."

I wiped the tears from my face.

I pushed out my Finding Sense and immediately felt queasy.

I moved toward the far wall and ran my hand over it and the wainscoting. Bile started to rise when I touched a loose trim piece and pushed it. The wall popped out about two inches. The bile subsided, and I knew I had found the hidden room.

Seren hurried over.

"You found it."

I tugged the wall open. The scraping sound echoed as the wall moved across the floor. This was the sound I heard when we entered the house. The boy closed the secret door while hiding. Inside the hidden closet, the desiccated body of a child lay on the dusty floor wrapped in a blanket—a musty odor wafted from the small room.

I peered closer inside, and in the right corner was the ghost of a boy, his knees pulled up to his chest and his arms wrapped around them, trying to look as small as possible. A yellow toy truck with splayed tires sat beside him.

I said to the child's ghost, "Hello. Can you come out?"

He didn't move and continued to cower in the corner. His round, terrified eyes stared at me.

Seren asked, "You can see him?"

"Yes, he's in the far corner, but doesn't want to come out. He's frightened."

"What're you going to do?"

"I could force him to come out, but I don't want to do that. Let's go over here, sit, and wait a while."

I removed the tarp from the furniture in the center of the room and pulled out the brown sofa.

"He's scared. We'll have to be patient," I said.

I called the boy, "Please come out and talk to me. We won't hurt you."

We sat and waited. Nothing happened.

I put a bit of force behind my words, "You can trust me; you know you can. I'm here to help you. Please come out."

A head peeked around the corner and shot back.

"Come on. It's okay."

The ghost said, "What about her? She might be bad."

"No, she's not bad. You can trust both of us."

I coaxed the boy gently; my voice filled with warmth and reassurance.

He peeked out again and moved toward the couch, anxiously peering around. Slowly, the child crept forward in hesitant steps, his ghostly form flickering with fear.

I said, "No one else is here. It's okay."

The child's emaciated body, just skin and bones, with a head of scruffy blond hair, was as he appeared when he died. He advanced in short bursts toward us, searching around with each move.

"Come and sit next to me."

He hesitantly sat on the sofa and stared at the floor.

I took Seren's hand and whispered.

"I'm going to touch him. Hold my hand, and you'll be able to see and hear him."

"Okay."

She wore a perplexed expression, having never encountered anything like this before. She placed her soft, delicate hand in mine, and it felt natural. I rested my left hand on the ghost's arm.

I told the boy, "My name's Orion, and this is Seren. We are here to help you. What's your name?"

He said, "Johnny."

Seren flinched when she saw and heard the child's ghost.

"What's your last name?"

"Newman."

"How old are you, Johnny?"

"Five."

"How long have you been here?"

"I don't know—a long time. Mommy was supposed to come back after a few days, and she didn't. I'm waiting for her."

"I know you are. You are incredibly brave to stay here all this time. You did exactly what your mother asked you to do. I'm sure she would be very proud of you."

"Do you think so? I was really mad at her for a while when she didn't come back. But then I thought something must have happened to her. She wouldn't just leave me here."

"I'm sure she wouldn't. Do you have any idea what might have happened to her?"

"I think Daddy might have hurt her. He was so mean."

"What's your Daddy's name?"

"Earnest."

"Earnest Newman?"

"No, he has a different last name; I can't remember it."

"It's okay."

I glanced at Seren with a questioning look as tears streamed from her eyes.

"Do you think I should tell him?"

She nodded and wiped the tears away.

"Johnny, new people own the house now, and you must leave."

"I can't go. I have to wait for Mommy. I promised."

"I know you did. But something has happened, and she's not coming back."

He began to cry, his shoulders trembling with anguish. Johnny's sobs were heart-wrenching, echoing with raw pain. I held him close, my tears falling freely as a surge of empathy overwhelmed me.

"I'll find her. I promise," I said. "But you have to come with me. I can keep you safe."

He gazed at me.

"You're going to find her?"

"Yes, and I'll bring her to you. But not here. You'll have to come with me to my house."

He jumped up, ready to run away, but I placed my hand on his arm, and he stopped and sat back down.

"Johnny, you don't have to be afraid. You know I'm telling you the truth."

I sent him sensations of gentle reassurance and protection.

He stared at me with huge, sad eyes.

"Yeah, you're telling me the truth."

"My *God* father sent me dreams about you so I could come and help you because you're special."

"He did?"

His voice was small and unsure.

"Yes, he knew you were here alone, scared, and needed help. That was why he sent me."

The child hugged me, and I patted him on the back while holding Seren's hand. She squeezed it gently with sympathy.

I peered down at the boy, "Johnny, you know, you're dead and a ghost, right?"

He gazed over at the desiccated body in the secret closet.

"After the light tried to pull me away, that thing was there."

He pointed to his dead body under a dirty, ragged, old gray blanket.

"Is that... me?"

"Yes, that's your body."

"Is Mommy dead too?"

"No, I don't think so. I would know if she was."

Somehow, I knew she lived. I didn't get the usual deep-in-my-soul sensation when determining if someone was dead.

"Is that why she never came back ... because she knows I'm dead?"

"Oh, Johnny, I don't think that's the reason. I think something happened to her, and she couldn't return."

The boy cried, burying his face in my shirt, missing his mother.

I continued, "You have to come with me. I can carry you inside me and protect you."

"You can?" he asked, his voice trembling with cautious hope.

"That was one of the powers my *God* father gave me."

He hesitated, "But how do I do that? It sounds yucky."

"It's not," I assured him, with kindness in my voice.

"All you need to do is walk into me and give a gentle push. I'll help you."

After a moment of hesitation, Johnny stepped into me, his ghostly form flickering before dissolving completely as he entered. I blinked, my senses thrown off as the new presence within me took hold. Seren gripped my hand even tighter, her eyes brimming with awe and amazement.

In my mind, I told Johnny, '*That was easy, wasn't it?*'

'*Yeah, but it feels weird.*'

'*I know; it is weird.*'

With my eyes closed, I smiled. I'm sure Seren was wondering what was happening.

Chapter 13
The Police Arrive

Shocked by Orion Labauve and his extraordinary abilities, she couldn't believe what she was seeing. He didn't merely see or speak to ghosts—he could physically touch them. When he clasped her hand and communicated with the child's spirit, it materialized with such vividness that she nearly mistook it for a living child. The raw, overwhelming emotions radiating from the boy's ghost shattered her composure. Tears streamed down her face.

Orion's powers, he explained, were bestowed upon him by a mysterious godfather. Seren, vividly recalling the voodoo talismans he held at the shop, made her suspect this godfather was likely one of the elusive Lwa—the potent voodoo spirit entities. The mystery surrounding his abilities only deepened, leaving her with more questions than answers.

Even more intriguing was Orion's uncanny ability to contain a specter within himself without succumbing to its overpowering presence. Determined to understand how he achieved such a staggering feat, she stood near, focused intently on his every action. From the moment she stepped into the shop and felt his overwhelming presence, she sensed a power unlike anything she'd ever encountered, electrifying and formidable. What other extraordinary abilities did he hide behind that calm veneer?

Seren released my hand and asked, "Is he inside you?"

"Yes, he's here."

I turned inside and said, '*Johnny, say hi to Seren. You can use my voice.*'

Johnny's greeting came through in a high-pitched, childlike

version of my voice: "Hi, Seren."

"Hi, Johnny," she replied softly, her eyes narrowing as if trying to peer beyond the veil between worlds.

"I think you're pretty," Johnny said.

"Thank you, Johnny."

Before answering Seren, I spoke to Johnny in my mind.

'I have to speak with Seren for a while; please be quiet and let us talk. But you can talk to me in my mind.'

He said, *'Okay.'*

"Seren, what should we do about that?" I said, pointing to Johnny's body.

"I'll call Detective O'Reilly and inform him of what we found."

She went to the phone and called the police.

While waiting for the police, Seren's curiosity got the better of her.

She asked, "Have you always been able to do this?"

"Yes, since I was three, I've been able to see, speak to, and touch ghosts. After my twenty-fifth birthday, I discovered that I was a Spirit Speaker and learned of other powers related to interacting with spirits. Carrying them inside me is one of those abilities."

I hesitated. Why was I revealing so much? Was it our connection from a past life?

"So, you were born a Spirit Speaker?"

"Not exactly. I can tell you more details later."

I didn't want to say too much with Johnny inside me listening.

"Duke Shamedi endowed me with extraordinary abilities as a Lwa Spirit Speaker, but I didn't gain access to all of them until I turned twenty-five."

She nodded, as if she understood, but I'm sure she didn't. Who could?

I inquired, curious about her past.

"Doris told me that you have worked with the Shreveport police department on a couple of cases."

"Yes," she answered with a slight smile.

"That sounds interesting."

"It was, but it took a lot out of me doing it. You should consider working with the police. With your finding ability, you could probably help close many of their open cases."

"That might be interesting, but let's not tell them how easy it would be for me. I don't want to be hounded constantly. I always told the people I did Finding Jobs for that it exhausted me to perform the job to keep them from calling too much."

"Is it okay if I mention it to Detective O'Reilly?"

"Yes, but please downplay my abilities. A case here and there would be alright, but I don't want constant work. I don't think the Duke gave me these powers to work for the police."

She nodded.

Flashing lights illuminated the front windows as several cars screeched to a halt outside. Seren opened the door, stepping back as policemen rushed in. I moved to the stairs, sitting quietly while Seren directed the officers to the hidden closet where Johnny's body lay.

Johnny's spirit quivered with fear.

'*It's okay,*' I assured him. '*The police are here to help. They have to take your body away.*'

Johnny said, '*But Mommy won't know where to find me.*'

'*I'll show her when I find her. You don't have to worry. I'll bring her to you.*'

A police officer approached me and asked several questions. I answered all of them but omitted everything about speaking with Johnny's ghost and holding him. Several officers glared at me as they passed; I knew they were receiving ominous vibes from me.

A man with messy brown hair and a cheap suit burst into the house. His eyes locked onto mine with an accusatory glare, reminiscent of how Sheriff Titus in Madreville always glares at me. He strode over quickly and stood beside Seren, scrutinizing Johnny's lifeless body lying on the closet floor.

She hurriedly explained how we discovered the body before tugging him to the opposite side of the room. They huddled together, whispering fiercely, their glances flickering at me with suspicion and tension.

"Brian, come over here. I need to speak with you," Seren implored. He followed her to the far corner.

"What's going on here?"

He glanced over her shoulder at the curly-haired man sitting on the stairs. A strange feeling radiated from him.

She urgently explained to Brian that she couldn't succeed in exorcising the ghost for the Masons, but she remembered meeting Orion Labauve, whose business card proclaimed him as a ghost expert. Desperate for help, she called him immediately. She poured out every detail about the spirit, only to discover that Orion already knew more—his familiarity with ghosts was more profound than she could imagine.

"You think he killed the kid?"

Brian's glare shot toward Orion, sharp with suspicion.

"Oh, no. He had been dreaming about the kid's ghost being here, but he couldn't figure out where the house was until I showed him. He knew about the secret room and that the boy's mother had left to go and speak with his father."

"Did he exorcise the ghost?"

Glancing again at the curly-haired young man.

"No, he's holding the ghost inside of himself."

Detective O'Reilly's expression darkened as Seren recounted the events.

"You mean he's channeled the kid's ghost?"

Seren said, "No, he's holding it."

"He's actually holding the spirit inside him?"

The detective's voice was rising with each word, drawing the attention of some of the other officers in the room.

"Yes, he really did it."

She almost couldn't believe what she was telling Brian.

"You saw the ghost?"

He only half believed what she told him.

She nodded.

"Yes, when Orion held my hand, I could see and hear the child's spirit. It looked and sounded alive."

"Really? I've never heard of that ability before. My mother never said anything about this type of supernatural ability."

"Yes. It's all true. You know me. I can tell if people are lying. He's not making this up. He can also find things and people; that was his job for several years."

"Do you think I could ... talk to the kid?"

Brian's voice lowered, the weight of the case creeping into his tone.

"Let's go over and ask him."

They both approached Orion. He was leaning against the wall facing the stairs with his eyes closed.

Seren said, "Orion."

He didn't answer.

"Orion."

She touched his arm, and he jerked, opening his eyes.

Chapter 14
Interviewing Johnny

Two people from the coroner's office arrived carrying a body bag and what appeared to be a toolbox. They opened the box, pulled out small plastic bags and jars, and took samples from the corpse and inside the closet. They carefully lifted the body and placed it inside the bag. A brown, stuffed bear fell to the floor as they lifted the tiny corpse. It had been under the blanket covering the body.

Johnny saw the toy fall from the blanket and cried out, '*Tommy Bear!*' and attempted to bolt for the bear. I held him back.

One of the coroner's techs picked up the stuffed animal, placed it in the pouch with Johnny's body, and zipped it closed.

Seeing the coroner carry the bag with his body and Tommy Bear inside, grief overtook him, and he broke into uncontrollable sobs. Tears blurred my vision as a surge of helplessness washed over me. It was becoming difficult to control Johnny. I quickly stood and pressed my shoulder against the wall, turning away from the door to shield him from the sight of his body and Tommy Bear loaded into the van. The weight of the moment pressed heavily on us both.

I kept telling the boy, '*It's okay. It's okay.*'

He finally calmed down.

Seren and the detective approached me. I was preoccupied, trying to calm Johnny, and didn't notice until Seren touched my arm, and I jerked.

"Orion, I want to introduce you to Detective Brian O'Reilly."

O'Reilly held out his right hand, and I shook it. His eyes widened as he took my hand, feeling the unusual sensations from me.

The detective asked, "Can we go back here and talk?"

I followed them into the kitchen. He pulled a chair from the table and asked us to sit. He removed a small notebook and a pen from the pocket on the inside of his jacket.

He asked, "Could you please provide your full name, phone number, and address?"

I gave him the information.

The detective furrowed his brow and asked, "Why is your name so familiar?"

"You may have heard how I found the Rowan kid that was missing for two weeks up in Madreville several years ago."

"Yeah, that's it. The kid was down a well or something."

I nodded.

"That was you who found him?"

I nodded.

"Okay. From what Seren told me, you're a ghost expert."

"Yes, you could call me that."

I had never thought of myself in those terms, but compared to the rest of the occult community, I guess I am a ghost expert.

"You can see and speak to them."

"Yes…," I said hesitantly.

Seren noticed my hesitation.

"It's okay. He knows about occult stuff. His mother was a witch."

O'Reilly said, "But nobody on the force knows that. I'd never hear the end of it if they did. I understand that you are holding the child's spirit inside you."

"Yes."

Johnny squirmed inside, and I twisted my torso to compensate.

"Can I speak with him?"

His expression of curiosity was evident.

"I'll ask him."

I closed my eyes and asked, '*Johnny, the policeman wants to talk to you. It will help to find your mother.*'

Johnny answered, '*Okay.*'

I nodded.

"Yes, he'll talk to you."

I allowed the boy to come forward.

O'Reilly cleared his throat, never having interviewed a ghost before. He allowed his professional side to take control.

"Hello, I'm Detective Brian O'Reilly, and I need to ask you some questions about what happened. Is that okay?"

Johnny's voice came through me as a child's version of my voice.

"Orion said you're a policeman, but you aren't dressed like the other policemen."

"That's right. It's because I'm a detective. I search for the bad people and figure out what happened. Here's my badge."

He removed the badge clipped to his belt and handed it to Johnny. Johnny took the gold badge in his hands and carefully examined it.

"That's neat."

He gave it back to O'Reilly.

"Thank you. What's your full name?"

"Johnny Newman."

"What's your mother's full name?

"Darlene Newman."

"What's your father's full name?

"Earnest… something. I don't remember."

"Could it be Newman?"

"No. It's different. It's a long name."

The detective wrote things in the notebook.

"How old are you, Johnny?

"Five."

"How long have you been here?"

"A long time. I don't know how long."

"Can you tell me why you are here and what happened?"

The child's spirit hesitated, and, looking at the floor, he began.

"Okay. Mommy and I lived in a big house. Daddy would come over sometimes. Sometimes he was happy and gave us presents. He called me his little man. But a lot of times he got mad and hit me. He pushed me down. Mommy tried to stop him, but he hit her, too. One night, Mommy came into my room and told me to get out of bed. She said we were going somewhere else. I grabbed my Tommy Bear and a truck. We got in the car, drove a long way, and then we were here.

"We stayed in the house for a little while. We played games and had fun, but sometimes she looked sad. She told me I could never go outside because someone might see me and tell Daddy. She showed me the secret room and said that if anyone came into the house, I should hide there until they left. They might be mean people that Daddy sent.

"Then, one day, she said she had to go talk to Daddy and work things out. I didn't know what that meant. She said she would only be gone for a couple of days. She made me promise to stay in the house and not let anyone see me. I promised, and I've been waiting for her to come back. I think Daddy did something to her."

His voice cracked, and he started to cry, "I just want my mommy."

Johnny whimpered, his sorrow mixing with my own. Tears burned my eyes as I clenched my fists against the ache of his loss—and mine.

Seren rubbed my back, "It's okay, Johnny. We're going to find your mommy."

Detective O'Reilly said, "Thank you so much. This'll help us a lot to find your mommy."

I came forward, still crying, "I'm sorry. He's upset, and I'm struggling to control him."

I took my wallet from my back pocket, retrieved one of my business cards, and handed it to the detective.

"If you gather more information about where Johnny's mother might be, please call me. I promised the boy I would track his mother down."

Brian took the card and read it. He pulled out one of his cards and handed it to me.

"And you call me if you find anything about her. I mean it. Phone me."

I nodded.

Seren suggested, "Why don't you go sit in the car? I'll finish talking to Brian, and then we can go."

After Orion left, the detective turned to Seren.

"That was so strange. I've been around channelers, but they were nothing like this. He actually has the kid's spirit inside him?"

"I know. I've never met anyone with these abilities either."

She looked in the direction Orion had exited.

"And the vibes he gives off kind of leaves me with the creeps."

The detective gave an exaggerated shiver.

"After spending some time with him, the sensations ease, but there is always something lurking in the background. He mentioned that he has been able to do this since he was three."

"I wish my mother were still alive; she would have loved to meet him. She told me that the strongest psychic she ever met was the Voodoo Imperatrice, but I bet he's stronger than her."

"He may be," she agreed.

A flash of the psychic battle between Orion and a voodoo priestess jumped into her mind again. Was this the Voodoo Imperatrice?

"Do you think he can actually find the boy's mother?"

Brian's voice carried a mix of curiosity and doubt, as though the idea itself was too extraordinary to grasp.

"It sounds like he can find things. He found the hidden room here in about fifteen seconds," Seren said.

"If he goes looking for Johnny's mother, can you go with him?"

"I guess so. But why?" she asked, unsure why Brian would ask this of her.

"I want to know if he's really doing the things he says or if he's somehow linked in a different way to this whole situation."

"Okay, I'll ask to work with him to find Johnny's mother."

"If you can, and you find out he's involved with something bad, you get out immediately. This guy might be crazy."

"I'll see what I can do."

She left for her car, thinking, 'I don't think Orion's crazy, but there's so much more to him.' She was sure of that.

I walked to the car, looking away whenever police officers glared at me, not wanting them to see me crying. I sat in the Toyota, pulled a handkerchief from my pocket, blew my nose, and wiped the tears from my face. Johnny was still upset and crying.

I reassured him, '*You did great talking to the detective. I'm sure what you told him will help find your mother.*'

Johnny asked, '*I thought you were going to find Mommy?*'

'I am, and Detective O'Reilly is, too. Now, there'll be two people looking for her. So, one of us should find her.'

That seemed to make him feel better.

After about ten minutes, Seren emerged and got into the car.

"Are you okay? How's Johnny?"

"I'm okay. He's concerned about his mother."

She nodded and pulled out of the driveway.

"Can you drive with Johnny inside you?"

"Normally, yes, but I don't think it would be safe with him getting upset. Can you take me home? I'll send someone for the Rolls later."

"Sure, where do you live?"

"Near Madreville. Do you know where that is?"

"Yes. It's up north, right?"

I nodded, and she headed up the highway in that direction.

The child became upset occasionally and would start crying again during the drive to my home.

I told him, "Come out and sit on my lap."

He came out, hugged me, put his head on my shoulder, and cried. I rubbed his back.

I sat with my head resting against the side window, talking to Johnny about my family. Seren listened to my story the entire time.

She said, "Your life is definitely unusual."

I said, "That's for sure. When my mother inherited the plantation and we moved in, it was the best thing that had ever happened to me. Before that, we lived in drug flophouses. I was afraid all the time and would often hide. I understand what Johnny's going through."

Tears streamed down my cheeks in slow, relentless waves, some because of Johnny, but some from haunting memories of my fear in the flophouses. Despite my mother being only upstairs, it felt as if she vanished whenever she drank or used drugs. I was fortunate, in a way, to be raised by my ghostly family.

She remarked, "You only have a slight southern accent; I thought you said you've lived in Louisiana all your life."

"That's right, but Nanny Helen at the plantation taught me proper English, as she called it, and I've tried to maintain what I learned from her."

"You had a nanny?"

"Yes, she was a spirit, but she's gone to the other side now. I miss her."

Seren didn't ask any other questions during the drive.

When we arrived in Madreville, I gave Seren clear directions to L'Enfant Haven plantation. She pulled up to the gate, and immediately, the porch light pierced through the darkness, casting our shadows onto the mansion's front yard.

The lower-floor lights blazed through the windows, a warm, unmistakable glow announcing that my family was already there, waiting. They would have sensed my return and turned on every light, igniting the house in a welcoming brilliance. The fans whirred to life, pulling cool night air inside, as if the house itself eagerly prepared for my arrival.

Seren peered through the car's front window.

"Wow," she breathed, eyes sweeping over the mansion's gleaming façade. "It's beautiful—like it's frozen in time."

I said, "It kind of is."

She looked at me, not understanding what I meant by this statement. After the Labauve signet was destroyed, the Duke reinstated the Lwa that protected the house from aging. The curse protected the home as a place for the cursed ghosts to stay forever. Now with the curse no longer active, the house will last as long as a Labauve heir lives in it.

Johnny said, "Neat house."

I smiled.

"Come on in," I said stepping onto the porch and holding Johnny in my arms. "There are some people I'd like you to meet."

SPECTRAL PROMISES

Chapter 15

Johnny Comes Home

I walked up to the front door, holding Johnny in my arms. I pushed on the large teak door; confident my family would unlock it. As it creaked open, I ran my hand over the brass lion head knocker, feeling the worn metal beneath my fingers.

Johnny tilted his head, his curiosity sparked by the ornate knocker.

"Go ahead, rub the lion's nose," I said with a grin. "He likes it."

Johnny reached out to rub the lion's nose. A delighted smile spread across his face. Following closely behind, Seren chuckled softly before quickly swiping the lion's snout.

I closed the door and gently set Johnny down. He clung to my leg. The ghosts filled the vestibule. Johnny's gaze darted upward, his small hand gripping my leg as he pressed his face against my jeans. I tousled his hair.

"It's okay, buddy. I'll introduce you to everyone."

Seren shifted uneasily, her gaze sweeping the room as if sensing something just beyond the veil of sight.

"I can't see them, but I feel… something."

"I can fix that."

I took her hands.

"Close your eyes."

She complied. Closing my own eyes, I murmured the incantation to awaken her Spirit Sight. Warmth radiated from my palms as I placed them over her eyes and ears.

"Now, look around," I instructed.

She gasped softly as her surroundings transformed. Her eyes widened, and a radiant smile spread across her face as my family appeared to her for the first time.

"Everyone, this is Seren Griffyths. She owns the Star Occult Shop."

I placed a hand on Johnny's shoulder.

"And this is Johnny Newman. He'll be staying with us for a while. He's been waiting for his mother for years, and I promised to find her. Please introduce yourselves."

Each ghost stepped forward and introduced themselves to Seren and Johnny. The boy beamed with a big grin as the spectral figures shook his hand.

After the introduction, Johnny peered up at me, his brow furrowed in thought.

"Are they all dead, like me?"

I nodded gently.

"Are they waiting for their mommies, too?"

His innocent question hung in the air, momentarily stealing the room, before soft, affectionate chuckles rippled through the spirits.

"No, Johnny," I said, crouching down to meet his gaze. "They were given a choice: enter the tunnel of light or stay here to help me. They all chose to remain. They're my family. They've been with me since I was three."

Johnny's expression shifted to wonder.

"Wow! That's neat."

"Hey, there's a playroom on the third floor with toys. Do you want to go and play? Paul will play with you."

Johnny glanced at Paul. He smiled at the child, and Paul said, "I used to play with Mr. Orion all the time when he was little. I know all the good games to play."

The boy's face lit up, and Paul took his hand, moving toward the stairs. The boy stopped and glanced over his shoulder at me.

I said, "It's okay. I'm right here. I'm going to speak with Seren for a while."

He smiled, feeling the comfort of our bond, and continued up the stairs with the yardman.

Cyrus asked, "Is this the kid from your dreams?"

"Yes, it's heartbreaking what this child has been through."

Doc approached.

"How long do you think he'll be here?"

"Just until I find his mother. I can sense she's still alive, but I don't know where she is yet. It may take some time to locate her. I'll place a protective Lwa over Johnny to ensure his safety and prevent him from leaving the property. He gets upset sometimes, and I'm afraid he might try to leave and return to his mother's house if I'm not here. He can go outside to play, but only within the yard."

Doc nodded.

Throughout this, Seren remained silent and in shock. I could see the uneasiness in her eyes.

"Are you okay?"

She nodded.

"In all my years as a psychic and studying the occult, I have never seen anything like this. How on earth are you doing this?"

I took her to the couch and sat down with her.

"When we have more time, I'll explain it to you."

"Okay, I can't wait."

"Rose, can you make us some tea and something to eat? I missed lunch and dinner. I'm starved."

I asked her, "Are you hungry?"

Seren nodded.

I said, "I had better do that protection spell for Johnny."

"Are you going to do a Voodoo ceremony?"

"No, I don't need to do a ceremony. I have semi-direct access to the spirit realm. I only need to perform the correct magical movements to summon a Lwa. Watch."

I strode into the heart of the vestibule, needing ample space for my movements. I closed my eyes, centering on myself and homing in on my connection to the spiritual plane. My hands moved with purpose and fluidity, carving intricate patterns through the air that shimmered with a faint, otherworldly glow as I channeled my energy.

When I opened my eyes, Seren gasped audibly.

"Your eyes—they're golden!"

I didn't answer, allowing the sacred rhythm of the divine language to cascade from my lips. Mystical energy erupted through the room, a fierce vibration pulsating against my skin. A portal rippled open like water shattered by a stone, and a blazing blue orb emerged, glowing with an intense, ethereal light.

The Lwa hovered before me, its presence commanding yet serene. I gave it instructions, my voice steady despite the awe thrumming in my chest.

'*As you command, Small Duke,*' it said, its voice like wind through chimes.

It vanished, leaving a faint ripple as it zipped to Johnny's side upstairs. It would stay with Johnny until I released it from the task, or the child went to the other side.

Seren stared at me, her mouth partially open.

"That was... incredible. Were you able to call a Lwa over?"

She searched around the room for any signs of something unusual.

"Oh, yes. He's up with the boy now," pointing my head upstairs.

"I didn't see anything."

"You can't see Lwa. Even the ghosts can't see them, but I can."

"Amazing. Just amazing."

She shook her head in awe.

Rose came in with a tray of sandwiches and a pot of tea. Seren and I ate.

She asked about the house and its history.

I explained, "The Labauve family moved to the area from France in the 1790s and purchased the plantation. They owned hundreds of acres and about 70 slaves, making it one of the largest plantations in the region. In 1813, a tragedy occurred when one of the Labauve children died. A slave named Paul was accused of killing the child.

I pointed to the kitchen and said, "Rose cursed the plantation after that. She cursed the place so that anyone who died on the property and had injured or killed a child would have their spirit remain here until the curse was lifted."

"So, that means each of the ghosts I can see here harmed a child somehow?"

"Yes, except for Rose and Paul. Paul was already here when the curse was activated, and my grandmother, the Voodoo Imperatrice, summoned Rose from the other side. Rose returned to this plane because she wanted to find a way to release her son, Paul, so that he could pass over."

Seren asked, "But how can all the ghosts here do so much, like everything they did when alive? I've never seen that anywhere else where I've encountered spirits."

"It's because of how Rose structured the curse. The house doesn't age—well, it ages very slowly. The transfer of a large amount of energy from the mystical realm also makes the ghosts more tangible, allowing them to interact with items on the property. If there's a Labauve heir nearby," I pointed to myself, "more energy is transferred. When they are away from the property, they can't freely interact with their surroundings. If there is residual psychic energy in an area, they may be able to do small things, but not much.

"So, is that why Johnny could open and close the hidden closet door? Sufficient psychic energy resided in the house to allow it?"

"Probably, but without knowing the house's family history. It's hard to say."

"That's truly amazing."

She sat and stared at the table momentarily, digesting all the information I gave her.

She stood.

"I had better head home, call the Masons, and let them know their house is no longer haunted. Oh, I never asked what you charge for your services."

"Nothing. This was a job the Duke sent me, so I'm supposed to do this anyway."

"Okay, I'll call you tomorrow."

I walked her to the gate. Seren lingered, her car keys dangling loosely from her hand.

"Thank you for walking me out," she said softly.

I nodded, my chest tight with unspoken words.

"Bye. Talk to you tomorrow," I managed to say.

She hesitated, her eyes locking with mine, and for a heartbeat, I thought she might step closer. I ached for her to—God, how I wanted her to—but the weight of my fears held me frozen, paralyzing me, and pushing her away.

Finally, she turned and hurried to the Toyota. I watched her taillights fade down the driveway, a knot tightening in my stomach. I desperately wanted to call out for her to come back. I cherished every moment I spent with her and already missed her presence.

'God, I have to stop thinking like this. It's only going to make me feel worse, something I don't need to complicate my life further.'

Back inside, I leaned against the door, heart pounding as I listened to the joyful stomping of tiny feet upstairs. I hurried up the steps, every footfall echoing loudly. I entered the hall to find Johnny racing wildly with a toy plane in his hand, soaring through the air. His laughter was ringing off the walls. The blue Lwa trailed behind him, a watchful guardian, silent but intense.

I knew, for the first time in years, Johnny was happy. I smiled, pushing aside my turmoil. At least, for now, he could have this.

Chapter 16
What an Incredible Man

The sky was an inky black as Seren sped home, her mind racing from the day's emotional storm and incredible revelations.

Orion Labauve filled her thoughts; his lean, muscular frame, almost flawless, was impossible to ignore. The magnetic pull toward him was undeniable, yet she fought it, convincing herself it wasn't her desire; it was Chloe's. She told herself this was just the echoes of a life she had long forgotten. But despite her logic, the ache in her chest refused to be silenced.

She could sense his shyness, the way his words hesitated, tentative and unpracticed. During their drive, he revealed fragments of a harrowing life story that sounded unbelievable yet placed him in painful isolation. Raised in a house filled with ghosts, with an addicted mother just a floor away, he had been abandoned in every way that mattered. The idea of growing up surrounded by spirits rather than people sent a shiver down her spine. Her experiences with ghost exorcisms had only exposed her to ghosts stuck in loops of emotional trauma. The ghosts at L'Enfant Haven were like complete people. Perhaps that's how he managed by rarely having relationships with live people.

And that mansion was the same ominous structure from her haunting vision—the place where he battled a voodoo priestess in a fierce, otherworldly clash. It also loomed large in several of her visionary paintings, each echoing intense mysteries. At some point, she knew she would have to confront him and ask if that psychic battle had truly occurred. If it had, it would redefine everything she thought she knew about spiritual power.

Why had no one ever heard of anyone possessing such extraordinary powers? Despite her deep knowledge of the occult, she had never found a single record of someone with powers like his, leaving her both awestruck and hungry for answers.

Orion's connection to the spirit world was unlike anything she had ever encountered. He didn't just speak to ghosts—he commanded them, bridging realms with an effortlessly authoritative presence that shattered her understanding of the supernatural.

The way he summoned the Lwa spirits was mesmerizing, almost hypnotic. His eyes glowed with an intense, golden fire, as if illuminated from within, and his arms moved in a sweeping, hypnotic dance—part invocation, part ritual—each gesture precise, potent, and otherworldly. She recognized traces of East Indian mudras in the hand and finger formations and motions, mingled with cryptic symbols she couldn't even begin to understand, forming a language of raw power that left her in awe and trembling.

A chilling ripple of air swept through her as he moved his arms with deliberate intent, tracing intricate, arcane patterns. The room's temperature plummeted, a sharp drop that chilled her bones, and the surrounding space seemed to shimmer and distort like water under the light of a ghostly moon. A faint, purplish glow clung to his clothes, flickering and sparkling as if possessed by a life of its own.

As the crackling energy finally stilled, the room snapped back to its usual quiet, yet Orion remained perfectly still, his piercing golden eyes locked onto something beyond her perception.

"I summoned a Lwa," he declared, his voice carrying an unearthly weight.

And she believed him—without a doubt. She didn't need to see it to feel the raw, unfiltered power that still pulsed palpably in the air.

Until now, she believed Lwa could only be called through elaborate voodoo rites. Having participated in a few rituals and sensed the spirits's energy, nothing compared to what she felt when Orion manifested a Lwa to protect Johnny.

The full realization hit her like a lightning bolt. He actually summoned a spirit entity from another plane with just a few gestures. His physical magic was undeniably real—at his command, anything was possible. What astonishing power was he truly capable of?

Orion mentioned having a godfather who endowed him with unique powers. He must be referring to a God, not a human godfather, but an actual deity. It was most likely a Voodoo God since he refers to the spiritual entities as Lwa, which voodoo practitioners call them. He mentioned the Duke. Could that be the Voodoo God, Duke Shamedi? This was truly astonishing. She wanted—no, was compelled to learn more about him.

Her attraction to him was undeniable, surpassing even their shared past lives. There was an inexplicable pull about him, something she couldn't quite pinpoint, that drew her in. It wasn't simply curiosity about his powers; it was something deeper, more compelling.

Over the last few years, her business had flourished, and she had formed friendships with many people in the occult community in Shreveport, individuals with diverse mystical interests and abilities. Still, none were anywhere near Orion Labauve's.

Seren intimately knew hardship. Her father, a U.S. Marine, never returned from the Vietnam War. Left to raise their daughter alone, her English mother passed away when the girl was eleven, as cancer took her far too soon. She was thrust into New York City's foster care system—a world that swiftly taught Seren how to survive on her own.

Her mother's death left her vulnerable, adrift in a world that didn't understand her. Early on, she learned to hide her psychic gifts; the scorn and mistrust of others taught her this lesson well. Children whispered cruel words behind her back, and adults kept their distance, unsettled by what she knew but shouldn't. Isolation became her shield.

She had always been psychic, intuitively sensing things about people and places, a gift that set her apart. This ability terrified many, driving her to silence her thoughts, fearing rejection or worse. Her mother warned her to hide her perceptions, cautioning her to stay silent.

Yet, as a child, this was nearly impossible—hidden truths often slipped from her lips before she could stop them. To cope, she began drawing the visions that haunted her, always carrying paper and pencils, transforming her secret fears into art.

When transferred to a girls' reform school, her world changed forever. It was there that she discovered her psychic abilities and became a member of a secret occult club. In this supportive environment, she didn't have to hide her powers; instead, she was encouraged to push the boundaries of her potential. Driven by newfound confidence, she began offering tarot and psychic readings to the public after her release from the institution.

As Seren matured, her visions became vivid and powerful, inspiring her to create striking, ethereal paintings that captivated all who viewed them. Her artwork gained incredible popularity, fetching substantial sums and cementing her reputation as a visionary artist.

After exploring various mystical practices and religions, she decided to open an occult shop. However, New York City was too expensive for her to start a store. She researched different locations across the country and found a strong occult community in Louisiana, along with affordable property prices. She saved her money and moved to Shreveport, where she found a small store with an apartment upstairs. It was perfect; she felt nothing but positive energy from the location and knew this place was exceptional. She performed a blessing ceremony on the property and opened the store.

Seren pulled into her parking space at the back of the shop and climbed the stairs to her apartment. Everything she experienced today left her exhausted. She needed to relax and get some sleep. After taking a shower, she collapsed into bed, deciding to wait until tomorrow morning to call the Masons. As she drifted off, another past-life vision took over.

Chloe traveled with her father to Le Havre to pick up supplies for his candle-making business. While her father haggled over the price of beeswax, she slipped away and hurried down the lane to the shipping office. She entered the building and approached the tall counter, where a middle-aged clerk with gray hair bent over carefully examining documents. He knew she was waiting but showed no sign of stopping his work.

Finally, he glanced at the young woman and recognized her beauty.

He brightened and said, "How may I assist you, Miss?"

Chloe anxiously said, "I need to know when the next ship from Saint Dominque is expected."

He pulled out a massive ledger book, opened it, and scanned the pages.

"Ah, here it is. If the weather is good, in two weeks."

Chloe smiled, delighted that this date was earlier than she had sensed.

"Oh, thank you, sir."

She turned sharply and skipped back down the street, her heart pounding with excitement at the thought of Abelard's return. But the Fairy Queen's warning flashed in her mind like a lightning bolt.

Her pace slowed, and she clutched her hands in desperation, praying fervently, 'Please, don't let anything bad happen to Abelard.'

Her father stepped out of the shop where she had left him and said, "Ah, there you are."

Noticing her worried expression, he asked, "What's wrong?"

"I went to the shipping office to find out when to expect Abelard back, and the clerk said it would be two weeks."

"Well, that's good; why do you look so glum?"

"I just have a bad feeling that something happened to him while on Saint Dominque."

"Don't think that way. He'll be fine. You'll see."

As they rode the cart back to Falaise village, Chloe couldn't shake the chilling sensation that something sinister had happened to the man she loved.

It had been over a month since Chloe visited the Le Havre shipping office. Her mind wandered, thinking about Abelard, while she packed candles into a container for a customer's order. The doorbell rang. She turned, grasped the edge of her apron, and wiped the wax from her hands before heading to the front to greet the customer.

She glanced up from wiping her hands as she rounded the corner, and the most wonderful person in the world blocked her path—Abelard Ozanne, with a grin that lit up his face. Without hesitation, she threw herself into his arms, and their mouths instantly met in a fervent kiss. He lifted her effortlessly off the floor as their passion ignited, each savoring the intense heat of the other's lips—something they had both craved desperately.

He gently let her down to the floor.

With a chiding look, she said, "You're late."

"Yes, I missed the first ship and had to come on a later one," he said, still grinning broadly, obviously happy to be back.

"Come with me now."

"Oh, yes. I'll tell Mother I'm going out."

She hurried to the back of the shop and told her mother she needed to go out for a while.

She returned, and Abelard stood waiting with a basket in his hand.

She asked, "What's that?"

"I thought we might go for lunch in the fields," with a flirtatious glint in his eyes.

Chloe understood what that meant and smiled, a spark of anticipation lighting up her eyes. A thrill of excitement surged through her veins. For them, lunch in the fields was more than just a meal—it was their secret escape, an intimate moment in the tall grass where nobody could see them. They hurried out of the shop, their hearts pounding, and quickly made their way to the edge of the village, heading toward the old stone wall, eager for their clandestine rendezvous.

Abelard climbed over the stone barrier and helped Chloe over the wall. He took off his coat and laid it on the grass behind the wall for them to sit on. He pulled out a bottle of wine and uncorked it. They both took drinks from the bottle. Something felt different about him, but she couldn't quite pinpoint it.

He leaned over and kissed her. His blue eyes now sparkled with tiny golden flecks. She knew every part of his body, but his eyes had never shown such flecks before. He kissed her again, more passionately this time, and his kisses felt different, too. He pulled her down onto his coat, causing a wave of excitement to rush through her. She welcomed this change.

He began untying her bodice and loosening the ribbons. He kissed and licked down her neck and across her chest above her perfect breasts. The ribbons were now so loose that her ample mounds poured out, wanting to be free for him to fondle. He took one in his mouth and gently flicked his tongue over the nipple as he massaged the other breast. She sighed with pleasure. Why did it feel so much more enjoyable than before he left?

He pulled his shirt off, revealing his muscular chest. Each muscle was more defined and prominent than she had ever seen. She ran her hands across his muscular back as he kissed and fondled her breasts. His right hand explored under her skirt, slowly sliding his fingers up and down the inside of her thighs and between her folds, making her moan with pleasure. She wanted him now. His aroused member pressed through his pants and shifted against her hips.

She pleaded, "Now, now!"

He rose to his knees and frantically unbuttoned his breeches, pulling them down to his knees. Chloe anxiously watched Abelard expose his member. Was it larger now? No, it had just been too long since she last was with him.

Lifting her skirts to reveal her charms, he paused briefly to admire her beauty. She lifted her hips, eager to welcome him. As they made love, she moaned and noticed it was definitely larger. She cried out with him as they both reached ecstasy. She hit her peak much faster than ever before. Yes, he was different, but it wasn't a bad thing. Afterwards, he lay with his head between her breasts, breathing deeply. She silently thanked the goddess for her love's return. He was finally home with her.

Seren awoke abruptly, her body slick with sweat, her breath ragged from the vivid, intoxicating vision of making passionate love to Abelard. This dream was a continuation of one from that morning, when she was making tea for Orion. It was unlike any dream before— more intense, more real. The image of their lovemaking lingered fiercely in her mind, as if pushing beyond the boundaries of her subconscious. Was it because she now knew Abelard's reincarnation was residing in the handsome young man?

She rolled over, still haunted by the sensation of his movements inside her and the lingering glow of their intimacy. As exhaustion pulled her under again, she couldn't help but wonder—was Orion experiencing similar visions of them together in his sleep?

Roused by a strange sensation on her nose—something tickling her softly. Seren blinked her eyes open and caught sight of an eight-inch fairy hovering right before her face. Its delicate pinkish gossamer wings fluttered tirelessly, shimmering in the streetlight entering through the bedroom window. The fairy's androgynous, nude body had a faint bluish glow, giving it an ethereal presence.

With an urgent gesture of its tiny hand, it beckoned her to follow. Its high-pitched voice was so faint and strange that it was almost impossible to understand yet filled with unmistakable urgency.

Seren rose and wrapped the robe around her body. The room was icy. Her breath formed clouds from her nose. The psychic knew who summoned her.

She followed the blue fairy into the living room. The air shimmered with shifting hues, colors that changed like spilled oil. Lounging on the couch was the Fairy Queen, Bridette. Her bright red hair and pale alabaster skin glowed with an ethereal light. Her iridescent green wings enveloped her naked form, draped over her like a semi-transparent short dress. Around Bridette, the mist pulsed as if alive, curling and unfurling like a sentient veil. Several fairies and pixies flitted about the room and the goddess.

The Queen gestured for Seren to sit beside her in a chair that usually resided on the other side of the room. She complied and took a seat.

The Star Occult Shop was erected atop a sacred site—an ancient stone circle that served as a fragile boundary between the Fairy realm and the mortal world. Seren had immediately sensed the delicate, trembling edge of this veil when she first stepped into the building with the real estate agent, and it was this very mysterious thinness that compelled her to buy the property.

After moving in, fairies and pixies regularly appeared, flitting about her apartment and sometimes in the store after everyone departed, and it was closed. She never told anyone about these supernatural sightings.

The Fairy Queen had appeared twice before, each time bringing startling news—once warning Seren of an approaching stranger, and another time revealing he was the one she sought. This was her third appearance. She was never frightened; only happy that the Fairy Goddess had chosen to visit her.

During the previous appearances, she possessed Seren briefly and simply wandered around the apartment as if testing what it would be like to be human. This time, she did not possess the psychic. Now, as Seren's mind raced, she wondered with tense anticipation: what could the Fairy Queen be warning her about?

Bridette's emerald eyes sparkled as if she could see into Seren's soul.

"Yes," she said, soft yet commanding, "Orion Labauve is critical to you. However, his significance extends beyond your connection. He plays a role in matters you will come to understand in time."

She leaned closer, her wings glinting with a surreal, shimmering light.

"Don't be afraid to reach out to him, but tread carefully. He carries wounds that will take time to heal. The Duke has burdened him heavily, and much of his reluctance comes from that. Guide him, Seren. Help him find the path he was meant to walk."

The mist thickened into a suffocating fog, obscuring Seren's view of the Fairy Queen. Bridette vanished without a trace. Seren's lips curled into a subtle smile as a newfound clarity dawned—what she felt in Orion's presence was real, genuine, not just Chloe's thoughts echoing in her mind.

Memories flashed of Orion mentioning something about the Duke. Wow, the Fairy Queen knows a Voodoo Spirit God like Duke Shamedi? Do they talk together in the spirit realm?

SPECTRAL PROMISES

Chapter 17

Bunny's Protection

I approached Johnny, engrossed in playing with a toy airplane.

"Hey, sport," I said gently to get his attention. "I'm heading to bed. Could you keep it down? Paul or any of the others can play board games with you."

Johnny stopped.

"Oh, okay. I was having fun," he said, chewing on his lip and his voice dropping to a whisper.

Openly playing was something he had craved for so long.

"I know you were, but running up and down the hall was making quite a racket."

"Oh, no."

Remembering that creating too much noise was forbidden in his mother's house.

"It's okay. I need to sleep, and your running will keep me awake. Tomorrow, you can make as much noise as you want."

He looked up with a broad grin. Being told he was no longer under the tight restrictions he suffered through for the last five years delighted him.

I said, "Good night."

As I headed down the stairs, I noticed Paul standing to the side. Having overheard my statement, he nodded in silent agreement. He would keep Johnny quiet for the rest of the night.

I went to bed, exhausted from the day's unusual activities. I fell asleep when my head hit the pillow.

Sometime in the dead of night, something jostled me awake, shifting the sheets and snuggling against me. I shot a glance over. It was Johnny. A blinding flash of lightning illuminated the room, and a deafening roar of thunder rattled the windows immediately after. The child burrowed under the covers, practically lying on top of me, his tiny frame trembling uncontrollably.

I instinctively wrapped my arm around him and softly asked, "What's wrong?"

"I don't like storms." His voice quaked.

"I don't like them, either."

In my mind, I called for Milly, '*Please bring Bunny to me.*'

Within seconds, Milly opened the door and handed me Bunny. The 18-inch-long, brown, plush stuffed rabbit was my nightly companion from the age of three to ten. Nanny Helen gave me the toy on my first stormy night in L'Enfant Haven.

Holding the stuffed rabbit again flooded me with memories. As a child, he was my comfort, protector, and the one to whom I whispered secrets when the world felt overwhelmingly big and confusing. The stuffed rabbit and I would have conversations. He spoke to me when I was young. As I got older, he stopped talking to me. I always thought that was just my kid's imagination. After all the strange things that have happened in this house, I now wonder if it was something else that spoke through the rabbit, something supernatural and more real.

I looked down at Johnny, his round, frightened eyes gazing up at me.

"This is Bunny. He helped me when I was young and afraid of many things, especially storms. When the lightning flashed, I would push my face into his tummy so I couldn't see it. Like this."

I buried my face in Bunny's plump belly, the soft fur enveloping my cheeks.

Johnny smiled.

"Like Tommy Bear."

"Yes, like Tommy Bear. You can use Bunny while you're here; he likes you, I can tell."

The boy took the toy with his small, trembling hands, and at that moment, lightning flashed. He pressed his face into the plush rabbit's tummy, his small body shaking in fear. He calmed down and lifted his head to peek out, ensuring that the flash was no longer there.

I smiled.

"See, he helps."

The boy's ghost nodded and hugged the stuffed rabbit tightly.

"Can I stay here with you? I'll be quiet."

"Sure, that's okay."

The child snuggled close beside me, and Bunny nestled securely between us. I wrapped my arm around him, my fingers trembling slightly as I tried to reassure the frightened child. Closing my eyes, I struggled to drift back into sleep, but the storm's aftermath lingered, leaving my nerves frayed. Bunny's steadfast, protective presence once again wrapped around us like a shield, calming my restless mind. I hadn't hugged Bunny in a long time; his quiet strength was a comfort I desperately needed. I resolved to carve out a special space for him in my room, a sanctuary where my protector can stay close, always.

As I tried to relax, I remembered when I almost lost Bunny.

Mr. Butler arrived with two pairs of hand-me-down shoes from his grandson, Darren, who was sick with a virus spreading through the schools. The attorney visited the ill child, who was in bed with a fever. He never thought about washing up before coming to the plantation. He always hugged me when I was little and visited the mansion. I was four years old at the time.

He sat me on the couch and placed a pair of used red sneakers on my bare feet. He pinched my toes, and there was too much space between the ends of the shoes and my toes. That size was too large.

He slid another pair over my feet, closer to the correct size.

"There you go, try those out."

I stood up and ran down the hall to the kitchen, returning with a smile.

"How do those feel?" he asked.

"I like them, Mr. Butler," I said, laughing as I jumped up and down.

I didn't often get new things—at least not new to me. I dashed out the back door and ran around the house several times in my sneakers.

A week later I became sick from a virus I unknowingly contracted from the attorney, who transmitted it from his grandson. Naturally, my mother didn't notice until the ghosts dragged her from her room up to the nursery on the third floor.

I began to feel unwell, with my stomach upset and aching, so I informed Nanny Helen, and she placed her hand on my forehead.

"Oh, my. You feel warm. Off to bed with you. I'll call the doctor."

Placed in bed, I immediately vomited on the floor as Milly changed me into my pajamas.

Doc arrived with a thermometer and took my temperature.

"101. That's high. We'll keep him in bed and watch him closely."

My fever rose rapidly, causing Doc Albert to appear visibly concerned. Cold compresses and alcohol rubs were ineffective in reducing my temperature.

I don't remember much of it; I mainly experienced fever dreams. When I woke up, one of the ghosts would give me water and a few spoonful's of chicken soup to eat. All I wanted was to hold Bunny tight and sleep.

My temperature reached 104, and Doc said, "That's it, we must get him to the hospital. Go downstairs and bring Marie up here."

Hugo, the ghostly property maintenance man, and Walter, the ghost chauffeur, went to my mother's room and shook her shoulder, but she did not respond. They jarred her more vigorously, and finally, she awoke to perceive vague outlines of the ghosts. She screamed and pulled the covers over her head.

Hugo and Walter exchanged grim looks.

"We need to get her upstairs to see Ory," Hugo said.

Without hesitation, Walter roughly yanked the sheets back, ignoring her desperate protests. She lay on the bed, trembling violently and shrieking in terror. The two spirits seized her arms with an unnatural grip and hoisted my mother from the bed. They dragged her by her arms up the stairs to my room, placing her beside my bed. She fought wildly, screaming bloody murder all the way. Finally, she collapsed to her knees, crouching on the floor, tears streaming down her face.

I woke up to the sound of sobs, unsure of their source. My head swam. I leaned over and saw my mother cowering on the floor, weeping.

I whispered, "Mama, I'm sick," and that was all I could manage to say.

She raised her head and crawled over to me. She knelt by my side and placed her hand on my forehead.

"Oh, my God, you're burning up."

It finally dawned on her that something was wrong with me.

She gazed around, but no ghosts were in sight. She knew the specters transported her up there to take care of me. The ghosts waited in the playroom to prevent her from freaking out again and listened to her statements.

"Baby, I'm so sorry. I should have checked on you."

She took the thermometer from the nightstand and inserted it into my mouth. It now reads 105.

"Oh, God. I'm going to call Mr. Butler."

She ran down the stairs, called her attorney, and told him how sick I was. Mr. Butler phoned the ambulance.

Mr. Butler arrived twenty minutes later. He rushed into the house and up the stairs to the third floor. Mother knelt beside my bed, crying and unsure of what to do.

Her red-rimmed eyes looked up, and she cried out, "His temperature is 105. He's going to die."

He knelt beside her.

"I called the ambulance. He must have the flu that's been going around. I might have brought it with me when I delivered his shoes. My grandson was sick with it."

They both waited. Mr. Butler wrapped his arm around her as she sobbed on his shoulder.

One of the ghosts left the front door open for the EMTs.

When they arrived, the two men rushed in and shouted, "Hello, the EMTs are here!"

Mr. Butler rushed to the banister and shouted down at them, "Up here on the third floor!"

My mother explained that my temperature was 105 degrees. One emergency tech took a thermometer from his shirt pocket and confirmed the reading.

He said, "We need to cool him down."

He picked me up and carried me to the ambulance. I vaguely remember this, holding Bunny the whole time. The emergency technicians surrounded my body with cool packs and began checking my other vital signs. One of the EMTs tried to take the toy away, but I wouldn't let go of my protector.

The EMT said to his partner.

"This kid's got a death grip on the rabbit."

The other EMT gently said to me, "It's okay. You can let the rabbit go. He'll be right here next to you."

I released my hold on Bunny, and they placed the stuffed animal on the gurney beside me. After that, I passed out and didn't remember anything until I woke up the next day in the hospital.

After they settled me on the gurney, the ambulance took off, heading for Shreveport, with Mr. Butler and my mother following.

I stayed in the hospital for two days. My mother remained with me the entire time. I was grateful that Mama was with me in this strange place, filled with weird noises and people in blue pajamas constantly coming and going. I didn't realize that Bunny wasn't there with me.

Returning home, I still had to stay in bed for the next few days. I missed the toy and started looking for him.

I told my mother, "Mama, I want Bunny."

She said, "Okay," and searched for him.

She came back a little later.

"I'm sorry, Baby. I can't find him. Where did you leave him?"

"He was in bed with me."

She knelt and searched under the bed but couldn't find Bunny.

"He's not there. I'm sure he's somewhere in the house. It's okay; we'll locate him later. You should go to sleep."

She pulled the cover over me and left the room.

I wanted Bunny. Where was the rabbit? Sleep overcame me due to the illness. When I woke, I rifled through the blankets looking for Bunny.

I called Nanny, and she appeared.

I asked her, "Nanny, where's Bunny?"

"You took him in the ambulance with you. Was he left at the hospital?"

"I didn't see him at the hospital. I thought he was here."

Then I realized that Bunny was lost, and a wave of panic and fear overtook me. I began to cry loudly and uncontrollably, tears streaming down my face. I cried for what felt like forever, overwhelmed by worry, until I finally decided I had to tell Mama. I crawled out of bed and hurried to her room.

I shook her arm gently, but urgently, until she slowly woke up.

"Oh, Baby," she said sleepily, "what are you doing up? You should be in bed."

"I want Bunny. Bunny is lost. He must be afraid."

My stomach twisted.

I began to cry and scream for the stuffed rabbit. My protection was gone. The toy I loved most disappeared; it was nowhere to be found in the house. My tiny world imploded. Mama pulled me next to her and held me as I cried for the toy. I would doze off briefly and wake up screaming for him. This continued through the night and into the next day.

This kind of stress was too much for my mother, and I'm sure she wanted to take her pills and forget all of this, but she didn't. I could feel her shaking, but I only cared about Bunny.

Mama called Mr. Butler, not sure what to do.

He arrived half an hour later. My mother explained that the stuffed rabbit was missing, and I wouldn't stop crying.

Mr. Butler said, "He had it in his hand when the EMTs placed him in the ambulance. I remember seeing it. I'll call the ambulance company."

He went downstairs and called emergency services. He returned and said, "I left a message for the EMTs who came here about the stuffed rabbit. They'll return my call when they are off their shift. I'll phone and let you know what they say."

He returned to his office. I continued to scream for Bunny the rest of the day and into the night.

The next day, Mr. Butler arrived just before lunch, clutching Bunny. Relief surged through me as I snatched him up, pressing his soft, familiar fur fiercely against my face, as if to anchor myself in that moment of reassurance.

Mother asked, "Where did you find it?"

Mr. Butler said, "The EMT called me back and said it fell off the gurney when they rolled Ory into the hospital. They found it beside the ambulance on the ground and brought it back to the receptionist at the hospital.

"I drove there this morning and told them what I was looking for. A shift change had occurred, and thinking it was a donation, the new receptionist delivered the toy to the children's ward playroom. I located him in the arms of a little girl. She didn't want to let him go. I finally coaxed her to trade for another even bigger stuffed animal."

I took Bunny to the playroom. I placed him on my lap and looked into his glass eyes.

"Don't you ever get lost again." I scolded him.

I don't know if it was my imagination or if he actually spoke, but I remember him saying, "I'm sorry."

I hugged him fiercely and rocked back and forth.

I desperately clung to Bunny for the entire week, terrified he would vanish again at any moment.

Chapter 18
Jogging with Johnny
& Seren's Arrival

Seren woke up earlier than usual. After her encounter with the Fairy Queen last night and the somewhat cryptic message she left, she became more determined to return to Orion's house and discuss plans to find Johnny's mother, hoping he would allow her to join him.

She placed the kettle on the stove and went to take a shower while the water heated. The kettle's whistle sounded from the kitchen as she stepped out of the tub. She dried herself, wrapped a towel around her hair, went back to the kitchen, and turned off the burner. She put on her robe, sat down, and enjoyed her tea and strawberry yogurt.

As she slowly sipped her tea and savored each spoonful of yogurt, her mind replayed the events with Orion from the day before. He was an utterly intriguing person—an enigma that beckoned her curiosity. Bridette confided in Seren that Orion was more than important to her; he was vital. His extraordinary abilities only heightened his allure, yet his shyness created an impenetrable barrier, making it nearly impossible to uncover the depths of his true self.

He mentioned that people deliberately avoided his company because he emanated unsettling, almost toxic vibes. Yet, to her, these feelings were not frightening; they were striking—an unmistakable, compelling distinction. Her psychic abilities revealed no sinister or malevolent energy, nor did she experience profound impressions that she had never encountered from anyone else. Perhaps this incredible gift was what the fairy goddess alluded to in her cryptic, tantalizing remarks.

The psychic wanted to learn more about Orion, including his background and any other powers he might possess. She also aimed to understand how he was in bed. She couldn't help but wonder if those extraordinary sensitivities extended to passion, leaving her breathless at the thought.

Other men she had been with were adequate. Still, she could always tell that they mainly focused on their feelings during intimate moments and didn't care much about how it affected her. They were fun to be with for a while, but they usually wanted to move on after just a few days. She could sense they were nervous when she made coffee exactly how they liked it, even though they hadn't said anything to her.

She understood this and accepted her situation, acknowledging the unlikelihood that she would ever find someone to love her as she was. She enjoyed the experiences in bed but never expected them to develop further. However, Orion was unique. She wanted this relationship to evolve, but it must be for the right reasons, not because she loved a past version of his soul.

She went to the phone and called his number. No one answered. She decided that she would have to make the first advances due to his shyness. She left a message on his answering machine saying she would be there at about nine, without asking if that was okay.

As soon as she hung up, the telephone rang again. It was Jenny. The two friends were so in sync with each other that this often happened. Seren had intended to call her next.

"Oh, hi, Jenny. I was going to call you. Can you open the shop today? I'm going to Orion Labauve's to work on the ghost case with him. I'll probably be gone for quite a while."

"Yeah, right, the ghost case, huh?" she said with a slight chuckle. "I'll open and close the store. But you'll owe me some time off for this."

Seren hadn't mentioned anything about closing the shop, but her friend always knew what she was thinking.

"Of course. No problem."

"So, what is it with this guy? There's something unusual about him."

"That's only half of it. He possesses exceptional abilities, and I want to learn more about him. I'll tell you more later."

"Okay, you better, and I want all the dirty details. Bye."

She hung up the phone, went into the bedroom, and put on a white, low-cut, tight tank top that exposed considerable cleavage, along with a blue flowing skirt. She wanted to impress him with her assets. She hurried down the back stairs, jumped into her car, and headed for the L'Enfant Haven plantation. L'Enfant Haven—'Children's Shelter.' The name struck her as odd for a plantation, its mystery lingering in her thoughts.

When I woke up the next day, my young friends Johnny and Bunny were both gone from my bed. I heard shuffling on the third floor, which told me they were nearby. I put on my jogging clothes and headed up the stairs. As I climbed, I could hear Johnny's playful 'Whooo! Whooo!' echoing through the hall.

He was in the playroom, pushing the wooden toy train across the floor, with the rabbit perched on the attached caboose, clearly enjoying the ride. The boy looked up, his face lighting up with a big smile upon my arrival.

I said, "Good morning. I see you're having fun."

"Yes, Bunny likes riding on the train."

"I can see that."

"I'm going for a jog around the plantation. I'll be back after a while."

The boy seemed concerned.

I said, "It's okay, I'll only be gone for about an hour."

"Can I come?"

I'm sure he feared I would not return like his mother.

"Sure, if you can keep up."

"I can. I know I can."

A huge grin appeared, and he jumped up, ready to go wherever I went.

"Okay, let's go."

We ran through the damp grass beside the muddy plantation road from last night's rain, making squishing sounds with each step. Johnny stayed right next to me, not running but appearing and disappearing in spurts.

The boy, who had been confined indoors for five long years, was finally experiencing the awe of the outside world. Every detail became a precious discovery, a new treasure to chase. The simple act of jogging with me transformed into an expedition filled with wonder—every object an astonishing marvel. He would often pause, eyes bright with curiosity, to inspect intriguing sights—a fragile butterfly, a slithering garter snake crossing the path, leaves drifting silently in the ditch water—before eagerly catching up; his spirit ignited by each new encounter. His world expanded dramatically when I was near, serving as his steadfast guide into this exhilarating realm of freedom.

We circled the plantation four times. That was about all I could manage. I needed to work my way back up to ten laps around the plantation, which I used to do.

Approaching the house, I decided to go to the backyard to check on the chickens. When we entered, the birds quickly scurried away, flapping their wings and squawking in alarm as they were startled by our presence. Still catching my breath, I grabbed the egg basket from the back porch and stepped into the chicken coop. Johnny followed closely, wide-eyed at the sight of eggs nestled in the straw, as if discovering a hidden world.

He asked, "Why are eggs out here?"

"Because eggs come from chickens. That is where baby chickens come from. Baby chicks hatch if you don't collect the eggs soon.

His eyes widened.

"I didn't know that. Does that mean I ate a baby chicken when Mommy made eggs?"

"Not really. They didn't sit long enough, and a rooster must be nearby. But you don't have to worry about that now because you don't eat anymore, being a ghost."

"Oh, yeah. That's right."

He chuckled.

However, as we approached the house, a shadow of sadness crossed Johnny's face, a clear indication that he was thinking about his mother.

He asked, "When are we going to look for Mommy?"

His voice carried a mix of hope and longing, a testament to his deep-seated desire to reunite with his mother.

"I need to gather some maps and talk to Seren. Her abilities might lead us closer to your mom."

I planned to acquire a U.S. map and several local maps to pinpoint a general location to search for Darlene Newman. I wanted Seren to come along because her psychic abilities might also help—at least, that was what I told myself.

We entered the kitchen through the back door, and I handed the eggs to Rose. The room was warm from the heat of the stove, with pans of various simmering delectables occupying each burner. Many things were prepared from scratch, so there were always food at different stages of preparation scattered around the kitchen. The aromas, a delightful mix of home-cooked meals, filled the air, making my mouth water.

Rose began washing the eggs in the sink. Johnny stood beside her as she explained why the eggs needed to be cleaned.

"We need to wash the eggs because sometimes the chickens have poop on their feathers, which can get onto the shells. When the egg is cracked open to eat, it might come into contact with the outside and end up with poop in the egg. Nobody wants to eat poop,"

Johnny chuckled and shook his head.

As I walked away, she called out, "Do you want breakfast?"

"Yes, that would be perfect."

I headed upstairs to shower and noticed the message light on the answering machine blinking.

I rewound the tape and listened.

"Hi, Orion. It's Seren. I plan to arrive around 9:00 this morning. See you then."

I glanced at the ancient grandfather clock in the hall; its hands pointed to 8:55. A surge of urgency whipped through me—I had to get ready, and fast. The thought of Seren's imminent arrival sent a thrill through my veins, fueling my haste. I showered and shaved with frantic urgency, every second ticking away.

As I swung open the bathroom door, wearing only a towel low on my hips, I almost collided with her—the stunning woman suddenly standing there, her eyes meeting mine, intensifying the moment.

She squeaked, "Oh, sorry."

Her gaze flickered over me before she promptly looked away, her voice a flurry of nervous words.

"I needed to use the toilet. One of the maids said the restroom was upstairs."

I moved aside abruptly, letting her slip inside. The door clicked shut behind her. I chuckled softly, a mixture of adrenaline and curiosity, as I retreated to my room, still tingling from the encounter. Nearly colliding with Seren while barely dressed sent a jolt through me—a sharp, electrifying thrill I couldn't quite shake. I took a few deep breaths, trying to steady myself.

As I dressed, I couldn't help but smile at the sound of the redhead hurrying down the stairs, her presence lingering in my mind. When I finally made my way downstairs, I moved with casual ease, hiding the nervous flutter in my chest, eager yet anxious to be near her.

Seren parked the white Corolla in front of the mansion's gate and hurried to the door. She should have used the bathroom before leaving. She knocked on the lion head knocker, her legs pressed together; her need to urinate growing stronger.

One of the maids opened the door.

Seren said, "Hi, I'm here to talk to Orion, but I really need to use the restroom."

The ghost pointed up the stairs. Seren's urge to pee set her heart pounding as she approached the closed door beside the bedroom on the left, knowing instinctively where the bathroom was without needing guidance. She reached out, her fingers trembling, to grasp the doorknob when, without warning, it swung open with a loud creak. Standing in the doorway was a stunning male figure, wrapped only in a towel that clung barely to his hips. It was Orion—almost entirely naked, his gaze locking onto hers with an unsettling intensity.

A squeak escaped her lips.

He said nothing and stepped aside. She hurried in and slammed the door. She lifted her skirt and sat down on the toilet.

While sitting in the bathroom, she realized how embarrassing the situation was. He was almost naked right in front of her. His body was incredible, so muscular and fit. Her stomach jumped, and she wanted to run her hands across the rippling muscles. She longed to rip the towel off him and head straight for the bedroom. Her heartbeat increased as she imagined what that would be like.

Then she realized that the maid who answered the door was a ghost; however, she appeared solid and alive. She had never been able to see ghosts that clearly before, not until yesterday when Orion gave her what he called Spirit Sight.

She washed her hands, hurried down the stairs, and sat on the couch. Seren closed her eyes and took several deep breaths to calm herself.

Then, a child's voice said, "Hi, Seren."

She opened her eyes to find Johnny standing there with a big smile.

"Hi, Johnny, how are you?"

She knew that the boy probably hadn't smiled much in the last several years.

Johnny's face lit up as he enthusiastically recounted his adventures on the plantation.

"Paul took me to the playroom, and I played with a lot of toys. The room is filled with toys and games to play with. I had a lot of fun until the storm came."

A scared expression flashed across his face for a moment, then he continued.

"I don't like storms. I ran to Orion's room and climbed onto his bed, under the covers with him."

Seren wished she could be under the covers with him.

"He gave me Bunny. Bunny is like Tommy Bear, but Tommy Bear is gone now."

A sad look appeared for an instant.

"The police took Tommy Bear away with my body... but now I have Bunny."

He grinned.

"This morning, Orion and I ran around outside. I saw a lot of things while we ran. It was fun. Then, he showed me the chickens and the eggs. Did you know that eggs come from chickens? I didn't know that. Rose is cooking eggs for breakfast."

Seren said, "Wow, that all sounds like fun."

Orion appeared behind Johnny as he listed his many activities.

The young man said, "Johnny, why don't you play upstairs? Seren and I have a lot to discuss."

"Can I go outside?"

"Yes. There are children's ghosts by the old cabins in the back. You can play tag with them."

"Really? Okay!"

A huge smile spread across his face as he ran out the back screen door, which banged loudly when it closed behind him. She knew that the thought of playing with other children must have excited him immensely.

Chapter 19
Making Plans

Rose entered and announced, "Breakfast is ready."

I glanced at Seren, the morning light catching the fiery strands of her red hair. Her white tank top hugged her figure—curves I tried hard not to notice.

I swallowed hard, keeping my voice casual.

"Would you like some breakfast?"

"No, I had some yogurt before I came here."

"You don't mind if I grab something, do you?"

"Not at all."

She stood and trailed me into the kitchen. We sat at the table, and Rose placed a plate of eggs, bacon, and toast before me.

She turned to Seren.

"Coffee? Cream and sugar?"

Seren said, "Yes, please."

Rose served the coffee and left the room. All the ghosts were aware of how attracted I was becoming to the redhead and left us to our own devices.

We talked while I ate.

I said, "Thanks for coming out here. You didn't have to drive all this way just for me."

She said, "Oh, it's okay. Jenny's watching the shop today."

"I'm happy you came. Your psychic abilities may help me to track down Johnny's mother."

"Oh, really? From what I saw, you don't seem to need much help."

"Maybe, but I feel you'll be crucial at some point. And I think you sense it too—otherwise, why would you be here?"

"You're right. I did sense that I could offer some assistance. I feel so sorry for Johnny. I want to help find his mother."

"Good, so we are both thinking and feeling the same thing."

Our shared mission to find Johnny's mother seemed to unite us in a common purpose.

"Do you have a plan on how to start searching for her?" she asked, seeming eager to begin our quest.

"First, I'll review the Louisiana map and see if I detect anything."

"How will looking at a map help you to locate Darlene Newman?"

"I pass my hands over it, and if the person is in the area my hand is over, I feel a pulling in my stomach."

"Oh, okay. That's interesting."

"I'll have Walter bring the Louisiana map in from the garage."

I glanced to the side and asked, '*Walter, please bring in the Louisiana map.*'

Walter's voice echoed in my mind: '*Do you want me to bring in the condoms as well?*'

Heat rushed to my face, tightening my jaw.

'*No, just the map.*'

Seren looked at me with curiosity, but I avoided her gaze.

The ghost chauffeur appeared next to the table, and she jumped, startled by his sudden appearance.

The spirit put out his hand, and she shook it.

He said, "Nice to meet you again."

Walter said in my mind, '*She's beautiful. Don't let this one slip away.*'

I took the map and replied, '*Get out of here.*'

He disappeared.

Seren asked, "Were you speaking with him telepathically?"

"I guess you could say that. I can only do it with my ghostly family, no outside ghosts," I explained, feeling a growing sense of trust and connection with this woman.

I finished breakfast and said, "Let's lay this out on the dining room table."

We passed through the swinging door into the next room. I shifted the china dishes from the center of the table to the side, unfolded the map, and held my hand about an inch above the print. I moved it all over the surface—no sensations surfaced in my stomach.

I said, "Nothing. She's not in Louisiana."

Seren asked, "Really? You know that for sure?"

"Yes. I'll have to go to Marti's and get a bigger map."

"What's Marti's?"

"Marti owns the local gas station and repair shop."

I mentally instructed Walter to bring the Rolls around to the front.

Walter remarked back, '*It's not here.*'

I said out loud, "Oh, that's right."

"What's right?"

"The Rolls is still at your place. Maybe Andy and Doris can pick it up. I'll give him a call."

I walked over to the phone and called my friend. The secretary answered the phone.

"Hi, Doris. It's Orion. Can I talk to Andy?"

"I'm sorry he's out of town for another client. Is there anything I can do?"

"No, that's okay. Talk to you later."

I hung up, a little disappointed.

I told Seren, "Andy can't pick up the car. I hate leaving it there."

She suggested, "Why don't you drive back with me? You can get it then."

"Okay, we can stop at Marti's on the way to your place. Let's tell Johnny that I'll be out for a few hours. He gets anxious when I'm not around. I'm sure it's because of what happened with his mother."

I went out the back door and called the boy.

He came running up.

I told him, "Johnny, Seren, and I have to go to the store to buy a map and get my car from her place. I'll be back in a couple of hours."

He looked concerned.

"Johnny, you'll have to get used to my being gone. When searching for your mother, I may be away for several days or even weeks. You'll be here with my family. You'll never be alone. Do you understand?"

His lips quivered.

"Mommy said she'd be back in a few days… but she never came back."

His voice was soft, barely a whisper.

"What if the same thing happens to you?"

His fear echoing the uncertainty of his past experiences.

"As I said, you'll never be alone. My family will always be here for you. I promise I'll be back."

He gave me a big hug and followed me to the front porch.

We walked to her car. He watched us drive away and waved, attempting to appear brave.

Seren said, "I feel so sorry for the child. He's been through so much in such a short life and after."

"I know. I feel sorry for him as well."

I empathized with Johnny's situation, much of which was similar to my own early life.

Marti stepped out of the garage, a cigarette dangling from his lips as he rubbed grease-stained hands on a blue shop cloth. He exhaled a stream of smoke and nodded at me.

In his southern drawl, he said, "Orion. Long time no see. What brings you out this way?"

"Hi, Marti. This is Seren Griffyths. Seren, this is Marti Graceland."

They shook hands.

"Marti, I need to get some maps. I'm working with her on a missing person job, and they aren't in Louisiana."

The gas station owner asked, "Do you know what state they're in?"

"No, I don't."

"Well, in that case, you should get the big Rand-McNally book."

I understood what he meant. The book featured maps of all fifty states, displaying all the primary, secondary, and some tertiary roads for each.

"That sounds perfect."

We walked into the front office, and he pulled a new book from behind the counter.

"Great. How much do I owe you?"

"Don't worry about it. I'm making enough from the research on the Jaguar parts that a few more dollars don't matter. About the research, I've got some people calling England. We should be able to obtain the final parts from there."

"Fantastic."

While discussing the Jaguar, Seren wandered to the other side of the room, looking at the various displays.

Marti whispered, "Ory, she's gorgeous. Are you going out with her?"

"No, it's strictly business," I replied, trying to hide the fact that I was developing feelings for her.

"Don't miss an opportunity to be with someone that beautiful. Make a move," he prodded with a big smile.

Marti was one of the few friends I'd had since I worked for him at eighteen. He always advised me on how to interact with customers because he knew I was shy and struggled with being around people. Despite our age difference, he treated me like a younger brother and always supported me.

Seren turned and approached.

I quickly said, not wanting her to hear us discussing her, "Thanks, Marti. We'll talk about the Jaguar later. Bye."

I opened the door for her, and we returned to her car.

While driving to the Shop, she asked, "So, is he a friend?"

"Yes, I used to work for him after I graduated from high school, before I started doing the Finding Jobs. He has always tried to help me."

"He's not afraid of the sensations you give off?"

"He never seemed to be, but he got jumpy the few times he came to the house. I always figured he was sensing the ghosts."

"He probably has some psychic abilities and has felt strange things from people. I felt something while I was there. That's more than likely why he could sense the presence of the spirits."

"Really? You think he's psychic?"

That made sense. Marti had never acted upset or jumpy around me.

"Probably, from what I could tell."

I smiled upon hearing that.

While we drove, Seren asked, "I heard you say something about a Jaguar. Is that a Jaguar sports car?"

"Yes, I was in an accident with the Jag back in April. It was really messed up, and so was I. Walter and I have been trying to repair it, but some parts are hard to locate. Marti has been researching for us and tracking down the components."

"That's nice of him. To change the subject, can you tell me about the first time you saw a ghost?

Talking with her was so easy. I opened up and shared what happened when my mother and I first entered the L'Enfant Haven mansion. I explained how I believed the spirits were other people who lived in the house and how friendly they seemed. I told her how I felt safe and protected, never scared like I had been when we lived in the drug flophouses.

We were pulling up behind the Rolls when I finished speaking. Time flew by, and I didn't even realize I had been talking the entire trip. I had never spoken that much to anyone, alive or dead.

I said, "Oh, we're here so soon. I'm sorry I was talking the whole time and never gave you a chance to say anything. I never do that," shaking my head.

"That's okay. You must have needed someone to talk to, and your life is so interesting that I could listen all day."

She smiled at me, and her eyes showed sympathy and understanding.

I exited her car, leaned down, and said through the open window, "I'll call you tomorrow morning when I figure out where Johnny's mother is."

She grinned at me again.

"Wonderful. Talk to you tomorrow."

I entered the Rolls and pulled away. I smiled the whole way home, thinking about being near Seren and almost bumping into her with only a towel on. I fantasized about that moment, and I wondered what it would have been like to pull her into the bedroom and make love to her. Again, the hour-long trip went by quickly.

When I returned to the mansion, Johnny ran up and wrapped his arms around me.

I laughed and patted him on the head.

"See, I wasn't gone too long."

He gazed up at me with sad brown eyes, so thankful I had returned.

"Did you get the map?"

"Yes, I've got it right here," I replied, holding out the expansive book.

"Wow, that's a big book," he said, his eyes widening at the size.

I smiled at the child's wonder at everything new to him.

On the dining room table, I opened the book and flipped to the Texas map first. Slowly, I ran my hand over it. No queasiness occurred. I opened Arkansas; no sensations manifested—next was Mississippi, but nothing. Finally, Alabama gave me something. A tightening in my stomach happened when I turned the page to Alabama. A sharp pull twisted in my gut as my hand hovered over the southwest corner of Alabama. My pulse quickened. There, near Mobile.

"There she is... somewhere near Mobile," I muttered, unaware Johnny was still beside me.

He asked excitedly, "Where? Where is she?"

He jumped beside me and intently peered at the open book. I pointed to Mobile.

Johnny's small hands clutched the edge of the table, and his eyes shone with desperate hope.

"Can we go now? Can we go get her?"

"No, that's a long way away, and besides, you can't come with me while I am searching for her."

His sad eyes were on the verge of tears.

"I told you it may take me days or weeks to find her. The area I pointed to on the map is large and tracking her down may take some time. You must be patient and wait here."

"I know."

His voice quivered, the faucet opened, and the spectral tears started pouring down his cheeks.

"You have been brave and did everything your mother told you to do. Now, you must do everything I tell you so I can find her. You can do that; I know you can."

He nodded and stared at the floor, then threw his arms around me, face buried against my leg, still crying. I patted his back until he calmed down.

Rose walked in and asked, "Would you like some lunch?"

"Yes, I'm hungry."

I asked Johnny, "Why don't you play outside for a while?"

He said, "Okay," and ran out the back door.

After lunch, I stepped out onto the back veranda and observed him sitting on the ground, cradling a baby chick, gently petting it, and whispering to it. I wondered what he was saying to the bird, but I didn't want to disturb him.

Chapter 20
Preparing for the Trip

I ran my fingers over the Alabama map, focusing on Darlene Newman's location—northeast of Mobile. I would need a more detailed map once I arrived, but at least I had directions to follow now.

I called Seren. She answered the phone.

"Oh, hi. Have you figured out where Johnny's mother is?"

"Yes, somewhere northeast of Mobile. I've decided to drive there. Driving makes more sense than flying—I need the freedom to move on my own terms, with no rental car restrictions and no waiting around."

"You're not seriously taking the Rolls, are you? It must guzzle gas like a beast; you'll have to stop a lot. And if she's in trouble, wouldn't you want to be… less conspicuous? A Rolls is about as subtle as a neon sign."

I thought about what she said.

"You're right. I should rent a car."

"Why don't you take mine? I wanted to come with you anyway."

"Smart thinking," I said.

I was hoping she would want to come and stay the night here. Although I didn't expect anything to happen, just having her nearby made me feel better.

"I can come later this evening and spend the night, if that is okay. That way, we can leave early in the morning, and you won't have to wait for me."

"That's a wonderful idea. When can you get here?"

"Let me manage a few things here; make sure that Jenny can watch the store for a few days, and then I'll head out. I should be there later this evening."

"See you then."

Excited to spend more time with Seren, I sensed she was someone I could genuinely open up to—she seemed non-judgmental, which put me at ease. My curiosity about her background increased. I hoped she'd share her story. I was sure it would be fascinating.

I thought it wise to bring one of the ghosts to scout areas I can't access without being seen. Cyrus was always a great lookout and skilled at locating other spirits in buildings I couldn't enter. He was my companion for fourteen years and invaluable in many of my Finding Jobs. But could he keep his mouth shut while Seren and I talked?

I called him down from the attic. He appeared with his head lowered, guilt keeping his eyes from mine; he knew how angry I still was.

"Want to come on a Finding Job with me and Seren?"

His head shot up, and the biggest grin I had ever seen spread across his face.

"Yes! Oh, yes! I want to go."

"All right, but you must stay quiet while we talk. If you need to say something, ask first—unless it's an emergency. Deal?"

He was so excited that he started gushing, "Sure, sure! No problem. I can keep quiet. Thank you so much. I've been in the attic for a long time—well, not as long as 160 years—but still long enough. Are we searching for the kid's mother? He's a nice kid. He reminds me of you in some ways. I feel sorry for Johnny and what he has…"

I cut him off.

"That's enough. Seren will be here this evening. We'll leave in the morning."

"Okay, I'll be ready."

He smiled and popped back into the attic.

I turned and headed upstairs to tell the boy about the plan. Having taken Johnny under my wing, he was now looking to me for guidance and support.

The child was playing with the red truck I loved at his age. Bunny was in the back as he rolled it between the other toys, creating an obstacle course. I hated disturbing him while he was having fun, but I needed to let him know I would be leaving tomorrow.

"Johnny, I need to talk to you."

I sat cross-legged and patted the floor beside me for him to sit. He settled next to me with a questioning expression.

"Seren and I will leave tomorrow morning to search for your mother."

Johnny's face lit up.

"Can I come?"

I sighed.

"Johnny, we talked about this. It's a long trip, and I must focus on finding your mother, not worrying about keeping you safe."

"I know, but I want to see my mommy," he pleaded.

"You have to be patient. I know it's hard, but you can do it. I know you can," I reassured him, understanding his impatience and longing for his mother to be nearby.

He pouted, looking at the floor.

"Yeah, I can do it."

"You think you'll be able to settle down tonight? Seren and I need some rest before the trip."

"Yes, Doc said he would read The Wizard Oz to me."

"That's *The Wizard of Oz*, and it's a good book. I enjoyed reading it when I was young.

I knew Johnny was upset, but it couldn't be helped. I stood and went to my room to pack some things.

Seren arrived around 4 p.m., earlier than anticipated. The knock at the door jolted me—I knew it was her. I tried not to hurry, but my feet had other ideas.

I smiled when she came in, so glad she was near.

"Have you had dinner yet?"

"No."

"Good. Rose is making my favorite fried chicken. It's Bertha's prize-winning recipe."

"I love fried chicken. Who's Bertha?"

"She used to be the cook here; she was one of the family ghosts who decided to go to the other side to be with her children. She was one of the best cooks in the parish 80 years ago."

"Good, I can't wait to try it."

"Here, I'll take you to the room where you can stay tonight."

I escorted Seren up the stairs to my old bedroom. As she passed, a trace of coconut and jasmine lingered in the air. Shampoo? Lotion?

Whatever it was, it suited her.

I said, "This was my room from age ten to twenty."

"It doesn't look like a boy's room."

She must have expected posters covering the walls and things piled up everywhere. I was never like that. The most I had were a few books scattered around and a couple of trophies I won while on the high school track team.

"Yeah, we cleaned all my stuff out and set it back to how it looked before I moved in."

She set her case on the bed.

I said, "I'll leave you to settle in," and closed the door.

I returned downstairs and studied the maps further.

A short while later, she came down and asked, "So, what route are we taking to Mobile?"

I showed her the quickest route to the city in Alabama.

While examining the map, she remarked, "Too bad we aren't traveling along the coast; it's supposedly beautiful."

"Yeah, but that would take longer to travel there."

"I understand. Well, maybe we can go that way another time."

I glanced at her. Was she suggesting more trips together? Before I could dwell on it, she chuckled.

"I'm just kidding."

But that smile… maybe she wasn't.

I smiled back and said, "Sure, sometime after that trip to Hawaii."

She laughed with that familiar sound I loved. No, that was what Abelard adored.

Then she said, "Well, I refuse to drive to Hawaii. We have to fly," and crossed her arms.

Now I laughed; something I hadn't done in a long time.

Rose came in and said, "I'm glad to hear you two are having fun, but the girls would like to set the table for dinner."

I said, "Oh, sure."

I picked up the map book and went into the living room, where Seren continued to study it.

"Are you looking for something in particular?"

"Oh, anything interesting to stop and see along the way?"

"This isn't a pleasure trip."

I furrowed my brow a little.

"I know, but we should stop at times to stretch our legs, and if there is something cool to visit at the same time, well, all the better."

I had never thought about that before. Whenever I was on a Finding Job, I arrived at the site quickly, completed the task, and came home right after. I'm constantly worried about how people react when they're near me, so I never want to stay around anyone for very long. It would be nice to see some interesting things.

I smiled.

"That would be nice. I've never done that."

"Okay, I'll review the route and suggest some stops."

I nodded and smiled back at her, knowing this trip would be unlike any I had ever experienced.

Milly announced dinner, and we entered the dining room. Fried chicken, mashed potatoes with gravy, honey-glazed carrots, and biscuits were laid out on the table. The aromas were heavenly, making my mouth water. I took my seat at the head of the table, with Seren's place setting to my right.

She commented, "It's been a long time since I've had homemade fried chicken. This looks fantastic."

We both ate the tasty meal without saying much.

Seren said, "Oh, my God, I'm stuffed. I haven't eaten that much since last Thanksgiving with Jenny's family. If I eat here very often, I'll have to keep myself in check, or else I could gain weight fast."

Is she planning to come over regularly after we find Johnny's mother? That would be wonderful if it's true. I smiled.

We went out to the back veranda but didn't say much; instead, we enjoyed the coolness of the evening. Sitting beside her felt natural, as if I didn't have to start a conversation. I usually feel uncomfortable around people, unsure whether to start talking. Most of the time, I didn't bother. But this seemed different, almost as if it were meant to be this way.

Seren looked at the punching bag and weights.

"I see you work out," she said, tipping her head toward the equipment on the other end of the veranda.

"Yeah, but not as much as I should. I'm trying to teach myself some martial arts moves and need to practice them daily, but with everything that has happened, it's been difficult to maintain a regular workout schedule."

"If you're serious about learning, you must join a dojo. That's what I did."

"You're training in martial arts?"

This fact made her even more interesting, and it completely surprised me.

"I joined a year ago, Red Dragon Dojo, after Master Mike Wang became a member of my Occult Cabalistic Club. I'm only a brown belt, but I'm working on it. You should join."

"Oh, I don't know. They probably wouldn't want me around, disturbing the other students from concentrating."

"You might be right, but I bet you could set up some private lessons with Mike. He's psychic and probably won't be disturbed by your power."

I thought about this. It would be interesting to learn more about martial arts. I can now afford to pay for private instruction.

"Okay, I'll look into it when we get back."

Seren said, "I have a question for you."

"Okay, shoot."

"When I picked up your business card, I had a vision of a psychic battle between you and perhaps a voodoo priestess. Was that real, and did it happen here at this plantation?"

Her insight caught me off guard. She really was powerful.

"Yeah," I admitted, feeling a mix of relief and residual tension. "That happened a couple of months ago. The voodoo priestess was my grandmother, the Voodoo Imperatrice. She was trying to take the Labauve signet from me. She wanted to use it to control spirits, me, and my abilities. Luckily, I managed to hold her back and destroy the seal."

The memory of the event still haunted me.

"Oh, my God! That was a recent episode, unbelievable? Here?

"Yeah."

"Do things like that happen often with you?"

She tilted her head with curiosity.

"No, that was the first and only time. I hope nothing like that happens again. It nearly destroyed me."

I pray I never have to face anything so terrifying again.

Flashes of the battle jumped around in my mind, and I shivered.

"I'm sorry I asked that question. I can see that the event really upset you."

"It's okay. I know I should talk about those things instead of bottling them up inside."

"You're right. Keeping things bottled up isn't healthy—I hope you feel lighter now."

She gazed into the distance as if she were witnessing something significant and added, "Similar episodes will occur, and you'll need to learn how to deal with them."

She stared toward the family graveyard, her voice distant, as if weighed down by something. I think she's probably right, unfortunately.

She blinked rapidly, eyes darting around. Did she just have a vision?

She stretched, then stood.

"I think I'll turn in. We've got an early morning."

Her voice was light, but something in her eyes lingered, maybe excitement.

"Yeah, we probably should get going early."

"Good night," she said, leaving through the back screen door, which screeched as it opened and closed.

I stayed up a little longer, enjoying the cool evening air. Traveling with her tomorrow was definitely going to be an enjoyable experience.

SPECTRAL PROMISES

Chapter 21
Arriving at Saint Dominque

I woke up at 6 a.m. and slipped on a robe, something I rarely did. But it seemed like the right thing to do with a guest in the house. I opened the bedroom door to the sound of running water—Seren was already in the shower. I went back to my bedroom and lay down on the bed, waiting for her to finish. As I lay there, an image of Seren formed in my mind—water cascading down her body, skin glistening. Desire fluttered in my stomach, but before it could take hold, a past-life vision burst into my mind.

Dinner with Captain Marcus was surprisingly enjoyable, especially considering the ship's dwindling food supplies so close to the end of our journey. The captain was a charming gentleman who often entertained his passengers with amusing stories. The other passengers, mostly fellow merchants, and I played cards late into the night.

Afterward, I lay in my berth, dreaming about Chloe, the woman I loved—her red hair and beautiful body. I wanted to make love to her, but masturbation must suffice until I returned and could wrap my arms around her.

I went up to the Sainte Marie's deck in the morning and paced. The wind whipped my hair into my face. Annoyed, I pulled a leather ribbon from my pocket and tied my hair back with it at the base of my neck. We were near the Caribbean island, the ship's destination, and the air was warm. I didn't need my wool coat, so I wore only a linen shirt with the sleeves rolled up to the elbows.

A crewman's voice rang out—"Land ho!"—sending passengers scrambling to the rail. Two dark humps broke the horizon, still hours away but promising an end to the monotonous journey.

I returned to my stateroom and packed everything into my small trunk, eager to leave this cramped space; the smell was becoming unbearable. Now I could finish the business I came here to resolve for my father. I planned to board the next sailing vessel back to France on the day the contracts were signed and agreed upon.

Chloe didn't want me to take this trip, and an uneasy feeling swept over me after the Sainte Marie left the harbor, making me wonder if she might have been right. I would return as soon as I could to be with my love and ease this anxiety.

Many people crowded the dock, waiting for the passengers and crew of the Sainte Marie to disembark. I didn't know who would meet me from Mr. Pasteur's plantation. A crew member followed me down the gangplank, carrying my trunk.

A handsome, brown-haired young man with a slave following nearby approached.

"Are you Mr. Ozanne?"

"Yes, I'm Abelard Ozanne. Are you Mr. Pasteur?"

"I'm James Pasteur. Philippe Pasteur is my father."

"Glad to meet you."

I extended my hand, and we shook, smiling at one another. The young man's hair was cut short. He wore no long coat, only a linen shirt and a silk vest. I thought this must be to compensate for the heat and humidity.

"This way to the carriage."

The slave took the trunk from the sailor and rushed ahead to load it into the back of the ornate conveyance.

James inquired, "How was the trip? I hope the weather was good."

"Yes, it was surprisingly good."

I shrugged off my heavy coat, sweat already trickling down my temples and under my arms, and stepped into the carriage. We sat silently as the black man drove us to the plantation.

The landscape we passed through was incredible, and I wished Chloe were here to enjoy it with me.

The carriage pulled up to an exceptional house with exquisite gardens. Two slaves stood outside, ready to help the master's son and me.

An older slave stood off to the side, assessing me with curious eyes. From the corner of my eye, I noticed James glancing over at the old slave. The old man glared back and nodded.

I jerked out of the vision when a knock came on my bedroom door.

"Yes."

"I'm done in the shower. You can use it now."

"Thank you," I replied.

She knew I'd been waiting—she didn't even need to ask. I smiled. I liked that about her.

After showering, I shaved, brushed my teeth, and headed downstairs to the kitchen. Seren sat at the table, sipping coffee, with a small serving of scrambled eggs and chopped fruit on her plate. As I sat down, Rose brought me a plate of eggs, bacon, fruit, and toast.

I smiled and said, "Good morning. Did you sleep well?"

"Yes, all right. But it did take me a while to fall asleep. I guess I'm kind of excited about going on a 'Finding Job,' as you call it."

She slowly picked at her breakfast.

"Me, too. I've never had a job with so little information as this one. I usually receive more background details about the items or person I'm searching for. We'll head to Mobile and may have to drive around until I find something useful."

"You're sure she isn't dead?"

"Oh, yeah. I would know that immediately."

"How do you know that?"

Her brow furrowed in curiosity.

"I have been feeling sick when I search on the maps, so she is alive somewhere near Mobile. I wouldn't feel anything if she were dead."

Rose walked up with a brown paper bag.

"Here, I've packed some snacks for the trip."

"Thank you," I said.

Seren said, "That is so thoughtful of you."

Rose frowned.

"Be careful. I'm getting a sense of danger with this trip."

The psychic asked, "Can you tell us what type of danger?"

Her eyes were wide.

The ghost replied, "No, I'm just getting danger."

"Maybe I should do a tarot reading before we leave."

I chuckled.

"Does that really work?"

"When read by someone with psychic abilities, the cards can warn and indicate possible futures. Go into the dining room. I'll get my deck."

I finished my breakfast and walked into the dining room. She returned with a large, colorful stack of cards in her hands. She sat down, closed her eyes, inhaled and exhaled slowly, then shuffled the cards. Rose stood off to the side, intrigued by the reading.

Seren split the deck into three stacks and reassembled them in a different order. She pulled out three cards face down.

She flipped over the first card.

"The Tower."

A bolt of lightning split the sky on the card's surface.

She explained, "Crisis. Upheaval. Destruction. A sudden, unforeseen change."

The illustration on the card depicted a tower crowned with flames, bursting from its windows, set against a stormy sky, with people plummeting from its heights.

She turned the middle card over.

"Death. It signifies endings, failure, letting go of attachments, mortality, profound change, and severe illness."

This card featured a skeleton in armor riding a horse.

She turned over the third card.

"The Lovers signifies love, unions, partnerships, relationships, choices, romance, balance, and unity."

This card depicted a man and a woman holding hands.

Seren elaborated, "Rose is right; this trip could be dangerous. We should be careful. However, the lovers ultimately predict a good outcome."

I asked, "But what about the Death card? Is someone going to die?"

"No, it usually means big changes and releasing something that may hold something or someone back. It can mean death, but I don't think so in this case."

I said, "Okay, we'll have to watch out. I'll tell Cyrus to be extra vigilant."

She asked, "Why are you going to tell Cyrus?"

Her brow slightly furrowed.

"He's coming with us. He used to travel with me on Finding Jobs. He's a good lookout and can get into places I can't."

I called Cyrus down from the attic.

"Oh. It sounds like he would be good to have along."

But her brow remained furrowed slightly.

He materialized with a smile.

"Are we ready to go?"

"Soon. Seren did a tarot card reading, and it appears that this trip may be dangerous, so I want you to be extra cautious."

"Okay, I'll keep my eyes open," he said, his eyes narrowing with concern.

I entered the library and took out three thousand dollars from the money stash.

I thought, 'This should be enough, and I always have the credit card.'

I returned to the living room and told Seren, "I'm going upstairs to say goodbye to Johnny."

I ascended the steps to the third floor, hearing the boy laughing.

I entered the playroom, and the boy sat on the floor, laughing and watching Paul. Dressed like a scarecrow, with straw hanging from the sleeves of his shirt and an old hat with straw spilling out, Paul danced around the room. The child glanced up and noticed me enter.

"Orion, look. It's the scarecrow from *The Wizard of Oz*."

"I can see that."

Paul stopped dancing around.

"Johnny, Seren and I are leaving now to search for your mother."

The boy frowned.

"Everything will be okay. You don't have to be afraid. My family will be with you while I'm gone."

"I know. I'm just afraid that you won't come back like Mommy."

His eyes saddened with fear.

"That won't happen. I promise."

"Okay."

He stood, and we went downstairs together.

Seren waited next to the front door with her suitcase and Cyrus stood beside her with my bag.

Johnny saw Cyrus with the bag and said, "Is Cyrus going too?"

I answered, "Yes, he helps with my Finding Jobs."

"Why can't I go too?"

He pinched his lips together and pulled his arms behind his back as if almost ready to lash out.

"I told you that it would not be safe for you. Cyrus has done these many times. He knows how to be safe."

Cyrus crouched beside Johnny.

"I always watch Orion's back. I'll protect him this time, too. I promise."

He gently touched Johnny's arm, gave a smile, and a comforting look.

The boy's round eyes stared at Cyrus. He nodded but still frowned.

We all left and got into Seren's car, with Seren driving, me in the front seat, and Cyrus in the back. I watched the child ghost wave goodbye, trying to be brave. As we drove down the road, I glanced back and saw the boy burying his face in Rose's skirt and knew he was crying.

We filled the tank at Marti's station and headed toward Alabama. We drove down Interstate 20 heading for Jackson, Mississippi, stopped for gas, and switched to US 49 South.

I watched out the window as we traveled through the countryside— lush green fields filled with various crops and cattle grazing on the rich, succulent grasses.

None of us spoke for the first half hour until Seren finally said, "Hey, let's get to know each other a little better. Why don't we each share something about our childhood that we wish could have been different?"

Cyrus snickered from the back.

"This might take days."

I shot him a look of 'Don't start.'

He raised his hands in surrender, grinning as he leaned back.

Seren said, "Orion, why don't you start?"

I thought about the many episodes I wish had been different. I chose one.

At six years old, during the summer before I started school, I met the only person my age I could call a friend. His name was Sammy Hammond—a Black boy who ran away from home. I found him in one of the slave cabins in the back.

Paul appeared beside me.

"Ory, there's a kid in slave cabin one. I didn't want to spook him, so you should go instead.

"Oh, okay."

I had never been with another kid and wasn't sure what to do. This was before I started school, and no children ever came to the house. Nobody visited except for Andrew Butler Senior and, on rare occasions, his son, Andy. The boy probably wouldn't have seen Paul, but he might have noticed the door opening by itself. That would have been enough to scare him.

I went to the shack, knocked on the door, and said, "Hello, is anyone in here?"

No answer.

I slowly opened the door and peeked inside. The cabin was about 120 years old. The old gray wood slats were distorted, leaving gaps between them, through which light beams shone onto the floor. Giant cobwebs hung in the corners. An ancient cabinet leaned against the back wall. I approached it and looked behind. Crouched in the corner was a boy with his knees pulled up to his chest, trying to hide.

I said, "Hi."

The kid didn't respond.

"Why don't you come out? I'm not going to hurt you."

With a strong Southern accent, he said, "No, I want to stay here."

He trembled, his eyes searching around.

"Why would you want to do that? It's dirty and cold here at night."

"I don't want anyone to find me."

His voice quivered.

"Why?"

"If my stepfather finds me, he'll beat me."

He jerked as he made this statement.

"Why would he do that?" I asked, tilting my head to the side.

"I don't know, but he always does it when my mom is gone."

"Come on out. I won't tell anyone you're here," I implored.

"What about your mom and dad?"

He looked around as if someone might jump out and grab him.

"I don't have a dad, and Mom is always upstairs asleep. She never comes down."

He peeked over his knees and crawled out from behind the cabinet. He was skinny and filthy from head to toe. His torn T-shirt looked as if someone had grabbed and ripped it. The knees of his jeans were worn through, and his once-black sneakers, now mostly gray with grime, were barely held together by double stitching.

We sat on the floor and stared at each other.

I asked him, "What's your name? Mine's Orion Labauve, but everyone calls me Ory."

He said, "I'm Sammy Hammond."

He was skinny and looked hungry, so I asked, "Are you hungry?"

He nodded with a hopeful expression.

I said, "I'll go get us something to eat. I'll be right back."

I dashed out to the kitchen and told Bertha, "There's a boy in the cabin who is very hungry. Can you make something for him to eat?"

"Oh, lordy. Why, of course."

She grabbed bread, peanut butter, and jelly, made four sandwiches, placed them on a plate, and poured a glass of milk. I tried to hurry back to the cabin, but I nearly dropped the plate and spilled half the drink on the ground. I slowed down and handed the food to Sammy. He devoured three of the sandwiches, and I had one.

He chugged the milk, wiped the milk mustache away with his arm, and said, "Thank you. I haven't eaten anything for two days."

We talked for hours as the sun sank low. He revealed why he ran, how his stepfather would strike him when his mother wasn't home. He hid in alleyways, rummaging through trash cans for leftover fast food. At one point, he climbed into the back of an old dump truck. He was trapped inside for hours when it drove off. When it finally stopped for gas, he jumped out and sprinted down the road. He stumbled upon the plantation with cabins tucked away in the back.

I found him there, after he had been hiding. Neither of us was sure what to do.

He asked, "Can I stay here for a while?"

I didn't see why he couldn't. At only six, I didn't understand that children couldn't live independently.

I replied, "Sure."

I went to the basement and picked up a blanket and an old, stored pillow. Then, I headed to my room to find a pair of shorts, a T-shirt, and an old pair of sneakers that no longer fit me. I carried everything out to Sammy. He changed his clothes and was happy to be in something clean. Luckily, it was summer, and the evenings were warm, so staying in the cabin wasn't too bad.

Every day, Bertha made a second plate of food, which I took to him. I grabbed a couple of board games from the playroom, and we entertained ourselves for hours.

Then, one day, I decided we should visit the creek and play with the boats. I gathered a few toy boats from the playroom, put them in a box, and headed to the shack.

I said, "Come with me. We're going to the creek."

He said, "I don't think I should go out. Someone might see me."

I told him, "No one will see you. No one ever comes here."

Sammy carefully followed me down the road, searching around and over his shoulder the whole time. The stream was small because it hadn't rained in a while. A bridge had been built over it 100 years ago, and Great Aunt Gretchen rebuilt it about 20 years ago. Across the ditch that led into the creek, and beneath the viaduct, it was cool in the shade, and no one could see the two kids playing underneath the overpass.

We each put a boat in the water and watched as the current carried them under the bridge and out the other side, where a bend happened, and the stream followed the road for about a quarter of a mile.

We didn't let the boats go that far. We stopped them before the bend by wading barefoot into the knee-high water to catch the toys. We had races with the boats. This was great fun, and we played for several hours until both of our stomachs started growling.

Returning to the plantation house, Bertha left chicken salad sandwiches for us on the kitchen table. Sammy felt nervous as he entered, glancing around and expecting an adult to jump out at any moment.

He asked, "Who made the sandwiches for us?"

"Bertha, the cook."

"Where is she?"

Searching for her.

"Oh, she's around."

Even at that age, I understood that most people couldn't see ghosts and were afraid of them. I didn't want Sammy to feel scared, so I never mentioned the spirits to him.

He stayed at the plantation for a month. We developed a strong friendship and enjoyed playing and chatting together.

Then, one day, it happened. We were in the backyard playing ball, yelling, and having a good time when Mr. Butler suddenly appeared from around the side of the house.

He saw Sammy and yelled, "Hey, who are you?"

Sammy sprinted for the cabin.

I ran to Mr. Butler and said, "He's my friend, Sammy."

He narrowed his eyes and said, "When did you get a friend?"

I didn't know how to answer that. Mr. Butler followed Sammy to the shack.

I hurried ahead of him, my chest tightened; something was going to happen.

"What are you going to do? He's not doing anything. We're just playing."

"That's okay, but I need to know where he came from."

He kept walking toward the cabin. I realized I had to stop him somehow. I positioned myself in front of him to block his path. He lifted me, moved me aside, and continued on his way.

I yelled, "Stop! Stop! Leave him alone. He hasn't done anything."

Mr. Butler entered the ancient cabin and found him hiding behind the cabinet.

The attorney was very gentle with him.

"Son, please come out and talk to me. It's okay."

Sammy crawled out and stuttered.

"M…Mister, please don't take me home. My stepfather will hit me."

Mr. Butler exclaimed, "He beat you! Why?"

"He always hit me," and the boy began to cry.

He wrapped his arm around the boy as he wept. I observed this from the doorway and cried too.

Mr. Butler asked gently, "Where do you live?"

"In New Orleans."

"How did you get up here?" he asked, surprised the child was this far north.

"I hid in the back of a dump truck."

"Sammy, you can't stay here. I'm sure your mother is worried about you. Don't you want to see her?"

"Yes. But when she goes to work, then Ethan starts hitting me."

"That's not right. I'm going to the Sheriff and tell him about you. We can make sure that your stepfather doesn't hurt you anymore."

Sammy's eyes peered up at Mr. Butler and questioned, "You can?"

"Yes, we can. I want you to stay with Ory until we figure things out."

Sammy nodded, tears streaming down his cheeks. Mr. Butler got up, walked past me, and left. I went over to Sammy and sat beside him.

With his head hanging down, he asked, "Do you think he can make Ethan stop hitting me?"

I said, "I don't know. He can do a lot of things. He found Mama and me and brought us here. It's way better than where we used to live."

Sammy said, "Maybe he can make it so I can live here too."

"I don't know if he can."

I felt that wouldn't happen for some reason, but I didn't say anything to Sammy.

Two days later, Mr. Butler arrived with the Sheriff, their expressions unreadable. They returned to the cabin where Sammy stayed. I ran to the shack and listened as the two men spoke with my friend.

Mr. Butler said, "Sammy, we have spoken with your mother. She reported you missing to the New Orleans police, who have been searching for you. Your mother was very relieved to hear that you were okay. We'll take you back home. Your stepfather is no longer living with her."

"He's gone?"

A big grin formed on his face.

"Yes, he left. We told her why you ran away and she kicked him out. Do you want to live with your mother?"

"Yeah. As long as Ethan is gone, it's good."

Sammy hesitated at the Sheriff's side.

"Goodbye, Ory. I had fun. Maybe I can visit sometime?"

His voice was hopeful, but I already knew the answer.

I said in a shaky voice, "Sure, okay."

I didn't want him to go; he was the only friend I had as a kid. I ran into the house, went to my bedroom, and cried all afternoon. Somehow, I knew he would never come to visit. Nobody ever went to the plantation. Nanny Helen entered and rubbed my back. She didn't say much; she understood how I felt and knew there was nothing she could say to make it better. I never saw Sammy again, and I wish he could have come to live with me at the plantation.

Cyrus piped in and said, "I remember seeing you and the boy playing in the backyard. I looked through the attic window. The two of you seemed to enjoy yourselves."

Seren asked, "Didn't you have any friends at school?"

I replied, "No, I never did. I was excited about going to school a month later, thinking I would meet other kids like my friend, but I never did. I got into a fight on the first day, and no one wanted to be around me, not even the teachers, because I gave them all the creeps."

"That's too bad."

She gave a slight frown.

"Yeah, it's all because the Duke gave me these 'Special' abilities that ruined my life."

"But Sammy never was bothered by your abilities?"

"He never seemed to be."

After sharing this story, I gazed out the window as the countryside whizzed by. I realized how much I missed Sammy. I have never had a true friend; not even Andy counts as a close friend. We've never done anything fun together, and I've never been candid with him. Perhaps with Seren...No, I could never be that lucky.

SPECTRAL PROMISES

172

Chapter 22
Life at the Winston School
& Car Trouble

Seren said, "I guess I'm next. My story isn't so much about what I would have changed as it is about how, if this hadn't happened, I wouldn't be where I am today."

Cyrus piped in from the back seat, "Do I get to tell my story?"

I turned and scowled at him.

"No!"

He knew I was angry, so he closed his mouth, put up his hands, and said, "Okay!"

Seren said, "I would like to hear Cyrus's story. He can do his after mine."

Agitated, I said, "No, I told him the only way he was coming along was if he kept his mouth shut."

She said, "That's not very nice," with her brow furrowed.

My snide retort to Cyrus upset her, and I didn't want that to happen.

"It's a long story. I'll tell you some other time."

She acquiesced, "Okay. But I really want to hear it."

She started what I was sure was to be a fascinating narrative.

After Seren's mother died when she was eleven, she had no living relatives, and the state placed her in the foster care system in New York City. This was tough because most people who accepted foster kids did it just for the money. She moved from home to home because the foster parents disliked her, and she knew about their schemes to use the payments they received from the city for personal gain. Too young to keep her feelings to herself as visions appeared unbidden—glimpses of deception and greed—the truth slipped out before Seren could stop herself.

When she turned fourteen, the system transferred her to the Winston School for Young Ladies, a reform institute for girls. Due to the horrendous reports her foster parents provided about her no one would take her in. Of course, those reports were all lies, but she could never prove it.

While at the Winston School, word spread that she could uncover details about people, making most students reluctant to associate with her. They feared she might discover something they were doing or had done and report it. As a result, Seren was often left alone.

She learned a lot about some of the kids there. Most of them came from abusive families and were just trying to get by. Sometimes she would draw what her visions showed her. She always carried a sketch pad with her.

The students weren't the only ones with secrets; the teachers also had many things they preferred to keep hidden. As Seren became aware of these secrets, she kept them to herself or sketched them in her pads, knowing they would eventually prove useful.

Things were quiet during the first year she lived at Winston. Time passed in an endless routine: waking up at 6 a.m., showering, getting dressed, eating breakfast, attending classes, having lunch, engaging in recreation, returning to classes, having dinner, free time, and bed at 9 p.m. Then, Natasha O'Brien entered Seren's dorm room.

When Rachel Martin turned eighteen, she became a legal adult and left school, which resulted in an available bed in Seren's dormitory room. There were four girls per room.

A week later, Natasha O'Brien entered the room. She was fifteen, beautiful, with ice-blue eyes and a cascade of golden hair, but as tough as nails. The intense teen stormed inside, threw her bag onto the bed, and looked around the room with a fierce glare.

"No one, I mean no one, touches my stuff. You do, and something bad will happen. Maybe not today. Maybe not tomorrow. But it will."

The other girls in the room nodded, their faces pale with fear after Natasha's stern warnings. Seren watched intently as the new girl pulled her clothes from the bag, stuffing them into the small dresser drawers. Seren sympathized with the young woman; she sensed Natasha had endured a harrowing past, having lived on the streets for a year. Though she said nothing, Seren's hand moved instinctively, sketching a few fleeting scenes in her notebook, capturing the unspoken stories she envisioned.

The first day Natasha entered Mr. Hanson's—the 'Lech', as the girls called him—literature class, he couldn't take his eyes off the new girl. Seren knew there would be trouble. The Lech always stood too close to all the girls. He would purposely walk around the classroom, lean over a student, and put his face next to hers, asking ridiculous questions just to get near the girl.

He tried to approach a few young women, but most students knew what he was doing and avoided him. Seren knew that he had some successes in the past. He always acted as if the young women were interested in him. Natasha was his next target.

The bell rang, and chairs scraped against the floor as students streamed toward the door.

Mr. Hanson's voice echoed: "Miss O'Brien, stay behind. We need to discuss your coursework."

She sensed there was another reason why he wanted the new girl to stay late. Catching glimpses of his thoughts made her stomach turn. Seren left the classroom but hesitated outside the door. Natasha picked up her books and went to the Lech's desk with a disgusted look.

He said, "Put your books down and come here so I can show you what you need to do."

The blond young woman deliberately dropped the books on the corner of his desk, leaving a loud bang echoing in the high-ceilinged room. She came over and stood next to him as he pointed out the areas of study the new student needed to catch up on. While Natasha looked at the list, he wrapped his arm around her waist and pulled her closer.

She growled, "Hey, get your hands off me," and pushed at his shoulder.

He held on.

He said, "If you want to do well in my class, you have to make me happy," still holding her tight to him.

She yelled, "Stop! No! Let me go!" pushing at him to move away.

He held tighter and moved his other hand under her skirt.

She shouted again, "Stop, stop!"

Her arms shaking, she pushed, attempting to break his grip.

Seren stepped in the door and shouted, "You better let her go."

The Lech glared at Seren while clutching Natasha tightly and exclaimed, "You'd better get out of here. You didn't see anything. If you say anything, I'll say you two were in cahoots and made the whole thing up."

Seren's voice was cold.

"I'll tell them to check your right pocket for the panties you stole from the laundry room. Do you think no one sees you sniffing them?"

His eyes wide in shock, his hand shot out from under Natasha's skirt and went to his pocket to verify that the precious item was still there.

Natasha saw this reaction and realized that what Seren announced was true. She started to laugh. He immediately let her go. She picked up her books and ran over to her roommate.

Seren said, "If you ever touch any of the girls here again, I'll tell the Dean about you sneaking into the laundry room and stealing panties from the girls' dirty clothes bags. I'll also tell him about all the places where you're hiding the underwear around the school and in your car. You even have a pair on right now."

He turned beet-red, his mouth agape. The two girls left the room. He never approached any of the students again.

While hurriedly walking down the hall, Natasha asked, "Was all that you said about him true?"

"Yes. He's a sick man."

"I should have seen it coming," she said, shaking her head and pursing her lips.

"Why would you expect something like that?"

"Because it happened to me before when I lived on the streets. How do you know all of that?"

"I get visions about people. That's why a lot of the kids don't like to be around me."

"That's so cool." She smiled and asked, "What else do you know about?"

"I don't like to say things unless I have to, like this situation."

"Oh, okay. I understand."

She nodded.

After that, Natasha and Seren grew close over the next two years. They talked often and shared their stories. Seren described some of her unusual experiences, while Natasha discussed the challenges she faced while living on the streets.

The former street urchin learned to pick locks to break into stores and steal food and supplies. She taught Seren this valuable skill. The two friends often sneaked out of school at night to go downtown and hang out. The redhead would point out who was safe to associate with and who seemed dangerous.

They snuck into rock and roll clubs at fifteen to dance and have fun. Seren always knew when the bouncers were onto them and when to leave before getting caught. The two teens enjoyed a good time together.

One evening, Seren, now sixteen years old, and Natasha decided to explore a new club rumored to be hidden in a far-off part of town. As they approached, she felt a mixture of excitement and strange anticipation. They arrived outside an old warehouse where a flickering sign announced a free gathering hosted by the "Open Life and Light of Truth Tabernacle."

Seren was instinctively pulled toward the door. That night, the event featured Helen Overmeyer, a renowned psychic and channeler, who was scheduled to speak and offer revelations that could potentially change everything.

Seren said, "Let's go in," and moved toward the door.

Natasha replied with disgust in her voice, "You have got to be kidding; I'm not going to church."

"It's not a church. A psychic is talking."

Seren said excitedly.

"I'm going to the club down the street. Come on," she said, pleadingly.

An overwhelming compulsion washed over Seren.

"No, I think I need to go here."

She pushed open the door, but Natasha didn't follow. The young woman stepped in confidently and took a seat at the back, remaining for the entire session and the subsequent Q&A. Some topics Helen discussed resonated deeply with the sensitive teenager, even though she initially struggled to understand them. That night, she discovered answers to many of her questions about her extraordinary abilities, igniting a new fire within her.

A small gathering occurred after the Q&A session, and Seren stayed, wanting to hear more. Helen Overmeyer noticed the young woman standing in the corner and approached her.

She took Seren's hands and said, "Honey, you need to return. Don't run away. Complete your education. If you run away, you'll regret it for the rest of your life."

Seren was utterly stunned. She had been contemplating running away for weeks, secretly planning every detail with Natasha. They had mapped out multiple steps for their escape, each more daring than the last. Yet, despite their careful planning, an uneasy knot tightened in Seren's stomach, and she hadn't yet made a final commitment to this risky decision.

The psychic continued, "Here, take my book and read it. I think it will help you."

The woman opened her large purse, pulled out a book, and handed it to the teen—Following the Path of the Light Road. Seren took the book. Helen smiled, turned, and walked away.

The young psychic finally understood what she truly was. She spent the next few days reading the book that Helen had given her, and her life changed forever. Eager to learn about psychic abilities, the occult, and alternative religions, she joined the Open Life and Light of Truth Tabernacle and attended as many meetings as possible.

She learned a great deal from other Tabernacle members, many of whom remain her friends. Two years later, Seren left Winston School and got a job at a bookstore owned by a member of the Tabernacle. She started giving psychic and tarot readings in the store's backroom and, over several years, earned enough extra money to buy her own shop.

Seren didn't see Helen for ten years. Their second meeting occurred at a Psychic Awareness Conference in New Jersey. The young woman was getting ready to move to Louisiana to open her occult shop. She explained to Helen how meeting her and reading her book transformed her life.

I asked, "What happened to Natasha?"

"She ran away, and I never heard from her again. But I would have never seen that sign about Helen Overmeyer speaking at the tabernacle if I hadn't met her at the school, and we didn't start sneaking out at night."

By the time our stories wound down, Jackson, Mississippi, was already behind us, and the road stretched endlessly ahead. We were heading south on US 49 when the car's engine started making a horrendous knocking noise, and smoke began billowing from under the hood.

"Damn it! What now?" Seren groaned, her grip tightening on the wheel, frustration boiling over.

I leaned over and noticed the engine light was blinking, and the temperature was in the red on the dashboard.

I said, "Pull over. It's overheating."

She pulled over onto the shoulder of the road.

I opened the door and said, "Pop the hood."

She leaned down and pulled the hood release. I opened it and brushed the steam away with my hand to inspect the engine. I took out my handkerchief and removed the dipstick. The stick was clean—no oil was visible.

I asked Seren, who was standing next to me, "When was the last time you changed your oil?"

She hesitated.

"I don't know. I never think about those things."

I shook my head in disgust. How could someone not consider changing the oil in their vehicle?

I said, "Well, we aren't going anywhere now."

The words hung heavily in the air.

I thought, 'I should have rented a car.'

A regret I couldn't shake.

"Yeah, you're right. You should have rented a car," she said with a knowing smile.

Did she just read my mind?

I shook my head.

"No telling how long we'll have to wait for somebody to stop. The last town we passed was ten miles back, and I think it'll be several miles until the next one."

"I don't think we'll have to wait long for some help," she said and smiled.

Ten minutes later, a tow truck pulled up behind Seren's Toyota. I looked at her with raised eyebrows; she just smiled and shrugged. A short, fair-haired young man in dark blue, stained coveralls hopped out of the truck, approached us, and said in a strong southern drawl, "Y'all need some help?"

I stepped forward.

"Yeah, the engine overheated, and I'm not sure what else is wrong. It sounded like it might have thrown a rod. She forgot to change the oil for a long time."

The young man chuckled.

"Well, you're in luck. I'm heading to my uncle's repair shop in Alexandria, just down the road a bit. I can tow you in, and I'm sure Uncle Bob can fix what's wrong with the car. My name's Perry."

I extended my hand. Perry shook it, but his fingers twitched, and his expression flickered with discomfort—he felt it. That strange pull people always got from me.

"My name's Orion and this is Seren."

"Nice to meet you two," he said hesitantly.

He returned to the truck, positioned it in front of Seren's Toyota, and hooked it up. We all got into the truck's front seat with Seren in the middle. I didn't want Perry to feel more uneasy sitting next to me. After twenty minutes, we pulled into Bob's Auto Repair. All this time, Cyrus remained in the back seat of the Toyota.

We sat in the front office while Cyrus wandered around and Uncle Bob checked the damage to the Corolla. He came in with a frown on his face.

"Not good news. You were right; it threw a rod."

I asked, "How long will it take to fix it?"

"Oh, maybe two and a half days. I'll have to order parts, but those may take a few days to arrive unless you want to pay my nephew to drive over and pick them up."

"I'll pay for that," I said, knowing Bob was extending the time factor. "I can give you a little extra if you shorten the repair time."

"I'll see what I can do. This whole job is going to be pricey."

He smiled widely, knowing he would profit well from this work.

"That's okay. I'll pay. We have to get it repaired and out of here."

"Okay, I'll continue working on this while Perry picks up the parts. Y'all can get a room a block down the road at the Minute Motel, or if you'd like a nicer place, Perry can take you to the lake where you can stay in a cabin. My cousin owns the resort. It's really nice and quiet."

Seren's eyes lit up.

"A cabin by the lake? That sounds perfect."

Seeing Seren's excitement about a cabin by the lake, I said, "Thanks. We'll do that."

Seren was all smiles, even though these setbacks and problems were entirely her fault. Her tarot card reading did indicate failures and changes.

She smiled at me and said, "Failures and changes."

All I could do was smile back and shake my head.

Perry dropped us off at Lake Blanc Resort. During the twenty-minute trip, Seren and I sat in the front seat with Perry, while Cyrus held onto the towing mechanism in the back of the truck. The resort consisted of several log cabins arranged around a central parking area. They appeared well-maintained and clean from the outside. One cabin had an "Office" sign above the door, and a larger one next to it displayed a "Restaurant" sign. Only four parked cars were in the lot.

The lake was a short distance from the office, and the woods surrounding the pond and among the cabins consisted of various pine trees.

Approaching the office, Seren said, "This is beautiful. I get a good feeling from this place."

I smiled at her; I felt good vibes as well.

We entered the office and were immediately greeted by a heavyset woman with gray hair and glasses, wearing a floral muumuu dress and smiling widely.

She roared, "Welcome to Lake Blanc."

I said, "Hi, we're having our car repaired at Bob's, and he recommended this place while we wait."

"Yeah, Bob's my cousin. I'm Tabitha Blanc, the owner. So, you want a one-bedroom for one night?"

"Maybe two nights, and we need a two-bedroom."

The woman looked at Seren and raised her brow.

I explained, "She's a business associate."

"Oh, yeah, sure. I got a nice two-bedroom right next to the water. The restaurant's open for dinner from 5-8 p.m., and breakfast is served from 7-10 a.m. You just missed lunch."

I signed the register, and she gave me the key to cabin five.

Seren and I followed the signs along the path toward cabin five. Cyrus walked behind us but drifted closer to the lake, approaching someone who was standing there. It was another ghost. It's not unusual for a spirit to linger near a place like this. It was likely someone who drowned in the lake or had some other tragic story.

The cabin featured a living room furnished with simple 1970s decor and a kitchenette in one corner. Two small bedrooms and one bathroom were centrally located to the right.

Seren headed for the first bedroom and said, "I'm going to take a nap before dinner."

"Okay."

I went to the other bedroom and took out the book from my bag. I opened the sliding glass door and stepped onto the patio, a cement slab with two white Adirondack chairs. I was about to sit down when I noticed several lounge chairs on a dock by the lake. They looked much more inviting. Trees shaded the area near the shore, and the sounds of frogs and buzzing insects filled the air. I settled in and began to read my book. Cyrus had been wandering around the grounds. He took a seat in the other lounge chair.

I read for a while, but I became distracted by the sound of fish jumping in the water. Perhaps we could rent some fishing gear and go fishing tomorrow. It had been a long time since I last fished. Andrew

Butler Sr. would occasionally take me when I was young.

The lake shimmered under the afternoon light, its surface rippling like liquid gold. A sense of peace settled over me, familiar yet distant. It reminded me of the ocean, the view from the second-floor balcony at the Pasteur plantation. And just like that, I was there.

SPECTRAL PROMISES

Chapter 23
Abelard and the Duke

I stood on the second-floor balcony, holding a cup of tea as the full moon rose over the horizon. Its silver reflection stretched across the calm Atlantic, displaying my path home from Saint Dominque. The next day, I would return to France and Chloe, the love of my life. I missed her so much. I rushed the merchandise sales negotiations to return as quickly as possible.

The Pasteur family was charming and begged me to stay longer, making the trip feel like a holiday. I couldn't wait. An emptiness grew in my stomach from missing Chloe.

James Pasteur, Philippe's oldest son, approached.

"So, Abelard, you're really leaving tomorrow."

"Yes, I am," I said with determination.

"Well, in that case, we should do something interesting tonight. Have you ever seen a voodoo ceremony?"

"No, what's that?"

My curiosity was piqued.

"The slaves have a sort of religion and regularly have ceremonies that they perform. The ones during the full moon are exciting. We should go."

"A church?" I asked, frowning.

James grinned.

"No, they hold their rituals out in a clearing beyond the fields. Come on—you'll see things you won't believe."

I momentarily declined, and Chloe's warning that something would happen surfaced. Nothing had happened; her vision wasn't real.

Then I decided to do something fun before leaving.

"Okay. Let's go."

"I'll get you something to wear."

"What, this isn't good enough?"

I looked down at my casual attire.

"It's too formal. I'll be right back."

The young man left for a few minutes and returned with a pair of white linen drawstring pants and a loose-fitting shirt similar to what the slaves wore.

I stared at the clothing, a little shocked.

"You want me to dress like the slaves?"

James chuckled.

"Yes, that's what everyone wears to these ceremonies. They see it as evidence that everybody is equal in the eyes of their Gods."

"Gods? They believe in multiple Gods."

"Yes, they have Gods for everything. I think tonight is a ceremony for Duke Shamedi, the god of the dead and spirits. They perform this ritual on the full moon because the veil between the living and the dead is thin now, or so they say."

I hesitated.

"Well, okay."

I changed clothing and went out front.

A worn buckboard stood waiting, the wooden frame creaking under the weight of the slaves perched in the back.

James bounded down the steps dressed in white clothes, and headed for the wagon.

He jumped onto the back and shouted, "Come on!"

I hopped up next to him.

I asked the young man, "Do you do this often?"

James answered with a big smile, "I've been doing this since I was twelve."

I glanced over his shoulder, and all the slaves smiled at me. A chill slid down my back—not from the night air.

Upon arriving at the ritual site, everyone jumped out of the cart and hurried toward a large bonfire. Many people were already there, standing around the fire. Drummers off to the side played a rhythm, and all the attendees hummed and swayed to the beat.

I followed James to the middle of the crowd.

My host pointed out the priest and said, "There's the voodoo priest, King Pappa. We call him Brutus."

The old slave appeared to be in his fifties, wearing multiple necklaces made from various handmade items, including twisted vines, corn husks, wooden links, ceramic beads, and other unidentifiable trinkets.

I recognized him as the old man who was staring at me when I arrived at the plantation.

The man scattered chalk around the bonfire. Then he picked up a stick, carved with strange, mysterious symbols, and dug into the ground, filling the carved depressions with chalk. He nodded, signaling two other female slaves to pour something from ceramic pitchers into wooden bowls decorated with painted symbols. The women passed the bowls to the crowd, where each person took a sip before passing it on.

Someone passed the bowl to me. I examined the mixture, with bits of plant matter floating on its surface. It emitted a foul odor. I scrunched up my nose and handed it to James.

James nudged the bowl back toward me.

"No, you have to drink."

I recoiled.

"It smells like rot."

The young master took a sip, smirking.

"See? It won't kill you."

I took the container back and forced a small amount down my throat.

"Oh, my God, this is terrible," I gagged, almost to the point of vomiting.

James chuckled and passed the cup to the next person.

"It tastes better later on."

"What, we have to do this again?"

This was becoming too much.

"Oh, come on. Stop being a baby."

I didn't like being called a baby, so I stayed quiet.

I started to feel dizzy, and the drumbeats became more intense. The rhythm seemed to push me to move with it. I swayed to the beat with the other participants. Suddenly, another container appeared out of nowhere, and I took a sip from it.

James said, "Take a bigger drink this time. You'll feel better."

I took a large gulp, and James was correct. It didn't taste so foul this time.

The ceremony intensified as the voodoo priest danced wildly around the blazing fire, weaving in and out of the circle with frantic energy. He shook eerie dolls, shards of bone, and shouted in a guttural, ancient language. The ceremony sent shivers down my body. The slaves in the crowd shimmered with surreal colors, some with faces twisted into distorted images.

Another bowl appeared, and someone urged me to drink it all. I felt a strong compulsion to obey and drank everything in the bowl. This time, the flavor was floral, and the scent was intoxicating. I smiled.

My body began to jerk uncontrollably, and my vision blurred. Dizziness hit me like a wave, threatening to pull me to the ground. Someone grabbed my arms and dragged me to the front. My eyes refused to focus. Colors swirled into madness.

Then, out of nowhere, a tall, black figure dressed entirely in black appeared within the circle—a face painted stark white like a skull. Where did he come from? He wasn't there a second ago.

The painted man grinned, his teeth gleaming unnaturally white. He drifted toward me, his legs motionless as if floating in the air. The stranger in black extended his hand and gently pressed against my forehead. Unable to stay upright, I fell backward, but someone caught me and carefully placed me on the ground inside the circle with my arms outstretched. The only thing in my vision was the pale painted face of the ominous figure and the dark pits of his eyes. They terrified me, and I screamed. My eyes rolled back in my head, and I convulsed. I rose above my body and watched, unsure of what was happening to me.

The convulsions stopped. A slow, unnatural smile spread across my lips. I was no longer in control of my body. Laughter, deep and hollow, burst from my throat—the spirit God possessed my body.

Watching from above, my possessed eyes shifted from blue to golden, shining with an inner light. I spoke in a strange language, and the voodoo priest replied, "Yes, Lord."

I had no control; I was helpless, powerless to intervene. My mind and emotions were frozen solid—completely numb, unable to react or feel anything at all.

King Pappa went to the other side of the fire and returned with three beautiful young slave girls. The priest leaned down and undid the knot holding my pants closed and pulled them down to expose my erect cock. The first girl raised her dress and knelt over my hips and sighed as she mounted my substantial member.

We moved rhythmically to the beat of the drumming. My arms were still splayed out at my sides. The crowd's shouting grew more frenzied. The girl and I shouted out as we reached ecstasy together, and the crowd erupted in jubilation. The woman rose, revealing my engorged member ready for the next offering.

The next woman came forward, raised her skirt, and mounted, what I somehow understood was a God's cock. Again, we moved in unison to the beat of the drums. The woman shivered as we both achieved an orgasm. The crowd yelled and screamed.

The third offering stepped forward, and the ritualistic coupling continued.

The young woman leaned over him after the ritual and kissed the God, saying, "Thank you, lord."

The God smiled back at her.

When this girl stood up, my member was now spent and flaccid, no longer capable of engaging in the act of sacred coupling.

The God, from within my body, turned my head and addressed King Pappa in the God's language with a low, booming voice, saying, "The offerings were excellent. The boy is a suitable avatar for my purposes. The women are all pregnant and will give birth to offspring who will possess exceptional abilities. You must teach the children the Lwa way. They will pass this knowledge on to their children, and their children's children will serve me later on this plane."

King Pappa kneeled and said, "Thank you, Lord. It will be done."

The God shouted in French, "James Pasteur, come to me."

James, trembling, moved forward, his eyes wide with fright, and shakily knelt, never believing he would speak with a God.

"You have provided the boy I needed, and for this, your plantation will thrive for many years."

The young Pasteur bowed his head and cried, "Thank you, Lord, thank you, thank you," his voice quaking.

The God said, "I have finished here."

Yanked back into my body, I felt a surge of panic as my whole frame started to tremble uncontrollably. My eyes snapped upward, then wildly rolled back down. When they finally focused again, I knew my irises had returned to blue.

I screamed in terror and spiraled into darkness, my body convulsing uncontrollably with wild, frantic jerks.

James and a slave lifted me by the arms and gently laid me on the back of the buckboard. They returned me to my room at the plantation. The white garments were removed, and I lay naked in the bed.

I slept fitfully for sixteen long hours, tossing and turning as wild dreams haunted me—drums pounding, people screaming and pleading, slave girls wailing, and a terrifying man with a ghostly, white-painted face. I tried to run from him, but no matter how hard I tried, I could never escape his chilling presence.

I woke up to sunlight pouring through my window, impossible, my room faces west. I tried to remember how I got to my room and what happened during the ceremony. All I could recall was drinking a foul-tasting mixture, and after that, everything was a blur. I sat up quickly, my stomach churning—the ship. I missed it. No!

I rolled out of bed and dropped to my knees. My stomach twisted, and I vomited a thick, reddish fluid onto the floor.

The door opened, and a slave girl entered, carrying a tray with several items. She placed the tray on the table and hastily ran to me, helping me to stand. I realized I stood naked, but this didn't seem to bother the slave. She helped me to bed, and I quickly covered myself. She poured a glass of water from a pitcher on the nightstand and offered it to me. I greedily gulped down the water, realizing how thirsty I was, while she cleaned the mess I left on the floor with a towel.

I stared at the girl; a gnawing sense of familiarity gripped me—too familiar. A jolt of fevered desire and raw ecstasy surged through my body. No, this couldn't be real. I shook my head, desperate to dispel these images.

The girl asked, "Are you alright, Sir?"

I gazed at her, attempting to determine if this vision with her was real.

"Sir, sir, are you good?"

"Yes, I'm good. I'm sorry I was unclothed when you came in."

"No worries, sir, I have seen all the Masters naked. I'm the bathing slave."

"Bathing slave?"

"Yes, I prepare the bath for the Masters and Mistresses. I came in to bathe you."

Then I remembered that this service had been offered during my visit, but I declined, preferring to bathe myself.

I glanced at the tray on the table, which contained a basin, pitcher, cloths, and soap.

"Would you like to be bathed now? You were sweating fiercely when they put you to bed last night."

I leaned back against the headboard, attempting to recall what had happened, but only a jumble of nonsensical images surfaced in my mind.

The slave asked again, "Would you like me to bathe you?"

I thought that sounded good.

"Yes, please."

The girl poured warm water into the basin, wetted a cloth, and lathered it with soap. She pulled me to a standing position and ran the soapy cloth over my body, cleaning every inch. I stood in ecstasy. The soft cloth gently moved over my body, removing the sticky sweat residue. She rinsed and dried me off and then put me back in bed.

As she left the room, she said, "I'll tell Master James you're up."

Still feeling uneasy and confused as I lay in bed, I berated myself for agreeing to attend that ridiculous ceremony and for missing the return ship to France. Now, I'd have to wait another two weeks.

James burst into the room with a broad smile, followed by two slaves carrying trays laden with various foods.

"Well, it's about time you woke up," he exclaimed.

The young plantation heir upset me.

"Why didn't you wake me so I could board the ship? Now it's weeks before the next one is available."

"I'm sorry, but you reacted badly to the Worshipping Drink. It usually makes you feel free and open, seeing lots of colors. At least, that's what it does for me. But you went a little crazy and started fucking a few of the slave girls. If you wanted to do that, all you had to do was ask me. I could have brought you a girl."

"I don't remember that. I get flashes of weird things and a guy with white paint on his face. Then I woke up here."

His eyes went wide when I said that. Did he think I was crazy?

"We didn't want to dump you on the ship. If you had any further problems, we thought it prudent to have a doctor available."

I shook my head and scowled at James.

The man retorted, "Oh, don't be that way. I promised you something interesting, didn't I? Have some food."

"I'm not hungry. My stomach's upset."

"Well, at least have some broth. It can help with upset stomachs."

"Okay."

I sipped the cup of broth offered by one of the slaves. It tasted good, and my stomach settled down after a few minutes.

As James and the others left the room, he looked over his shoulder and said, "Why don't you get dressed and come downstairs? The rest of the family is worried about you."

"Maybe in a little while."

He closed the door.

I sat in bed, still trying to remember what happened at the ritual, when a voice said, '*You did good last night, boy.*'

Where did that come from? Wait, had I heard that same voice at the ceremony? I looked around, but no one was in the room.

I jumped out of bed and immediately dressed. I suddenly didn't want to be alone.

I jolted out of the vision. Someone shook my shoulder. I looked up and saw Seren. The book I had been reading had slipped from my lap and onto the dock.

Seren's voice pulled me back.

"Orion. Orion."

My eyes snapped into focus. She leaned over me, concern shadowing her features.

"You were gone," she murmured. "A vision, wasn't it?"

"Yes, I was Abelard, on the island of Saint Dominque. I was taken to a voodoo ceremony, drugged, and possessed by Duke Shamedi. It seems I can never get away from him. He took control of me even in past lives."

"That must have been why Chloe didn't want him to go. She knew something bad would happen."

"How do you know that?" I asked, raising my brows.

"I've had my own visions as Chloe."

"So, we did know each other in another life. It seemed you had been Chloe, but I wasn't sure."

"Oh, yes. We were very close."

I thought, 'That's why I'm so attracted to her, why she looked so familiar the first time I saw her.'

Seren said, "Let's go to dinner. I'm starving."

We walked to the restaurant and enjoyed an excellent meal. Afterwards, we returned to our room and sat on the patio. I shared with Seren what happened to Abelard, and she told me about some of her visions as Chloe.

I said, "We seem destined to be together, but this isn't a good idea. My grandmother, the Voodoo Imperatrice, could harm you to exert control over me. I don't want anyone to be harmed."

She said, "Tell me about the Voodoo Imperatrice."

"It's a long story, and I still don't understand why she's doing the terrible things she does. I don't want to go into that right now; maybe some other time."

I didn't want to break our wonderful evening together with something upsetting.

"Okay, whenever you feel like telling me."

I stood and said, "I'm going to my room and will read for a while. The mosquitoes are getting too thick out here. Good night."

I went to my room and thought about my visions and what Seren shared about her experiences. We had once been lovers. And God, I wanted nothing more than to be hers again—to run my fingers along her skin, to tangle my hands in her hair, to enjoy the softness of her lips. But I couldn't. It was too risky. Loving her would make her a target. I fell asleep and didn't wake until the sun rose.

Chapter 24

A Day at the Lake

The next day, after breakfast, I called Bob to check on the progress of the repairs. I didn't like what I heard—the Toyota wouldn't be ready until tomorrow. I hung up with a frown.

I decided to call Andy to let him know what was happening. Since it would be a long-distance call, I went to the pay telephone in the far corner and made a collect call through the operator. Doris answered and said she would accept the long-distance charges.

"Hey, Doris. Is Andy around?"

"Nope, still out of town."

I sighed.

"We're at the Lake Blanc Resort in Mississippi. Her Toyota threw a rod, and it is being repaired. It should be ready tomorrow, so we'll head for Mobile then."

"Is there anything else I can do for you?"

"No, just let him know when he gets in."

"Okay. Call us when you get to Mobile."

"Okay, talk to you later."

I hung up the phone, and Tabitha exited the back office.

She asked, "Are your car repairs completed?"

"No, probably not until tomorrow. Anything to do around here while we wait?"

"Oh, plenty. We've got hiking trails, rowboats, and fishing. Vincent will clean and cook fish of a decent size for you if you catch something. You can even go swimming in the lake."

"I'd love to swim, but I didn't pack a suit."

"Oh, that's okay ... there's no one else here right now, and your cabin is far enough from the others that you could just skinny dip."

I smiled and asked, "Can we rent some fishing gear? I haven't been fishing in ages; that would be nice. Oh, and a six-pack of Pepsi."

"Sure thing, I'll set you right up. Do you want two sets?"

I pondered the offer, curious if Seren had ever gone fishing. Being a city girl from New York, she probably didn't know how to fish. I could teach her; that would be fun.

"Yes, please."

Mr. Butler Senior occasionally took me fishing and taught me how to fish. I cherished our time together. I would bring home my catch, and Bertha, the ghost cook, would clean and prepare the few fish I caught. I liked eating fish because it was something different from the usual chicken offered. We were always short on money for food, and raised chickens in the backyard. My meals typically consisted of chicken and vegetables prepared in various ways. Bertha was very creative.

Tabitha disappeared through a door behind the counter and came back with two fishing poles, a net, a small plastic case filled with various hooks, lures, and bobbers, and a bag overflowing with squirming night crawlers.

I went back to our cabin with the fishing supplies and a six-pack of Pepsi. Seren stepped out of the bathroom, towel-drying her hair. Her eyes focused on the gear and widened.

I smiled, held up the fishing gear, and said, "Let's go fishing."

The anticipation of the adventure ahead was palpable in the air.

"I don't know how."

She tilted her head and stared at the gear with a smile.

"I'll teach you. It's easy," I reassured her.

"Okay, this should be interesting."

We stepped out of the sliding glass door and embarked on a journey along the lake's path to the boat dock. I helped her on the rowboat, and we set off. As I rowed the boat across the lake, she clung to the sides, her excitement and apprehension blending into a mixture of emotions.

"Haven't you ever been in a rowboat before?" I asked with a smile.

"No, I haven't," she confessed, her lack of exposure to outdoor activities resonating with me.

"Oh, it's safe. Look."

I leaned side to side, causing the vessel to rock in and out of the water. She let out a shriek and a laugh, holding on to the edges even tighter.

"Stop that!" she shouted.

"Okay, okay," I reassured her, chuckling. "This seems like a good spot."

She nodded, a playful glint in her eyes.

"I hope we catch something nice," she said, her voice brimming with anticipation.

I opened the box, removed a few items, and attached the bobbers and hooks to the lines. I took the bag of wigglers and pulled one out, anticipating it would be fun to watch her reaction.

I said, "Let me show you how to put the worm on the hook."

Her face scrunched up as the nightcrawler wiggled in my fingers. I pushed the hook shaft through three times and wrapped it around, leaving the tail end dangling.

"See. Easy. Now you try one."

"Oh, no. I can't do that."

She shied away from the squirming creature I offered her.

"Come on. It won't hurt you."

She hesitated, then pinched a nightcrawler between her fingers. The worm curled around her hand, and she shrieked, flinging it to the bottom of the boat.

I couldn't contain my laughter.

"Give it another try."

She shot me a playful glare. I picked up the bait and handed it back to her. With bravery, she pierced the creature, her expression a mix of determination and disgust, creating a moment of pure amusement.

"That's good. Now try it again."

She stabbed it a second time and quickly wrapped the crawler around the hook.

"Okay, that should be fine."

I demonstrated how to lower it into the water and reel the line in and out.

We sat quietly for a while. I offered her a soda. She nodded, and I pulled the tab for her.

She took a big sip and asked, "How long does it take to catch a fish?"

"Sometimes soon. Sometimes, all day."

"What? I don't want to sit here all day. I'll be a crispy critter. I didn't bring any sunscreen with me; I didn't know we'd be out in the sun."

"Be patient. We'll see how they're biting."

As the words left my mouth, my line tugged.

"I've got a bite already."

I pulled on the pole, and the line played out. The hook was set. As I reeled in the catch, I explained what I was doing. When the fish got close to the boat, I lowered the net into the water and scooped it out. A twelve-inch crappie thrashed around in the net, and I placed it at the bottom of the boat. Once it stopped flopping, I removed the hook from its mouth.

While this was happening, Seren watched with wide eyes. Suddenly, her fishing pole jerked. She gasped and held it tighter. I gave her instructions, which she followed closely, concentrating hard and furrowing her brow. She pulled the fish toward the boat, straining a little. I grabbed it with the net and reeled it in. Her fish was slightly bigger than mine.

A big smile appeared, and she shouted, "Let's do it again."

I laughed; she glanced at me and laughed as well.

"That was fabulous! I never knew that doing something like this could be so much fun."

I baited my hook while she performed hers independently. We fished for about an hour. Her fair skin was beginning to turn red.

I said, "I think we should go in now; you're starting to burn."

She glanced at her arms and said, "You're right. I was hoping I could stay out longer. If we come back here, I'll bring sunscreen and a sun hat."

She continued speaking as if we had a future beyond this job. My heart twisted at the thought—I wanted that future too but dared not believe it could happen.

We stowed the fishing gear, and I rowed us back to the dock.

She carried the fishing gear to the cabin, while I took the fish we caught to the restaurant and spoke with Vincent, the chef, about preparing it for dinner. While there, I asked him to make two turkey sandwiches to take back for lunch.

Seren was happy to see the sandwiches.

"Oh, good, I'm starving."

We munched on our lunch and quietly stared out the sliding glass door.

She suggested, "Let's go for a walk on one of the hiking trails through the woods."

"That sounds wonderful," I said.

We found directions with distances for the different paths on a sign nearby. We chose the 3.5-mile trail that circled the lake.

The trees shaded the trail, and the lake's views were occasionally visible where the underbrush thinned. As we walked, winding through the woods, the silence between us was thoughtful. Then she broke it.

Seren asked, "Can you tell me what happened with that psychic battle between you and your grandmother?"

"Sure, but I have to give you some background first."

As we slowly strolled, I recounted the harrowing events that led to the battle: my grandmother's relentless attempts to take control of my unknown powers, the shocking discovery of my newfound abilities, Rose's terrifying possession of me and the deadly terrors I faced, my ominous trip into the spirit realm, my chilling realization that the Labauve signet was Cyrus's cursed amulet, and finally, the brutal confrontation at the mansion that left me hospitalized for weeks.

She listened silently, absorbing every word. When I finished, we were back at the cabin.

She said, "That's an incredible story, and to think it's all true. And you actually went to the spirit world?"

"Yes, it was amazing, but not as much fun as you might think. When the Duke anointed me, as he called it, it was one of the most agonizing experiences of my life."

"I can't even imagine what you have been through," she said, placing her hand on my arm.

Heat radiated through me where she touched my arm. The warmth drew me closer to her and her soft, red lips. Her eyelids flutter...

"What do you want to do now?" I ask at the last moment, snatching myself upright.

"I think I'll take a nap before dinner."

"I guess I'll read."

Two hours later, she left the bedroom.

I placed my book on the coffee table and said, "Are you ready for dinner?"

'Yes, I am."

We walked to the restaurant. Vincent had cleaned the fish and baked it with a wonderful lemon sauce. Our meal included fish, roasted potatoes, steamed vegetables, and a salad.

Seren said, "That was marvelous, and to think we actually caught the fish."

I smiled, seeing the enjoyment in her eyes.

We briefly discussed what we would do when we found Darlene Newman. I had only planned to bring her back to the plantation and let her and Johnny be together for a while before he had to go to the other side.

After we returned to the cabin, she said, "I'm going to take a shower."

"Okay, I'll take one after you."

The water splashed behind the bathroom door. I stood at the glass door, staring at the lake, but my mind was elsewhere, imagining rivulets sliding over her bare skin.

It was twilight, and the moon rose above the horizon. It pulled me into another past-life vision.

Seren stepped out of the bathroom, her pink robe cinched tightly. Orion stood at the glass door, motionless, bathed in the moonlight reflected from the lake. The scene felt surreal, but something was off. Orion's stance, the stillness of his shoulders; unease prickled up her spine.

She said, "Orion?"

He turned, but he wasn't Orion anymore.

The young man approached her and said in French, "Chloe, my love."

Before she could react, he swept her into his arms and carried her toward the bedroom. He set her down gently. Slowly, he peeled the robe off her shoulders. It dropped to her feet as she stood fully exposed. Her body trembled with anticipation.

Chloe wrapped her arms around his neck, and their lips met in a fiery, passionate kiss that ignited the room.

SPECTRAL PROMISES

Chapter 25

On Fairy Hill

I watched the full moon begin to rise above the horizon from my second-floor bedroom window. Its pale glow shot long shadows across the room. The voice inside my head returned. It relentlessly haunted me since the voodoo ceremony, gnawing at my mind.

'*It's time, boy. Go to Chloe. Take her to Fairy Hill.*'

I should never have let James Pasteur talk me into attending that pagan ritual. She was right from the start. She warned me that something terrible would happen, and I shouldn't have set foot on the Caribbean island.

The entity with the stark white face whispered constantly, its voice echoing in my mind. I was powerless, compelled to obey its commands. I couldn't escape.

I clutched my head, fingers digging into my temples as if I could claw the voice out.

"No!" I shouted. "I won't go to her. You're going to do something to her."

'*No, boy, I would never harm her. She's precious to me. Go now.*'

I dropped my hands. In a daze, I moved to the door and hurried downstairs, feeling forced to follow the spirit God, Duke Shamedi's instructions.

I ran to the barn, quickly saddled a horse, and raced to the small house behind the candlemaker's shop. It was dark by the time I arrived. I led the horse beside the window above Chloe's bed. I tapped on the glass once. No response. Twice.

The window creaked open, and there she was. Chloe, the most beautiful woman in the world to me, poked her head out and said, "Abelard, what are you doing?"

I didn't understand what the demon possessing me wanted to do with her. I had to bring her along. I struggled to restrain myself. My hands trembled uncontrollably.

I hesitantly said, "Chl...Chloe, come with me. We have to go to Fairy Hill."

"What? Why?"

She frowned, seeing my eyes blink erratically, my hands clenching and unclenching into fists.

"Just come; we have to go now."

She hesitated, then crawled out of the window in her long white nightgown. The air was chilly, and she wrapped her arms across her chest. I leaned down and lifted her onto the saddle with one arm, holding her securely with one arm while tightly gripping the horse's reins with my free hand.

I kicked the horse into a gallop and raced toward Fairy Hill. She looked up at my face. My jaw clenched in apprehension, my eyes intense, and I stared straight ahead. I could do nothing else. She must have been wondering why we were heading to Fairy Hill. The moon rose higher above the horizon.

We reached the base of the hill. At the top stood the ancient megaliths, about four to five feet tall, arranged in a circle. The boulders were roughly rectangular in shape. No one understood how the incredibly heavy sentinels could have been moved and placed there. The carved stones had been there for as long as anyone could remember. Most people were too afraid to approach them, claiming that strange things had happened there and that fairies could sometimes be seen. Bad things happened when fairies were nearby.

The hill never frightened Chloe. She told me she could sense waves of energy there and knew she could sometimes communicate with the Fairy Queen on that spot.

I helped her down from the horse, took her hand, and pulled her firmly behind me. She stumbled up the hill, her bare feet wet with dew, trembling in the night air. She stood in the middle of the circle, shivering. I took off my coat and draped it around her shoulders.

"Abelard, why are we here?"

She pulled the coat closed with trembling hands.

"It's time, my love. The veil is thinnest now."

My voice sounded different, deeper, as if it was coming from far away. It was now the voodoo God speaking through me and controlling my body. He moved to the edge of the circle, facing the rising moon. The moon was half-visible.

The demon forced me to remove my vest and shirt, dropping them on the ground. I stood there, bare-chested with my arms out, my head lifted, and my eyes closed, as if soaking up the moon's silver rays.

"Abelard, what are you doing?" Chloe called me.

"Can't you feel it? Can't you sense the veil dropping?"

Excitement washed over my body. My voice was jubilant.

Chloe felt something: a prickling sensation across her back. A small blob of light appeared out of nowhere and fluttered around, always staying within the stone circle. A few more lights flickered into view. She watched them with curiosity. One floated close to her. She reached out to touch it, but it zipped away. The moon had risen higher and was nearly fully visible. How had it moved so quickly?

She looked at Abelard. He now stood completely naked with his arms outstretched, awash in the full moon's light.

Chloe's senses flared with a subtle, tingling alarm from behind. She spun around just in time to confront the Fairy Queen, who hovered effortlessly beside her. Her iridescent wings, edged in shimmering emerald green, flickered and fluttered with mesmerizing grace, releasing a dazzling wave of iridescent colors with every movement. The Queen's fiery red hair floated weightlessly around her, as if immersed in water. At the same time, her lean, alabaster body radiated an intense, divine glow that seemed to pulse with otherworldly power.

The Fairy Queen's fingers barely grazed Chloe's forehead, but that gentle touch unleashed a blinding surge of shimmering light that engulfed her. Her breath hitched painfully in her throat as a wave of dizziness overtook her. She staggered, fighting to stay upright. When her eyes finally fluttered open, they were no longer only hers—glowing with an eerie, unnatural green hue.

The girl dropped the coat with a trembling hand and pulled the nightgown over her head, her transformation now complete.

The now-naked girl approached the man and took his hand in hers.

He turned his head, peered at her with a broad smile, love radiating from his golden eyes, and said, "Wife."

She replied, "Husband."

Her iridescent green eyes also reflected her passion for the God she held hands with. At last, they could touch each other, something they could never do in the spirit realm.

He picked her up, carried her to the man's coat on the ground, and gently laid her on it. He lay down on top of her and kissed her passionately.

He pushed up and said, "We don't have much time, Bridette, my love. This is the best I can do for now. Later, I will be able to do better. I have plans for the future in motion. Things will be perfect then."

"It's good now. I love every second we can be together."

Love flowed toward the possessed man with each word.

She touched his face, and the Duke's dark skin beneath the avatar's white flesh showed through.

Their bodies entwined beneath the moon's glow; energy crackled around them. Magic surged and stars flickered. Reality itself seemed to bend and warp as the couple reached a state of divine ecstasy.

The magical storm remained confined within the ancient stone circle. Not a soul in the village could ever comprehend the intensity of love and passion that erupted on Fairy Hill.

I jolted awake, my body feverish and my mind reeling. Another vision—but this one felt different. Too real. I rolled over, and Seren lay naked on the other side of the bed. I jerked back, shocked to see her in my bed. I looked around; no, I was in her bed.

Images of the two of us making love flashed in my memory. No, it wasn't Seren and me, but Abelard and Chloe. No, it was the Duke and Bridette.

This couldn't have happened. What did I do? Did I force myself on her as Abelard? I sat naked on the edge of the bed and put my hands over my eyes.

"Oh, God. No."

My pulse pounded in my ears as I gripped my head. Had I lost control?

I quickly got up, picked up my clothes from the floor, and entered the bathroom.

I relieved myself and thought, 'I'll take a shower. Maybe that will clear my head.'

As the water pounded on my scalp, I kept telling myself, 'That didn't happen, that didn't happen.'

But it felt so real. This is probably the last time I'll see her, the last chance to be with a woman like her. How could she ever want to be with me after what I did?

I dried, dressed, and stepped out of the bathroom. Seren sat on the sofa, staring at me.

I couldn't look her in the eyes, so embarrassed by what had happened between us, that I stared at the floor and said, "I'm sorry about what happened last night. I...I... had no control. Abelard took over, and then the Duke. You had no say in what occurred. I'm sorry. The Duke takes over my life no matter where or when I am."

I turned to go to my bedroom when she said, "Orion, it's okay. You didn't hurt me. I wanted to be with you, as Chloe, Bridette, and myself."

I stood with my back to her, unable to look her in the eyes.

"It doesn't matter," I said, my voice hollow. "It shouldn't have happened. I won't risk this again. I told you about my grandmother. She could hurt you. We can't be together ...that way."

I walked into my bedroom and shut the door. Sitting on the edge of the bed, I stared at the floor, beating myself up for what I had done. God, I hate the Duke so much. He even controlled me in past lives. I seethed.

Cyrus approached and said, "I don't understand why you're so upset. You've wanted to be with her since the moment you saw her. Now that you have, just look at you. I've never seen you this depressed. What's going on?"

"Don't you understand that wasn't me making love to her? It was Abelard and the Duke. She didn't do it because she wanted to be with me. She did it because Chloe and Bridette wanted to do it."

"But she said she wanted to be with you."

"I know she said that, but was it real or just leftover feelings from the others? Besides, I can never have anyone I care about, or else my crazy grandmother would go after her. Stop talking about this and leave me alone!" I shouted at him.

When Orion turned, his eyes had transformed. His movements were no longer Orion's familiar grace, but something more ominous. It wasn't Orion at all; it was Abelard.

A vivid past-life vision unfolded before her eyes. She found herself on Fairy Hill with Abelard, when everything shifted, the very fabric of reality changed. The Fairy Queen now possessed her, and Duke Shamedi possessed Abelard. As divine beings, they made passionate love atop the hill, an encounter filled with indescribable intensity and power.

After the Gods vanished into the night sky, Chloe and Abelard lay on his coat, their gazes fixed on the luminous moon now hanging high above them.

Abelard gently turned to her, his voice trembling with emotion: "I'm sorry that happened."

Chloe said, "I'm not. It was amazing."

His eyes shut tight, trembling as he confessed, "I had no control over myself—the pagan God that possessed me from my time on Saint Dominque took over."

"I know. It was enjoyable, but not the same as with you."

He gazed into her eyes, a deep love shining within him. With a confident smile, he rolled over and pressed his lips to hers in a passionate kiss. Their connection ignited as they made love with fiery intensity, fully embracing their human vulnerability and desire.

Seren opened her eyes, and Orion was making love to her with closed eyes.

She thought, 'I think he's still Abelard.'

She didn't want it to stop and let him continue as Abelard. The coupling intensified, reaching a passionate crescendo—something she had desperately longed for since her very first encounter with Orion. After he finally rolled off her, exhaustion quickly claimed him, and he fell into an instant, restless sleep.

She paused, a gentle smile curling on her lips as she closed her eyes and drifted into sleep, her heart hopeful that this encounter would continue in the morning.

When she woke in the morning, Orion was gone, leaving only the faint scent of his musk. She heard the shower running, a sound that resonated loudly in the quiet room. She got up slowly, dressed with deliberate care, and sat on the couch, her eyes fixed on the bathroom door, waiting for him to come out. She desperately wanted to tell him just how much she enjoyed last night, her heart pounding with anticipation.

He emerged from the bathroom, avoiding her gaze, his voice trembled as he apologized for the event.

He turned away from her, saying they could never be together because of what his grandmother might do, and entered his bedroom, closing the door behind him.

She sank onto the couch, her heart heavy with sadness and confusion. Last night had been a whirlwind—strange yet exhilarating. How could he be so paralyzed by fear of his grandmother that he couldn't even allow himself to enjoy sharing a moment with someone else? The Fairy Queen had confided in her about his deep-rooted issues, revealing a struggle that was more profound than she had imagined.

A single tear escaped her eye, tracing a silent path down her cheek for Orion. She returned to her bedroom, collapsing onto the bed with a heavy sigh, her mind racing with desperate ideas to save him from himself.

I lay on the bed until the sun rose. I didn't feel like eating breakfast, and I didn't hear Seren leave her room, so I assumed she didn't want breakfast either.

Around 8 a.m., a knock sounded at the door of the cabin.

I opened the front door, and Perry stood there with a big smile.

"Good morning! Uncle Bob told me to come and pick ya'll up. Your car is ready."

Still depressed by the previous night's events, I said, "Okay, we'll be out in a few," and closed the door.

I turned, and Seren was standing in her bedroom doorway.

I said, "Perry's here. The car's done."

"I heard."

I started to move past her, but she grabbed my arm.

"Orion, about last night. You did nothing wrong. I wanted to be with you."

I shook my head, freed my arm from her grip, and went to my bedroom to pack. I quickly stuffed everything into the small suitcase and hurried outside.

I approached Perry, who was standing by his tow truck.

"I need to pay the bill. I'll be right back."

He nodded. I turned and saw Seren leaving the cabin. I looked down, unable to make eye contact with her, and walked to the office.

Tabitha stood behind the desk with her usual big grin.

I said, "We need to check out. Can I get the bill?"

"Here you go. Did you and the young lady have a good time?"

She handed me the invoice. Noticing my sour expression, she furrowed her brow, wondering what was wrong.

I said, "Yeah, it was okay," as I reviewed the document.

I noticed the charges for the fishing equipment.

"Oh, I left the fishing gear in the cabin. I'll go and get it."

She said, "Don't worry about it. I'll pick it up when I clean the cabin."

I paid and left with her following me. She stood in the driveway waving as the truck drove by.

We said nothing during the drive to Bob's Auto Repair. When we arrived, Bob exited the garage, wiping his hands on a red shop towel and smiling, knowing this was a big payday for him. Seren went to the car, and I accompanied Bob to the repair shop office. He reviewed the invoice with me. Based on my experience with automobile maintenance, I recognized the exaggerated times for some repairs, but I didn't argue with him. I paid the bill and went to the Toyota. Seren had already packed our suitcases in the trunk.

She asked, "How much was the bill? I'll repay you when we get back."

"Don't worry about it. This is my Finding Job, so I'll pay for it."

She nodded and got into the driver's seat, me in the passenger seat, Cyrus in the back, and we left, heading east for Mobile.

We said nothing for quite a while, and then she attempted to start a conversation.

"Orion, please don't feel bad about last night. Everything is fine."

"I don't want to talk about it."

"But, Orion, you should talk about it. You shouldn't hide your feelings inside. It's not good for you."

I raised my voice, "I said I don't want to talk about it. And besides, how do you know what's good or not for me? We barely know each other."

"Okay. Cyrus, is he always like this?"

Cyrus said, "Yes, as long as I've known him. He keeps things bottled..."

I turned, anger flaring in my eyes at Cyrus, and shut his mouth for him. He slammed back against the seat, his lips tightly pursed, and his eyes bulging with fear.

Seren stared at me.

"Did you make him stop talking?"

She glanced back at Cyrus and recognized his wide, frightened eyes. She shouted for me to stop—twice, louder each time. I didn't stop. She pulled the Toyota to the side of the road, tires screeching as she made a quick stop.

"Let him go. Now."

Her hands gripped the wheel, knuckles white.

"Or you can walk to Mobile."

Anger blazed in her eyes; at a level I had never witnessed before. While others merely disliked me, she was truly furious. I hated seeing her anger directed at me. I hated having to confront my feelings. All I wanted was for Cyrus to shut up and stop rambling.

I gave in and let him go. The ghost relaxed.

She asked, "Cyrus, are you okay?"

"Yes, I'm okay. It's okay."

He turned and stared out the side window.

Seren continued, "How can you do that to him? He's your friend. Wait a minute, you don't know how friends behave around each other; you've never had one. Well, let me explain how friends act..."

She went on a tirade for ten minutes.

"Do you know how childish that was? You've never learned how to interact with people..."

She continued about how friends are supposed to behave.

I sat and listened, knowing she was right about most of it.

She calmed down and asked, "Do you have anything to say?"

"No, I don't know what to say. I've never had anyone speak to me that way. I'm sorry."

I wasn't sure how to react.

"Okay, just think about what I said. This conversation is over. Let's keep heading to Mobile and find Darlene Newman."

She pulled back onto the highway, and we silently continued to Mobile, Alabama.

I reflected on her words, a flash of realization hitting me hard. I'd never spent this much time with anyone since I was six, and Sammy stayed with me. Outside of school, I had always been alone, navigating life's obstacles on my own. But now, everything felt different, more vulnerable, more real. It hit me then, stark and undeniable.

Yes, I attended school, surrounded by many people, yet I kept my distance. I avoided interaction, instinctively retreating from their reactions because of my strange emanations. I didn't know how to connect with people carrying their own pain.

The ghosts tolerated me because of the guilt they carried—being somehow involved in the death of a child. They taught me not to get angry, so I buried my emotions deep inside. That suppression finally erupted during Rose's possession when she was trying to find the Labauve signet. Now, with power over the spirits, I realize that any emotional outpouring has a direct impact on them. I must learn to control and harness my emotions before they control me.

Maybe, just maybe, she could help me become more than just a vessel for ghosts or a God.

SPECTRAL PROMISES

Chapter 26
Apologies and the Lockwood Institute

Humidity thickened as we crossed the border into Alabama.

Seren asked, "Once we're in Mobile, what's the plan?"

"Stop at a gas station, and we'll pick up a more detailed map."

"All right. There's one. I'll stop now," she said as she pulled over.

I got out, filled the tank, and went into the station's office to pay and buy a map. At the car, I unfolded the document across the hood and traced our route. Seren stood beside me, watching. As I followed Highway 65, a dull ache crept into my gut. South of Andalusia, my stomach twisted violently.

"Right there. Somewhere around there."

"You're sure?"

"Oh, yeah."

"That's at least another hour away. Let's grab lunch first."

"Okay."

We went up the road and stopped at a burger joint. Starving, I loaded up on burgers and fries while she kept it simple. We sat in the restaurant and ate lunch. Cyrus stayed in the car, still upset about what I had done to him.

Seren asked, "Have you thought about some of the things I said to you?

Embarrassed and overwhelmed, I averted my gaze, nervously scratching at the worn tabletop.

"Yes, I have. You're right; I don't know how to treat a friend. Can you help me?"

This was incredibly hard for me to say. I timidly looked up into her worried eyes, feeling the weight of vulnerability.

"Yes, I can. I'll let you know when you're doing something wrong."

I smiled.

"Thank you."

I felt a surge of relief that she hadn't given up on me. Maybe I wasn't as irreparably broken as I had always convinced myself.

We returned to the car. Sitting in the front seat, I turned to Cyrus and let out a sigh.

"I'm sorry," I whispered. "I let my anger get the best of me. I shouldn't have taken it out on you."

Cyrus stared at me.

"Oh, okay. I understand. Besides, you have every right to be angry with me after what I did to you."

Seren smiled, "Now, see. It wasn't so hard to apologize to a friend. But, Cyrus, what is that about—he has a right to be angry with you?"

Seren looked confused.

"Why on earth would you say that?"

Cyrus shot me a probing look, his eyes asking for more. I simply nodded in response.

As we drove up Highway 65, Cyrus told her how he had always been selfish in his life and revealed that he was gay. He was so self-focused that he pushed his nephew down the stairs, causing the boy's death, and he blamed Paul for it. Rose was so furious that she cursed the plantation; she said anyone who hurt or killed a child and died on the property would have to stay there as a ghost.

He also revealed that after discovering the Voodoo Imperatrice had been hunting for the Labauve signet just months earlier, he realized the sapphire on his amulet was the last vital piece of the family seal. Yet he kept this secret from everyone, knowing they would all have to cross over once the curse was lifted. He refused to abandon this world; his only true desire was to stay with Orion, with whom he had fallen deeply in love.

Cyrus sighed, shoulders slumping.

"I put everyone at risk so I could stay. I let my selfishness control me. And now? I know what's waiting for me on the other side. Hell, probably. Whatever Orion does to me, I deserve it."

Nobody spoke for a few moments.

Finally, Seren began. "Cyrus, I'm sorry you had a difficult life, but at least you now understand that you were largely responsible for most of your issues. I don't believe it was entirely your fault. Much of it likely stemmed from how you were raised during that time. People weren't familiar with psychology back then. Now, you are trying to improve. Have you learned lessons from your experiences?"

"Yes, I should have told Orion how I felt about him and what the amulet was."

"Being open about things is the best for most situations."

She glanced at me; I knew her words were also directed at me, but I still couldn't summon the courage to tell her how I felt. I believed she was the most incredible woman I had ever encountered—her appearance, her emotional depth, her intellect—all of it simply took my breath away. Every night since I met her, I fall asleep imagining what it would be like to make love to her, my mind consumed by it. I just stared out the window and said nothing. I'm an idiot. I know.

My stomachache intensified as we traveled along the highway. I rubbed my stomach and closed my eyes.

Seren noticed this and asked, "Is your stomach getting worse?"

"Yes, it is."

"So, that means we are getting closer."

"Yeah."

We passed the exit for a county road, and the ache diminished somewhat.

"Turn around. It's decreasing. We're going in the wrong direction. We passed a county road back there. We have to go that way."

Seren found a turnaround on the highway and returned the way we came. She turned south on the county road, and my stomachache intensified.

"Yes, this is the right way."

We followed the road for several miles, and the ache began to diminish again. I gave her directions. She turned onto another road.

We took a left onto another road, drove for about two miles, and then turned right onto a dirt road. A sign next to the road read, 'PRIVATE DRIVE.' She started to slow down, but I signaled to her to keep going. She sped up, and we continued.

My stomach convulsed violently. We were here.

A massive wrought-iron gate loomed at the top of the hill; its dark metal twisted into sharp, intricate designs. A brass sign gleamed in the dimming light: LOCKWOOD INSTITUTE FOR THE MENTALLY CHALLENGED.

Seren slammed on the brakes. The Corolla skidded to a halt in a cloud of dust.

This was it. Darlene Newman was in this building. I promptly opened the car door and puked on the dirt, wishing I had never eaten those burgers.

Seren asked, "She's here? A mental institution?"

Wiping my mouth, I said, "Yeah, she's definitely here."

We all stared in stunned silence through the window at the imposing building. Further up the hill loomed a red brick colonial-style mansion, its thirty-foot-tall white columns reaching toward the sky and a second-floor balcony hinting at faded grandeur. A vast porch lined with white wicker chairs in small, haphazard groups stretched across most of the house's front, giving it charms despite the institution's ominous purpose. Metal bars covered every window, a stark warning of the dangers inside. Clearly, extensions had been added over time, transforming the mansion into a structure three times larger than its original size.

Seren asked, "What should we do?"

I said, "I guess go in and ask for her."

"Okay, I'll say I'm her sister. Hospitals usually won't allow non-family members to visit patients."

"That sounds good. Cyrus, while we're talking to the staff, you sniff around and see if you can figure out where she is."

He said, "All right, just like the good old Finding Job days," and he produced a huge smile.

I smiled back at him, seeing how happy he was to be part of a team again.

Pointing up the hill, I said, "Let's go."

Seren slowly drove the car through the open gates, onto the gravel driveway, and parked in the small visitors' parking lot in front of the hospital. Another lot was on the east side of the building, where several cars were parked.

We went up the steps to the front door. I grabbed the handle, but it didn't budge. Serem tugged on my sleeve and pointed to a sign above a speaker grill with a green button below it. The sign read, "PUSH BUTTON FOR ACCESS." I pressed the button.

The intercom crackled to life, a woman's sharp, impatient voice cut through the static.

"Yes. What do you want?"

Seren shouted to the speaker, "Hi, I'm here to visit Darlene Newman. I'm her sister."

Nothing happened for a few moments, then a loud buzz and a 'thunk' echoed from the door. I grasped the door handle, and it opened. I let Seren enter first.

Across the front lobby, paved with institutional green and gray checkerboard linoleum, stood a high, curved counter. The walls were painted a pale gray, or perhaps they hadn't been painted in so long that the white had faded to a grayish hue. The place had a musty smell and a faint background odor of disinfectant.

Behind the counter loomed a nurse in her 40s, with dishwater-blond hair tightly pulled into a bun. Deep lines etched her forehead, suggesting the stern furrow on her brow was a permanent fixture. She glared at us with an unyielding stare, as if she took no nonsense from anyone. We approached with smiles, but she remained unmoved, her piercing gaze unwavering. The name tag read 'Blanche.'

A six-inch-square speaker sat on the countertop, with a foot-long box containing toggle switches marked with numbers and an old-fashioned microphone positioned to its right. Along the wall behind her, there were rows of small, square cubbyholes, like those in hotels used for storing room keys. Keys were also placed in these compartments. Each spot displayed a number or a label: Pat Acc, Sol 1, Sol 2, Sol 3, Exam 1, Exam 2, Food Stor, Ice B, Shower, etc.

On the right side of the hall, three wooden doors with frosted, opaque windows on the upper half had names stenciled across them. I assumed these were the offices for the facility director and doctors. To the left, a metal door with a prominent lock stood.

Seren began, "We would like to see Darlene Newman."

She flashed the nurse her brightest smile ever.

"We were in the area and thought we'd stop by to check on how my sister is doing. Darlene and I haven't seen each other in over five years."

She looked at me and asked, "Isn't that right, honey?"

I said, "Yeah, I think that's right. We stopped by her house and visited her and Johnny."

She nodded and waited for the nurse to respond.

Blanche glowered at us.

"You should have called ahead. You can't just walk in here and see a patient."

Seren replied, "Like, I said, we were in the area and decided to stop by at the last minute."

"I'm sorry, but you can't see her. She's in a bad state, and interaction with people would upset her."

At that moment, the metal door clanged and opened. Out stepped a huge black orderly; 'Martin' was on his name badge. Voices, loud talking, and yelling resonated from the opening.

He closed the door and said, "I'm going out for a smoke."

He walked to the front door, and Blanche flicked the number one switch. The loud buzz sounded, and the 'thunk' of the lock being released echoed through the high-ceilinged hallway. He pulled the door open and stepped out, already grabbing the cigarette pack from his pants pocket.

As I stood there, I knew something was wrong. I felt several ghosts in the area. An orange Lwa orb flickered through the wall and hovered in the upper corner. Then, a few others appeared. They didn't like us being there. I sensed we had to leave before something terrible happened, especially to Seren. The Lwa were unhappy we were there and started bouncing off the walls. I didn't think they could do anything to me, but they could hurt her, depending on what power they had been tasked with.

Seren started to say something—I took her hand and said, "Honey, I'm sorry, but you can't see your sister. I know you really wanted to, but we don't want to upset her."

I glanced at the nurse.

"Thank you so much for your help."

I held Seren's hand and led her toward the front door. A buzz and a 'thunk' sounded. I opened the door, and we stepped outside. Seren pulled her hand away from mine as we came onto the spacious veranda.

She exclaimed, "Why did you do that?"

I noticed Martin sitting in one of the wicker chairs on the porch, smoking his cigarette and staring at us. She saw me peering over her shoulder and turned to see Martin.

Then, she turned to me and said, "You're right, honey. We shouldn't bother her."

We hurried down the stairs to the car and drove out through the gate.

Blanche Franklin trailed the strange couple to the exit, her eyes sharp as she watched their exchange on the porch. Something about them was off—especially the man. Handsome, yes, but his unsettling gaze kept darting around and sweeping up at the ceiling as if he were searching for something invisible. Why were they asking about Darlene Newman?

The head nurse decided to call Mr. Charbonnet and tell him that people were there asking about his wife.

SPECTRAL PROMISES

Chapter 27

Planning the Breakout

I told Seren, "Pull over to the side so we can wait for Cyrus."

She pulled onto the grass.

Seren glared at me.

"Why did you want to leave so soon? I had more arguments to hit 'Nurse Ratched' with."

"Lwa were in that place, and they weren't happy we had walked in. I hope they didn't do anything to Cyrus."

At that moment, my ghost friend popped into the backseat.

"Phew! That was close."

I asked, "Were the Lwa after you?"

"Not at first. I think they assumed I was just one of the other ghosts. I couldn't see them, but I could feel them. It started getting uncomfortable. They pushed me to the gate. I don't think they can go past the gate."

Seren exclaimed, "There were other spirits in there?"

"Yes, quite a few. They mostly hang out with specific people. Those poor people see the ghosts and think they're going crazy," Cyrus said.

She said, "The ghosts must have been what I sensed. But it was hard to tell what was there with all the heightened emotions."

I said, "I sensed the spirits there, and when Lwa showed up, not knowing why they were there, I figured we had better get out."

"What are we going to do?" Seren asked.

"I don't know yet. Let's find someplace to stay for the night, and I'll think about it."

She pulled back onto the dirt driveway and returned to the county road. Eventually, we arrived in Jonestown and booked two rooms at a motel, one for Seren and one for me.

Across the street from the motel was a local diner called 'Mama's Place.' Every small town seems to have a restaurant serving typical

American home-style meals, so we went there for dinner. I ordered the pot roast dinner while she had a large chef's salad.

As we ate, Seren asked, "How are we going to rescue Darlene?"

"I don't know yet. Cyrus, did you find her while you were snooping around?"

Cyrus sat in the booth beside me. I looked across at Seren while speaking with Cyrus so people would think I was conversing with her.

"Yes, I saw her. Her name was on the clipboard hanging next to her door. She's in Solitary Confinement, room three, on the third floor. When I peeked in, she seemed out of it. I read her file. They have her on a strict regimen of drugs, loading her up in the mornings and late afternoons."

Seren grimaced when she heard about the drugs. I shook my head, feeling sorry for the woman.

I turned to Cyrus and gave him a big smile.

"Good work," I said, trying to be more open with my acceptance of Cyrus' contribution to this Finding Job.

He smiled back.

Seren noticed my attempts and smiled at me.

She said, "So we have to get her out before her morning meds or just before her afternoon meds, when she's most cognizant."

"That's good," I said, rubbing my jaw. "But we need to get in through the locked doors, retrieve the patient ward keys, locate Solitary 3, take Darlene, and escape back to the car—all before anyone sees us."

I shook my head, unsure how to achieve this monumental task.

Seren commented, "First, we should ask the question: why is she in that type of hospital? If she's there for a mental health reason, maybe we shouldn't break her out?"

Cyrus replied, "From what I could tell, most of those people were being tortured by the ghosts. I don't think they're there because they should be."

I said, "And since Lwa were also present, those people were probably cursed. Lwa tend to associate with individuals because of a curse or for protection. Based on Cyrus's description, I don't believe they were being protected. We must assume that Darlene is being held there against her will."

The others nodded in agreement.

After dinner, we returned to my room. I sat next to the window in the 70s-style floral-print vinyl chair and stared out, thinking about how to extricate Darlene with my unique powers. Seren and Cyrus sat on the bed, bantering ideas back and forth. Most of them were impossible, which is funny considering what I had in mind.

Seren peered at me and snidely said, "You're not offering any ideas. What's on your mind?"

"I've got some plans."

"Well, let's hear them."

I turned the chair around and outlined my idea, focusing on my unusual abilities.

I explained that I would call the Lwa in Lockwood and release them from their duties. I would call Lwa to use as a diversion to get all the staff away from the patients. I would assign Lwa to protect and hide us while we locate Darlene and release her.

Seren exclaimed, "Well, that sounds like a plan, as long as you can do all the incredible things you said."

"All I can do is try. Theoretically, the plan should work. We'll have to arrive there early in the morning. So, I recommend we go to bed early and get up at about 4 a.m."

I was determined to get Darlene out of that horrible place.

"Why so early?" She asked.

"I must prepare and call Lwa over from the spirit plane before we head out."

She nodded, got up, and moved for the door.

"Okay, I'll see you in the morning."

She smiled and went to her room.

Cyrus asked me, "Can you do everything you said?"

"I think so. Here's what I need you to do. Please stay with Seren and Darlene. Do whatever you can to assist them. I know you're limited by not being near home but do your best. At the very least, let them know if someone is after them."

"You'll be there. You can protect them."

"But if something happens to me, you help them. Promise me."

"I'll do what I can."

"While searching Lockwood, did you see a back door or any other way to get out other than the front door?"

"Yeah, there's a door exiting to the side from the basement, but it has one of those electric locks."

"Was there a speaker with a button below it?"

"Yeah, and the number four was printed above it."

"Good, that probably means switch number four opens it. That should work. That's the way I want you to take Seren and Darlene out of the building."

"Okay."

I went to bed but had a hard time falling asleep.

I asked Fuzzbucket to help. He has stayed with me ever since I called him to help heal my arm. He's usually perched on my right shoulder. No one, not even a ghost, can see him.

'Fuzzbucket, please help me fall asleep. I need to be alert tomorrow. And if anyone gets injured, I want you to heal them as quickly as possible.'

'Yes, Small Duke. Fuzzbucket will heal everyone.'

The small Lwa rolled across my forehead, humming and vibrating. This calmed me, and I drifted off to sleep.

I awoke with Cyrus shaking my shoulder.

"Orion, it's four o'clock. Wake up."

"Okay, okay."

I sat up and rubbed the sleep from my eyes. I went to the bathroom, brushed my teeth, shaved, and got dressed. Seren knocked on the door. I let her in, fully prepared for the mission ahead.

I said, "Good morning. Did you sleep last night?"

"Not very well. I think I was too excited."

"I can understand that. I asked Fuzzbucket to put me to sleep."

"What's a Fuzzbucket?" she asked curiously.

"Oh, haven't I told you about Fuzzbucket?"

She shook her head.

"It's a healing Lwa that I called to this plane to help heal my broken arm. He stayed after the Duke healed it with a piece of fruit from the Tree of Life. I like him. I have told him that if we mortals are injured, he should heal us as quickly as possible."

"Okay. Where is he now?"

Her eyes were darting around.

"Right here on my shoulder."

I pointed to my right shoulder. The little guy twirled around when I pointed at him. Seren looked at the spot and shook her head.

She asked, "So, what do we do first?"

"I have to meditate and call Lwa over."

I sat cross-legged on the bed, closed my eyes, and began deep breathing to calm myself in preparation. Seren sat in the chair, watching intently.

I opened my eyes, aware of their golden glow. The air around me shimmered, magic rippling like heat waves. I rose, moving my hands with urgent precision—carving potent, unseen symbols into the very fabric between worlds. My voice, deep and ancient, boomed with authority, calling out names only gods could comprehend: Protection, Glamour, Action—the Lwa responded instantly, energy thrumming in the air.

Moving my hand forward, I formed a fist, grasped a few Lwa energy tails, and pulled the entities closer. I repeated this five times. The spirit entities floated before me as I explained what I wanted them to do in the God language.

In unison, they all responded, '*Yes, small Duke.*'

I relaxed, exhaled, and closed my eyes. When I opened them again, they were blue once more. I stumbled back onto the bed, dizzy after calling Lwa.

Seren stood and hurried over to me.

"Are you okay? Did you pull the Lwa over?"

"Yes, they're here."

While holding my arm, she glanced around the room.

"I can only make out a few shimmers."

"That's better than most people who see nothing. Let me lie down briefly to clear my head before we go."

I lay back and rested my spinning head on the pillow. I fell asleep for a while, and when she touched me, she jerked back and yelped.

I jolted awake.

"What happened?"

"I went to wake you and got a shock. Was that just static electricity or the Lwa?"

"I think it was the Lwa. They get a little protective."

I leered at the Lwa hovering above me and said, *"This is Seren; she's, my friend; you are not to harm her. Does everyone understand that?"*

'*Yes, Small Duke,*' the chorus chimed.

I gestured to the blue Lwa.

"You. Protect her at all times."

It zipped toward Seren, hovering just above her head.

'*I protect Seren, mate of Small Duke.*'

It puffed up, practically vibrating with pride.

I hesitated. Should I correct it? No, it's best not to confuse things.

I said to Seren, "There, you are now protected. You can't be cursed or injured by a mortal or animal. The protection should work in most situations, but it may not work completely if a lot of action is going on."

She smiled.

"Thank you."

I pointed to another blue protection Lwa and said, "You protect me."

It hovered above my head, puffed itself up, and said, '*I protect Small Duke.*'

It flew in circles around my head, happy with the assignment.

"All right, let's head out and break out Darlene Newman."

Cyrus grinned.

"Our first prison break job."

Seren chuckled. I smirked. As the motel door clicked shut behind us, I exhaled. It was time.

Chapter 28

The Breakout

Cleetus Broux and his twin brother Clive lounged against the brown Lincoln Continental, cigarettes dangling from their lips. The orange flare of their cigarettes briefly lit their scarred faces. The night air reeked of stale tobacco and gasoline. Neither man was happy about their assignment.

Bald, six-foot-three, and built like linebackers, the twins weren't paid to think; they were paid to break bones. And right now, they are bored as hell.

Earnest Charbonnet Jr. answered his ringing phone at about 5 p.m. The information that he received upset him. He was in a foul mood after that and started yelling at everyone.

Something was going on at Lockwood. Everyone there was handsomely paid just to stay silent about the patients locked inside. Most of these patients weren't sick—they were carefully kept alive and sedated for reasons known only to him and his business associates. Then, out of nowhere, someone came asking about his wife, turning everything upside down. He had to know what was going on.

"Cleetus. Clive."

Charbonnet's voice was sharp, impatient.

"Get to Lockwood. Watch for any outsiders snooping around. If someone shows up, stop them and find out what they want. If they ask for Darlene Newman—"

He cracked his knuckles.

"Bring them to me."

Cleetus said, "Okay, boss. How long should we stay?"

"Wait a couple of days; if no one shows up, come back here."

"You got it, Mr. Charbonnet."

They drove to the 'Crazy Shack,' as they called it, and went in to talk to Blanche.

The twins approached the counter.

Cleetus, the one who did most of the talking, said, "Hey, Blanche, the boss told us to keep an eye out for strange people. Did someone come by and mess with this place or something?"

The head nurse found the twins disturbingly like oversized pit bulls that reeked of garlic and spoke like sewer rats. But right now? They were precisely what she needed.

She said, "Yesterday, a weird couple dropped by out of the blue, asking to see Darlene."

The brothers exchanged a look that said it all. This was bad and would upset the boss.

Cleetus commented, "That's real bad news. Mr. Charbonnet's gonna lose his mind."

Blanche agreed, "I know, that's why I called him."

"What did they look like?"

"They were a young couple, mid-twenties, both good-looking. She had long, red hair; he had black, curly hair with a single white curl at the front. She claimed to be Darlene's sister. I was never told that she had a sister. Oh, and they were driving a white Toyota Corolla with Louisiana plates."

"Okay, we'll wait outside in the parking lot and keep a lookout. We'll grab'm if they come back."

"We don't have any spare rooms for you to stay in overnight."

"That's okay. We brought the Lincoln; there's lots of room in the back to sleep."

"I'll have the cook bring y'all food when it's mealtime."

Clive said, "I have to use the John."

Blanche pointed down the hall toward the kitchen and said, "On the right."

While waiting for his brother, Cleetus said, "Maybe later tonight, we can hang out and have some fun."

The nurse wasn't particularly attractive, but not a dog. He wasn't a picky man.

The nurse scowled at him.

"You're disgusting."

Cleetus laughed at her expression. Clive walked up and they left the lobby.

Clive asked, "What were you laughing at?"

"I asked Blanche if she wanted to fuck later tonight."

He was still smiling.

"You've got to be kidding. It hasn't been that long since you fucked someone."

"I know. I just wanted to see her reaction. You should have seen the look on her face."

He laughed out loud again, and Clive chuckled with his brother.

The two thugs waited in the car all night. The cook brought them dinner. They ate everything but complained about how terrible the food was. They took turns sleeping in the back seat of the luxury automobile. Nothing happened the entire night except for a scream or cry from a patient coming through an open window.

We returned to the Lockwood Institute, turned the car around to head in the right direction for a quick exit, and parked in the grass alongside the dirt road.

I turned to Seren.

"I need to show you how the glamour works."

I pointed to the two yellow Lwa.

"You with Seren, and you with me. You both will glamour us to blend in with the background."

They replied.

'As you command, Small Duke.'

"Watch this."

I lifted my hand, palm facing me, and passed it slowly over my face and down my chest. My image faded—blending into the car seat and side window until I was only a ghostly outline.

Seren sucked in a sharp breath.

"Oh, my God. You're almost invisible."

"That's right. Unless someone is specifically searching for us while glamoured, they won't be able to see us, especially if we're against a wall or something. If we find ourselves in the middle of a room or a large area, that's a bit trickier. Somebody might catch a glimpse of movement. So be careful."

"How do you stop the glamour?"

"You do the same thing only in reverse."

I placed my palm over my chest and moved it to the top of my head. I was now fully visible.

"That's amazing. This truly is magic."

"Okay, I'll glamour myself and run over to that oak tree on the right. Then I'll remove it so I can call the Lwa to me from inside the institution. Seren, glam yourself and wait at the gate. I'll release the Lockwood Lwa and send them back to the spirit realm. They'll be gone and unable to do anything to you. Then I'll re-glamour, and we can move to the building."

"How are we going to get in?"

"You'll see when we arrive. Okay, let's go."

We both glamoured ourselves and hurried to the gate. I ran to the oak tree with the troop of my magical entities following me, stood behind it, and removed the glamour. I inhaled deeply, centering myself. Raising my hands, I traced precise patterns in the air, my voice low and commanding.

"All Lwa in the Lockwood Institute—come to me."

The entities began to manifest before me. There were about twenty.

"You have all completed your tasks. I release you and return you to the spirit plane."

A small portal of golden light appeared, and the Lwa popped out of existence one at a time.

I waved for Seren to come over. I couldn't see her clearly until she was right next to me.

"Okay, let's slowly move to the front door."

I glamoured myself, and we made our way toward the building and ascended the stairs.

"Now what?" Seren whispered.

"Watch."

I turned to the eager Lwa hovering nearby.

"All of you—hit the kitchen. Burst pipes. Collapse shelves. Do anything to raise hell."

"You—"

I pointed to a golden Lwa.

"When the hospital staff is in the kitchen, flip the number one switch on the switch box at the counter. This will unlock the front door for us, and you can then join the others for the fun. You will all be released to return to the spirit realm when I leave the building."

All the Lwa were buzzing with excitement, eager to cause trouble for the people inside.

I peered at Seren, just able to make out her outline.

"Seren, when we enter the building, hug the wall and move to the patient door. I'll retrieve the keys from the cubbyholes and unlock the Patient Access door. I want you to run up the stairs to the third floor and find Solitary Confinement three. I'll be right behind you."

"Okay, I'm ready."

"Lwa, now go!"

I gestured toward the door.

The Lwa passed through, leaving small flashes of light as they phased through the massive wooden doors. We stood outside, listening for the door buzzer. Crashes reverberated through the halls—yells, frantic footsteps, and a distant scream. Then came a sharp buzz and a metallic 'thunk'. The lock was released.

We entered and moved to the wall. The staff's voices yelled and shouted, and a couple of screams echoed from the kitchen. A sound like a shower and water splashing could be heard. A loud crash rattled through the hall.

The Patient Access door swung open, and Martin ran into the front lobby and down the hall toward the kitchen, shouting, "What the hell is going on?"

I rushed to the key cubbies and grabbed the keys for Patient Access and Solitary Confinement 3. I unlocked the metal door, and we hurried inside.

The stairs to the upper floors were immediately to the right. On the left, a large entryway led to an expansive room where the patients stayed. Against the wall, a cart filled with tiny paper cups containing the patients's medications and a pitcher of water. Martin must have just begun distributing the morning medications.

The unfortunate incarcerated individuals wore pale green hospital gowns and had dirty, unkempt hair. Some sat at tables, others rocked back and forth in chairs, while some walked around in circles. Several ghosts were also present. The specters stirred, turning their hollow gazes toward me. Then, one by one, the patients followed suit, their vacant eyes locking onto mine. Something inside them recognized me.

Cyrus was already halfway up the stairs and waving at us to follow, "Come on, you'all. This way."

Seren and I glanced at each other, realizing we needed to take action on behalf of these people.

We hurried up the stairs, following Cyrus. The third-floor hallway had several doors on both sides, each marked with a number. At the end of the hall was Solitary Confinement 3. I inserted the key and unlocked the door. We stepped into the room, where Darlene Newman sat up in the squeaky metal bed.

Darlene flinched, her eyes darting wildly.

"Who's there?"

The door seemed to open by itself, then swung closed again. She gasped, scooting against the wall, trembling.

The room was roughly six feet wide and eight feet long, featuring a bed, a chair, and a small table. The sheets were filthy and hadn't been changed in a long time. The odor of urine lingered in the air.

I removed my glamour and said, "I'm Orion Labauve, and this is..."

Seren appeared beside me in a shimmer of fading glamour.

"Seren Griffyths."

"Darlene Newman," I said. "Johnny sent us. We're here to take you home."

Shaking, the woman cried, "Oh, my God. I really am going crazy," and sobbed into her hands.

Seren ran over to the woman and put an arm around her shoulder.

"No, you aren't. This is real. We are real. We came to find you. Orion promised Johnny that he would find you."

Darlene lowered her hands and gazed up at me.

"Johnny's okay? He's alive?"

I didn't want to tell the woman her son was dead and a ghost, so I just said, "He's at my house."

She started to cry again.

I said, "Come on. We have to go. The commotion the Lwa are producing downstairs won't last long."

She looked up, obviously knowing something about Lwa.

"You brought Lwa with you? Are you a voodoo priest?"

"Not exactly, but I'll tell you later. We have to get out of here."

Seren helped the poor woman to her feet. I re-glamoured, and Seren did the same. Darlene appeared to be standing alone. This wasn't going to work.

I exclaimed, "I should have assigned another glamour; she's exposed."

Seren said, "And a protection Lwa."

"You're right. Damn! I should have thought of that."

This was my first rescue mission, so I didn't think of everything.

I un-glamoured and un-protected myself and told the Lwa, "You are now assigned to glamour and protect Darlene."

The two entities moved to Darlene's shoulder. I showed the frightened woman how to proceed, and she performed the glamour movements.

Seren's voice worriedly asked, "But what about you? Now they'll be able to see you."

"Don't worry about me; I can take care of myself. Cyrus, please show them the way to the basement exit you mentioned. When you're down there, buzz me, and I'll flip the unlock switch."

Seren protested, "You can't do that. They'll catch you."

"Hopefully, the problems in the kitchen keep them occupied. Now go. Get back to the car fast. If I'm not there within the next ten minutes, take off. Get her back to the house."

"I'm not leaving without you," Seren said.

"Yes, you are. Now go! Go!"

I could hear their footsteps rushing down the hall to the back staircase, where Cyrus signaled for them to follow. As they descended the stairs, I prayed they would reach the car safely. I ran down the front stairs and stood at the metal door, listening to determine if anyone was on the other side. Someone touched my shoulder, and I jerked around.

A woman's ghost smiled at me and said, "Who are you? I've never seen you here before."

She appeared to be in her thirties with blond hair. One of the patients lingered beside her, her eyes bulging with a wild look. She was exactly what I needed.

I said, applying a bit of emphasis.

"Can you help me? I need to find out if anyone is in the lobby or at the counter. Can you check?"

The spirit said, "Sure, I can do that," and she disappeared.

Other ghosts started moving toward me.

Whispers filled the air.

'*Help us.*'

'*Free us.*'

'*Please—before it's too late.*'

I stared at them, realizing they were being held here and wanted to move to the other side. I had to free them.

The first ghost reappeared and said with a broad smile, "The staff are still busy in the kitchen."

I said, "Thank you."

I unlocked the metal door and rushed to the counter. I could hear Seren's voice calling my name through the speaker.

I flipped the switch on the microphone and whispered, "I'm unlocking the door."

I toggled switch number four.

Seren urged, "Hurry!" through the speaker.

I reopened the metal door and returned to the patient area. More patients were acting agitated and milling around.

I said, "I'm going to help you all."

The ghosts became excited and shimmered in and out of view. Several patients didn't understand what was happening and grew more restless. I had to move quickly before the staff left the kitchen. I took two deep breaths, calmed myself, and performed the hand and arm movements to open the tunnel of light to the other side. I carved the air with my hands, forming a shimmering circle of light. The passage irised open—glowing gold, pulsing with unseen energy.

A ripple passed through the room. Some of the poor people gasped.

How could they detect it? I didn't understand how they could perceive the tunnel; perhaps it was all the drugs they were being given that opened their third eye.

Spirit families from the other side gathered in the tunnel, their arms outstretched to welcome the ghosts. The spirits held at the Lockwood Institution, probably by the Lwa curses, were now free to enter the passage and be with their loved ones. They moved down the tunnel of light, which then closed.

Two of the more lucid patients approached me and said, "Thank you."

I shouted to everyone, "I'm going to get you all out of here!"

Some understood what I said, but most didn't.

I opened the metal door and could still hear loud noises and shouting coming from the kitchen. Rushing over, I flipped the number one switch before running out the front door, down the stairs, and across the lawn toward the gate.

My heart pounded as I hurried to the gate. Behind me, a car door slammed, followed by the roar of an engine starting up.

I put on the steam and sprinted full out for the Toyota. The car engine hummed, and Seren stood next to the open door.

As I sped towards her, I shouted.

"I'm driving! Get in!"

She ran around to the passenger side and hopped in.

I skidded to a stop, crashing into the open door, jumped in, shoved it into first gear, and stomped on the gas pedal. The Toyota lurched forward, the momentum throwing Seren and Darlene back against their seats.

I yelled, "Buckle up! Someone's chasing us!"

SPECTRAL PROMISES

Chapter 29
Making Our Escape

Early the next morning, Cleetus leaned over the seat and shoved his brother.

"Wake up! It's your turn to watch."

Clive rubbed the sleep from his eyes and sat up.

He said, "I need to take a piss."

He walked toward the oak tree at the end of the parking lot. They had both agreed it would be the designated spot while they were there. He went behind the tree and relieved himself.

As Clive zipped up his pants, Cleetus shouted at him.

"Clive! Get back here!"

Clive ran back to the Lincoln parked in the middle of the lot. His brother waved his arm at him to get over there fast.

He hurried to his brother.

"What's wrong?"

Cleetus pointed.

"It's him!"

He pointed to a dark-haired man sprinting for the gate.

"Get in the damn car—NOW!"

The twin ran around to the other side and hopped in.

The big goon started the engine, and Clive frantically asked, "Shit! Where did he come from?"

"I don't know; he just came running out of the front door."

Like a shot, Cleetus backed up and drove down the gravel driveway toward the gate. The man was already outside the gate.

Clive remarked, "Man, that guy can move."

As they approached the front gate, a white Toyota sped down the dirt road, kicking up a cloud of dust and pebbles that obscured the vehicle as it careened out of sight.

Cleetus shouted, "That must be the white Toyota Blanche said those people came in!"

The Lincoln bounced along the dirt driveway, with the men inside jumping in their seats; the luxury vehicle wasn't made for this type of pavement. They reached the asphalt road and stopped, unsure which way the white car had gone, as the dust haze obscured their view. They spotted it further down the roadway on the left. The thug screeched the tires on the pavement in pursuit of the mystery man.

I stomped on the gas pedal, and the Toyota spun out on the wet grass before gaining traction and hitting the dirt road. Speeding down the driveway, the Corolla kicked up a massive cloud of dust and pebbles behind it.

"Cyrus!" I barked. "Eyes on the rear—tell me when they're too close to breathe."

Darlene looked around and shouted, "Who's Cyrus?"

Seren shouted back, "He's a ghost!"

Darlene's eyes went wide, but she didn't have a chance to ask anything more. The women were trying to buckle their seatbelts but were struggling because the car bounced on the dirt.

We reached the asphalt road, and I turned left, the tires screeching on the hard pavement.

Seren yelled, "What's going on?"

I loudly answered, "Guys were waiting in the lot. They saw me— now they're after us."

I slammed the stick into gear.

Seren shouted, "Who is it?"

"How am I supposed to know?" I shouted back, pushing the small Japanese vehicle to speeds it wasn't designed to handle.

I crammed it into the next gear, and the engine screamed in protest.

Cyrus whipped his head around.

"Shit—brown Lincoln. And they're closing in. FAST!"

Darlene said, "My husband must have put men on watch."

Seren asked, "Your husband, who's that?"

"Earnest Charbonnet Jr."

Seren paled.

"Oh my god."

"What?" I snapped, still focusing on the road.

"Charbonnet. Earnest Charbonnet. He's not just anyone—he's the biggest criminal kingpin of the Southeast. Detective O'Reilly told me about him."

I thought, 'Great, now we have a crime lord after us.'

I knew the county road was approaching quickly, but I had to return to a dirt road that the Lincoln couldn't navigate easily. I downshifted and slowed to turn right onto the county blacktop, as the Toyota's rear end skidded back and forth around the corner. I promptly shifted back through the gears to extract the most power from the small 4-cylinder engine.

I recalled that there were several farmers's access roads on the right. I slowed down and drifted around the corner onto one. The rear left tire hung a few inches over the drainage ditch. I floored it and got the vehicle straightened out.

Cyrus shouted and laughed, "The Lincoln missed the turn. They'll have to stop and back up."

I continued to accelerate down the farm road, and a T intersection loomed ahead. I grabbed the emergency brake handle, pulled it up, and executed a bootlegger turn. The rear end veered to the right, pushing us into a left turn around the corner.

I cried out, "Cyrus, do you see them?"

"No, maybe they gave up!" he shouted back anxiously.

A dust cloud appeared on the left up ahead. Someone was barreling down another dirt road toward us. Could it be them? We were getting closer, and whoever it was was approaching us quickly. I slammed the gas pedal to the floor. If only I had the Jaguar right now.

We zoomed past the dirt access lane, and I caught a glimpse of a vehicle in my peripheral vision.

Cyrus yelled, "It's them! They must have found another road."

I kept going.

He yelled again, "Shit, they're on our tail."

I shouted back, "Cyrus, do something."

He disappeared.

Another dirt roadway was coming up fast on the right. I yanked the wheel and pulled the emergency brake—gravel kicked up as we skidded sideways into another bootlegger turn, the Toyota's tires barely holding traction. I straightened the Corolla up and kept the pedal to the floor.

Cyrus popped back onto the back seat and burst into laughter.

"Ohhh, YEAH! They tried to follow but ended up ditching themselves sideways! They aren't getting out of there without a tow truck, and they'll have to hoof it to a phone."

I asked, "Was that because of you?"

"Yeah, I may have moved the steering wheel a little when it shouldn't have moved."

I laughed.

"Good work."

I kept going for a mile or so and then stopped to check on how the girls were doing. There had been several instances of screaming during the frantic chase, but I couldn't focus on that while driving. I glanced over at Seren and back at Darlene. Seren's knuckles were bone-white, still clutching the dashboard. Her breath came in short, panicked gasps.

I said, "It's okay; It's over."

I gently placed my hands on hers, "You can let go now."

She peered at me, her eyes still wide with fear. Tears began to well up. She released the dashboard, grabbed my shirt, and buried her face in my chest, crying. I wrapped my arms around her and rubbed her back. I liked how this felt; I always want to protect this woman.

I peeked over the seat back at Darlene. She seemed to have managed the harrowing trip better. She was breathing heavily, but not in the same way as Seren.

I asked, "How are you?"

She said shakily.

"I'm okay. I haven't been through something like that since I was a teenager."

She smiled back at me.

Seren looked up and asked, "How do you know how to drive like that?"

"Walter taught me. He used to be a dirt track race driver."

She smiled and sat back.

I asked, "Is everyone okay?"

They both nodded.

"Alright, let's head home."

I followed the dirt road, and we eventually returned to a county road. From there, we found Highway 65 heading back toward Mobile.

I said, "Maybe we should go to a police station and report what we've discovered at Lockwood."

Darlene shook her head, eyes dark with fear.

"No. No cops."

"Why not?"

"Because Charbonnet owns them. Every last one. That's how he can get by with so much and never get caught. That and the voodoo protection spells."

Surprised, I asked, "Did you say protection spells?"

"Yeah. He has several voodoo priests and priestesses working for him."

"That's why you knew about Lwa."

"Yeah. Earnest told me about them."

I asked, "If the police are on the take, how can we protect you?"

"I have to go to the FBI. They have been trying to get Earnest for years. I can offer information about my husband's operations in exchange for witness protection for Johnny and me."

I winced and glanced at Seren, mouthing, 'Should we tell her?'

She shook her head no.

"All right, there should be an FBI office in Mobile."

"No, not Mobile. He has too many eyes in Mobile. We need to get out of Alabama."

"Alright. We'll keep going and try to get home."

Everyone nodded, still a little shaken by the harrowing event.

Chapter 30

Darlene's Story

Once we were out of Alabama, we all relaxed a bit. We stopped for gas, grabbed some food and drinks, and used the restroom. Darlene still wore the thin, crumpled hospital-style gown from Lockwood. She shivered in the crisp early morning air. Seren took her hand and led her to the facilities with a suitcase in tow.

When they came out, the escapee looked different—now in jeans, a sweatshirt, and sandals. Although still unwashed, her hair—pulled back into a ponytail—gave her a semblance of dignity. We returned to the Toyota and headed up US 84 while eating the sandwiches and sodas I bought for all of us.

As I drove, I considered the possibility that the guys in the Lincoln would continue to search for us or stop. I had to keep an eye out for cars following us.

Seren asked her, "How did you get involved with Charbonnet?"

Darlene said, "Oh, that's a pathetic story."

And she outlined her life with the crime lord.

Darlene Newman's father, Buford Newman, worked for the Charbonnet crime syndicate in Mobile. He primarily served as a bagman but did whatever Earnest Charbonnet commanded him to do.

Charbonnet took control of the Forester gang in Mobile amidst a storm of bullets and blood. By the time the dust settled, his gang was the only one left standing—and everyone recognized that Mobile now belonged to him.

One day, her father came home with a young man in his mid-twenties, Earnest Charbonnet Jr., who had started working for his father in Mobile. Everybody called him Ernie to differentiate him from his father. Buford was to show him the ropes.

At eighteen, Darlene fell hard for Ernie. He had the kind of looks that belonged in old gangster movies—tall, rugged, wavy dark brown hair, and scars that hinted at a dangerous life. But his smile captivated her, charming and effortless, making her feel like the most important person in the room.

The young criminal rose quickly through the ranks; he was smart and didn't take shit from anyone. If someone didn't pay up, he would have no hesitation in getting the money out of them, in whatever way it took. His father didn't play favorites, and his son had to work through the organization. Charbonnet was proud of the young criminal he raised.

After a few years, Charbonnet suffered a heart attack, and Earnest Charbonnet Jr. took over the crime syndicate. Ernie insisted that everyone now call him Earnest after that.

While this was happening, Darlene and Ernie continued to date regularly. She knew her boyfriend was high in the Charbonnet syndicate but didn't know exactly what his job involved.

After Ernie became the top dog, he asked her to marry him. She was overjoyed and said yes. This arrangement did not make her father happy. Buford was present during several of Charbonnet Jr.'s bouts of rage, striking out at anyone nearby. He didn't want his daughter exposed to such episodes.

Earnest told Darlene, "Don't worry, honey, I'll talk to your father."

That night, Earnest took her father out for a few drinks, and when they returned, her father said, "Darlene, I give you my blessing to marry Earnest."

Yet, he still didn't look happy. He appeared frightened.

Darlene pleaded, "Daddy, what's wrong?"

"Nothing, dear, nothing."

Yet, the fear persisted.

Two weeks later the couple married and Ernie bought a substantial colonial mansion in Mobile for his new bride. They moved in, and life was good for a while.

Then, one day, Earnest came home, and Darlene asked her husband, "Ernie?"

She was the only one allowed to call him that.

"What's wrong? You look so upset."

He scowled, anxiety evident on his face.

He explained. His voice grew louder and angrier as he spoke, "I found out that Joey Johnson, someone I thought I could trust, was operating behind my back and started his own protection racket without giving me a cut.

"I can't put up with anything like that. I had to show everyone they can't do that, so I killed him. I didn't want to do that. I liked the guy. Why did he make me do that?"

He picked up a vase full of flowers and threw it across the room. The ornate porcelain shattered on the floor. He stomped off to his office and slammed the door, causing the pictures on the wall to rattle.

Darlene felt sorry for her husband and followed him through the door.

"Honey, I'm sure Joey would have given you a cut. Did you ask him?"

Earnest prowled the room like a caged animal, his anger barely contained. At Darlene's question, something snapped. His eyes darkened—not with rage, but with something colder, crueler. The first blow came out of nowhere, a sharp crack against her cheek. Pain exploded across her face as she hit the floor before she could react to another strike. Then another.

"Don't you EVER question me!"

His voice was like steel, each word punctuated by the sting of his hand.

Darlene's body displayed several bruises from the beating. Ernie had never struck her before. She had never seen him so angry. She stayed away from him and went to bed early. Later that night, she felt him crawl under the covers and put his arms around her. She tensed up, unsure if he would strike her again.

He felt her reaction and said, "Darling, I'm sorry I hit you. I was just so angry I couldn't control it. I'll never do that again. Do you forgive me?"

Fear curled up her spine like a snake. If she said no, what would he do? What would he become?

"Yes," she whispered, her lips brushing his—not out of love, but survival.

He smiled, and they made love. The next day, a huge flower arrangement arrived at their house.

Earnest was in a good mood all day and told her that Nanny Adelice managed to calm him down. Adelice was his Nanny and practically raised Ernie after his mother had mysteriously disappeared. A voodoo priestess, Nanny Adelice, taught Ernie a great deal about the religion.

Rumors circulated that Charbonnet senior probably killed his wife and hid the evidence, but he told his son that she ran away and left him. Little Ernie was angry when he heard this and threw his toys around his bedroom. How could she leave him? He hated her for it.

Earnest explained to Darlene, "Nanny will be over in a few days with some of her followers. She's going to do a ceremony to protect me."

Darlene said, "Are you sure you want to get involved with things like that?"

Anger again flared in his eyes, and he yelled, "Why are you asking this? Don't you want me to be protected? You don't understand what kind of danger I'm in out there."

He stomped toward her and raised his hand to strike her. She cowered, holding her hands over her face, but he didn't hit her and marched out of the room. She didn't talk to him for the rest of the day.

Adelice and her entourage arrived two days later. They moved the furniture in the living room and performed the ancient ceremony. Darlene stayed quiet and watched the ritual from the back of the room. Afterward, Ernie was exceedingly happy, and the next day, he took his wife on a shopping spree.

Things were calm for the next few weeks. Ernie would come home and tell her about the many details within the organization. Drug deals, rival gangs being killed, etc. The information terrified her, but she never said anything. She just listened.

Then she began to feel unwell in the mornings and visited the doctor. She was pregnant. Earnest was ecstatic over the news.

She was three months pregnant when Earnest came home in another rage, throwing anything he could get his hands on around the room and breaking a few windows. He headed for his wife. She ran, and he cornered her in the laundry room. She cowered against the far wall.

He raised his hand to strike her, and she shouted, "Don't, the baby!"

A flash of recognition came over his face, and he stepped back, stomping out of the room. She stayed away from him for several days. It wasn't until weeks later that she discovered the reason for his anger. Adelice, the Nanny, had died of a heart attack.

Things with the organization started going downhill, and Earnest Charbonnet Jr. became increasingly paranoid. He hired several voodoo priests and priestesses to perform protection spells for him, and he also had them send curses to the Voodoo Imperatrice. He believed that she caused Adelice's heart attack.

Earnest was angry most of the time, but he never beat Darlene while she was pregnant. Her husband was overjoyed at the birth of his son and named him John after his grandfather.

Little Johnny was a quiet baby, thank God. There is no telling what the crime lord would have done if the baby had cried all the time. The boy was three the first time Earnest struck the child.

The crime lord came home in one of his foul moods, yelling and shouting, "How did they screw up the transfer? How did the New Orleans police find out?"

Johnny ran into the room, hearing his father, and hoped for a new toy that his father would often bring back after being away on long trips.

The boy cried out happily, "Daddy! Daddy!" and grabbed his father's leg.

The innocent child gazed up at his father, love in his eyes for the man, and said, "Where's my present?"

To Earnest, the boy's outstretched arms weren't love—they were need, expectation, another demand. His rage boiled over. With one shove, the child flew backward, his tiny body slamming against the wall with a sickening thud. A high-pitched wail pierced the air.

Earnest approached his wife and shouted, "Shut that kid up, or I'll shut him up!"

She picked up Johnny, ran to his bedroom, placed him in his bed, and told him, "Stay here, honey. Daddy's mad and does bad things when he's mad."

She closed the door and went downstairs. Now she was angry. How dare he hit their son?

She yelled, "Ernie, how can you hit Johnny? He's a child happy to see his father."

He turned and backhanded and punched her two more times with his fist, then tramped off to his office. Lying on the floor in pain, she could hear him screaming at someone over the phone.

The next day, Earnest went out to his car and returned with a toy truck. He had brought a toy for his son but forgot about it during his rage. Now frightened of his father, the boy stayed close to his mother, his right arm wrapped around her leg.

Earnest squatted to the boy's level and said, "Johnny, I'm sorry I hit you yesterday. Here, I bought you a new truck."

He handed it to the child. Johnny hesitantly took it. Earnest opened his arms for a hug. Darlene gently guided the child to his father. The boy peered up at his mother with frightened eyes and slowly moved to his father. Earnest hugged his son with what appeared to be genuine remorse for what he inflicted on the boy. She hoped this was the last time her husband harmed her son, but it wasn't.

Darlene received a letter from a lawyer stating that her Aunt Wilma died and left her the house in Shreveport, Louisiana. She remembered the happy times she had there as a child. Her father would drop her off to stay with his sister for two weeks each summer. The house always gave her a strange yet protected feeling.

Darlene called the attorney and discussed the particulars. He came out, papers were signed, and the old white Victorian house was officially hers. Darlene didn't know what to do with the house, but something told her not to tell Ernie about it. She hid all the paperwork and opened a bank account to cover the home expenses. Earnest never found out.

Earnest's bouts of rage and anger continued. Johnny would run to his room whenever the madness happened, having learned not to come out when his father was like this. A few times, his father burst into the boy's room yelling about a toy left somewhere in the house and would smack his son several times.

Once, Darlene jumped on his back, trying to make him stop hitting their son. Her crazed husband turned on her. She ran from the room, hoping he would forget about Johnny and pursue her instead. He did and she suffered bruises from head to foot from the beating. The following day, she found Johnny in his closet, asleep, curled in a ball, hugging Tommy Bear.

Over the next couple of years, these episodes happened regularly. She knew something must be done. Charbonnet would be gone for two weeks. It was her only window of opportunity to escape her husband's abuse.

Darlene emptied the checking account—every last cent. She purchased an old brown 1970 Ford Maverick from a no-questions-asked dealership, paid in cash, and parked it in a pay-by-the-day lot—a getaway car waiting in the shadows.

Two days later, when the housekeeper, maid, and gardener were all out for the night, she packed clothes for herself and Johnny in a small suitcase. Earlier in the day, she went to the store and bought coloring books, crayons, and food, which she stored in the used vehicle. That night, she rousted her son out of bed and took him, along with the two toys he insisted on bringing, to the Maverick. They drove to Shreveport and her Aunt Wilma's house.

She and Johnny stayed there for about a month. She knew that Charbonnet would be searching for her and Johnny. She showed the secret room to her son, just as Aunt Wilma had shown her when she was little. Wilma told her that back in the late 1800s, a series of murders occurred in Shreveport that were thought to be caused by witchcraft, but they weren't.

Members of the Newman family were witches then and created a secret room for protection. They also placed unique spells on the house to protect the family. Darlene instinctively knew nothing could happen to them as long as they stayed in the house.

She tried to make Johnny's situation as easy as possible. They always played games and were happy together, but she knew she had to do something. Charbonnet would eventually find them, which would be worse if he did. She didn't want to subject their son to even more trauma, so she decided she must talk to her husband and work things out.

She told Johnny he must stay in the house and not let anyone see him. She thought she would only be gone for a couple of days. She didn't know Charbonnet had issued a call across the entire Southeast to be on the lookout for her and the boy, along with pictures and a reward.

Darlene checked into a small motel.

She called her husband.

"Ernie, it's me."

"Where the fuck are you, and where's Johnny?"

"He's safe. He's with people who won't harm him."

She said this to attack Earnest's conscience if he had one.

"I want you and Johnny back here, now."

She could hear the anger in his voice.

"Ernie, I'm not coming back if you continue to beat your son and me. You have to stop. We can't take it. Do you know your son is terrified of you? Is that what you want?"

"No, you get in the car and come back here immediately! Do you hear me? You're not leaving me like my mother did," he screamed over the phone for several minutes.

The motel door exploded inward, slamming against the wall. Three men filled the doorway—hulking shadows, their faces impassive, their presence screaming danger. She knew they were men working for Charbonnet. She screamed and struggled, but they grabbed her and threw her into the backseat of a Lincoln Continental with one bald guy sitting on each side of her.

The third took the receiver and said, "Mr. Charbonnet? We've got her."

He listened.

"No, sir. The boy isn't here."

The crime lord gave further instructions.

"Yes, sir. We're on our way."

He hung up and closed the door.

They drove her back to the colonial mansion in Mobile. During the six-hour trip, all Darlene could think of was Johnny in the house by himself. Earnest stood at the front door when they arrived. Fists clenched, rage boiling in his eyes. The goons dragged her in and threw her on the sofa.

Charbonnet snapped, "Wait outside!"

He leaned in, glaring at his wife with icy intensity.

"Why did you leave? I gave you everything!"

She shot back, voice trembling with anger and hurt, "You beat Johnny and me. Is that how you show love?"

His jaw clenched, voice strained with frustration.

"You know my job's hard, and I get angry."

She held her ground, eyes blazing.

"You don't need to take it out on us—on a child."

After a tense beat, he finally whispered, "You're right. I shouldn't have done that. I'm sorry."

But she didn't believe him. She knew, deep down, it would happen again.

He looked around, desperation flickering in his eyes.

"Where's Johnny?"

She crossed her arms defiantly, resolutely.

"I'm not telling you."

Anger burned in his eyes as he struck her.

"Tell me where Johnny is. Right now!"

"Or what, are you going to kill me? Go ahead. Kill me. Then you'll never find out where he is."

He yelled in rage, swinging his fist several times until she was unconscious.

Charbonnet shouted at his men outside, "Get in here!"

The goons hurried into the house.

"Take her to Lockwood. Maybe after she's locked away there for a while, she'll talk."

The men picked her up and drove to the Lockwood Institute. Placed in a small room and shot up with various drugs, Darlene didn't understand what was happening.

People would come in regularly and ask, "Where's Johnny?"

All she would say is, "He's safe."

She lost all sense of time while under the influence, the drugs muddying her mind completely. When she overheard Martin, the orderly, talking about a vacation and how perfect June would be in Florida, her heart sank with horrifying clarity—her son was dead, unless he had somehow escaped, left the house, and sought help, that was her only weak hope. But if that had happened, Ernie would have known and come to gloat, like he always did. He never arrived. He never found Johnny. She knew her son was gone forever.

Distraught, she sobbed for days but never told any of the staff why she was crying. They didn't care. They didn't get paid to care.

Chapter 31
Hiding Out at Lake Blanc

Darlene's story answered several questions about what happened to her and Johnny and introduced another layer of complexity to the situation.

Darlene said, "But now I know that Johnny isn't dead. You said he's at your house. When did he leave my aunt's house? How did you find him?"

Seren glanced at me, and I nodded, knowing we should tell her about her son.

She looked back at Darlene and said, "I have bad news. Johnny's dead and has been for over four years."

Darlene's eyes filled with tears, her fists clenched, her voice rising in anguish, "Then why did you say he was at your house?!"

Seren continued, "Because his ghost is at Orion's house. People bought your house, and Johnny's spirit couldn't stay there. Orion took the boy's ghost to his house."

Her expression twisted, torn between confusion and grief.

"Johnny's a ghost?" she whispered.

I piped in, "Yes, he asked me to find you. That's what I do: find people and things."

"You spoke to him?"

Her voice broke on the verge of outright sobbing.

The psychic told Darlene about the Masons's call and the haunting of their new house. She explained the spirit wouldn't leave, but she knew it was a child. She called Orion because he's a ghost expert and can see, speak, and carry ghosts inside him. He took her son's spirit to his house and promised Johnny that he would find you.

Darlene asked, tears still coursing down her cheeks.

"Are there other people there who can see him?"

I said, "Yes, my ghostly family. They are watching him and taking care of him. I also put a protection Lwa around him."

"A Lwa? So, you're also a voodoo priest?"

"Not exactly, but the Lwa Spirit God Duke Shamedi gave me powers to call and use Lwa. Oh, and my grandmother is the Voodoo Imperatrice."

"Your grandmother is the Voodoo Imperatrice?" Darlene said incredulously. "She's the one who has been causing Ernie and his father problems for years. That was one of the reasons he contracted all of those voodoo ceremonies to be performed to protect himself and his businesses."

This surprised me, and I asked, "Why's she after him?"

"Because Ernie's father killed her aunt and uncle. That's all I know."

I didn't say anything. I never knew my grandmother had an aunt and uncle who would have been my great-great-uncle and great-great-aunt. Staring out the window as I drove, I remembered her saying something about discovering why she did what she did. But when did she say that?

Seren asked, "Orion, you have a strange look. What's wrong?"

"I remember my grandmother saying I would want to help when I found out why she was doing the terrible things she was doing. It seemed like it was from a dream or something."

Red and blue lights flashed in the rearview mirror, sending a shock over me. Shit!

"Oh, shit, it's the police. Seren, Darlene, activate the glamour Lwa. That way, he'll only see me. If he works for Charbonnet, it might throw him off when there's only one guy in the car. Cyrus, when the cop stops, go to the patrol car and listen to what he reports."

Cyrus said, "You got it."

Darlene asked, "Oh, yeah. Who's Cyrus?"

She never had a chance to learn more about Cyrus amid all the excitement.

"I'll explain later."

I pulled over and took a couple of deep breaths to calm myself. I sat and watched through the side mirror as the cop slowly got out of the police car and sauntered over to the Corolla with his hand on the handle of his gun. I looked out the window as the police officer leaned down. He searched inside the Toyota but didn't see anything but me.

I innocently asked, "Hello, officer. Was I doing something wrong? Was I speeding?"

The officer glared at me and said, "Driver's license and registration."

I pulled out my wallet and removed my license. I leaned over, popped open the glove box, and found the registration sheet. I handed him the documents and again asked, "What's wrong, officer?"

He studied them and asked, "Why is the car registered to a Seren Griffyths?"

My pulse quickened. I hoped he'd accept this explanation.

"Oh, that's my girlfriend. My car's in the shop and she let me borrow hers for work."

"What's your job?"

"I find things. I was working for the Murphys in Montgomery. I found some lost jewelry."

He didn't seem to be listening to me and walked back to the police car, still studying the documents. I knew Cyrus was listening.

Seren whispered, "Girlfriend, huh?"

"It was the only thing I could think of," I whispered.

Darlene said, "I hope he isn't working for my husband."

Cyrus popped back in.

"They're looking for a white Toyota with one male and one, maybe two females. I think he's going to let you go."

I exhaled and relaxed a little as the police officer returned.

He handed me the license and registration and said, "Watch your speed."

With a big smile, I said, "Thank you, officer. I will."

My hands shook as I tucked the license away and pulled onto the road, carefully using my turn signal and keeping my speed below the limit.

The ladies removed the glamour.

Darlene said, "That was close."

I said, "A little too close. I've got to drop you girls off somewhere. I have a bad feeling about that. Darlene, you didn't hear what Cyrus said. They're looking for a white Toyota with one male and two females. To answer your previous question, Cyrus is a ghost. A friend of mine. He's sitting next to you."

When I said this, she moved away slightly and peered at the space beside her.

I explained further, "He scouted out Lockwood before we broke you out. That's how we knew where you were."

"Do you always have ghosts around you?"

Her voice was shaking slightly. She leaned closer to the car door away from the side Cyrus sat. The idea of a ghost being nearby frightened her.

I had always had ghosts nearby. Not being around living people, as is normal, I often forget that this idea terrifies most of them.

"There for a while, I used to, but now, only when I want them nearby. I brought Cyrus along because he's experienced in assisting me with several Finding Jobs. Anyway, those guys saw only me leaving Lockwood. Eventually, they will start looking for just me. I'm going to drop you two off at Lake Blanc. Seren, when you get there, call Andy Butler. His phone number is on my card. You still have that, don't you?"

"Yes, I've got it."

She picked up her purse and rifled through it, pulling out the business card.

"Tell him what's going on. Then, call the FBI. I'll continue driving toward Shreveport and keep them away from you two. If they catch me, they can only hold me for trespassing on Lockwood property."

Darlene said, "If the police are working for Charbonnet, they'll hand you over to his men. There's no telling what they'll do."

Seren said with concern, "Orion, you should remain at Lake Blanc with us and wait for the FBI."

"No, I want Charbonnet's men as far away from you two as possible. I can take care of myself. Cyrus, you stay with Seren. Help however you can. Keep a lookout for any strange people."

Cyrus said, "But, Orion, I want to be with you to help you."

"No! Stay with her."

I put some force behind my words, not wanting to argue with him.

I wanted to muster any advantage I could to protect the woman I cared for. Having Cyrus nearby as a lookout would be beneficial.

He sat back.

"Okay."

It took another half an hour to reach Lake Blanc. When we arrived, Seren exited the Corolla, leaned back in, and said, "Orion, be careful. I don't want to lose you. Something bad is going to happen. I can feel it."

I glanced back at her and recognized her anguish. She was on the verge of tears. I didn't want to lose her either.

"I will."

She shut the door, and I headed back for the highway.

Seren and Darlene watched as the filthy vehicle, covered in dark-brown dirt from their harrowing race over the farmer's dirt roads, rapidly moved down the access road.

Seren thought, 'He should have stayed here with us. Something terrible is going to happen to him.'

Darlene said, "Seren, let's get a cabin."

The psychic looked at the woman and nodded. She had a bad feeling. Orion was in danger.

The two women entered the office. Tabitha Blanc sat behind the front counter as usual. She stood and immediately produced a big smile.

"Ah, you're back so soon and you brought a friend. Where's Mr. Labauve?"

She said, "He has to take care of some business. He'll be back later."

She thought to herself, 'I hope so.' Yet, the sense of danger continued to envelope her.

The resort owner asked, "So, two cabins?" with a note of curiosity.

"No, one two-bedroom."

Tabitha smiled.

"Sure thing. I'll give you the same cabin. You just missed dinner. But there are some sandwiches available in the refrigerator."

While Seren registered, Darlene pulled sandwiches and sodas from the cooler. They walked to the cabin, where Darlene practically fell onto the couch.

"I'm exhausted, but I need a shower, and we have to call the FBI."

The psychic said, "Take a shower. I'll contact Andy Butler."

"Who's Andy Butler?"

"He's Orion's business partner and lawyer. I've never met him. But if Orion says he can help, I'm sure he can."

"Okay."

Darlene went to the bathroom, and the redhead returned to the resort's office to make the long-distance phone call.

She entered the office and beelined it for the telephone booth. While waiting for the operator to make the collect phone call, she mentally ran through what she wanted to tell the lawyer.

The phone rang, and a woman answered, "Andrew Butler Jr., attorney's office, how may I assist you?"

The operator said, "Will you accept a long-distance telephone call from Seren Griffyths on behalf of Orion Labauve?"

"Yes."

"Hello. My name is Seren Griffyths, and I need to speak with Andrew Butler immediately about Orion Labauve."

"Oh, Seren, it's me, Doris. What's wrong?"

The psychic's voice was frantic and agitated.

"I think Orion's in danger. He told me to contact Andy."

"Okay, I'll get Andy for you," Doris said urgently.

The secretary jumped up and entered Andy's office.

"Andy, Seren Griffyths is on the line. She says Orion's in danger. She wants to speak with you."

"Put her through and listen in."

"You know I will when it involves Orion," the secretary said.

The witch punched the button to transfer the call and held the receiver to listen to the conversation.

The attorney answered the phone, "Hello, this is Andrew Butler."

"Hello, I'm Seren Griffyths, and Orion told me to call and let you know what's happening."

"Go on."

She outlined everything that had happened to them since they left the mansion. She told him how worried she was and about the possible danger he was in.

Andy said, "Thank you for telling me this. You're right. He should have stayed with you two at the resort and waited for the FBI, but he never listens to anyone. I'm getting on a plane to Mobile and renting a car. It'll probably take a few hours before I arrive. Don't go anywhere."

"Alright. Thank you," Seren said to the attorney.

She stood looking down at the floor. The sense of impending doom surrounding Orion grew with each minute. What else could she do?

Detective Brian O'Reilly popped into her head. Perhaps he could help. She knew he wasn't on Charbonnet's payroll, what with everything he told her about the crime lord. She made another collect long-distance telephone call.

Before she could say anything after the call went through, the detective immediately shouted, "Seren, what the hell's going on?"

Seren's voice broke, and she began to cry, "Brian, I need help, and I don't know what to do."

"Okay. Calm down. Tell me what's going on. Is it that weird guy, Orion?"

"Yes! He's in danger, and I don't know what to do."

"Tell me what's happening."

Seren proceeded to tell the detective about what occurred over the past few days, how they helped Darlene Newman escape from a mental institution called the Lockwood Institute, controlled by Earnest Charbonnet Jr., that Darlene Newman was Charbonnet's wife, about the car chase, and how they were waiting at the Lake Blanc Resort in Mississippi and were going to call the FBI.

"Darlene is ready to give state's evidence against her husband, but she'll only speak with the FBI because she says most of the police around here are on Charbonnet's payroll."

The detective shouted, "Holy fuck. You've really stepped into a shit storm. I told you to watch out for this guy. I knew he was trouble."

"I'm going to call the FBI after I get off the phone with you."

"No, I'll call them. They may not believe you. But if I call and say I have a credible informant, since I'm another law enforcement officer they'll listen to me. Charbonnet is on their hot list. They'll be all over this so fast your head'll spin."

"But what about Orion? He took off in my car, trying to take them off Darlene's trail."

Her voice shook with each word.

"I'll let the FBI know that. Give me your car's make, model, and license number."

Seren gave him the information and the address for Lake Blanc, and they ended the call. Seren turned and saw Tabitha standing at the front desk, her eyes huge and amazed at what she overheard.

She begged, "Please don't say anything to anyone about what you heard."

"No, honey. I won't. I know people who have been fucked over by Charbonnet. I hate that sicko. So the FBI will be coming here?"

Seren nodded.

Tabitha commented, "It'll probably be a couple of hours before they arrive from Mobile or maybe Jackson. I'll call Vincent back in. Those guys will be here for hours and will be hungry and thirsty."

"Don't tell Vincent it's the FBI. Just say a big party is coming in late."

"Sure thing, honey."

She picked up the phone and called the resort's chef.

Seren returned to Cabin Five and discovered Darlene sitting on the couch, her right leg bouncing up and down nervously.

"What took you so long? I was getting ready to head to the office, thinking something had happened to you. I need to call the FBI."

"Don't worry about it. I called a detective friend in Shreveport, who I know isn't on Charbonnet's payroll, and told him what's going on. He's calling the FBI. He said they were more likely to believe him than us."

Darlene sat back, relaxing a little.

"Thank God."

"I also called Andy Butler, Orion's attorney. He's coming here, but it will likely be a few hours before he arrives. Tabitha said it would take a couple of hours for the FBI to arrive from Mobile or Jackson."

Darlene said, "In that case, I'll take a nap while we wait for everyone to get here."

"I'll stay up. I couldn't sleep if I wanted to; I'm too worried about Orion. I know he's in trouble."

"Don't worry so much, honey. Orion seems like he can take care of himself."

"You don't understand. I'm psychic; I read the tarot cards before we left. They warned us of danger. I can feel it, and it's worsening each minute."

Darlene nodded and shuffled off to the bedroom.

Seren gazed out the sliding glass door at the lake reflecting the moon. She recalled being here just a few days ago, in this exact cabin, and how Abelard's personality seemed to take over Orion. He carried her to the bedroom and they made love as Orion and Seren, Abelard and Chloe, and Duke Shamedi and Bridette the Fairy Queen. The experience was incredible, but Orion became upset afterward, feeling he took her without her permission, even though she told him the opposite, that she wanted to be with him.

She knew he longed to be with her, but he feared what his grandmother, the Voodoo Imperatrice, might do to her, which was what held him back. If they survived this ordeal—no, once they survived it—she needed to find a way to help Orion move past his fear and embrace a more fulfilled life, even if it meant they couldn't be together.

A sudden, searing pain lanced through the back of her skull. Seren gasped, gripping the table for balance. Orion. Something-or someone—had struck him hard.

Andy Butler thought, 'Oh, my God, Orion has somehow gotten involved with the Charbonnet Syndicate.'

As an attorney, although not a criminal lawyer, he had heard horror stories of the gang's criminal activities from some of his legal associates. Now, they may be after Orion. He was sure Orion had no idea what he was up against.

Andy yelled, "Doris, get me a flight to Mobile and rent a car!"

Doris shouted back, "Working on it!"

Andy called his wife, Vivian, and told her he had to go to Mobile to help Orion. He didn't give her any details about it because he didn't want to worry her. His voice was firm, and his determination to assist Orion was unwavering.

Vivian didn't ask questions. She never did.

"Just be careful," she said.

Andy promised he would—and hoped he wasn't lying.

He hurried to the closet and grabbed the extra clothes he stored at the office in case of an emergency. This habit started when he was forced to work with the Voodoo Imperatrice, and his stomach would often get so upset that he regularly soiled his clothes by vomiting. He pulled out his small overnight bag and began packing quickly.

Doris rushed into her boss's office.

"Okay, I have you on the next flight with Republic Airlines to Mobile. It leaves in an hour and a half. You should be able to make it. And you have a car rental with Hertz."

She handed him the note page with the reservation numbers. He stuffed it into his jacket pocket.

He looked at Doris and said, "Can you believe this?"

"With Orion, yes, I can. Call me when you arrive."

She rubbed the crystal around her neck, a nervous habit, hoping Orion was okay.

Andy saw her rubbing the crystal and moved his hand over the one she had given him for protection. He always wore it beneath his undershirt, despite having a protection Lwa that Duke Shamedi assigned to watch over him.

"I will."

The attorney hurried down the stairs, jumped into his new Cadillac, which he had recently bought after Orion had significantly increased his retainer, and sped off to Shreveport.

Arriving at the airport, Andy paid for the flight and ran through the facility to catch the plane, his chest heaving from the exertion.

The last passenger to board Republic flight 282 to Mobile, Andy, plopped into his seat, panting from the run, and quickly buckled his seatbelt. Luckily, the trip would only take an hour and a half to

Mobile, but then he faced at least an hour's drive to this Lake Blanc resort, wherever that was.

SPECTRAL PROMISES

Chapter 32
Captured

The Toyota engine roared as I sped toward Jackson, Mississippi. My pulse raced nearly as fast as the wheels beneath me. It had been about half an hour since I dropped off Seren and Darlene at Lake Blanc, but my mind was still reeling. I couldn't shake the fear that something might happen to Seren—my protectiveness deepened after the car chase.

When she buried her face in my chest, crying, my heart ached. All I wanted was to stop, hold her close, and shield her from everything. She trembled from the terror of it all. I gently rubbed her back, trying to soothe her, feeling the raw intensity of the moment—every second was crushing, yet somehow perfect and natural in its chaos.

A line of flashing lights ahead snapped me out of my thoughts. My pulse quickened. I hit the brakes, scanning the road. There was a blockade. Cop cars lined the highway in front, their lights dazzling in the darkness. My stomach clenched—more flashing lights appeared in my rearview mirror. They had found me.

I slowed the Corolla and stopped in front of the police cars. Two officers stood in front of their vehicles, their guns drawn and aimed at me. Three more patrol cars arrived behind me and parked sideways on the highway, blocking my way. I sat and waited, afraid that if I moved, someone might shoot. Through the rearview mirror, I saw the police officers standing behind my car pull their guns. My stomach tightened with dread, and I raised my hands.

The door yanked open with a screech. A tall, thin, dark-haired cop loomed over me, gun aimed.

"Out! Now!" he snapped.

I slowly stepped out with my hands raised. Another pudgy officer put away his gun, seized my right arm, forced it behind my back, and roughly pushed me toward a police car. He slammed my face onto the back of the vehicle and cuffed me. I stood there. My anger simmered beneath the surface. I noticed a large, bald, muscular man with facial scars who wasn't wearing a police uniform.

He came up to me and shouted, "Where is she?"

"Where's who? What's this all about? Why are you doing this?" I shouted back.

He smacked me. My face stinging from the blow, I angrily lunged at him.

Then something hit me on the back of the head. Lights flashed in my eyes. My knees turned liquid and I fell to the asphalt.

Now two bald guys who appeared to be the same stared at me lying on the ground. Was I seeing double? Black spots formed in my vision, and I couldn't keep my eyes open. I fell unconscious.

I couldn't tell how long I'd been unconscious. Awakening, I found I was bound to a cold metal chair, the handcuffs biting into my wrists. A throbbing pain blazed through my head, making it hard to focus my eyes. Blinking desperately, I struggled to steady myself.

One bald guy yelled at the other.

"Cleetus, you hit him too hard. He should be awake by now."

Cleetus glared at me and said, "He's awake."

The first bald thug grabbed my shirt, shook me violently, and shouted, "Where is she?"

He shook me so violently my head flopped about, causing flashes of light in my eyes, and then everything went black again. When I awoke the second time, the two guys were still arguing about how hard I had been hit.

A third deep voice with an authoritative tone shouted, "Shut up!"

My head hung down; it seemed to weigh a hundred pounds. I couldn't raise it. Steps approached, and a firm hand grabbed my face, pinching my cheeks, and forcefully raised it.

He leaned down, leered at me, and said, "Where's my wife, Mr. Labauve?"

He was in his early forties with a few scars on his face. His thick brown hair had streaks of gray at the temples. He was definitely the guy in charge. Anger and danger radiated from his piercing eyes.

I slurred, "How am I supposed to know where your wife is when I don't even know who you are?"

He let go of my face and walked away.

One of the bald guys grabbed my shirt and began smacking me across my face, saying, "You don't talk to Mr. Charbonnet like that, you fucking asshole."

Once again, my face was white, hot, and stinging. My ears were ringing. Angry, I kicked out, smashing my foot into the goon's balls. He gave a loud groan, backed away, and doubled over in agony.

The other guy jumped over and proceeded to punch me in the face several times. My face was a ball of pain, with lights exploding in my left eye as the thug pummeled me, and Charbonnet chuckled. I couldn't think straight; the beating so rattled my brain. I blacked out again.

I woke up gasping after they threw a bucket of cold water on my face.

One of the bald goons said, "See, Clive. I told you that would wake him."

With the water dripping off my face, I said, "Thanks for the shower."

Clive pulled his fist back to hit me again, but Charbonnet put out his hand and grabbed his fist as it moved in for another blow. My mouth filled with the coppery taste of blood, and I spat it onto the floor, just missing Charbonnet's shoes.

The thug pulled his arm back to start again, but his boss stopped him and said, "Mr. Labauve, now you know who I am. Where's my wife?"

"I don't know. She went with the FBI," I whispered, barely able to form the words with my jaw not functioning correctly, and pain shooting across my head with each movement.

"The FBI?" he shouted, his brow furrowed with anger.

I continued, "She called them, and they picked her up."

I knew this was the plan, but I wasn't entirely sure if she had left with them.

Charbonnet stomped to the other side of the room, running his right hand through his hair. Upset by this information, his face distorted in anger and rage.

Sweat dripped down my back. I gazed around the place with my good eye, the other unable to focus correctly, and realized I was being held in a Quonset hut metal barn with various types of farm equipment scattered about.

Charbonnet said, "That doesn't matter; I still have my protection. That should keep them off my back, no matter what she tells them."

I heard this and remembered Darlene's words about his voodoo protection spells. I sharpened my gaze, peering more intently at the criminal kingpin through my Lwa sight. There they were—about twenty Lwa of various colors, shapes, and sizes, swirling around him like a protective aura. He was right; with that much protection, nothing could touch him. A surge of awareness and intimidation washed over me as I realized the formidable barrier surrounding the crime lord.

Charbonnet stood with his back to me, obviously thinking. Then he turned.

"Okay, where's Johnny?" he asked.

I told him the truth.

"He's dead."

"No, he's not. I know he's alive. I've been assured."

"No, he's dead."

Charbonnet nodded his head to the bald goon, and the creep proceeded to beat me in the chest and stomach. The blows forced air from my lungs and I gasped. A rib cracked with white-hot agony coursing through the left side of my chest. I let out a loud groan and oomph with each blow. The gorilla smiled as he pounded in the same area again.

The crime boss yelled, "Stop!"

He moved toward me and said calmly, "Now, Mr. Labauve, this can go on for a long time. You'd better tell me where my son is."

In short gasps, I answered, "I told you he's dead. He's been dead for over four years. He died of starvation when your wife didn't come back to get him."

I was having a hard time breathing; each breath produced flashes of agony.

The crime lord said in a tone that revealed his uncertainty about whether I was telling the truth, "But she said he was with people taking care of him."

"She lost track of time from all the drugs they had her on at Lockwood. She didn't realize she had been there for over a month. When she was able to think a little, she realized Johnny was dead. She would have told you if you hadn't placed her on those drugs. After that, it didn't matter; she continued to let you think he was alive, knowing it would drive you crazy."

Charbonnet's anger increased as I outlined this. Veins bulged on his neck and forehead, and he began panting. He picked up a can of something on a table and threw it across the room, where it hit the wall, the lid popped off, and white paint splashed down the corrugated metal panel.

Upon seeing this, I thought, 'Oh shit! Now, I've done it. He's probably going to kill me.'

The goon I kicked in the balls cracked his knuckles, a slow, deliberate sound.

"Want me to break him some more, boss? He's got plenty left to snap."

At that moment, a young black man with a short afro entered the barn and whispered something to Charbonnet Jr.

He glared in surprise, but then a broad smile spread.

"Oh, really."

"The messenger nodded and left.

Well, Mr. Labauve, I have just been informed that you are the grandson of the Voodoo Imperatrice. Is this true?"

Now it was my turn to be surprised. I wasn't sure how to respond. Darlene told Seren and me that my grandmother has been after the Charbonnets for years. That must be one reason he has so many Lwa around him. She must really scare him. Maybe I can use this.

I slurred, "Yeah, you'd better let me go or else you'll be in for it from her."

I don't think I came across as very convincing. I'm not used to playing games with people like this.

"Are you trying to scare me? That's funny."

Charbonnet chuckled.

"Your grandmother has been trying to get my father and me for decades and hasn't succeeded yet."

His face turned red, and he shouted, "Why are you here? Why did you take my wife? Did your grandmother think she could hold my wife to get to me?"

I didn't know what to say.

All I could say was, "No, she didn't send me. She doesn't even know I'm here."

"I don't believe you. Break a finger."

He pointed at Cleetus with a slight smile.

I struggled and kicked out, attempting to push them away. The two thugs came at me from the side. One held my hand down, and the other grabbed my right index finger. He pulled it sideways until it snapped. I screamed at the top of my lungs.

In a calm voice, Charbonnet asked, "Now, Mr. Labauve, why did the Voodoo Imperatrice send you to kidnap my wife?"

Tears were coursing down my cheeks. My heart pounded in my broken digit, and with each beat, pain rushed through my hand and up my arm.

"She didn't send me. We don't talk. I hate the bitch."

The words burst out of my mouth with vehemence and loathing. Here I was being tortured again because of her, because of the things she had done. Situations I had no involvement with. All I wanted to do was help a kid find his mother. Why am I always being blamed for something I didn't do? People or entities were constantly using me for their personal agendas. Things that I care nothing about.

Charbonnet shouted back, "Then why did you kidnap my wife?"

I told him, "Because Johnny asked me to find his mother."

"Oh, so now you are saying he's alive."

"No, he's dead, but he's a ghost. His spirit asked me to find her."

Charbonnet pursed his lips in frustration and said, "He's lying, break another."

My eyes bulged with fear, knowing the pain that was coming. The big goon smiled and broke my middle finger. Again, I screamed from the agony that ran through my hand. This time, I openly sobbed from the pain. My head hung, tears dropping onto my jeans.

"Mr. Labauve, there are eight more fingers to go through if you don't tell me the truth," the kingpin explained calmly.

I said, pleadingly, "I am telling you the truth. I can see and speak with ghosts. I talked to Johnny."

"On the other hand," Charbonnet said this as casually as if he were ordering a steak at a restaurant.

The goons switched sides and places as one of them said, "It's my turn this time."

I struggled again, yelling, "No! No!"

And the index finger on my left hand went sideways. Pain exploded in my hand. My vision swam. A rushing sound filled my ears—like water, like static. My body sagged, darkness swallowing me.

From the farmhouse's porch, Sammy could hear Mr. Charbonnet in the barn swearing a storm because the prisoner passed out again. When the call came in that Orion Labauve was the Voodoo Imperatrice's grandson, it shocked Sammy. He remembered Orion, 'Ory,' from the time he ran away and stayed for a month at the plantation house. He hated what was happening to Ory and wanted to do something to help him.

He decided to tell the boss that he knew Orion from when they were little and friends. Maybe if he could get Ory to tell him the truth, and they would stop beating on him. He entered the barn and explained how he thought he could get his friend to tell him the truth.

"Okay, kid, go ahead, and if you get the truth out of him, you'll get a bonus."

Sammy smiled.

"Thank you, boss."

Sammy Hammond entered the small room where Orion was being kept. The room had been the farmhand's room before Mr. Charbonnet bought the place to use as a personal hideout. The room contained an old metal bed with a thin mattress, one chair, a toilet in the corner, and a deep, old washbasin. An ancient naked-lady poster from a girly magazine hung on the wall beside the bed.

The young man gasped, seeing his childhood friend lying in horrible shape. Blood was all over his face, most of the left side bruised and swollen. He was breathing in short gasps. His broken fingers were at angles they shouldn't be, swollen, black, and blue.

Sammy found an old towel hanging on a nail next to the sink. He took the cloth, wetted it with water, and proceeded to wash the blood from Orion's face. His friend started to moan and woke.

I don't know how long I was out this time, but someone called my name, "Ory, Ory. Wake up."

I woke, and the black guy who brought the information about my grandmother leaned over me. Seeing him close now, he seemed familiar.

He said, "Ory, sit up and have some water. Here."

I lay in an old bed. He held a metal cup with water. I tried to move, but every part of my body screamed in pain. I moaned as he helped me up to drink. I greedily gulped, tasting blood mixing with water in my mouth.

The young man said, "Ory, you have to tell him the truth, or he'll continue to hurt you."

Why was he calling me Ory, as if he knew me?

"Do I know you?"

"Don't you remember me? I'm Sammy Hammond. I stayed at your place for about a month when we were little."

"Sammy, that's you. Huh, I was just talking about you the other day. You're working for Charbonnet?"

"Yeah, I make decent money. I have to care for my mother, she's sick. But Ory, you have to tell him the real story."

"I am telling him the truth. Everything I said was the truth."

"You mean you really can see and talk to ghosts?"

"Yes, it's all true."

"I don't know what he's going to do with you. I heard him say he didn't want to kill you yet."

As he said this, I became dizzy, my vision peered down a tunnel. The tunnel kept getting smaller until blackness closed in from the sides, and I was out again.

Sammy was convinced beyond any doubt that Ory was telling him the truth. There was no reason for him to invent such a fantastic story. He remembered the old plantation they stayed at, its eerie atmosphere lingering in his mind—like someone was watching them. He remembered Ory talking alone multiple times, with no one in sight. Ory must have been talking to ghosts even back then, and Sammy couldn't shake the feeling that something unseen was always lurking just out of view.

When Sammy exited the room after speaking with Orion, Charbonnet was waiting for him, crouched on a wooden chair, nervously wringing his hands.

The crime lord stood and asked, "Well, boy, did you get the truth?"

"Yes, sir. He really is telling the truth. He really can see and talk to spirits, and your son's ghost asked him to find his mother."

Charbonnet stood there, surprised by this revelation. He could tell that the young man believed what he said.

He thought, 'Oh, well, Labauve is still the Voodoo Imperatice's grandson. I may be able to take advantage of this. It makes sense that he would have special abilities, being the grandson of one of the most powerful voodoo priestesses in the Southeast. I'll keep him around for a while.'

"Okay, Sammy. You go on home to your mamma and tell her hi for me."

"Yes, sir. I will. Thank you, sir."

Sammy walked away with a smile, got in his old red Ford, and headed home. His mother would be shocked to see him so early.

Charbonnet crossed his arms. A slow grin curled his lips.

"Well, well… Looks like you might be useful after all, Mr. Labauve. But, damn, I want more information now!" and stomped out of the barn.

Chapter 33

The FBI Arrives

Seren rubbed the back of her head, the ache a ghostly echo of Orion's pain. Pacing the floor, she fought the growing anxiety, unsure what to do.

Cyrus said, "Why don't you calm down?"

"I would love to, but I know something has happened to Orion. Can't you sense it?"

Her voice trembled.

"No, I think he's too far away for me to feel what's happening to him."

He stared off as if trying to sense Orion somehow.

Seren sat on the sofa, wanting to do something, anything. Concern and anxiety etched on her face.

Cyrus peered at Seren and said, "You really care about him. Don't you?"

"Yes, I do. At first, I was afraid of what I was feeling because I thought it was actually Chloe's feelings from a past life, but now I believe these emotions are mine. The day before I left the shop, the Fairy Queen visited me and told me that Orion would be extremely important to me. She also explained to me that he had emotional issues and was reluctant to start a relationship."

"Boy, that's on the nose. He's had a hard life."

"Can you tell me about his life? I know it'll never come out of his mouth."

"No doubt about it. If Orion finds out I told you, he might actually force me to cross over."

"I won't tell him. I'll say I had a vision."

Cyrus smiled and said, "Okay. Where should I begin?"

The ghost stood, staring at the floor, weighing which parts of Orion's past to reveal. He decided and outlined a few of the worst things that had happened since Orion was eleven and he started staying with the boy when he possessed the amulet. He had heard of a few other incidents from his early childhood from the other ghosts, and he told her about those as well.

Seren listened with rapt attention to the incredible story Cyrus shared, her heart aching fiercely for Orion and the harrowing life he endured. She understood why he was so reticent—why he kept others at arm's length, terrified to let anyone get close. Determined to offer genuine reassurance, she desperately wanted to be a steady presence for him, an unwavering constant amid his turbulent world, someone he could finally confide in whenever he needed. He only opened himself slightly to her, revealing a fragile vulnerability, the walls surrounding his heart mostly remained intact. Breaking down those barriers would require time—perhaps longer than she hoped—and some might never be crossed.

The psychic stared out the sliding glass window; someone was coming, several people were coming. She hoped it wasn't Charbonnet's men. Her determination to rescue Orion was unwavering, and she was ready to face any challenge.

A heavy knock pounded through the cabin, rattling the walls. Seren froze—another knock—louder this time. A chill crept through her body.

Then a voice, firm and commanding: "Federal agents. Open up."

She opened the door, and four tall men in dark suits stood on the cabin's small front porch.

The one in front asked, "Are you Seren Griffyths?"

"Yes."

Her voice quivered. Were they really federal agents?

"Ma'am. We're with the FBI."

They each held out badges.

"A detective, Brian O'Reilly, called and said that the wife of Earnest Charbonnet Jr. is with you."

She exhaled with relief; they were finally here.

"Yes, sir. She's here. Come in."

The agents entered and searched around, verifying that nothing dangerous was visible.

She said, "Darlene is taking a nap. I'll get her."

The psychic went to the bedroom and woke the woman.

"Darlene, the FBI is here."

Darlene opened her eyes and groggily said, "Good."

She stretched and said, "That was the best sleep I've had in years."

After rubbing the sleep from her eyes, she followed Seren into the living room. Entering the room, the psychic felt a sudden stinging as if she had been smacked on her face. Her eyes widened and watered; she knew Orion was experiencing this torture. She rubbed her left cheek, feeling the heat from the slap.

One of the federal agents noticed her surprised expression and her stroking her face.

He asked, "Are you okay?"

She answered, still staring off into the distance, "Yes, I'm fine."

The agent in charge stepped forward. He was in his late forties, with short-cropped brown hair speckled with gray and intense brown eyes.

He shook Darlene's hand, "Nice to meet you, Ma'am; I'm Special Agent Henry Upton. I understand that you're Earnest Charbonnet Jr.'s wife.

"Yes, I'm Darlene Newman."

"You never took your husband's last name?"

His eyes narrowed with suspicion.

"No, he never wanted me to. He said it was to protect me."

He pointed to the couch for her to sit on and sat in the chair across from her.

"I understand that you want to provide State's evidence against your husband in exchange for witness protection."

"Yes, that's correct."

Darlene held her hands in her lap, trying to keep them from shaking, as she was nervous about what the next steps might entail. Her bravery in facing the FBI was evident.

"Well, ma'am, you may know that we have been trying to gather evidence against your husband for several crimes for years but have never been able to make anything stick. Why do you think the information you have will be sufficient to put him away?"

"I can tell you where to find his business information and documents at our house, where he hides them. I can provide the names of people he has either killed himself or ordered to be killed. Would something along those lines be acceptable?"

Agent Upton's eyes widened.

"Well, ma'am, that depends on if it all pans out."

Upton looked up at one of the other agents and said, "Bill, why don't you take Miss Griffyths into the other room and get her story?"

The young blond agent moved his hand towards the bedroom; Seren entered and sat on the bed. Her wrists ached as if being pinched by something, and her fingers tingled. She rubbed her wrists and flexed her fingers. The agent watched her doing this, wondering why.

He said, "I'm Agent Bill Harman. Can I ask you some questions?"

Seren answered, "Yes..."

He pulled a notepad and a pen from his jacket. She stared off, realizing that these unsettling feelings came from Orion. Harman could see that the beautiful redhead wasn't paying attention to him.

He cleared his throat and said, "Miss, can you tell me how you know Darlene Newman?"

Seren nodded and glanced up, "Oh, I'm sorry. I just met her earlier today when we broke her out of the Lockwood Institute for the Mentally Challenged."

This answer surprised the young agent.

"What do you mean, you broke her out? Out of a mental institution?"

"Yes, Orion figured out that she was at Lockwood, and we devised a plan to break her out."

"Who's that?"

This was the first time he heard the name.

"Orion Labauve. He finds people and things."

Seren paced the bedroom as she answered the questions.

"You mean he's a private detective?"

The agent watched the woman. Seren noticed him watching her. She thought, 'He's probably wondering why I'm so nervous. Should I tell him?'

"No, he gets hired to find people. He has a unique ability to track people down," she said.

"Who hired him to locate Mrs. Newman?

"Her son, Johnny. Well, not really her son, he's dead. We found his body in a house I was exorcising. There were drawings on the walls that Johnny made of his mother driving away."

The agent scribbled the information down.

"You said he was dead. Who killed him?" the agent asked.

"No one. He died over four years ago, of starvation," she answered.

"Why did you say her son asked Mr. Labauve to find his mother, if he's dead?"

"Because of the drawings on the walls—she was driving away, the boy in the picture crying. It was as if the drawings were speaking directly to Orion. He felt that she was still alive and somehow connected to him. He's psychic," she told the FBI man, emphasizing the word with a newfound resolve.

Orion's psychic abilities were different from hers, but no less real in his mind. In the South, believing in psychics is commonplace, so her words would resonate with many—yet for Orion, it was a truth that etched itself into his very soul.

The man frantically wrote everything in his notepad.

A sharp pain lanced through Seren's jaw. She gasped, clutching her face. She staggered, nearly losing her balance.

"Orion—he's being hit," she gasped.

Agent Harman grabbed her shoulders and eased her back down onto the bed.

"Ma'am, what's wrong?" Her face distorted.

"Orion is being hit in the face."

"But, ma'am, he isn't here. Where is he?"

She snapped at the young man because of the pain shooting across her jaw, "I know that. Someone has him. I think it's Charbonnet."

"How do you know this?"

His brow furrowed, not believing her statement.

"Because I'm psychic, and I feel things. Orion dropped us off here so we could call the FBI. He took off to pull the cops away from finding us. Darlene said that Charbonnet has most of the cops in this area on his payroll. I know Orion has been caught, he's in danger, and they're beating him. That's what I'm feeling."

"Why don't you wait here, Miss Griffyths? I need to speak with Agent Upton."

He left the bedroom.

Seren lay on the bed, trying to calm herself. She had to get out of there and locate Orion. It was apparent that the agent didn't believe anything she said. If they weren't going to do something, she would.

Standing in the corner, Cyrus came up and asked with concern, "You said Orion's getting beaten?"

"Yes, I can feel it. It must be ten times worse for him. We've got to find him."

Cyrus asked, "Can you feel everything that is happening to Orion?"

Seren answered, "Not everything. I sense some things because I care for him and he's in danger."

He nodded.

"I need to speak with Darlene."

She furrowed her brow. She had to help Orion. She got up and peeked out the bedroom door. The FBI agents huddled in the kitchenette, whispering. Darlene sat on the couch. Seren realized that the glamour Lwa they used at the Lockwood was still with her. She pulled the glamour down and quietly moved toward the woman on the couch. She leaned against the wall so the agents couldn't easily see her.

Darlene recognized the shimmer as it left the bedroom and moved next to her. She knew it was Seren with a glamour.

The psychic whispered, "Darlene, it's me. I'm getting horrible feelings that Orion is captured and being beaten. Do you know where they may have taken him?"

Darlene thought momentarily, turned her head as if to look out the sliding glass door at the lake, and whispered, "Ernie has a farm south of Lockwood near the border with Florida. He called it his private hideout. I don't know its exact address."

"Thank you. That's okay. I'll find it. I need to help Orion. Can you create a distraction so I can leave without them noticing?"

"Do you really want to do that? If my husband catches you, he'll kill you."

"I can hide like this. I'll have Cyrus as my lookout."

"Okay, be careful."

Darlene got up, opened the sliding glass door, and walked out. The agents all turned and followed her, thinking she was attempting to escape.

Seren snatched her purse sitting on the coffee table, quietly left through the front door, and headed for the resort's office.

Special Agent Upton approached Darlene on the back porch and said, "Mrs. Newman, what're you doing? It might not be safe for you to be out here."

"Oh, I just had to come out and get some fresh air. I've been locked away at Lockwood for almost five years, and being stuck in that cabin is almost as bad."

Harman said, "Miss Griffyths said that she and an Orion Labauve broke you out of there this morning."

"Yes, that's correct. My husband had me incarcerated there and placed on drugs all this time. Everyone there is someone that he or his close associates want to have disappear but not die. The doctors and staff are all on his payroll."

Agent Upton asked, "Mrs. Newman, if you were in a mental institution, how are we to believe what you say?"

"At my house, Ernie had lists of people he put in there. If it were a legitimate hospital, why would someone like him have a list like that?"

The agents all looked at each other, knowing that this was big. Bill wrote it in his notepad.

Upton said, "Ma'am, please come back in and tell us more."

They all returned to the living room, and she told them some of the details about her horrendous experiences while at Lockwood. The agents all scribbled madly in their notepads.

When one started to get up and go to the bedroom, Darlene would stop them with, "Oh, don't leave, you'll want to hear this," and would begin on another juicy bit of info that she heard from another patient while at Lockwood.

Seren ran to the Lake Blanc office. Outside the door, she removed the glamour and stepped in. As usual, Tabitha Blanc sat behind the counter, reading a magazine. She produced one of her huge smiles as

Seren entered.

"Hi, honey. How's it going with the FBI? I saw them drive up."

"It's fine, but I've got to go and help Orion. They aren't going to let me leave. Is there any way I can rent a car?"

"Is Mr. Labauve in trouble?"

"Yes, I know he is. I'm psychic, and I can feel it."

"I knew there was something different about you two. Here, take my car."

The resort owner pulled her purse from under the counter and removed the keys.

"Here you go, honey. You be careful."

"Oh, Tabitha. Thank you so much. I don't know what I can do to repay you."

"You don't worry about it. Now go and help the man you love."

"You could tell?"

"Oh, yeah. Now go! It's the black Olds."

Seren smiled, and tears welled in her eyes from the generosity demonstrated. She ran to the only black vehicle parked near the office and left the Lake Blanc Resort, heading back to Alabama. Cyrus popped into the front passenger seat.

"If we get close to where Orion is, do you think you'll be able to find him?" she asked Orion's ghost friend.

"Yeah, probably. But can't your psychic abilities also track him down?"

"Psychic feelings aren't always very accurate. I think we can locate him if we work together as a team."

"I agree. If anything happens to him, I'll haunt Charbonnet till his dying days."

The ghost crossed his arms and produced a determined expression.

Seren said, "I love Orion too and feel the same way. Damn it, Orion. Why do you always do this? You always throw yourself into danger, always pushing me away. I can't lose you."

"I know you care for him. I only wish he knew it. It's something he's been looking for all his life," Cyrus said.

Seren swallowed hard, her fingers gripping the steering wheel until her knuckles turned white. She hated this feeling—this helplessness.

Every mile that separated them twisted in her chest like a knife.

"Hold on, Orion," she whispered. "We're coming."

After nearly forty-five minutes of hearing the incredible information Mrs. Newman provided to the FBI agents, Bill decided to check on Seren. He told Special Agent Upton about the fantastic story the redhead shared with him. Naturally, his supervisor didn't believe a word he reported about the psychic abilities. Harman began having second thoughts when Darlene Newman recounted the same fantastic tale of how they escaped.

He gently knocked on the bedroom door, assuming the young woman was asleep. She said she wasn't feeling well.

"Miss Griffyths?"

He received no response and stuck his head in the door. No one was there. He pushed the door open and hurriedly scoured the room.

"Henry! She's gone. Seren Griffyths isn't in the bedroom."

The young agent's voice was anxious.

Henry Upton glared at the blond agent, "What do you mean she's not there?"

"She's not in the bedroom or bathroom."

"Shit! She must have left while we were all outside. Go and find her!" Henry commanded.

Bill ran outside, searching up and down several of the walkways and paths. She didn't have a car; she couldn't have driven away. He entered the office, and a heavy-set, gray-haired woman sat at the counter with a big smile.

He hurried to her, "Have you seen Miss Griffyths? The pretty red-headed woman."

"Oh, sure, she was here about forty-five minutes, maybe an hour ago."

"Where did she go?"

"I don't know, honey. She borrowed my Olds and said she had to go and help Mr. Labauve. Nice, good-looking young man. I think they're in love."

He raised his voice, angry for losing Seren, "What kind of car do you have?"

"A black 1975 Olds Cutlass. I think that's what it is."

"License plate number?"

"Oh, dear. I don't think I remember that. NFT458, no, that was my husband's. Mark's gone now. He died three years ago. It was so sudden."

"That's too bad, ma'am. Please try to remember the number."

"FRP,... I know it has an F in it."

"Damn! Your name is?"

"Tabitha Blanc"

"Thank you."

The young agent stormed out of the office door and returned to Cabin Five.

Tabitha watched the man leave. She hoped she had stalled the FBI agent long enough to give Seren time to find Mr. Labauve.

Chapter 34
Finding Orion

Four hours after receiving the call from Seren Griffyths, Andrew Butler Jr. stood in front of cabin number five at Lake Blanc Resort and knocked on the door. A tall, blond young man dressed in a dark suit answered.

Andy said, "Hello, I'm Andrew Butler Jr."

The agent furrowed his brow, suspiciously glaring at a man in his early 60s with gray-streaked brown hair wearing a gray business suit and blue paisley tie.

"And why are you here?"

Having heard Andy's announcement from the couch, Darlene Newman shouted, "He's my attorney."

The young FBI agent stepped aside and Andy entered the cabin.

The FBI agent said, "Identification, please."

The attorney handed over his driver's license and a business card.

The man turned to his supervisor and said, "He looks legit."

Andy said, "May I speak with my client in private, please?" and pointed to the bedroom.

Darlene stood up and hurried to the bedroom. The attorney followed behind and shut the door.

He put out his hand, "Nice to meet you, Mrs. Newman."

She said, "Good to meet you. Seren told me she called you."

"Where are Orion and Seren?" he asked, raising his eyebrows and pursing his lips.

"Orion took off in Seren's car to keep my husband from finding me. Seren said she could feel that Orion was in trouble and went to find him. I told her about the farm that Ernie had outside Mobile."

"Have you explained this to the FBI agents?"

"No, I haven't. I don't know the exact address."

"How was she going to find it?"

"She's psychic. She thought she could do it."

"Okay, Orion can find things; maybe she can find him. But how was she going to help him?"

"I don't know."

She shook her head.

"We'd better tell the FBI, but don't tell them anything else unless you talk to me first."

"Okay."

Darlene was glad to have someone there to assist her. She wasn't sure what to tell the FBI and thanked God that Mr. Butler was there to advise her.

Andy opened the door and they stepped out.

He addressed the FBI agents, "Gentlemen, my client has given me some disturbing information. Two people are missing and may be being held against their will by Earnest Charbonnet Jr. You must locate them before she releases any further information."

Agent Upton stood and approached the attorney.

"Well, where are they? Do you know?"

Darlene said, "They may be on my husband's farm."

"And where is that? Can you please provide the address?"

"It's somewhere north of Mobile near the Florida border. We may be able to find the address at my house."

"We're acquiring a search warrant for your house. We can head over there now. We'll have it delivered."

Upton glanced at the other agents.

"Okay, men, we're returning to Mobile."

The agents, two cars, and Andy's rental left the resort, speeding down the black-top road. Forty-five minutes later, they pulled in front of the beautiful colonial mansion that had been Darlene's.

Darlene sat in the back seat of the FBI agent's car and stared out the window at the house where so many terrible things had happened to her and Johnny. There were also some good memories, but the horrible beatings overshadowed those.

Agent Upton opened the door for her, but she didn't move. He leaned down and peered at the woman.

"Are you okay?"

She didn't answer. Flashes of her husband's fist smashing her in the face, Johnny's small body flying through the air and crashing against the wall consumed her thoughts.

Andy approached and recognized the problem. He bent down and held his hand out to the distraught woman.

"Darlene, it's okay. Earnest can't hurt you anymore."

She looked up at Andy's caring eyes and took his hand. He helped her out of the car and put his arm around her shoulder, offering protection as they headed toward the house.

Agent Upton pounded on the front door and forcefully pushed the doorbell button, yelling, "FBI, open the door!"

The other agents stood close behind him with their hands inside their jackets, ready to pull their guns. After a few moments, Angela, the Black housekeeper, opened the door. Her eyes were wide with fear as she saw the men.

Upton said, "I have a search warrant for this property."

As he spoke these words, two more vehicles with flashing lights raced up the driveway and skidded to a stop.

Angela did as Mr. Charbonnet told her.

"May I see the search warrant?" she said.

Another FBI agent hurried to the door, waving a document.

"Here's the warrant," he said and handed it to her.

The housekeeper took the legal paper and stepped aside as the agents rushed past her.

When Darlene and Andy entered, the housekeeper exclaimed, "Mrs. Newman, I thought you were in the hospital! Mr. Charbonnet said you went crazy, and he had to commit you."

Darlene replied, "No, Angela, Earnest had me locked away at Lockwood and put on drugs."

Angela shook her head and started to walk away, but one of the agents pulled her into another room to ask questions.

Agent Upton asked Darlene, "Do you know where your husband stored his important documents?"

"Yes, they're in his office."

She moved cautiously toward the room, down the dim hall, and to the right. Her trembling hand reached out to grasp the door handle, but suddenly she paused, haunted by vivid flashes of lying helpless on the floor and Earnest's beating her pounding in her ears. Overwhelmed by fear, she jerked her hand back, turning sharply and collapsing onto Andy's chest, sobbing uncontrollably.

Agent Upton swung the door open swiftly, and the other agents stormed in, their eyes scanning every corner and tearing through the papers in a desperate search for answers.

Upton shouted, "We need to find the address of a farm somewhere north of Mobile, near the Florida border, immediately. Look for that first."

He turned to Darlene and Andy.

"Why don't you two go to the living room and rest while we search?"

Andy guided Darlene into the living room and insisted she lie on the sofa. Darlene looked around the room. Nothing had changed since the day she left with Johnny. The same ornate French-style furniture still filled the room, and the same expensive crystal chandelier hung from the center of the tall ceiling.

The attorney headed for the telephone on a sideboard. He first called Doris to tell her what had happened so far, admitting they still didn't know where Orion was.

Doris said, "I'll search with the crystals. Sometimes I can find clues through them."

Andy said, "Okay, call me if you see anything. I'll be at this number for a while."

He gave her the phone number listed on the telephone.

Andy then called his wife, Vivian, and explained that he was helping a friend of Orion's and would probably be away for a few days. He promised to call her later.

He went back to Darlene.

"How are you doing? Would you like some water or something else to drink?"

She nodded.

He located the spacious kitchen and rummaged through the cabinets for two glasses. He filled them with water and returned to the living room. She took the glass and sipped from it, still in shock over everything happening and being back in this house.

Agent Upton approached.

"We located a safe behind a bookcase. Do you know the combination?"

Darlene answered, "Yes," and gave him the numbers.

The code was Ernie's Nanny's birthdate. Henry Upton rushed back to the office.

Andy said, "I'm surprised your husband gave you the code."

"Oh, he didn't. I was in the office one day when he opened it, and I looked over his shoulder. I recognized that it was his Nanny's birthday. He always thought I was stupid and would never remember it. But I'm not stupid."

"Of course not," Andy said.

They trailed Agent Upton back into the office, their eyes fixed on his tense movements. He meticulously entered the numbers on the safe dial, each rotation heavier with anticipation. The dial stopped—then turned again—Click, Click, Click. Upton's hand grasped the handle and yanked it upward. The safe's door swung open with a creak, revealing its secrets. Darlene exhaled shakily, her heart pounding as the safe clicked open—inside the contents could spell salvation or doom for Seren and Orion.

Seren sped to the general area of Charbonnet's farm, where Darlene told her the hideout was located. She was astonished that the police didn't stop her.

Pain shot through her fingers on her left hand, and she screamed in agony. The Olds swerved to the side, heading for the ditch. Cyrus grabbed the wheel and yanked it, guiding the car back onto the road as she stomped on the brakes.

He shouted, "What's going on?"

"I think they broke Orion's fingers."

Tears poured down her cheeks. The pain was so intense, he must be near. She flexed her fingers.

They wandered the county roads, desperately hoping to feel

Orion's elusive presence once more. But nothing responded. Darkness was falling rapidly, shrouding the trees and structures in shadow, making everything more difficult to see. Frustration boiled over as she slammed her hand on the steering wheel, turning on the headlights.

"Cyrus, can you feel Orion anywhere?" she demanded, voice trembling.

"No, nothing," he replied flatly.

"Damn!" she cursed, her pulse pounding as the night closed in around them.

She accelerated slightly, moving the vehicle forward with purpose before sharply turning right onto the next dirt road. The roadway stretched ahead through a dense stand of trees on both sides for about a mile, the quiet only broken by the crunch of tires on gravel. At the T-junction, she slammed the brakes momentarily, her mind racing — which way to go? Closing her eyes, she desperately tried to sense Orion's presence. A sudden tingle in her left hand snapped her to attention, urging her to turn left. Heart pounding, she carefully inched down the lane, each movement heavy with anticipation.

Cyrus sat up quickly.

"He's close."

Another dirt road appeared in the headlights on the right. She turned and gradually moved the vehicle forward.

The ghost shouted, sitting erect in the seat, "He's here, I can definitely feel him!"

Seren switched off the headlights and cautiously moved forward.

Lights illuminated the porch of an old farmhouse. To the left stood a large metal barn, with various farm equipment parked behind it. Seren parked the Cutlass between a tractor and another piece of equipment she didn't recognize.

She slipped from the car and eased the door shut, soundless as a shadow. Cyrus vanished into the shadows. The Lwa still nearby, she instinctively pulled down the glamour, blending seamlessly into the darkness. Suddenly, the engine of a vehicle roared to life, headlights piercing the night, casting light on the driveway. She knelt beside the old Cutlass; eyes fixed on a faded car creeping along the gravel road. Seren moved like a whisper, circling the barn, her body pressed to the side for cover. No one was on the farmhouse porch.

The barn door swung open and slammed against the wall. Out stomped a middle-aged man, swearing profusely. He tramped across the gravel driveway toward the house.

Cyrus reappeared beside her and whispered—though he didn't need to, being a ghost.

"Orion's in a locked room in the barn."

She nodded.

Two more men exited the barn. They were big, bald men.

They shoved each other back and forth, saying, "You hit him too hard."

"No, I didn't."

"Yes, you did."

They entered the house, the screen door slamming behind them.

Seren approached the barn door and entered. Cyrus signaled for her to follow him.

He paused before a metal door and said, "It's locked."

She said, "Here are the keys."

A ring of keys hung from a nail on the wall next to the door. She took them from the hook and tried a few until she found the correct one. The door opened, and she hung them back on the nail. She entered the room, and the door closed behind her.

A single dim bulb hung from the ceiling, casting hazy light that barely pierced the shadows. In the far corner, an old iron bed rested, with someone lying on it. She cautiously approached, knowing who would be there.

SPECTRAL PROMISES

Chapter 35
Calling Lwa and Escaping

Someone shook my shoulder. Pain washed over my body like a thousand needles. I groaned. My eyelids fluttered, and the world blurred. Red hair and soft features appeared. A familiar voice. Seren?

"Orion! Orion! Wake up!"

Was that Seren's voice? I blinked several times as my vision cleared. It was Seren, the most wonderful sight to wake up to.

"Where am I?" I asked, confused.

"You're at Earnest Charbonnet's farm."

"What?"

Charbonnet owned a farm? I couldn't picture him on a tractor unless it were to plow someone into the ground.

"Seren, what are you doing here? He'll kill you."

I tried to move and fire lanced through my ribs. My hands, broken, stiff, throbbed in time with my heartbeat. I gasped and collapsed back, blinking against a wave of dizziness. The room tilted. A sharp pulse exploded at the base of my skull, sending black spots across my vision. I clenched my teeth, swallowing a groan.

Sympathetically, Seren said, "Stay down. You're in terrible shape."

"I'm thirsty."

A coppery taste lingered in my mouth. Though Sammy had given me water, the thirst still clawed at my throat. How long had it been since Sammy was here, or had that been a dream?

"Here, I'll get you a drink."

She picked up the metal cup on the floor and went to the sink to fill it.

She returned and lifted my head as I drank, the cool water easing my raw throat. Blood mixed back into the clear liquid from my split lip.

"I'm actually better than I was. Fuzzbucket has been working on healing my injuries as best he can."

"That's good," Seren said.

"My head doesn't hurt as much as when they first hit me."

"Yeah, I felt that."

She rubbed the back of her head.

"You did?"

She nodded.

I raised my hands to examine them.

"My broken fingers aren't as bent and swollen as they were, so the little guy is getting things done."

Cyrus leaned in.

"They still look terrible."

"Yeah, they hurt like hell. How did you find me?"

I wished they hadn't placed themselves in such a dangerous situation.

The barn door slammed outside.

I whispered, "They must be coming to check on me. Hide."

Seren pulled the glamour down and stood next to the wall. Now invisible.

Keys jingled as someone unlocked the door. I lay back and pretended to be unconscious.

The two gorillas walked in, one saying, "Sammy must have forgotten to lock the door when he was here. The boss is going to be mad when he hears about this."

They lingered by the bed.

One remarked, "He's still unconscious. You hit him on the head too hard."

It was the bald twins who had taken pleasure in beating me.

The other said, "You were pounding on him pretty good. You might have done a lot of damage inside."

The first chuckled.

"Yeah, I felt something pop a couple of times."

"I wouldn't laugh if I were you. The boss said to keep him alive. He has other plans for him."

"Yeah, no telling what those could be. He pissed Mr. Charbonnet off pretty bad. The sorry sum-of-a-bitch will get it bad for sure."

They left and locked the door.

Seren removed the glamour and told Cyrus, "Follow those guys and find Charbonnet. Find out what plans they have for Orion."

He nodded and disappeared.

She leaned down to me.

"We've got to get you out of here."

"But I've got to stop Charbonnet first."

"What do you mean, stop him? You're in no shape to confront him or his men."

"Not physically. Stop him. I have to remove all his Lwa protection. He's covered in Lwa. Darlene said he had all kinds of voodoo ceremonies performed, and I heard him say something about his protection that should keep the FBI away. I think he has his businesses protected as well."

"If he has so much protection, why didn't the Lwa stop me and Cyrus?"

"Maybe they didn't see you as any threat. I don't know."

"Can you remove the Lwa?"

"I'm not sure. I need to think about how to do it."

I stared at the ceiling, contemplating different possibilities.

I would have to summon a lot of Lwa and have them push his Lwa back to the spirit realm. That means I need to attract large, strong spirit entities. Can I manage this in my current state? I have to try. If Charbonnet isn't stopped, he'll come after Darlene, Seren, and me. If all his protection is gone, he'll have to use his resources to block the FBI instead of attacking us.

I glanced at Seren.

"I have an idea, but I need your assistance."

"I'll help any way I can. Darlene was talking to the FBI when I left over two hours ago. I'm sure they plan on doing something to Charbonnet by now."

"But if we don't remove those protections from him and his businesses, they won't be able to do anything."

"Okay. What can I do?"

"I have to call Lwa over from the spirit world to make Charbonnet's Lwa return to that plane."

"How are you going to do that with your busted hands?"

She must have remembered the magical hand and finger movements I used to summon Lwa for Johnny's protection and Darlene's escape.

"You'll have to do it for me."

Her eyes widened in surprise.

"What? How am I supposed to do that?"

"I can pull the magic in and pass it through your arms and hands. You're a strong psychic, so I think you can handle exposure to that much mystical energy."

Hesitantly, she said, "Alright…if you think that'll work."

"If it doesn't, I want you to leave. Leave me, go back, and tell the FBI where I am."

"But I can't do that."

She placed her hand on my shoulder. Her gentle touch warmed my heart in this difficult situation.

"You heard those guys. Charbonnet wants me alive, so he's not going to kill me, at least not right away."

Seren frowned and turned away. She stared at the floor, contemplating her options.

After a moment, she turned back and said, "Okay, what do you want me to do?"

"Do you remember the hand and arm movements I did to call the Lwa for Darlene's breakout?"

"Yes. I think so."

"Show me what you remember."

She formed her hands into the magical form to open a portal.

"That's close. Move your middle fingers down lower."

She followed my instructions.

"Good. Now, point your elbows higher. There you go … and straighten your arms out. Slower. Bring your hands back, meet at the center of your chest, and rotate your wrists. There, you've got it. You do that five times."

"What will you be doing?"

Her forehead wrinkled again, unsure if this would work.

"I'll stand behind you, hold on to your elbows with my hands as best I can, pass the magic into your arms and hands, and chant the spell in the God language. Hopefully, this should open a portal, and I can verbally summon the Lwa and tell them what I want them to do."

Her lips and chin trembled with fear, as she had never done anything like this in her life.

I reassured her, "It's okay. You don't have to be scared. I don't think this will hurt you."

"You don't think? You've never done anything like this before, have you?"

"Well, no… But I have to do something. If I don't, I know it'll be terrible for a lot of people."

A cold shiver ran over my body just thinking about it. She noticed the shiver.

"Are you having a vision?"

"No, I just get feelings."

"Okay, when do we start?"

"I need to find out what Charbonnet's doing. Cyrus, come here."

I pulled Cyrus to me, and he instantly manifested.

"Damn, Orion! Do you have to do that so hard?"

His eyes shot daggers at me.

"I'm sorry. We're in a hurry. What's going on? What's Charbonnet doing?"

"He's on the phone yelling at people. That seems to be the only way he talks to people. The other four creeps are out on the porch, smoking. None of them wants to be around him when he's like this."

"Okay. Seren and I are going to call some Lwa over to help. I want you to keep a lookout, and if any of those guys start to head over here, try to distract them. Do you think you can move some things and make a distraction?"

"Yeah, I think there's enough psychic energy around here to do something."

"Great. Okay, go."

He disappeared.

I began to sit up, but pain shot through my chest from the broken ribs.

"Can you help me get up?"

I groaned.

She bent down, took my left elbow, and helped me stand. I wobbled, my head spinning. Seren tried to steady me.

"Please stand with your back to my chest, and I'll lean on you."

I leaned against her back, trying not to put all my weight on her. My head was next to her left ear, her curly hair tickling my cheek. I closed my eyes and wanted to bury my face in it. Stop! Concentrate!

I said, "Okay, we both need to relax and slowly breathe in and out a few times. I'll begin to pull magic into me."

Waves of mystical energy swirled in the room. I knew my eyes must have turned golden. I raised my hands and held her elbows in my palms, trying not to bend or hit the broken fingers. I felt her shiver. The magic flowed into me. I gently pushed the energy through my palms and into Seren's arms. She shook, either from exposure to the mystical energy or possibly fear.

"Alright, start the movements."

She positioned her hands with precision, moving her arms exactly as needed. I chanted in the ancient, sacred God language. The fine hair on her arms stood erect from unseen currents of energy. A static charge sparked between her trembling fingers. We persisted, and the portal poured open, pulsating with raw, unearthly power.

The air shifted, thick with an ominous hum that shook the metal walls. Shadows stretched and twisted, reaching toward the ceiling. My hands throbbed with pain from my broken fingers. I pushed through the agony and winced, forcing myself to continue channeling the raw magic into Seren's arms. Her skin was now shimmering with an otherworldly glow. A gust of wind burst through the room, carrying ghostly whispers from the other side and whipping Seren's curls into my eyes.

Orbs appeared. Dozens of them flickered into existence, luminous and otherworldly, in various sizes, colors, shapes, and textures. The Lwa had arrived. They filled the small room.

She stopped the magical movements, and I commanded the Lwa to force Earnest Charbonnet's Lwa to return to the spirit realm. They were also to clear all Lwa around his businesses and homes. After Charbonnet's Lwa returned to the spirit realm, they were to stay and prevent any new spirit entities he might summon from helping him.

I grimaced as the chorus of Lwa responded with loud, high-pitched trills that hurt my ears, saying, '*As you command, Small Duke.*'

They zipped away, passing through the walls.

I said, "It's done."

My legs began to buckle. Seren grabbed my arm and helped me back onto the bed. I sat on the edge, trying to steady my breathing to ease the pain.

She frantically asked, "Did the Lwa come through?"

"Yes. They came through and took off to do what I commanded. Let's hope it works. If my Lwa aren't strong enough, they may not be able to push Charbonnet's out."

"That was incredible. I could feel something flowing and traveling along my hands and arms. Was that the magic?"

"Yes, it was."

"Amazing."

She had a big grin, having experienced something that very few in the occult community ever had.

Ready to move on, she said, "Alright, now that that's done, we can get you out of here."

"No, not yet. I have to rest for a while. I'm always exhausted after performing one of those calls. Let me nap for an hour or so."

"Orion, I want to get you out of here as soon as possible. I don't want those goons to return and continue beating you. They seemed too eager to do that."

"I know. But I'm so weak right now that I can barely walk. Just let me rest for a while," I pleaded.

She shook her head and stepped back, her scowl revealing her concern for me.

I fell asleep.

After what felt like just a few minutes, Seren was vigorously pushing my left shoulder.

"Orion, come on, wake up."

"Alright, alright!"

I groggily opened my eyes and blinked several times.

"How are we getting out of here? They locked the door."

"It won't be for long."

She ran her fingers through her thick hair and removed two large bobby pins.

"Remember, I mentioned that I learned how to pick locks."

She squatted next to the door, bent each bobby pin to a certain angle, and inserted them into the lock orifice. She wiggled them around, but nothing was happening. One of the pins slipped out of her fingers, fell to the filthy floor, and slid under the gap between the door and the floor.

She exclaimed, "Shit!"

She dropped to her hands and knees, slipped a finger under the door, and retrieved the fallen pin. She reinserted the two pins, wiggled them slightly, and then, 'CLICK,' the lock was released.

"You're not the only one with skills."

We both smiled.

I said, "Help me up."

She took my arm and helped me stand. My legs were still shaky, and flashes of pain radiated across my chest. I groaned.

She pulled down her glamour, making it difficult to see her. I leaned on her and put my left arm around her neck. She took my left hand in hers and wrapped her right arm around my waist. We hobbled to the barn exit. She peeked out the small window in the door.

"Damn, those goons are all on the porch."

It was dark, and they sat in chairs, smoking. A bright porch light illuminated the entire area. There was also a light over the barn door, making it easy for them to detect us.

I called, "Cyrus."

He popped into view.

"Can you create a distraction to get those guys off the veranda and into the woods?"

He smiled, "Sure thing," eager to stir up some mischief.

We waited, and a metallic bang echoed from the far side of the farmhouse. The crew drew their guns and sprinted off the porch and around the house.

Seren and I hurried out the door as fast as we could, which wasn't very fast, and around the side of the metal barn. We shuffled up the dirt road toward the back of the structure. I felt dizzy, and it was hard to breathe with my broken ribs.

Seren encouraged me.

"Come on, the car's behind the barn and the tractors."

A door slammed from somewhere behind us.

Shouting.

Heavy boots pounded across the porch.

Then—BANG!

A searing, white-hot explosion of pain tore through my right shoulder. My body jerked as if struck by a sledgehammer. I gasped, the world spinning around me. My knees buckled, and I collapsed forward onto a pile of sand, scraping my face against it. Everything dimmed as darkness rushed in.

I woke up a few seconds later to someone rolling me over. It was Charbonnet standing above me with a gun.

"How the fuck did you get out, Labauve? I'm not messing with you any longer."

He pointed the weapon at my head. Flashing lights illuminated his face. The roar of racing car engines approached from the road.

In short gasps, I said, "You're finished. That's the FBI. I stripped you of all your protective Lwa. Nothing shields you now."

Charbonnet's eyes bulged in surprise. He scowled at me in rage, holding the gun barrel just a foot from my head. I drew a shuddering breath, the pain in my ribs unbearable. Charbonnet sneered, his finger tightening on the trigger.

Seren—where was she? He would shoot her next.

The firearm roared—a blinding light.

Seren's voice—distant, panicked—calling my name.

Then, nothing.

Chapter 36
Rescued and Abelard's Final Act

Seren supported Orion's weight. He felt heavier than she anticipated, and they weren't moving as quickly as she wanted. With each step, he groaned in pain.

A door slammed behind them, followed by a shouted command—and then a deafening bang that echoed across the yard.

Orion stumbled and fell forward, pulling her down with him. She released him, and her chest collided with a wooden crate, knocking the air out of her. She lay gasping for breath on the ground.

Charbonnet stomped toward them, gun raised, eyes blazing with fury. He barked something at Orion, his voice muffled by the ringing in her ears. Orion groaned in response, but she couldn't make out the words. Seren's vision swam. She blinked hard.

No—no time. Charbonnet was pulling the trigger. Seren screamed, throwing herself forward and slamming into Charbonnet's wrist. The weapon veered off—but not in time.

BANG!

Orion's body went limp. Blood trickled down his temple, dark against the sand.

Cyrus popped next to Orion and gasped, "Orion!"

The crime lord stood, confused by what had just happened. What caused his hand to move at the last second? Flashing colored lights and roaring engines from vehicles advanced up the farm's driveway.

The crime lord sneered, looking upward at the flashing lights of law enforcement as they approached the farm's driveway. He turned around and ran to the Lincoln Continental parked next to the house. He jumped into the white luxury vehicle and sped down the dirt road into the woods.

Tires skidded across the gravel driveway. The rumble of engines roared above the howling wind. A storm had been brewing in the area all evening, and it finally arrived.

The four thugs, having heard Charbonnet's gun, rushed back to the porch, ducking for cover upon seeing the FBI's vehicles approaching.

Car doors burst open. FBI agents flooded out, guns raised.

"Federal agents! Drop your weapons!"

Gunfire erupted. Muzzle flashes illuminated the rain-soaked night. Bullets slammed into car doors and porch railings, splintering the wood.

Thunder cracked overhead, a deafening boom that swallowed the chaos for a split second—then the fight resumed.

Seren removed the glamour and crouched over Orion. Tears welled in her eyes. Blood was running down Orion's head, and a large red spot was forming on his shirt from the gunshot to his shoulder. It was growing with every second.

Rage manifested on Cyrus's face and he disappeared.

She cupped her hands around Orion's face and cried, "Orion! Orion!"

He didn't respond. The loud bangs and shouts from the gun battle felt distant. The only thought on her mind was the fear of losing Orion.

One of the FBI cars stopped in front of the two victims, blocking them from the confrontation. Bill Harman jumped out and leaned down.

He asked, "Miss Griffyths, is this Orion Labauve?"

She vigorously nodded her head, tears streaming down her cheeks.

Harmon asked, "Are you okay?"

She yelled above the loud gunshots, "I'm okay, but please call an ambulance!"

At that moment, a flash of lightning lit up the sky, and a half-second later, a colossal thunderclap filled the air. It immediately began to pour rain in buckets. Seren leaned over Orion's head, trying to shield him from the rain.

The FBI agent crawled into the vehicle and called for an ambulance using the car radio, explaining that the victim had multiple gunshot wounds and other injuries.

Cyrus appeared beside the thugs shooting at the FBI. He had to do something to stop this. He placed his hand on the muzzle of one big bald guy's gun and pushed. The bullet hit the edge of a vehicle's door, nearly hitting an agent.

Frustrated, he looked across the driveway and saw Seren leaning over Orion.

He thought, '*She has a lot of psychic energy, maybe I can pull enough from her to use.*'

He concentrated. Drawing energy from the psychic, he pushed on the gun, and it nudged ever so slightly—not much, but just enough for the expelled bullet to impact the ground in front of an FBI vehicle. He then approached another thug and did the same. The bullet from this creep also missed its target and hit the gravel. Cyrus smiled and moved from one goon to another, causing them to miss their targets.

The gun battle ceased and one of the four thugs walked off the porch with his hands raised. Two of the goons bore various gunshot wounds, with blood trickling down their arms and legs. Several FBI agents surged forward, forced the criminals to the muddy ground, and handcuffed them. The fourth thug lay dead. One of the agents sustained an injury to his shoulder.

Bill Harmon retrieved a blue plastic tarp from the car's trunk, opened it, and draped it over Seren and Orion to shield them from the rain while they awaited the ambulance.

Seren collapsed beside Orion, her breath coming in ragged sobs. Her hands hovered over his bloodstained chest, trembling. She pressed down, attempting to staunch the bleeding, her fingers slick with crimson.

"Orion, please—don't you dare die on me."

Her vision blurred with tears.

She clutched his hand, pressing it to her cheek.

"I lost you once as Abelard; I won't lose you again. Do you hear me?"

She shut her eyes.

"Please," she whispered, her voice cracking. "If anyone is listening—any spirit, God—save him. Take my life instead. Just save him."

Cyrus popped next to Orion and kneeled, with his head down, praying for Orion's life.

Thirty minutes passed before the emergency vehicle arrived. It felt like an eternity to Seren. The rain eased, but the storm continued to deliver a constant drizzle.

The EMTs examined Orion and treated his wounds as best as they could, trying to halt the bleeding. They gently placed him in the ambulance and set off.

Before they left, she asked one of the EMTs, "Where are you taking Orion?"

The EMT answered, "We're transporting him to Springview Hospital in Mobile because of his severe injuries."

Cyrus hopped into the back of the ambulance with Orion. Seren noticed this and felt relieved that Orion wouldn't be alone during the trip to the hospital. Of course, the EMTs remained unaware of it.

She turned to head for Tabitha's borrowed Olds. Bill, the young blond agent who spoke to her at the resort, stopped her.

Bill Harmon asked, "Can you answer a few questions before you go?"

"All right, but hurry."

"How did you know where to find Mr. Labauve and where Mr. Charbonnet was?"

She answered quickly, wanting this to be finished promptly, "Darlene told me he had a farm in this general area, so I headed here."

"But how did you find it? We didn't know the location until we visited Charbonnet's house and discovered it in his safe, along with his documents. Thankfully, Mrs. Newman knew the combination.

"It's like I told you before: I'm a psychic. I knew the general location and drove around until I could feel him."

"You said you thought he was injured."

"Yes, I felt it when he got hit in the head and when they were beating him in the face."

"How did you get in and get him out?"

"I waited until the goons left the barn, then I snuck in."

She didn't mention Cyrus, the ghost who was aiding her by signaling when the coast was clear.

"I have to go. I'll be at the hospital."

Seren turned and ran to Tabitha's car, then sped down the driveway towards Mobile.

Bill stood watching the car vanish down the driveway. His boss won't believe how she discovered the farm.

I was Abelard, heading to the village to meet Chloe and plan our wedding. My parents opposed the idea, but I was determined to marry the woman I loved. I told them I was willing to give up my inheritance if needed. Finally, they gave in—they had no choice, especially since she was pregnant.

It had been two months since our possession by Duke Shamedi and the Fairy Queen. During that time, we made love, an experience that was the most incredible of our lives. Chloe mentioned that she thought that was when she became pregnant.

I now understand why the voodoo spirit, the God, possessed me while I was in Saint Dominque. It was so he could be with the Fairy Queen on Fairy Hill. The pagan entity plunged me into torment, whispering constantly in my mind and sometimes taking control of my body. I thought I was losing my mind. After that night on Fairy Hill, the pagan God's voice disappeared. I felt like myself again, and life returned to normal.

As I entered the village, people filled the street near the candlemaker's shop. I spotted Chloe standing in the front doorway.

I approached and asked, "What's going on?"

She said, "You remember the boy, Claude? He became ill, and they don't think he'll recover."

I remembered the smiling eleven-year-old boy.

I thought, 'That's too bad. I wish there were something I could do.'

A sensation washed over me. I knew I could help him.

The doctor emerged from the tiny house and shook his head.

"The boy's gone."

The mother let out a raw, broken wail as she collapsed against her husband's chest. The villagers wept, while others whispered prayers among themselves.

Then the priest raised his hands.

"Come," he declared, his voice like thunder. "Let us pray for Claude's soul to ascend to heaven."

The crowd murmured in agreement, shuffling into the cottage and through the back door to the backyard.

A strange sensation rippled through me, a pull, as if unseen hands were reaching out. Something told me it wasn't too late.

I hesitated to enter. I walked into the cottage. A bed sat next to the fireplace. My gaze turned towards the child's body. The shape of the child, covered with an old, patched blanket, lay on the bed. It had only been about five minutes since the doctor had pronounced the boy dead.

Everyone went outside. I stayed in the hut, kneeling by the bed. I removed the blanket. The boy's body lay with his hands crossed over his chest. I moved his hands to his sides and placed my right hand on his thin chest, closed my eyes, and took a deep breath.

My soul soared, floated, calling to the child, and reached out for his spirit. The boy was moving toward the tunnel of light. My hand touched his shoulder, and he turned.

I gazed into his eyes and said, "You don't have to go now if you don't want to. I can take you back. What do you want to do?"

The boy's round eyes glanced at the tunnel and then back at me.

He said, "I want to go back."

I offered him my hand, and he took it. In an instant, we were both back in our bodies. A shiver coursed through me as I anchored my soul to the flesh.

Claude opened his eyes and gasped for air. He steadied his breath, and I assisted him to stand.

I asked, "How do you feel?"

He smiled, "I feel good, Mr. Ozanne."

"Alright, let's go out to your parents."

I took his hand, and we walked through the back door.

Most of the villagers were gathered around the priest, who shouted a prayer at the top of his lungs. I navigated through the crowd, holding Claude's hand. People recoiled and gasped as we approached Claude's parents. Chloe spotted me coming through the back door with the boy, her eyes wide with surprise. She followed us.

We entered the center of the circle. Claude recognized his mother and ran to her, wrapping his arms around her waist.

She glared at him in shock and screamed, pushing him away, shouting,

"Demon! Demon!"

Claude peered up at his mother with tears forming in his eyes. His lower lip was trembling.

His father pushed him away, yelling, "Demon, get out of here."

The boy stumbled and fell to the ground. His eyes were wide with surprise.

I hurried to him and helped him sit up.

I asked, "Are you okay?"

He said, "Yes," with tears coursing down his cheeks.

The priest raised the crucifix toward the child and shouted, "Begone, spawn of hell."

This terrified the boy, causing him to hold his hands over his eyes and sob more intensely.

I pushed the priest away and shouted, "Why are you doing this? The boy's alive. You should be happy."

He glared at me.

"Did you bring him back?"

I said, "Does it matter? He was obviously not dead. You should be happy he is here now."

The doctor said, "He was definitely dead. There was no heartbeat."

The priest now extended the crucifix toward me and yelled, "Only God can resurrect someone. You've been acting strangely ever since you returned from your overseas trip. People have seen you talking when no one was there. The Devil must possess you."

As this unfolded, Chloe rushed to Claude, helped him to his feet, and quickly led him away from the crowd. She guided him to her house behind the candle shop, laid him on her bed, and then hurried back.

The villagers all began to shout and scream, "Devil! Demon!"

I shouted back, "No, I'm not the Devil! I go to church every Sunday. You have all seen me there."

But they all continued shouting. No one was listening.

Several large stacks of stones and rocks lay piled across the area—a community project to build a protective stone wall along the cliff's edge. The rocks, collected from an old quarry, were ready for construction. Suddenly, someone picked up a stone and hurled it at me. I instinctively raised my arm to block it. The stone hit, sending a sharp pain through my arm. Almost immediately, others joined in, pelting me with stones and shouting relentlessly. Instinctively, I stepped back.

The wind picked up, with great gusts carrying spray from the waves below, which whipped up the cliff and buffeted everyone. The wind blew my hair over my eyes.

Retreating, I shouted, "Stop! Stop! I'm not a demon! I'm not the devil!"

The frenzied villagers tossed rocks at me, their anger unrelenting. I pushed my hair back and lifted my arms defensively, searching desperately for a gap to escape. None appeared. Lost in the chaos, I didn't realize how dangerously close I was to the cliff's edge.

Chloe's high-pitched scream cut through the furious shouts of the crowd.

"Stop! Stop, please!"

Two men seized her arms, pulling her back. She kicked, clawed, and struggled, but they held firm.

Her tear-stained face contorted as she screamed, "No! Abelard!"

A sharp pain shot through my skull, and everything spun around me. My vision flickered, and I stumbled. My foot found only empty air.

The last thing I saw was Chloe's horror-stricken face as I plummeted over the cliff, and she screamed my name, "ABELARD!"

A scream tore from my throat. Hands gripped me. My arms thrashed, instinct screaming, 'RUN.'

Pain raced through my body like fire.

I gasped for breath, my chest tightening.

Then—Seren's voice.

"Orion! Orion. Stop! It's okay!"

I blinked, my eyesight swimming. No angry mob. Just a hospital room, the sterile scent of antiseptic, and the beautiful redhead's face hovering over mine.

Chapter 37

Time in the Hospital

My vision swam before sharpening into focus—red curls, green eyes, a tear-stained face: Seren. Her hands held my shoulders, warm and firm, grounding me.

"Orion!"

Her voice wavered between relief and panic.

"You're awake."

I exhaled sharply, my chest tightening with pain. A groan escaped my lips. My body ached as if I had been trampled. Seren's grip loosened; her touch became gentle as she guided my arms down and cupped my cheek.

Tears were still streaming down my cheeks.

She asked, "What was going on? You were yelling and flailing around."

"I was Abelard."

The words stuck in my throat. My chest heaved.

"The villagers—God, they were screaming for my blood. I saved that boy. I resurrected him, and they called me the Devil."

Seren's hands tightened on mine.

"I understand."

I shook my head and swallowed hard.

"The stones hitting me, you screamed—No, Chloe screamed—as I fell."

I shakily exhaled.

Seren said, "I guess that's why Chloe said Abelard would die after returning from the Caribbean."

I nodded, still upset by the experience.

Andy and a nurse rushed into the room.

Andy said, "Oh, he seems to have calmed down."

I said, "I was having a bad dream," knowing it was more than just a dream; it was another past-life memory.

The nurse leaned over and asked, "Would you like something for the pain?"

I said, "Yes, please."

Despite not liking to use painkillers, this was one situation where I truly needed them. She gave me a shot.

As I lay waiting for the painkiller to take effect, Seren explained how she had been experiencing her own past life episodes as Chloe. She knew Abelard had fallen off the cliff and what had happened to Chloe after Abelard died.

After Abelard's death, his family moved Chloe and Claude to a village far to the north. There, she started a candle-making shop and told the villagers that her husband had died, which made it too painful for her to stay where they had lived before. She explained that Claude was her brother. When she gave birth to her son, she named him Abelard. Abelard's parents adopted the baby, recognized him as their own, and renamed him Jacques Abelard.

Chloe agreed to let the grandparents care for the baby because she knew they could provide for him much better than she ever could. He was sent to school and later to university. He married and had a daughter, Juliette, who married Lucas Labauve. Chloe married the village blacksmith, and they had four children together. One of her daughters married and moved to England.

I listened intently.

"So, I'm related to Abelard and Chloe, and you may be related to Chloe."

"So, it seems."

"Is there some sort of incest issue, since we…?" referring to our making love at the lake.

Seren smiled and said, "With about twelve generations between us and them, I don't think so."

My eyes were getting heavy.

"I wonder if we're also related to Abelard's children, who were conceived during the voodoo ceremony?"

I never heard her response because I fell asleep.

When I next awoke, I was moaning in pain. Seren turned from the window, her face breaking into a broad smile. Outside, the rain continued to pour, intensifying the somber mood.

"There you are."

She gently took my left hand, careful not to jostle the broken finger.

"How are you doing?"

"Better than the last time I was awake, but everything still hurts."

I closed my eyes.

Warmth. That was the next thing I felt before I realized her lips were on mine—soft, urgent, and real.

She kissed me as if I were something precious, something she nearly lost. I kissed her back, drowning in her, in the way she tasted like honey. For the first time since being at the Charbonnet farm, the pain dulled, pushed aside by something that made me want to hold on and never let go.

Footsteps creaked on the floor. She pulled back just as the doctor entered, and I struggled to subdue the urge to curse whoever ruined the moment. I glared with a flash of anger at whoever interrupted Seren from kissing me.

It was a doctor. He was tall, in his mid-forties, with gray hair and a broad smile.

"Mr. Labauve, at last, we get to meet. I'm Dr. Norman. I did the surgery on your head."

I blinked a few times, a little confused.

"I didn't know I had surgery."

Dr. Norman chuckled.

"Well, Mr. Labauve, you certainly like to keep us on our toes."

My mind was still foggy.

"What?"

"The bullet took a nice chunk of your skull when it hit. We had to replace that section with a small metal plate."

I stared at him. I raised my left hand to feel the bandage surrounding my head.

"I have a metal plate in my head?"

"Yep. And trust me, it's an upgrade."

He chuckled.

"You're lucky—no brain damage. But you've been out for a week. Your girlfriend here has been by your side every day."

I glanced over at Seren, who was smiling at me, and said, "Yeah, my girlfriend."

I smiled back at her, hoping this was real and not just some crazy dream.

The doctor continued, "You're actually making excellent progress, considering all the injuries you had when they brought you into the Emergency Room. The staff were taking bets on whether you would pull through."

He chuckled.

"I'm glad you're doing better. I'll be by tomorrow to check on you. Try to eat something, okay?"

He left smiling.

I turned to Seren.

"Girlfriend?"

"It was the only way they would let me stay with you. They would only allow family members in. I guess they consider a girlfriend close enough. Oh, and attorneys, because they let Andy in. I kissed you when I knew someone was coming to keep them thinking I was your girlfriend."

I smiled. I still liked the sound of 'Girlfriend.' That kiss was much more than play-acting. I could feel the intensity. Or was that just wishful thinking?

"I thought Andy was here."

"He was, but he had to return home for a few days to handle business for another client. He'll be back."

"Where is this?"

"You're in the Springview Hospital in Mobile, Alabama."

"I thought I was going to die. Charbonnet had the gun pointed right at my head."

"I pushed his hand away at the last second, so the bullet only grazed your head."

"Grazed, yeah, enough to take a chunk out."

"That's better than in your brain."

"Charbonnet didn't try to shoot you?" I stared at her.

"I still had the glamour on; it was dark, and he couldn't see me."

I nodded, now understanding.

"What happened to him, and where is Darlene?"

Seren described the events at the resort, including her calls to Andy and then Detective O'Reilly, the arrival of the FBI, and her use of Tabitha's car to locate me. She also recounted what Andy said happened when he arrived at the resort and how they went to Darlene and Charbonnet's house. The FBI agents identified the address of the farm and rushed over, hoping Charbonnet was still there and that you were still alive."

She continued, "Darlene's with the FBI in protective custody. They left a guard outside the door to protect you after I informed them of his attempt to kill you. Agent Upton knew that Charbonnet would send someone to finish the job. He doesn't like to leave loose ends, and based on what his henchmen said after their arrest, you really pissed him off."

"Yeah, he was pretty angry when I told him I took all his protective Lwa away. I think he'll be busy trying to protect his organization for a while."

I smiled, thinking about what I had accomplished.

I asked, "Did the FBI do anything for those poor people at Lockwood?"

Seren answered, "Yes, they raided the place just in time and caught most of the staff loading their personal belongings into cars. I guess they intended to leave all the patients unattended."

"That's good; they got those people out of there."

She frowned at me.

"Well, you need to start considering your own protection more. When you pulled the Lwa over to stop Charbonnet's protection, you should have kept one there to protect yourself. Then you might not have been shot."

"Yeah, you're right. I never think about myself. I should do that more."

"Yes, I don't want to lose you. I've lost too many friends and people I care about."

"I know what you mean; so, have I."

A nurse's assistant came in with a tray of food.

They raised my bed to a sitting position, and my head began to throb again. I grimaced and held my hand over the injured area.

Seren asked, "Is your head hurting again?"

"Yeah, I think it's because I sat up."

"Why don't you lie back down?"

"No, I'd like to eat something if I can. I'm hungry. I hope the throbbing calms down."

It was lunch, and they brought me something light: chicken noodle soup, crackers, and apple juice. I managed to get about half of it down before I felt nauseous.

I asked Seren, "Have you eaten anything today?"

"Yes, I had a big breakfast at the hotel down the street where I'm staying. I'll have dinner when I go back tonight."

We turned on the TV and watched a few game shows. Then Andy arrived with a couple of books and magazines under his arms. I was happy he was there.

Andy smiled.

"Good, you're awake. I brought you some things to read."

"Just like the other times I was in the hospital. Thanks," I said.

"You have to stop getting yourself into trouble."

"I don't do it on purpose. It just happens."

"Yeah, well, now you've got a major criminal after you, as well as a crazy grandmother."

"Speaking of grandmothers, did you know that the Voodoo Imperatrice has been pursuing Charbonnet and his father for decades? That was one reason he had Lwa surrounding him for protection."

Andy's eyes bulged in surprise.

"I never knew that. Seren told me you sent Lwa out to stop his protection. I wonder if she'll attack him again with his protection gone. Perhaps that'll keep both of them off your back."

Andy started talking to Seren about something, but I wasn't listening. I was thinking about why the Voodoo Imperatrice would be after the crime boss. What could he or his father have done to her?

Somewhere in my mind, I remembered her saying, 'If you knew what I was trying to do, you would help me,' or something like that. When did I hear that? It must have been when she captured me. Could that be related to something Charbonnet had done?

Wait, Darlene mentioned that Charbonnet killed her aunt and uncle. I guess that was what she was referring to.

While I pondered this, my left middle finger instinctively scratched the bedsheets. Cyrus gently placed his hand over mine, and I immediately stopped rubbing. He has always held my hand during anxious moments since he started spending time with me at age eleven. Although I couldn't see or hear him because of the pain medication I was taking, his presence was familiar and comforting, soothing my anxiety.

Andy said, "Orion, what do you think?"

"Huh, what? I'm sorry, I wasn't listening."

"I was saying, when you get back and feel better, I would like you and Seren to come to my place for a barbecue. Vivian hasn't seen you in ages, and I'm sure she would like to meet Seren."

Perplexed. Why was he acting like Seren and I were a couple? Why is everyone assuming that?

I said hesitantly.

"I guess so… That would be up to Seren if she wants to come."

Seren smiled.

"I'd love to come over."

Andy and Seren turned away from me. I think they may have been listening to Cyrus. I couldn't see or hear him.

I asked, "What's going on?"

Seren said, "Nothing. Cyrus was saying you look exhausted."

I did feel tired.

"Yeah, I am. Kind of."

She said, "Okay, we'll leave you to rest. We'll be back tomorrow. Come on, Andy, you can take me out somewhere decent to have dinner. I'm getting tired of the hotel food."

Andy said, "Yeah, sure. See you tomorrow. You rest."

The redhead picked up her purse. The attorney grabbed his briefcase, and they hurried out the door.

I was alone in the room, but I knew Cyrus was there with me. I tried to sleep, but my thoughts kept swirling in my mind as I nervously scratched at the sheet. Besides my grandmother's mysterious intentions, Charbonnet was also after me now. What am I supposed to do? Why does everyone act like Seren and I are a couple?

I wanted more than anything for us to be a real couple. God, I longed for it. But how could I ask her to stay? She deserved peace, free from the constant threats: Charbonnet, my grandmother, and the Duke's ominous plans to send me away to who knows where. I've already been in the hospital three times in just six months. How much longer can my luck hold out?

I exhaled heavily, my hands trembling. I couldn't bring myself to do that to her. Seren deserved more—more than this bleak reality, a better, brighter future free from my problems. She shouldn't be burdened by someone like me. I had to let her go, even though it shattered me inside.

I wondered what happened to her car when the twins caught me. She needs a new car. Even after the recent engine repairs, it was still not a good vehicle. She deserves something better. I'll ask Andy to buy her a new car when they return, and he can take the money from my bank account.

She should go back home. Poor Jenny has been stuck taking care of the occult shop all this time because of me, and that's not fair to her. I'll tell Seren to fly back to Shreveport and have Andy cover the cost.

Seren told me that Darlene was with the FBI, but when would she be able to come to L'Enfant Haven mansion to see Johnny and say goodbye? She needs to talk to her son. The boy needs to pass to the other side. The poor boy's been waiting all this time to see his mother. He must be frantic by now. He's probably thinking I'll never come back, like his mother.

Cyrus squeezed my hand, recognizing my anxiety.

I said, "It's okay. I was thinking about Johnny and what he must feel right now."

I wiped the tears away and closed my eyes, but sleep wasn't coming.

A nurse entered to check on me.

"Oh, they said you were asleep."

"I was trying, but it's not happening. There's just too much bouncing around in my head, and it's hurting."

"I'll be back with a pain pill and a sleeping pill."

She left and returned a few minutes later.

I stared at the ceiling as the painkillers took hold, and the sleeping pill was dragging me toward sleep. My mind reeled with unanswered questions.

When would Charbonnet come after me? Would my grandmother come after me again? And why did I feel like I had to push Seren away when I finally had a chance at something real with her?

I sighed, my fingers unconsciously scratching at the sheets. Cyrus's hand settled over mine, steady, grounding. His silent way of saying: I'm still here.

Darkness finally took me, pulling me into another night of uneasy dreams.

Renee Boussard, the Voodoo Imperatrice, sat at the small, ancient table in the dimly lit divination room within her red house in New Orleans. A small bronze brazier burned, releasing a potent smoke of sacred herbs that sharpened the priestess's Far Sight. In the corner, the drummer thumped out a steady beat, his rhythms echoing through the space, helping her plunge deeper into a meditative trance.

With unwavering focus and mystical power, she watched over her grandson, Orion, hoping to unveil some hidden truths.

She had been performing this ritual every day since she learned he was alive, from one of her informants, a nurse at the hospital he was sent to after the confrontation at the plantation. Her Far Sight granted her a precious few hours each day to watch him, to hear his every whisper and watch his every move, before it faded away. With each passing moment, her obsession grew stronger, knowing that he was truly alive and nearby.

Nothing much happened for almost a month; he aimlessly wandered the plantation mansion, haunted by the searing pain from his injuries after shattering the Labauve signet and being violently hurled onto the stairs. Then, unexpectedly, he met a psychic named Seren Griffyths, and everything changed. He was utterly smitten with her.

Over the past few weeks, he discovered a boy ghost named Johnny, rescued him from a dilapidated house, and vowed to find his mother. Determined and urgent, Orion, Seren, and Cyrus—a ghost from the plantation—set out on a trip to Alabama, driven by the hope of reuniting Johnny with his mother.

Her grandson located Darlene Newman inside a private mental institution and staged a daring rescue to free her. The three of them narrowly escaped, and Orion left the women stranded at the Lake Blanc Resort, their fate uncertain.

When the Imperatrice returned the next day to continue her Far Sight, she was horrified to find Orion being miserably tortured by Earnest Charbonnet Jr. Her rage erupted—a blazing storm of fury. She wasn't going to lose another family member to this animal. For decades, the curses she sent to him and his father were always blocked by the voodoo protections shielding them, leaving her helpless and enraged.

She watched with tense anticipation as Orion summoned Lwa from the spirit realm, commanding them to break Charbonnet's protection. This was the moment she had relentlessly worked toward. Her previous attempts to harness Orion's hidden powers had always failed. But now, against all odds, her grandson had achieved what she had long desired—despite being severely injured at the time.

She cried out with pure joy upon seeing this, her heart pounding with excitement. Without hesitation, she frantically prepared a ceremony to curse Earnest Charbonnet Jr., passion fueling her every move. But the curse was thwarted again—nothing happened. Whatever Orion had done now blocked her curses completely. Frustration and determination flared within her; she had to find out what he did, no matter the cost.

She continued her daily Far Sight ritual.

Chapter 38
Angry Magic

When Seren and Andy arrived the following day, I shared my thoughts.

"Seren, it's time you went home. Poor Jenny's been running the shop by herself for too long."

"Oh, no. I called and told her to close it until I return." She said.

"Well, see, that's not right. That's your livelihood. You must keep the store open to make a living, not stay with me. I'm fine."

"I'm okay."

"No, you're not. Andy, get her a plane ticket for Shreveport. Pay for it out of my account. Oh, and buy her a new car. I don't know what happened to her car."

Andy said, "We found it. It was impounded..."

I cut him off.

"It doesn't matter. She needs a better car. After everything she went through because of me, she deserves it. Buy her a car."

Seren's green eyes flashed.

"You don't get to buy me a new car like I'm some damsel in distress. And don't tell me how to run my business."

"Seren, let Andy purchase you a car. Go home and take care of yourself," I begged her.

"Orion, stop it."

Her voice wavered, but her gaze held firm.

"I'm here because I want to be, not because of anything you're doing."

I tensed, pain rippling through my battered body.

"Well, I don't want you here," I shouted.

The words spilled out, bitter and sharp.

"Just go home!"

She stiffened. Her green eyes flashed. She felt hurt, angry, and something more.

"Orion, I'm not a ghost. You can't just push me away like you do them."

No, she has to go, ripped through my mind. Something snapped. My pulse surged, and my body tensed even more. I wanted them to go away. I needed them out of here.

Anger coiled inside me, hot and unfamiliar—something dark, something powerful. It clawed at my insides, begging to be released. I couldn't stop it. I didn't want to stop it. Magic flowed through my veins, a sharp, electric hum beneath my skin. My vision blurred at the edges. My breath came fast and ragged. Without thinking, I raised my hand and pushed.

Seren and Andy slammed into the closet door, the thud echoing off the sterile hospital walls. They gasped, their eyes bulging with shock, staring at me.

Seren started to say something, but Andy gripped her arm, "I think we had better go."

They both turned and left my hospital room.

Each breath I took was quick and hard, like I had just run several miles. I heard them leave.

A few seconds later, the FBI guard assigned to watch over me stepped in and asked, "Is everything all right?"

"Yes. We just had an argument."

He nodded and returned to the chair outside my room.

What had I just done? Somehow, I pushed Seren and Andy. It was similar to how I pushed the ghosts, but I never had to pull magic in to do it to the spirits. I didn't even think about it; it just happened. I was so angry that they wouldn't listen to me. Magic seemed to pour in on its own. It buzzed and tingled through my body, and I released it through my hand. I could have hurt them. What am I becoming? My stomach twisted. My chest tightened like a vice. What had I done?

I gasped for air, but it felt like I was drowning, not from pain, not from exhaustion—from the terror of what I had just unleashed. My hands trembled violently. My unbound fingers clawed at the sheets, tearing through the fabric, but I barely noticed. I wasn't afraid of my grandmother. I wasn't scared of Charbonnet. I was terrified of myself.

Cyrus took my hand, and I squeezed it, knowing he was still here with me, no matter what kind of monster I was becoming. His touch calmed me, just like it had when I was young and upset. I mentally pushed away the two people I cared about most. Why did I do that? Tears streamed down my face.

Seren grabbed her purse and stormed out of the hospital room, rushing through the hall and heading for the elevator with Andy hurrying behind her. He grasped her arm.

"Stop! Stop!"

She stopped and shouted, "Can you believe what he did to us?"

"I know. Please keep your voice down. Let's go out to the car and discuss this."

He guided her to the white Ford rental, his hands trembling as he hurriedly unlocked the doors.

When they were both seated in the vehicle, Andy said, "Orion has never been able to do that before. Something is happening to him."

This statement surprised her and Seren's anger subsided. She didn't know the extent of his powers and thought this was something she had never seen before. It was something no one had witnessed until this morning.

She said, her voice cracking with concern, "Perhaps I should go back and talk to him."

"No, I think we'd better leave him alone for now. He has to think about what he did."

Seren clenched her fists and with an unwavering gaze, she stared out the windshield.

"He must be hurting. I should go back. Let him know I'm here."

Andy sighed.

"Seren, when Orion feels worried, he lashes out. That's how he's always been. If you push, he pushes harder."

She bit her lip, fighting the sting of tears.

"But I am here. And I don't care how angry he gets; I won't just— walk away."

Andy softened.

"I know. But right now, the best thing you can do for him is give him space."

She nodded.

"Okay. What should I do now?"

"I think you need to go home. I'll see how he's handling things tomorrow. I can't stay long. I have a meeting with Darlene and the FBI, which will take hours tomorrow. I'll phone you and let you know how he's doing."

"I'll call about a flight to Shreveport in the morning," she said.

She bowed her head, on the verge of tears.

"Don't worry about it. I'll call Doris and have her book a flight for you. Orion's paying for it, especially after what he did."

"Okay, but I feel so bad for him. I wish he would open up and talk about his feelings."

"He has always been closed. The only time I saw him open up was when he came home from the hospital after the battle with his grandmother and found out that his ghost family had all decided to stay with him. He was crying like a baby over that. He never cried that much, even when his mother died."

Andy drove Seren to the hotel. He was staying at the same place. He went to his room, called Doris, and told her what happened.

Doris said, "Oh my, the poor boy. More things happening to him?"

The next day, Andy went to Orion's hospital room early. He was still asleep, but his ghost friend stood watching him at the foot of his bed.

He walked in.

"Good morning, Cyrus."

Cyrus put his finger to his lips and moved to the room's far corner.

The ghost whispered, "Orion's really upset about what happened yesterday. He literally cried himself to sleep, like when he was little."

"Oh, no."

Andy turned his head and looked over his shoulder at his friend, worried about what he was going through.

"He has also started his scratching thing again. That started after he got out of the hospital the last time."

"What do you mean, 'his scratching thing?'"

"When he was little, he would sit in corners and scratch at the walls."

"He did?"

This shocked the attorney. But wait, he remembered Orion scratching the armoire wall while possessed, when he found him hiding inside.

"Nanny managed to break him of that by teaching him piano and ensuring he always has something to do with his fingers."

He nodded.

Cyrus continued, "When he went to school, he would pick at his desk and scratch his pants whenever he felt nervous or upset. His desk always had chunks missing from the corners, and his jeans were often holey and frayed at the thighs from where he scratched at them. Milly and Philly constantly repaired his pants."

"I remember the holes in his pants."

He had wondered why his father didn't buy him new ones. He probably did, but Ory kept scratching holes in them.

"As an adult, he appeared to have ceased the picking and scratching, but now it started up again. I doubt he realizes what he's doing. Haven't you noticed how the wicker chairs on the veranda all have fibers sticking out of the arms?"

"Yes, I did. I got stabbed a couple of times by them. I just thought they were getting old and falling apart."

"No, that's from Orion picking at them. Also, look at the arms of the sofa in the living room. The patterns in some spots are nearly gone because Ory scratched them off."

"Oh, my God. I never paid attention."

"Last night, he was so upset he scratched a hole in the sheet on the bed."

Andy shook his head.

"Why do you think this has come back?"

"I believe he's concerned about what his grandmother will do next, and now he has to worry about Charbonnet as well. He's scared, Andy, and believes he's the only one who can take action. He doesn't know what to do."

A voice sounded from behind them.

"Hey, guys. What's going on?"

Orion, having woken up, saw Andy and Cyrus whispering in the corner.

The attorney turned and smiled.

"Hey, buddy, how are you feeling today?"

"I feel better, not as much pain. I can even see Cyrus."

Andy said, "That's great."

"What were you whispering about?"

"Oh, we didn't want to wake you. I was telling Cyrus that Seren has gone home."

Orion visibly relaxed.

"Oh, thank God. That's one thing I don't have to worry about."

Andy glanced at the ghost, and the ghost raised his eyebrows in an 'I told you so' expression.

Orion asked, "What's going on with Darlene?"

The attorney said, "I can't stay long today because I have a meeting with Darlene and the FBI. We're working out the details of the witness protection agreement. I'm her lawyer now."

"That's good. She has to come to my house at some point to say goodbye to Johnny. He won't pass to the other side until he sees his mother."

"Okay, that's good to know. I'll think about how to put that into the agreement without sounding too weird."

"Good."

Orion gazed out the window at the rain, his left middle finger beginning to scratch at the sheet. Andy noticed the action. Recognizing it now, he remembered other instances where Ory had scratched at chair arms and various surfaces. Cyrus approached the bed and took Orion's left hand. Orion squeezed the ghost's hand and looked up at Cyrus with a smile.

"Andy, I'm sorry about pushing you yesterday. I didn't even know I could do that. I got angry and it just came out. Seren must think I'm a monster."

"It's okay. I don't think she feels that way. You should call her and apologize. I'm sure she'll forgive you."

"I hope so."

He returned to staring out the window.

The attorney picked up his briefcase.

"I've got to get to the meeting. I'll probably see you tomorrow."

Without looking over, Orion said, "Sure. See you tomorrow."

Seren returned to Shreveport the day after Orion psychically pushed her and Andy. Andy convinced her it was best to leave him alone so he could reflect on his actions. The attorney, who had known Orion all his life, probably knew the best way to handle him. She wanted to return to the hospital and speak with Orion. Instead, she chose silence, hoping he would find his way.

She called Jenny to pick her up at the airport. Her friend pulled up in her old Chevy, screeched the car to a stop in the passenger pickup lane, and jumped out. She ran to Seren and pulled her into a big hug.

"Oh, I'm so glad you're back. You look so tired. Let's get you home."

Seren said, "I'm glad to be home. And you're right, I am tired."

Jenny drove to the shop. Seren had called Jenny nearly every night, updating her on everything that happened. It was the most incredible story Jenny had ever heard.

"So, how's Orion?"

"I don't know. Andy said he'll call me and let me know."

When she arrived at her apartment, walking up the creaking metal stairs was exhausting; her legs felt as if they weighed a hundred pounds each. Her friend stayed for a while and made soup for lunch. They talked.

Seren told Jenny, "I think I'm in love with him, but I'm not sure it can work. He is so closed off and unwilling to open up or listen to anyone. Andy told me to wait and let Orion make the first move. I'm afraid I'll be waiting forever if I do that."

Jenny said, "Right now, I think that's all you can do. Wait and see what he does."

"But I want to help him, how can I do that if he won't talk to me or see me?"

Her voice cracked, and she started to cry. Jenny put her arms around her friend's shoulders and rocked her back and forth until Seren sat up.

As she sat in Jenny's arms, Seren thought, 'I have to stop this. I have to move forward.'

Sniffling, she said, "You're right, I'll just have to be patient. If it happens, it happens. If it doesn't, it doesn't."

Jenny stayed until early evening, despite Seren insisting that she was fine and asking her to go home. She took a shower and was ready to go to bed early when the phone rang.

It was Andy. He informed her about Orion's condition and what Cyrus had said regarding his friend's stress, anxiety, and the scratching issue.

Seren said, "Yeah, he was scratching the tables at the restaurants we stopped at, and sometimes he scratched at the car door handle."

After they hung up, Seren's eyes filled with tears as she thought about Orion. He must be overwhelmed, burdened by the weight of the world on his shoulders. To protect those he loves he keeps them at arm's length, isolating himself once again. The loneliness he endures is incredible and her heart ached deeply for him.

She had to be patient and hoped he would call her when he calmed down.

Chapter 39
Leaving the Hospital

I spent another week and a half in the hospital. The doctors were astonished by the speed of my recovery. I knew Fuzzbucket was accelerating the healing.

I couldn't muster the courage to call Seren while I was in the hospital. I thought I would talk to her when I got home. I didn't want her to hate me; I just wanted her to be safe, and being around me wasn't safe.

Every day, I thought about how I can keep my grandmother and now Charbonnet from coming after me and those whom I care for. I was afraid the ideas I came up with aren't enough. The Lwa I summoned to fight my grandmother's Lwa weren't strong enough, and they were beaten badly during the psychic battle at L'Enfant Haven mansion.

I wasn't sure if the Lwa I called on to remove Charbonnet's Lwa were enough. Some of them had succeeded in banishing his Lwa from his house and the farm where he held me hostage. If they weren't strong enough, the FBI's raids wouldn't have been successful. But was the Lwa truly gone from him? I didn't know. If not, he'd definitely come after me. He probably wouldn't target Seren, since she was hidden behind her glamour. But if he discovered I cared for her through other means, he might go after her to reach me.

I did't need to worry about Andy and his family, because the Duke placed protection spells on all of them after the battle with my grandmother.

Seren should still have the protection from the Lwa I called to watch over her. Was it strong enough to withstand whatever my grandmother or Charbonnet might throw her way?

I loved everything about Seren—her green eyes that flared when she was mad, her challenges, and how she never let me push her away.

But I did push her away.

I swallowed hard. Did I say I…?

Yes, I did. I loved her. For the longest time, I had been fighting it—denial, confusion, fear—but it had been there all along. Then, the realization hit me, crashing over me, stealing my breath, and shaking my core. And the worst part? I could never tell her. Not now, not ever. I had to protect her from the chaos inside and around me.

Andy arrived at 2 p.m. to pick me up from the hospital. We finished the paperwork, and he pushed the wheelchair to the rental car. They wouldn't let me walk out of the hospital. We drove straight to the airport, where the FBI agent followed us in his vehicle and accompanied us through the terminal. He waved as we went up the stairs to board the plane.

Doris was waiting for us at the curb in her black Honda. We walked slowly toward her, and the crystal witch ran to me, hugging me a bit too tightly. I groaned.

She said, "Oh, I'm sorry. It's just so good to see you."

I smiled and said, "It's good to be back."

Andy helped me into the car, and we headed home. We pulled up to the mansion; the door opened, and I saw my ghost family standing in the vestibule, waiting for me, with Johnny out front. I slowly shuffled down the path with a big smile, seeing all of them, knowing there was nothing my grandmother or Charbonnet could do to harm them. Or maybe there was. I didn't know what it could be. I didn't want to think about it, so I smiled.

Johnny ran out to me and hugged me, almost knocking me over.

I said, "Careful there. I'm still not well."

He said, "Oh, I'm sorry."

He took my hand, and we walked the rest of the way to the house together.

I sat on the sofa while Rose brought me tea. Andy and Doris left. I shared everything that happened during this Finding Job as I had always done with my family, except for the incident involving Seren and Andy. I felt so ashamed of that action that I couldn't bring myself to tell them. There were gasps of concern over the horrible events.

Johnny remained still. His small hands formed into fists. Tears coursed down his pale face.

"Johnny," I said softly. "It's okay."

He looked up, eyes dark with sorrow.

"But when is Mommy coming?"

His voice trembled.

"She said she'd come back. She promised. You promised you'd bring her."

My chest tightened.

"She will, buddy. I swear."

But even as I said it, I wasn't sure if it was true.

The boy said, "But my Daddy was so mean to you and Mommy. I hate him."

He crossed his arms and furrowed his little brow.

"We got your Mommy out of that place and he can't hurt her anymore."

"I know, but when will I get to see her?"

"Andy is working on that and will let us know. Again, you have to be patient."

"Okay…" he said hesitantly.

He stared at the floor, so upset by this. What could I do?

He turned and went upstairs to the nursery.

I asked Doc Albert, "How's he been?"

"Not too bad, but sometimes he sits in the nursery's window and stares out for hours. One time I found him in the nursery armoire crying."

"I guess that's what he was used to, staring out the window and crying in a dark closet."

I felt sorry for the boy, but I couldn't get his mother here any faster.

Paul, Walter, and Hugo volunteered to maintain regular watches at the property perimeters in case Charbonnet sent someone here. They could warn me of any unwanted arrivals. I thought that sounded like an excellent idea. When I healed, I'd summon Lwa to carry out that function and protect the house.

I began to feel tired and didn't want any dinner. Doc helped me to bed, and I took two of the pain pills the hospital sent home with me. I quickly fell asleep and slept through the entire night.

SPECTRAL PROMISES

Chapter 40
Enlightenment from the Duke

I woke up the next day wanting to take a shower, but I needed help removing the bandages from my head and shoulder, as well as the Ace bandages from my fingers. Milly and Philly, the ghost maids, came to help me. After the dressings were removed, I looked at myself in the mirror. My face was still bruised in several spots, but it was healing.

What really startled me was my hair—or rather, the absence of it. The doctors had shaved my head for surgery, leaving only dark stubble all over. I had never seen myself like this before. My curls had always been a part of me—wild and untamed— but now I looked... different. Exposed.

The suture lines were jagged, a stark reminder of how close to death I came. A thin, dark line ran from my forehead, curving back across my scalp like a lightning bolt. I hoped my hair would cover the scar when it grew back. Or would I always carry this mark, a silent testament to everything that happened during this event?

The gunshot wound on my right shoulder was a dark, puckered purple scab with some yellow around it for about two inches. My face was still slightly purple in places, but the swelling had significantly decreased, and my left eye could now open fully. My fingers looked straight but were purple and ached. Purple blotches spread across my left chest, where the broken ribs still hurt with each breath. In other words, I looked like I had been through a horrible ordeal, called Cleetus and Clive.

The girls helped me into the shower, and I let them scrub me down. After the shower, I felt a little better.

As I entered my room, the air felt different—charged and humming with unseen energy. A fire crackled in the hearth even though I was sure I had never lit it. And there, the last person I wanted to see, lounging in the chair as if he owned the place—Duke Shamedi.

The warm room was welcoming. He glanced at me with a smile. It wasn't his usual big, toothy grin that always made me wonder what kind of mischief he was up to. This smile radiated friendship, perhaps even a little—dare I say—affection.

He said, "Come here, boy, we need to talk."

His voice sounded serious and concerned. I put on my robe and sat in the chair across from him. I didn't make my usual smartass comment because his expression was so different.

"You did good, boy. You got Johnny out of that house and to a safe place. You found his mother and pulled the protection off Charbonnet. Now, he can die as he was meant to."

The words landed like a blow, tightening something deep in my chest.

"What do you mean, 'He can die as he was meant to'?"

"With all the Lwa surrounding him, he may have never died. He was scheduled to go a few years ago, but because of the Lwa, he didn't, and his son did."

"What, you mean Johnny died because Charbonnet didn't?"

"He was never supposed to be born at that time."

A cold weight settled in my chest.

"What?"

"Charbonnet should have died years ago," the Duke continued, his voice steady and unyielding. "When he didn't, when the Lwa kept him alive, the balance of the spiritual-temporal lines was thrown into disarray. Johnny was an anomaly, a soul born out of time. And when the universe tries to correct an imbalance…"

I swallowed hard.

"Someone has to go. But his spirit is still here," I said. "So, you're saying that everything I did and everything that happened to me was to restore balance to these temporal lines. Is that why you granted me these powers to balance the universe?"

"That and other more personal reasons."

"Like what?"

I wanted to know what other life-threatening things he may expose me to.

"I can't tell you at this time. What surprised me," the Duke mused, "was you pushing Andy and Seren like that. You shouldn't have that ability yet—not for years."

My pulse stuttered.

"What do you mean… yet?"

He gave me a slow, knowing smile.

"Something else is at play here, boy. And it isn't me."

A chill crept over my body. If Shamedi wasn't the one pulling the strings, who was?

I asked, "But wait, you Gods are in charge of the Lwa … Why didn't you pull them off Charbonnet?"

"Only the individual, or God, who requested the service of the Lwa can dismiss them from their duties. Alternatively, if the individual dies, a God may come to release them, should it choose to do so. Additionally, a person with sufficient power can beseech the Lwa to perform tasks or free them from their obligations if the spirit entities deem the person worthy of their attention. However, this is quite rare."

"If that's true, how could I remove the Lwa from Lockwood and off Charbonnet?"

"That's what I mean. Something else is giving you powers you shouldn't have."

That answered several questions that had been lingering in my mind but raised many more. The Duke must have sensed my thoughts and continued with other comments.

"But don't worry about it. I'm sure it will all work out. You need to learn how to control your emotions. The ability to use magic initially stems from your emotions. You'll develop better control over time, but it may take a few decades. Merlin was nearly 80 before he could master it. Even then, he still didn't have complete control. If he had, he would have been promoted to a God."

I choked when he said Merlin.

"Do you mean the Merlin, as in Merlin, the magician? Promoted to a God? Can a human become a God?"

He kept talking and ignored my second question.

"Yes, there was only one. As a human, you need assistance to enhance your skills and emotional support. Without proper emotional regulation, dark entities—drawn to your mystical energy—may pursue you. Seren is equipped to help with this. Her capacity for love and psychic abilities can guide and assist you.

"I want to be with her, but I'm afraid that everything happening to me could endanger her. I don't want to put her or anyone else at risk."

"Don't be afraid, boy; you have the power to protect those you care about. With your loved ones close by, you'll find the motivation to do your best to keep them safe, drawing strength from within to fight the dark forces. Stay with her."

I stared at the fire and nodded.

He said, "You look terrible. You need to be prepared for everything that's coming your way, so I've brought you this."

He reached into his pocket and pulled out a white object. It was a piece of fruit from the Tree of Life. I took it from his hand and stared at the mystical item. The spiritual object shimmered and undulated in my palm. I knew it could heal all my physical injuries.

Staring at the piece of magical fruit, I asked, "Do you mean something else is coming soon?"

I looked up, but the Duke was gone, and the fire in the fireplace was no longer burning. It was no surprise that he would disappear without saying goodbye.

I popped the fruit into my mouth and savored its magnificent flavor.

Fruit from the Tree of Life. Yes, that was what it was—the taste of life itself—the rich, intoxicating flavor of all living things. The magic surged through my body with intensity, pulsating into every fiber of my being. I could now vividly sense the powerful magical waves crashing over me like a tidal force. Three brilliant flashes of light erupted from my chest, illuminating the dim room. The mystical energy, having fulfilled its purpose, could no longer be contained. Now, it must return to the vast, infinite universe.

I gained a clearer understanding of what occurred when I consumed the magical fruit. I sat in the chair, shaking and panting, with my heart racing, ready to pass on my part of life to something else. I called Milly and Philly. They appeared immediately, smiled, and knew what to do.

Chapter 41
Waiting for Mommy

The next morning, I called several Lwa from the spirit realm and assigned them as guards, early warning informants, and house protectors. I also included a personal protection Lwa—I named him Sylvester— and a glamour Lwa—Glam for short. This glamour entity was stronger, letting me appear as anyone I wanted. Seren was right; I needed to think more carefully about my own protection.

The next few days remained quiet around the mansion. Even Johnny didn't make much noise. He mostly sat in the nursery window seat, staring out and clutching Bunny tightly to his chest. I knew he missed his mother, but there was nothing I could say to ease that longing.

On the third day, Andy called.

"Orion, how're you doing?"

"I'm okay. The Duke dropped by with a piece of fruit from the Tree of Life, so I'm all healed. Even my hair grew back."

"That's great. I got word from the FBI. They'll bring Darlene over the day after tomorrow at about 10 a.m."

"Oh, wonderful. Johnny will be so happy. What did you tell them was the reason?"

"That was a tough battle. They were determined to keep her from going anywhere. We explained that she needed to meet with you at your house to express her gratitude and provide information that might help keep Charbonnet from bothering you. We made it clear that if she didn't get this opportunity, she wouldn't testify in court when they apprehended her husband."

"They must have really been upset about that."

I smiled, thinking about how angry the criminal lord would be when captured and his wife stepped on the stand.

"She also wants Seren to be there to thank her. Have you spoken to her yet?"

"No, I haven't."

I felt so bad about pushing her and was sure she wouldn't forgive me.

"Do you want me to talk to her?"

"No, I'll do it. I'll call her today."

We hung up, and I sat in the chair beside the telephone, hesitating to call Seren. The Duke said I should be with her, and oh, God, I want to be with her. But what did she want?

I dialed her number. The phone rang. Once. Twice. Three times. Every second felt like a countdown to something I wasn't ready for.

Then—her voice.

"Star Occult Shop, how may I help you?"

My throat closed. My fingers clenched the receiver. I opened my mouth, but nothing came out.

She sighed, exasperated.

"Orion, I know it's you."

I stammered, "Yeah, it...it's me."

"What do you need, Orion?" she said in a disgusted tone.

I quickly said, "Darlene will be over here the day after tomorrow at 10 a.m., and she wants to see you while she's here."

"Alright, I'll be there," she said before hanging up.

I sat there with the phone pressed to my ear, wanting to say more, but she had already disconnected the call. She must still be incredibly angry with me, and I didn't blame her.

I walked into the living room, turned on the TV, and reclined on the sofa, absentmindedly scratching the arm of the antique furniture as I tuned out whatever was playing on the screen. My mind swirled with indecision. Should I call her back, or would that only infuriate her more? What should I say? I'll talk to her when she arrives.

Johnny came downstairs, looking downcast.

I smiled and said, "Hey, sport. I just received a call. Your mother will arrive the day after tomorrow at 10."

Johnny's entire form froze. His eyes widened, lips parting in disbelief.

"She's... coming?" he said, his voice quaking.

I nodded.

A squeal of pure joy burst from his small frame as he bounced on his heels, clapping his hands together.

"She's coming! She's really coming!"

He hugged Bunny so tightly that I thought the poor stuffed animal might pop a seam.

Hugging Bunny, he said. "I'll wait right here for her."

I was glad to see him happy.

"Sure, you can do that."

"What room will Mommy stay in?" he asked excitedly.

My stomach sank. I hesitated.

"Johnny… she can't stay."

His excitement dimmed, his expression wavered, and his face fell. Joy snuffed out like a candle.

"You lied."

"I'm sorry, Johnny, but she can't live here. She's only coming to see you and say goodbye."

Tears welled up in his eyes.

"You said you would find her and bring her here. You lied!" he shouted.

He hugged Bunny, sobbing, burying his face in the rabbit's head and rocking back and forth.

I felt even worse about this than I already did about Seren.

"I'm sorry you didn't understand what I meant. You can't stay here either. You must pass through the tunnel of light. Your mother is coming to see you before you leave."

"But I want to be with Mommy," he cried.

His sorrow washed over me as it had at the house where I found him. Tears ran down my cheeks.

"I know you do, but you have to go to the other side because you're dead. We all have to go at some time."

"But your family is still here."

"That's a special situation and they will pass over when I do."

"Why can't I wait and go when Mommy goes?"

"No, Johnny. You can't stay. You'll be with your Mommy when she dies and goes to the other side. Then you'll be with her forever."

"But I'll have to wait a long time again."

"Time works differently over there. It won't seem like a long time, and you'll be able to do whatever you want to do."

This statement appeased him slightly.

"I will? Will I be able to eat candy again? I like candy."

"Yes, you can have as much candy as you want. It won't be bad there. You'll like it."

"How do you know all of this? Did you die and go there?"

I chuckled.

"I almost died once. I've never been there, but I've come close. I've visited the spirit realm, which is where the Gods and Angels live. Having been there, I now know many things about the other side, including ghosts and spirits, as well as how to help them."

He fell silent and remained on the couch, hugging Bunny. Everything I said must have overwhelmed the child's mind.

I went outside, sat on the veranda, reflecting on what I had learned over the past few weeks, and picked at the arm of the wicker chair.

Chapter 42

Darlene's Arrival

Two weeks had passed since Seren's return from Mobile, Alabama, with no call from Orion. She knew he was home because Andy had called her. Her frustration was growing, and she was becoming angry with him for not calling.

Finally, he called and told her that Darlene would be over at his place the day after tomorrow. She replied that she would be there and hung up the phone. Seren feared that if she spoke with him at that moment, she would yell at him for not calling sooner, and she knew that wasn't the right thing to do.

The day finally arrived for her visit to the plantation where she hoped to see Darlene and speak with Orion. Seren spent a long time contemplating what to say to Orion. She wanted him to know that she was there for him, should he choose to open up, and that she genuinely cared about him. Her most profound hope was that he would listen.

As she drove the new Ford Mustang that Andy purchased for her last week with Orion's money, a surge of anxiety gripped her. She yearned to be near him again—to gaze at those blue eyes, flecked with gold that sparkled in the right light. She craved the unique sensations only he could emit. Most of all, she desperately wanted to kiss him.

On the morning Darlene arrived, I informed the Lwa that visitors would be coming and to allow them to enter the property and house. I didn't want the FBI getting zapped by the Lwa.

Johnny and I sat on the sofa pretending to be interested in the flickering TV as we waited. The voices from the screen were just background noise, and our minds were elsewhere. Every distant sound, every creak of the old house, sent a shiver through me. My stomach was in knots and my fingers tapped nervously against the armrest.

Sitting beside me, the boy clutched Bunny so tightly it was almost painful to watch, his ghostly form vibrating with anticipation.

A branch snapped outside, making Johnny tense. I sprang up from the couch, my heart racing, and hurried to the door. But when I opened it, nothing. Just a stupid squirrel running across the yard. I exhaled sharply and smiled at him while shaking my head.

His shoulders slumped.

"Maybe she's not coming," he whispered, his voice trembling with fear.

"She's coming," I assured him, trying to quell my gut's slight, nagging fear.

I instinctively knew someone was at the door, so I hurried to open it. My breath caught in my throat at the sight of Seren standing on the porch. Her green eyes looked concerned, softening her features. She wore a deep blue peasant dress cinched at the waist, its fabric flowing around her legs like ocean waves. The low neckline revealed the gentle curve of her collarbone, while her skin seemed to glow in the morning light. Her usually wild auburn hair was pulled into a loose ponytail, with a few strands falling freely to caress her cheeks.

For a moment, all I could do was stare. My fingers curled into a fist, aching to touch her—to pull her close, to bury my face in her hair and breathe her in. But I couldn't.

I forced air into my lungs and cleared my throat.

"Hi."

She said, "Hi. You're looking good. Did you use a Lwa to heal yourself?"

"No, the Duke brought me a piece of fruit from the Tree of Life."

She said sarcastically, "Oh, he did, did he? Why didn't he bring that while you were half-dead at the farm?"

She looked disgusted as she entered. The familiar scent of jasmine and coconut shampoo accompanied her in.

Johnny darted forward, gripping Seren's legs with a childlike urgency.

"Mommy's coming," he whispered, his voice trembling with excitement.

His small hands clutched at the fabric of her dress, his spectral form flickering slightly with emotion.

Seren knelt, her own eyes shining.

"I know, sweetheart. You must be so excited."

She smoothed her hand through his hair.

"I bet she's just as excited to see you."

"Yeah, I miss her so much, but Orion said I can only be with her for a little while, then I have to go into the tunnel."

"That's right. It's hard to wait for someone you love."

She peered up at me. I looked away, knowing the statement was meant for me as well.

Seren continued, "But you can do it; I know you can."

The boy said, "I'll try."

He looked down with a sad expression.

The door opened and Andy Butler walked in with a smile, wearing jeans and a tan short-sleeved button-up shirt. He noticed Johnny and squatted down to his level.

"Hi, you must be Johnny. I'm Andy. I'm Orion's and your mother's friend. I've been helping her work with the FBI, so your daddy can't hurt her anymore."

The boy smiled and said, "Thank you, Mr. Andy."

Andy grinned back.

Andy stood and said to Seren, "How are you doing?" shifting his eyes toward me.

She said, "I'm fine," and returned with a slight head shake and pursed lips.

I observed this exchange, aware that they were making silent comments about me. I averted my gaze to the floor, not wanting to look either of them in the eye.

Johnny watched this unspoken conversation between the adults, confused about what was happening.

The sound of multiple vehicles racing up the driveway echoed from outside. I opened the mansion's door and three identical black Ford sedans pulled up and parked in front of the picket fence.

I looked down at Johnny, cautioning him, "Don't run out to your mother. She won't be able to see you yet. I'll help with that when she gets into the house."

Hanging on my leg and fidgeting, he said, "Okay."

The car doors swung open, and several men in dark suits and ties stepped out. Henry Upton, the supervising agent, along with two other FBI agents, approached the entrance. The remaining agents lingered on the path, scanning their surroundings suspiciously. Agent Upton recognized Andy Butler and Seren Griffyths, offering them a nod.

He held out his hand to me for a handshake.

"Nice to meet you, Mr. Labauve."

I took his hand and shook it.

"Nice to meet you."

The agent's eyes widened. He felt the ominous sensation I emit.

He said, "I saw you in the hospital, but you were pretty messed up. I'm amazed you look so well now."

"Yeah, I'm a fast healer."

He wouldn't understand or believe it if I told him what really happened.

"We need to search the house and property before we let Ms. Newman in."

"That's okay," I said.

He gestured for the two men with him to enter the house and turned to the other agents waiting on the flagstone path.

"You all check the grounds."

The two men moved swiftly, their gazes sharp as they checked every room and carefully cleared corners. Naturally, they wouldn't see the spirits, but that didn't stop my stomach from twisting whenever one of the agents brushed too close to a ghost they couldn't detect.

Johnny fidgeted next to me, his small hands gripping the hem of my shirt. He practically vibrated with impatience, his spectral form flickering at the edges.

"Why is it taking so long?" he whispered, shifting his heels.

I placed a reassuring hand on his head.

"They just need to make sure it's safe, buddy."

Agent Upton approached the middle vehicle, opened the back door, and Darlene Newman stepped out. They must have gotten her different clothes, as she wore a stylish brown dress with a wide tan belt. Her hair was now cut into a nice shoulder-length style. The agent escorted her into the mansion and then left, closing the door behind him.

SPECTRAL PROMISES

Chapter 43
A Mother Says Goodbye to Her Son

Johnny hurried to his mother, wrapping his arms around her. She couldn't see him and only felt a tingling sensation around her legs. The boy looked up at me with tears in his eyes.

"She can't see me."

I said, "Just a minute. I'll let her see you."

Darlene frantically asked, "Is Johnny here?"

"Yes, he's hugging you."

I pointed to her legs, where Johnny embraced her.

"Is that what I'm feeling?"

She looked down at his general location.

"Yes. I can allow you to see and speak with your son."

I approached her, took her hands, and said, "Please close your eyes."

She did.

I whispered the Spirit Sight incantation and placed my hands over her eyes, then her ears. This would allow her to see the ghosts at the L'Enfant Haven plantation.

"Okay, open your eyes."

Darlene's eyes flew open as she looked down at her son. Overwhelmed with emotion, she sank to her knees, clutching him desperately. Johnny nestled into her embrace, tears streaming down his face.

Between sobs, she gasped, "I'm so sorry I left you alone at the house. Your father wouldn't listen to me and put me in a hospital on drugs, so I couldn't get out and reach you."

Johnny looked at her, his eyes round with love and forgiveness.

"I know, Mommy. Orion told me what happened and how Daddy beat him up because he got you out. I hate Daddy."

"Don't say that, honey. Your father's sick, and because of that, I didn't tell him where you were. I should have told him; maybe then you wouldn't have… died. It's all my fault."

She fell into another fit of heart-wrenching sobs.

The boy said, "Mommy, I want to go with you."

"Oh, baby, I know you do, but you can't. You have to move on."

"That's what Orion and Seren said."

He frowned, spectral tears still streaming down his cheeks.

A wave of both joy and sorrow overwhelmed everyone in the room as tears flowed for the mother and son.

Darlene and Johnny sat on the floor and talked for about half an hour. Johnny told his mother about what he had done during his stay at my house. Darlene explained to the boy how the FBI was protecting her.

The tunnel of love and light emerged. Only the spirits and I could see it.

The boy glared at it, feeling the pull but resisting the urge to go.

I said, "Johnny, it's time."

He stood, stared at the tunnel, and said, "I don't want to go."

"I know you don't, but you have to. We talked about this. I explained it to you."

I smiled at the child.

"I know."

He turned and gazed up at his mother with longing.

Darlene's throat tightened as she knelt before her son, her body trembling uncontrollably. Her fingers twitched, aching to reach out and hold him one final time—but she couldn't.

"Johnny, baby… it's okay," she whispered, her voice breaking. "You have to go. But I promise I'll be with you again. Forever."

Johnny's lip quivered; his little fists clenched at his sides.

"But I don't wanna leave you."

Tears streamed down her face as she forced herself to smile through the heartbreak.

"I know, sweetheart. But you have to."

She pressed a trembling hand over her mouth to stifle her sobs, her body shaking as she watched him turn towards the light.

I knelt beside the boy.

"It won't be long before your mother meets you. So, you won't be alone I asked my mother to be with you while you wait. See, there she is."

"You mean the pretty lady with the pretty hair."

"Yes, that's her."

My mother stood in the tunnel, her hands reaching out to Johnny. As soon as the tunnel appeared, I instinctively called her, urging her to help Johnny cross to the other side.

I placed a hand on Johnny's back and gently steered him toward the glowing passage. He glanced over his shoulder.

"Bye, Mommy."

"Bye, baby. I love you," Darlene whispered, her voice trembling

My mother offered her hand to the boy and they moved down the tunnel. The passage to the other side snapped shut.

I said, "He's gone."

Darlene turned and collapsed into Andy's arms, sobbing uncontrollably against his chest.

I turned to look at Seren. She was wiping her eyes with a handkerchief; her face lined with emotion. Our eyes met and I offered her a reassuring smile. After everything that happened at the house where we first saw Johnny's ghost, we both understood each other's feelings more deeply.

I stepped closer, speaking softly.

"Could you stay a little longer after the others leave? I need to talk to you."

Seren's gaze settled on me, uncertainty flickering in her green eyes. For a moment, I feared she might refuse. Then she nodded slowly, offering a faint, uncertain smile.

Darlene calmed down and glanced at Andy.

"Thank you."

He nodded and smiled. She turned to me.

"I want to thank you so much for caring for Johnny, bringing him here, and allowing me to see him one last time. If it weren't for you, I would never have been able to say goodbye to him and would still be stuck in that awful place.

"I guess that's all. I'll never see you again while in the witness protection program. Thank you all for everything you have done for Johnny and me."

I said, "Darlene, if you ever need my help, you know where to call me or Andy."

She nodded and turned to the door.

Andy opened the door for her, and she stepped out. Agent Upton escorted her back to the car, and the vehicles turned around and made their way back up the plantation road.

Chapter 44
Together at Last

All of us, including my ghostly family, gathered anxiously in the vestibule. I explained what the Duke told me: Charbonnet should have died years ago, but the Lwa's protection kept him alive. Because of this, Johnny was conceived too early. In a proper timeline, Darlene would have married someone else and had Johnny later in life. He would have grown into a man. But since Johnny is out of sync with time, he had to die young to balance the spectral timelines.

Andy asked, "What are spectral timelines?"

I replied, "I don't know. I didn't understand half of what the Duke told me. All I know is that conditions have improved, but they still aren't quite right, and that's part of my role: to help restore everything to its proper state. Who knows what that means for the future?"

Andy shook his head.

"More weird things to watch for."

I nodded.

He continued, "I'm heading home. I'll talk to you later."

He left, leaving Seren and me staring at each other. My family knew we needed to talk and they vanished.

Seren's face showed a hint of sadness. Despite her evident anguish, her beauty still captivated me. Was she mourning Darlene and Johnny, or was her sorrow directed at us?

I needed to apologize to her for the psychic 'push' I unintentionally delivered at the hospital. I hadn't realized I could do that. My chest felt so tight that I could feel it pressing against my heart.

She asked, "So, what do you want to say to me?"

I took her warm, steady hands, grounding myself in her touch, though mine trembled against hers. I stared at the floor, my throat tightening, the words catching deep inside me. Apologies never come easily to me.

"Seren..."

My voice cracked as I swallowed hard, forcing myself to continue.

"I... I'm sorry. At the hospital, when I pushed you and Andy... I didn't even know I was capable of that. I wasn't trying to hurt you—I just... I panicked, scared. I thought that if I made you both leave, you'd be safe."

I glanced up, searching her face for anger, for rejection. But instead, I discovered something that stole my breath—sympathy. Understanding.

I exhaled and said, "The Duke told me I shouldn't be able to pull magic and do that for several years. I don't even know how I was able to do it. He said it was linked to my emotions now. Eventually, I would learn better control; however, it would take years. He also mentioned that I needed support to manage my emotions and the use of mystical energy."

I hesitated, looking up at the ceiling and biting my lower lip, unsure of how to ask for assistance and reveal my vulnerability.

She could see me struggling.

"Orion, it's okay. I'm listening. I'm here for you."

Yes, she was here, but saying, 'I need help,' was still hard.

I spent most of my life alone. My ghost family was always nearby, ready to help, but talking to a living person was something else entirely. I never quite learned how to express my emotions or connect with others. My feelings would often burst out at the worst moments, leaving me speechless. I stared at the floor, struggling to find the right words. We stood frozen as time moved on, but I remained suspended in place. Seren grew increasingly frustrated, eager to give me the opportunity to speak my mind.

She said, "It's okay. If you need more time, I'll go, and you can call me when you're ready to talk more."

She turned toward the door, and panic gripped me as I realized she was leaving. I felt the distance between us grow, stretching into an unbearable chasm.

I reached out, grasping her hand before I could stop myself.

"Seren..."

She turned, her eyes questioning and her lips parted as if she might speak. But I didn't let her.

I pulled her toward me and kissed her. My heart was pounding with a mix of desperation, relief, and longing. I poured all my emotions into that kiss, my fingers tangling in her hair as my body pressed against her, as if I had been waiting forever for this moment. Maybe I had.

She didn't pull away. Instead, she pressed herself closer, her hands winding around my neck as her lips parted beneath mine.

When I finally broke free, breathless, I looked into her eyes and whispered, "Please stay. I need your help."

She looked into my eyes and asked, "Was the kiss from you or Abelard?"

I shook my head.

"Oh, no. That was all from me."

She wrapped her arms around my neck and passionately kissed me back. We stayed in the vestibule, kissing and touching each other as our hands explored each other's bodies. This was what we both wanted, but we had been too afraid to pursue it. I shivered from head to toe, longing for this woman. I took her hand and led her upstairs to my bedroom and she followed willingly.

The moment we entered my bedroom, our restraint shattered. Clothes tumbled off us in a frantic, awkward rush. I reached for her, my hands tracing the curve of her back and the softness of her hips. She felt like silk and fire under my fingertips, her warm breath brushing against my ear.

I suckled her right breast, flicking the nipple with my tongue. She flung her head back and gasped as I kissed and licked all over her neck and chest.

She pulled me to the bed, her laughter breathless, her hands urgent. I kissed her—deep, slow, reverent—drinking her in like she was the first taste of life itself.

She grabbed my cock and massaged it. I was on fire, hot with desire for every part of her. She was breathing heavily, her eyes glowing with her passion for me.

I called out, "Walter, bring the condoms from the Rolls."

She said, "You don't need those. I can't get pregnant."

"What do you mean?"

"I have twisted Fallopian tubes."

She pulled me to her and I slid inside. She inhaled sharply, her skin flushed as I entered. She closed her eyes and moaned with pleasure.

Could a couple be so perfectly matched? We made love several times that day and night. Each time was as passionate as the first.

Finally, I was making love to a woman I genuinely cared for—something far more meaningful than a fleeting one-night stand. The experience was incredible—more exciting, sensual, arousing, stimulating, provocative, and spectacular—than I ever could have imagined.

We finally exhausted ourselves and sat in bed holding each other. I shared more of what the Duke told me with Seren.

She said, "The first time I saw you call the Lwa for Johnny, I told myself you were using real magic. I guess you were."

"I never thought of it as magic; I believed it was more like spiritual power. But after hearing the Duke, especially when he mentioned Merlin, I realize now it must be actual magic. When I connect to the spirit realm and my eyes turn golden, I see magic flowing through the air. Mystical energy surrounds us, constantly present in varying amounts in different locations."

"What does it look like?"

"It's like clouds of different colors with small particles inside them that sparkle. They float and swirl around, pushed by some invisible current."

She said, "I don't know how I'm supposed to help you learn how to control your emotions and magic. I struggle to manage my own emotions. I'll do what I can and always be here for you, no matter what happens."

I kissed and hugged her.

"That's all I care about," I said.

Pointing to the painting of the door on the wall, "Are there faces in the light coming through the door in your painting?"

She laughed.

"I tried to cover them up, but it didn't work. I had started an earlier piece that just wasn't working, so I painted over it with white, but it seems to have leaked through."

"I see faces looking through the light."

She got up and walked closer to the picture.

"You're right, there are faces in the light, but those aren't the faces I covered. I don't remember putting those there."

She returned to the bed.

"That's happened to me before, where something appears in a painting that I don't remember doing. I usually figure out what it is later."

I sat up.

"There's something else I have to explain to you. You may not like it."

She sat silent, waiting with her head tilted.

I continued, "You remember I told you that the Duke gave me a piece of fruit from the Tree of Life to heal my body."

She nodded.

"Well, when I eat it, my body isn't just healed, something else happens."

"What's that?"

Her head tilted in curiosity.

"I have to have sex immediately after or else I would go crazy."

She furrowed her brow.

"Who did you have sex with?"

"Milly and Philly."

"The ghosts?" she questioned.

Her eyes were wide with shock.

"Yes, but you have to understand that there is no relationship with them. They are doing what they were trained to do: to please a man. My multiple great-grandfather, Gregor, pulled them off the streets and had them trained in a brothel, then brought them here to be his private sex toys and maids. They died from bad abortions. Their lives were terrible.

"When I'm in that super aroused state after eating the fruit, it's like an animal in musk rises inside me. I have to do it no matter what. Milly and Philly provide my avenue for release. They do what they did when they were alive, just as the other ghosts do what they did when they were alive here in the house."

"Well, if that happens again, you can do it with me," she said, crossing her arms.

"No, I can't. When I'm in that state, I don't care what happens to the other person I'm having sex with. It can get violent at times. I can't hurt the ghosts. I can hurt you."

I lowered my head, embarrassed by this confession.

"Did you do it with them when not in...that state?" she asked

"Only when they taught me how to be with a woman when I was sixteen and one other time."

"They taught you how to have sex?" she said with her brows raised.

I nodded.

She smiled and said, "Well, they did a good job. You're the best lover I've ever had."

I smiled back.

"Thank you."

"If this thing with the fruit from the Tree of Life happens again, warn me ahead of time so I know to stay away."

"I will," I said and kissed her, thanking God that she understood.

We spent the next three days together, talking and making love. Seren called Jenny to close the shop until she returned. Jenny agreed to handle the opening and closing during that time.

We longed to be close. Whenever desire arose, we made love in different rooms, passionately and often. It felt like we were finally giving in to all the moments we had been reticent to share. Now, there was nothing to hold us back.

Seren was initially hesitant to venture out of the bedroom due to the ghosts.

"You don't have to worry about them. They'll leave. They aren't watching."

This reassurance cleared her mind, transforming any place into a playground for our passionate adventures. She was more experienced than I was in exploring intimacy and was incredibly creative, making every moment with her a delight. I later learned she was five years older than me, but that didn't matter.

While Seren and I were together, I never considered how Charbonnet or my grandmother might plan to disrupt my now joyful life.

The Duke told me I had the power to protect those I cared about—like Seren, whom I cared for deeply, I think, even loved.

Did I love Seren Griffyths? Yes, I did. But I didn't want to declare it until I knew how she felt about me.

On the third night of passionate lovemaking, we fell asleep. As sleep pulled me in that night, I sensed something shifting. A strange, lingering energy crackled in the air. Magic. Old, familiar. Then, warmth. A delicious, tantalizing heat wrapped around me. My eyes fluttered open, and through the haze of pleasure, I saw it—wild red curls moving rhythmically at my groin. But something was… different.

Smiling, I said, "You didn't get enough earlier, huh?"

There was no response, but she kept at it. I moaned, savoring every second. Suddenly, a jolt of pleasure made me jump. I somehow recognized what it was.

I asked, "Was that a ...?"

My head was forcefully pushed deeper into the pillow, as if something yanked on my hair, and my eyes rolled back in my head. It was the Duke.

A huge smile spread across my face.

"...a Fairy Flick? Wife, you always know what I like."

He laughed.

Chapter 45
Divine Intimacy

A slow, knowing smile curved her lips. For the first time, through the Duke's eyes, I realized—this was no longer Seren.

"Yes, husband," she purred, her voice layered, carrying echoes of something ancient, something eternal. "I knew that would bring you forward."

He said, "You passed through first. You must be eager."

He kissed her, igniting sparks between their lips. The Fairy Queen gently brushed her hand over Orion's cheek and his olive skin deepened to a rich chocolate hue.

"There you are, my love. It's been so long."

"I told you I had plans that would be perfect. The boy and girl are perfect avatars for us. We can stay as long as we want."

"We can't take their lives from them. They have their own unique destinies. You know that."

"Yes, I know, but we can be together much more than ever."

"They are still aware; should we put them to sleep?"

"No, let them enjoy this with us."

He rolled over onto her, and the two divine beings—Duke Shamedi, the Voodoo God of the Dead, and Bridette, the green Fairy Queen—made love as only Gods can.

The divine lovers hovered a foot above the mattress, her delicate gossamer wings unfurled and wrapped around them, tightening with urgent tenderness. Magical particles—black from the Duke and green from the Fairy Queen—flowed from the Gods, swirling around them in a mesmerizing dance of mystical energy, blending and intermingling in a vibrant display.

Once the Deities reached a state of ecstasy and rapture, reality itself seemed to bend. The bedroom dissolved into shadows, flowing in and out of the mortal plane. Magical, sparkling grains swirled into a vortex above the couple, spinning faster and faster. This tornado of magic drew in mystical energy from the surrounding area, invisibly piercing through the ceiling and roof of the L'Enfant Haven mansion.

At the peak of divine ecstasy—a state only gods can reach—four figures screamed in unison: two immortal beings and two mortals. From them, a radiant, golden light erupted, pulled into the swirling vortex, shooting upward into the clouds. The sky exploded with thunder and multicolored lightning, streaking across the horizon in a breathtaking display.

The magic faded, the gods abandoned us, and we collapsed onto the bed with a thud. I gasped, heart pounding, and rolled off Seren. Had we just shared something divine? I looked at her—her eyes were closed, her breathing ragged, and her skin faintly glowing. I glanced at myself, and my skin was glowing too.

I asked, "Are you okay?"

She said with a huge smile.

"Yes, I'm okay. WOW! Did that really happen? Did we make love possessed by Gods?"

"Yes, that was real. I can still feel the magic. Can you?"

I rubbed my left thumb and fingers together, and tiny sparks flashed between them. But as the sparks dissipated, the magic faded away. We no longer glowed, and a sheen of sweat covered us both.

She answered, "Yeah, I can feel it, but it's going away now."

I said, "So, now you know what it is like to have your body taken over by a God."

"Oh, that's happened to me a couple of times. But only for a few minutes. Nothing like this."

Shocked, I said, "The Fairy Queen possessed you before?"

"Yes, at my apartment. The building was constructed over an ancient fairy circle of stones. The Fairy Queen comes on rare occasions."

"Oh, that's why I felt something unusual when I entered. Why didn't you ever tell me about it?"

"You have your secrets. I have mine."

I smiled.

"Let's try to keep that to a minimum."

"I agree. If we stay together, we need to be more open with each other."

"Yes, I have a lot to learn in that area. That's one place where I need your help."

I yawned.

"Being possessed by the Duke always tires me. I'm going to sleep."

She rolled over, draping her right arm across my chest, and said, "Me too."

It felt wonderful having her lying next to me. I wrapped my right arm around her back, gently stroking her soft skin with my hand. We both fell asleep immediately.

I woke to Seren shaking my shoulder.

I groggily said, "Wha...What?"

She said, "Orion, you were having a bad dream or something. You were talking in your sleep and thrashing around."

"I was? I'm sorry. What was I saying?"

"I couldn't understand. It almost sounded like that God language you speak when calling the Lwa."

"I don't remember. I'm sorry."

I rolled over and went back to sleep.

In the morning, I woke up and turned, searching for the beautiful redhead. She wasn't in bed. She must have gotten up earlier.

Cyrus manifested and said, "No, she's in your old bedroom."

"Why's she there?"

"You kept talking and thrashing about in your sleep. Seren couldn't sleep, so she went to your room."

"Damn. I don't remember anything. I feel like I slept great."

I got out of bed, went to the bathroom, and went to my old room.

The fan was on in the window. There she was. To me, the most beautiful woman in the world. Her auburn hair partially covered her face, and a lock floated up as she exhaled. I smiled. It was so cute.

I tiptoed to the other side of the bed, slipped under the sheet, and pulled close to her. I wrapped my arm around her and kissed her shoulder. She stirred, turned her head, and smiled at me.

I said, "I'm sorry I kept waking you. I don't know why I was doing that."

She asked, "Have you done it before?"

"I don't think so," I said furrowing my brow, trying to remember.

"Let's hope it was only because of what happened last night."

"I hope so. I want to sleep with you in my arms every night."

"And I always want to sleep in your arms."

She asked, "Is that going to happen often to us? Being possessed by Gods?"

I replied, "I don't know. They said we were perfect avatars and that means they can possess our bodies for longer periods. If all they want to do is make love, that won't be too bad."

I smiled.

"Last night was incredible."

"I agree about last night, but I hope it doesn't happen all the time."

"The Duke has possessed me a few times, but not that often. I don't think it'll happen a lot. It's only a feeling."

We kissed. I was ready to resume our human lovemaking.

She pushed me away and said, "I have to go to the shop today; we can't continue this."

She rolled out of bed and shuffled off to the bathroom. I could hear the shower. I really wanted to shower with her, but I knew that if we started, one thing would lead to another, and she would be late leaving.

I went to my room, dressed in jeans and a T-shirt, then headed downstairs. Rose had breakfast ready and laid out on the kitchen table. I ate, feeling famished. Seren came down, her auburn hair still damp.

She took a few bites of the diced fruit and said, "I've got to go."

She walked to the front door. I rushed after her, took her hand, drew her close, and kissed her.

"Can't you stay just a little longer?"

We continued to kiss and she said, "Really quick here on the couch."

I produced a broad grin. We rushed, removed our clothing, and frantically made love on the couch.

Chapter 46
I Have a Girlfriend

Andy Butler maneuvered his Cadillac off the dirt road and parked behind Seren's striking red Ford Mustang. He had persuaded her to accept Orion's gift by emphasizing that Orion was a millionaire, making the car's cost trivial to him. Later, they visited a dealership in Shreveport and purchased the new vehicle, while Orion remained hospitalized in Mobile, Alabama.

Surprised to see the Mustang and discover that Seren was there so early, Andy thought, 'Good, maybe they're finally talking and working things out.'

Orion needed a girlfriend and Seren seemed like the perfect match. Her stunning appearance and psychic abilities meant that his strange emanations didn't bother her. She cared deeply for Ory, which is why she became angry when he engaged in risky antics. Unaware of his true capabilities, she misinterpreted his recent psychic push at the hospital as mere childishness and an attempt to push her away. Yet, that action was likely a sign: Orion's powers were clearly growing.

Andy approached the front door of the L'Enfant Haven mansion, grasped the door handle, flicked the latch with his thumb, and pushed to open the door. It halted after opening only a few inches.

Milly's face appeared in the crack, and she said, "You can't come in right now. Mr. Orion's busy. He will be done in a short while. You can wait on the porch."

Surprised by this, Andy exclaimed, "Oh, okay."

Moans of pleasure from a man and woman filtered through the crack in the door. Milly shut the door. The attorney smiled, now aware of what was happening inside. He sat in the wicker chair on the front porch, grinning, and waited, thinking, 'I guess they must have worked things out.'

Seren and I shared an intimate moment on the couch. As she began to get up and dress, I hurriedly slipped into my pants and T-shirt, not ready to let her go.

"Can't you go tomorrow?"

"No, deliveries are due today, and I must be there to accept them. If they are returned, I may not be able to receive these items again for months. You don't understand how hard it is to track down some of the unique items my shop specializes in."

I nodded, understanding but knowing I would miss her terribly while she was away.

I followed her to the door. When she opened it and turned to leave, I grasped her hand and pulled her into my arms. I then kissed her deeply and passionately goodbye. She pushed me away and we both walked to the end of the porch. That's when I saw the red Ford Mustang for the first time.

"Oh, so you did take me up on my offer to buy you a new car. Good choice."

She turned, smiled, and pecked me on the cheek.

She looked over my shoulder, recognized Andy, and said, "Hi, Andy. I got to go."

I shouted as she hurried down the path to her new Ford, "Call me when you get there."

She called back as she shut the vehicle's door, "I will."

I stood on the porch, gazing longingly after her as the Mustang sped down the dirt road, creating a cloud of dust in its wake.

My friend approached and said, "Wow! You've got it bad."

Still staring at the dust cloud that was Seren, I asked, "Got what bad?"

"You're in love."

I looked at him and smiled, "Yeah, I think I am."

I shook my head back to the present.

"What are you doing here?"

"We must review the charity donations and decide which ones and how much to send."

"Oh, yeah. I remember. There are a few other things I'd like to discuss with you as well. I want to make some changes to the house."

I HAVE A GIRLFRIEND

As we entered, Andy said, "Now that you have a girlfriend, I guess I can't just walk in without knocking anymore."

"I guess you're right."

Smiling, I shut the door. Yes, I have a girlfriend, and I finally feel good about my life.

SPECTRAL PROMISES

Epilogue

Duke Shamedi stood intent on the vision before him, while Bridette hovered before the sacred bonfire, its violet flames licking at the void between realms. They stood close, yet an unbreakable thread of space remained between these two celestial beings—forces that could never truly merge in the spirit realm without unleashing catastrophic celestial disruptions.

If mid-level gods physically interacted in the spirit world, the resulting magical feedback could cause chaos across multiple planes of existence. The last such event led to the catastrophic Tunguska Event.

In 1908, scientists believed a small asteroid exploded in the skies above the southern Siberian forest, causing an extraordinary event. Eyewitnesses said it was as if the sky split open, with fire pouring out. And that's precisely what happened: a massive mystical portal opened, connecting the magical realm with the mortal plane. The sacred bonfire grew enormous, flames towering above the trees. A surge of magical energy erupted from the passage, uprooting and toppling trees for miles around.

The two Gods watched with intense focus as their perfect avatars managed the aftermath of the divine union. Orion and Seren appeared unscathed. The Gods exhaled in relief, knowing that the mortals were safe. Over millennia, these Gods frequently took on mortal forms. During those times, many humans endured severe mental anguish or were falsely branded as witches or demons, often leading to tragic deaths. As they continued to observe, a growing fondness for their avatars developed.

The boy—as the Duke called him—began to thrash about in bed and speak in a strange language.

Bridette asked, "Why is he doing that? This one hasn't failed as well, has he?"

The Duke shook his head.

"I don't know," he said thoughtfully, "He has also begun to

manifest abilities he shouldn't have possessed for decades. Something else is affecting and advancing him."

"That language he's speaking, it's ancient. It almost sounds like..."

She paused and turned to the Duke.

"You don't think it could be..." trailing off with obvious concern.

"It might be. There could be other destinies for the boy that I don't know about. He might be being prepared for higher-level soul missions. I'll delve deeper into the boy's soul to understand what's happening when we return during the next full moon."

"We won't be back together for at least nine full moons."

"Why do you say that?"

He looked over at her, confused by this statement.

"The girl is pregnant with twins, a boy and a girl. We can't expose the children to that much magic."

"But she said she couldn't become pregnant."

"I'm the Goddess of women's health. Her female reproductive issues have been corrected."

She smiled and shrugged.

"It just happened."

The Duke laughed.

"So, when we were together, the children were conceived. But that exposed them to our magic when we..."

She nodded.

He paused, contemplating the implications.

"Yes, the children will be exceptional. We must keep a close eye on them," the Fairy Queen said.

He nodded, wondering which higher-level God was so interested in Orion Labauve and why.

The End

Acknowledgments

I would like to express my deepest gratitude to my friends and family for their unwavering support and encouragement throughout the creation of the second Orion Labauve novel. This project holds significant personal and professional value.

I am immensely grateful to all of my Beta readers for their invaluable support and the constructive feedback they provided, which significantly enhanced the quality of the novel.

And thanks to C. Musick for coming forward to produce the new Orion Labauve book cover and keeping me from panicking after the original cover artist tragically passed away. The loss of L. Givens, with her humor, talent, and wonderful personality, is deeply felt by everyone who had the privilege of knowing her.

374

About the Author

L. L. Blacke is an author specializing in science fiction, paranormal fiction, and horror literature. From an early age, she has been an avid fan and voracious reader of these genres, which have inspired her imaginative and captivating storytelling.

With over thirty years of experience in the science fiction and fantasy community, L.L. Blacke has not only attended numerous conventions but has also played a significant role in organizing them. Her deep involvement in these events has enriched her understanding of the genres and provided her with a wealth of inspiration and connections within the literary world.

Now, in her retirement years, L.L. Blacke has embraced her passion for writing, finding it to be one of the most fulfilling and enjoyable pursuits of her life. Her works reflect her lifelong love for the fantastical and the eerie, drawing readers into richly woven narratives that challenge the boundaries of reality.

When she is not writing, L.L. Blacke enjoys exploring new books, participating in literary discussions, and sharing her experiences and insights with aspiring writers and dedicated fans of speculative fiction.